We Could Be Heroes

PJ ELLIS

Harper North

HarperNorth
Windmill Green
24 Mount Street
Manchester M2 3NX

A division of

HarperCollins*Publishers*   HarperCollins*Publishers*
1 London Bridge Street   Macken House,
London SE1 9GF   39/40 Mayor Street Upper
                                            Dublin 1,
                                            D01 C9W8, Ireland

www.harpercollins.co.uk

First published by HarperCollins*Publishers* Ltd 2025

1

Copyright © PJ Ellis 2025

Dinkus: Shutterstock 'Wildest Dreams' by Taylor Swift lyrics © Sony/atv Tree Publishing, Taylor Swift Music, Mxm Music Ab 'Teenage Dream' by Katy Perry lyrics © When I'm Rich You'll Be My Bitch, Prescription Songs, Bonnie Mckee Music, Where Da Kasz At?, Mxm Music Ab, Kasz Money Publishing, Matza Ball Music, Songs Of Pulse Recordings, Songs Of Pulse Recording, Dtcm Blvd

PJ Ellis asserts the moral right to be
identified as the author of this work.

A catalogue record for this book is available from the British Library.

PB ISBN: 978-0-00-853931-3

This novel is entirely a work of fiction.
The names, characters and incidents portrayed in it are the work
of the author's imagination. Any resemblance to actual persons,
living or dead, events or localities is entirely coincidental.

Set in Bembo MT by Amnet

Printed and bound in the UK using 100% Renewable Electricity
by CPI Group (UK) Ltd

All rights reserved. No part of this publication may be
reproduced, stored in a retrieval system, or transmitted,
in any form or by any means, electronic, mechanical,
photocopying, recording or otherwise, without the
prior permission of the publishers.

Without limiting the author's and publisher's exclusive rights,
any unauthorised use of this publication to train generative
artificial intelligence (AI) technologies is expressly prohibited.
HarperCollins also exercise their rights under Article 4(3) of
the Digital Single Market Directive 2019/790 and expressly reserve
this publication from the text and data mining exception.

This book contains FSC™ certified paper and other controlled
sources to ensure responsible forest management.

For more information visit: www.harpercollins.co.uk/green

For the gays.

ACT ONE:
WHO WAS THAT MASKED MAN?

'Fame is only good for one thing – they will cash your check in a small town.'

Truman Capote

1

Patrick Lake glanced sideways at his stunt double and thought, *I'd do me.*

Ok – maybe that was an inherently weird idea to have about somebody decked out to look exactly like you. And it was surely *not* the kind of thing that Captain Kismet, everybody's favourite superhero, said to himself between takes. But it had been a long day.

'The trick to falling,' the stuntman said, 'is knowing how to land.'

Corey's words, however sage, were not for Patrick's benefit: the two of them were filming behind-the-scenes content, taking turns to demonstrate the simpler stunts they had planned for *Kismet 2*. Footage of the pair in their matching costumes would then be cut into polished thirty-second videos and used to advertise the movie on social media later in the year; a perfectly curated glimpse behind the curtain. It was the kind of thing Patrick could usually do in his sleep. Except all he could really think about was, well... sleep. They were supposed to wrap on the movie a week ago, yet new script pages kept showing up outside his hotel room door like bad omens, and at this rate Patrick felt as though he would die in this grim little city.

'Birmingham?' he'd asked his manager, Simone, when she told him where reshoots would take place. 'Like, Alabama?'

'No, thank God,' she'd replied. 'It's in England. Very cheap to film there, apparently.'

Cheap, it turned out, was the operative word. The famous auteur the studio had hired to direct the second instalment of the newly rebooted *Kismet* franchise had burned through much of the movie's budget before the first act was even in the can, leading to his rapid firing and replacement by Lucas Grant, whose resume largely consisted of TV commercials and a Pixar short. Grant was tasked with righting the ship and getting it to port without bankrupting the studio, which meant relocating production to an old factory town where accommodating the enormous cast and crew wouldn't cost an extra couple of million dollars.

Corey executed a perfect backflip, and Patrick applauded, mugging for the camera. 'Nicely done,' he said, truthfully. With his earnest eyes and back-clapping Aussie cheer, it was impossible to dislike Corey, even if Patrick was occasionally thrown by their uncanny resemblance. Same sandy hair, same muscular build, even something of a likeness in the jaw. It took some getting used to. Patrick's stand-in for the first movie had been a slightly terrifying former MMA fighter in a blonde wig.

'You got what you need?' Patrick asked the videographer, who gave him a thumbs up. 'Great. Nice work, Corey. Thanks, everyone!' He began walking out of the soundstage warehouse, back to his trailer. *A shower and then a nap*, he thought. A nap would fix everything.

'Hey, buddy.' Hector Ramirez greeted him as he entered; he was doing sit-ups between the sofa and the coffee table. Patrick was almost always pleased to see his trainer, but right now he felt a lot like a kid who'd walked into class having forgotten to prepare for an impending exam.

'Hey, Hector,' he replied. 'Did we have another session today?' They'd seen each other that morning, when they'd hit chest and back. The first time Hector had put Patrick through one of his workouts, prior to the first *Kismet* movie, he'd spent the entire next day feeling like he was recovering from minor surgery. Now it was… well, not *easy* exactly, but he gained real satisfaction from pushing his body and seeing how much stronger he could make it. Not that he was in the mood for pushing right now.

'Nah.' Hector completed his final rep and immediately launched into a set of air squats. 'I was just around,' he added, barely short of breath.

'Just around.' Patrick eyed him suspiciously. 'And wondering if a certain leading lady might also be… just around?'

Hector simply continued his rhythmic ascent and descent, gaze fixed on some spot to Patrick's left. 'Who?'

Patrick snorted. There was definitely only one actor in the room. Hector was cool, but lost his chill when it came to Audra Kelly, Patrick's co-star. And he couldn't really blame him. Beautiful, funny, charming – recently named 'Internet's Ultimate Girlfriend' by a men's magazine. Some guys really went in for that kind of thing.

'She's not here.' Patrick gathered his jacket and headphones. 'Just me and Corey today. I think Kismet and Sura's next scene isn't until Monday.'

'I don't know what you're talking about,' said Hector, who was doing a pretty shoddy job of hiding his disappointment. 'But since we're here,' he continued, 'how about some burpees? Just for fun.'

When Patrick returned to the hotel forty minutes later, limbs crackling like firewood, he was more desperate for a shower than ever.

After he'd made his way out of the elevator towards his suite, Audra spotted him and waved through her open door across the hall. Patrick leaned on the doorframe and stuck his head into

Audra's room. The Princess Sura to his Captain Kismet was pacing with earbuds in, talking to thin air about her beauty must-haves.

'I like to keep things simple. Chapstick, a good concealer, a tiny bit of mascara,' she said, her voice low and throaty, like she smoked a pack of cigarettes a day. Which Patrick knew for a fact to be true, although the morality clause in their contracts kept it from public knowledge. Movie stars who smoked used to be cool; now they were bad for the studio's brand. Role models didn't smoke, or swear, or screw. And Patrick was nothing if not a role model.

'One hair must-have...' Audra paused mid-pace, appearing to give this serious consideration. 'You know, I'm *such* a slob,' she laughed. 'I've been using the same drugstore shampoo since I was sixteen! Oh, and argan oil. I swear by it.'

Another pause.

'My absolute pleasure.' She smiled radiantly, as if the reporter were in the room with them. 'Thanks so much. You have a great day now. Byeee...' Audra hit a button on her phone and pulled her earbuds out, sighing in exhaustion. She handed the device back to her assistant, shooed her out, and as Patrick stepped into the room to let the girl pass, Audra turned towards the bar assembled in the corner of her suite.

'That was *Elle*,' she said, fixing herself a vodka on the rocks. 'Want to hear something funny?'

'Sure,' Patrick replied. Audra picked up a crystal tumbler and held it out to him with an inquisitive look. He smiled, shook his head *no thank you*, and took a seat on the expansive sofa.

'I would *never* use argan oil on my hair.' She ran her hand through her wavy blonde mane. 'I think it's gross. But now a whole bunch of girls are going to try it, and their hair is going to be all greasy and sticky, and they're going to say to themselves: "Why doesn't *my* hair look as fabulous as Audra Kelly's?"'

'I don't get it,' Patrick said.

'Oh, it's just a silly game I play with myself.' Audra waved a dismissive hand and threw herself dramatically down on the couch beside him. 'I mean, why would I give my actual secrets away? Until a makeup company pays me to shill for them, I'm just making up shit as I go. We can't *all* be the Girl Next Door.'

Patrick didn't know what to say to this – but that hardly mattered. Audra was on a roll.

'And that's just women's media. A walk in the park, I tell you, compared to the creepy fuckable-little-sister act the guys expect. Never mind the fact that I have an Independent Spirit award – the real performance of a lifetime is convincing everyone that I love pizza and beer despite looking' – she looked down at her tiny waist –, 'like *this*.'

'Oh right.' Patrick nodded. 'The *relatable* thing.'

'Yep! I've gotta be one of the guys and love sports, and comic books, and video games. But not other women, apparently. The average Wonderverse moviegoer doesn't like it when girls exist for themselves or each other. Makes them uncomfortable. Honestly, some days I would love nothing more than to tell them that I've never seen *Star Wars* and prefer caviar to hot dogs, just to see if their heads explode.'

'Now that I'd love to see.'

'Ugh. I just hate all this Pick Me bullshit, you know? You have no idea how exhausting it is.' She leaned back against the sofa cushions and exhaled forcefully, lifting her glass to cool her forehead.

Patrick bit his lip. *Don't I?* he thought. Affable, unflappable charm was his thing. In other words, a focus group put together by his manager Simone had determined he would be most appealing if he leaned into the laid-back, humble-but-not-disingenuous, well-shucks-I'm-just-a-boy-from-Jersey brand of heartthrob.

'What's wrong with being myself, and saving the acting for when I book a job?' Patrick had once asked. Simone had laughed a real laugh, a rare moment of authenticity, considering she tried not to convey more than twenty per cent of an emotion at any given time, if she could help it.

'Sweetie.' She had touched his arm with genuine affection. 'This *is* the job.'

He drew in a breath, ready to tell Audra that he knew how she felt, but she was still gesticulating with her vodka on the rocks as she pontificated to the ceiling.

'I was in the *TIME* 100 last year,' she said. 'Why the fuck should I have to be *relatable*? I don't want to be fucking relatable! I want to be stoned out of my mind on an island with Rihanna – preferably being fanned by men in diamond-encrusted thongs. But apparently that is *not* the kind of answer people like to hear you giving in "72 Questions With *Vogue*".'

'People want to feel like we're just like them,' Patrick offered weakly.

'Well, here's the very simple problem with that,' Audra said. 'We're not.'

Patrick's eyebrows shot up.

'Not that I'm saying we're *better*,' she added hastily. 'Just… richer. Prettier. More successful.'

'More neurotic, anxious and insecure, too,' Patrick added.

'Definitely not better,' she repeated. 'Maybe even worse, in some ways. I mean, we're fucking spoiled, aren't we? But we are certainly *not* just like them. For one thing, I bet if I were *just a regular girl*, I wouldn't have to consult with my management team before getting a tattoo or cutting my god damn hair.'

'Your hair? Seriously?'

'My *hair*, Patrick.' She flicked a honeyed lock over her shoulder for emphasis. 'But with all that said, what would I rather be doing with my life? Waiting tables? Acquiring crippling student debt?

Getting married to some lunk who resents that I'm smarter than him, then giving up my minimum-wage job because bam, he got me pregnant and we can't afford day-care?' Audra shuddered.

'Isn't there anything you miss about your life before fame?' Patrick asked. 'I don't know, being able to go for lunch with your family without someone taking your picture?'

'Please. One of the perks of this life is not having to deal with my mother.' She caught his surprised look before he could hide it, and tsked. 'Let me guess, Patrick Lake is best friends with his parents.'

'My parents are nice people,' said Patrick instinctively.

'Good for you.' Audra pursed her lips, swirled her glass. 'My mother doesn't have my phone number. When she wants to contact me, she goes through my agent.'

'Are you kidding?'

'He negotiated her down to a visit every other Christmas.' She looked up with a dry smile. 'That man is worth every cent I pay him.'

Audra knocked back the rest of her vodka and abruptly rose from her lounging position on the sofa.

'Get up,' she said, crunching on ice. 'We're going out.'

'Out?' Patrick didn't stir. 'What do you mean?'

'You know, that whole place that exists outside of your hotel room? Honestly, it's a good thing you're as handsome as you are, because you are not the brightest star in the sky.'

'But we're not—'

'If you say "we're not allowed", I might just slap you,' Audra said, flexing her right hand, which Patrick now noticed was bejewelled with several elegant but weighty-looking rings. 'It's Friday night! And we're the talent. What we say goes. Otherwise, what is the actual point of being a movie star?'

'I don't know about this…' Patrick reluctantly allowed himself to be pulled to his feet.

'Trust me, a night off from reading endless rewrites and scrolling through what people think of us online is exactly what we both need.'

'Oh, I try to stay off social media,' Patrick said.

'Very admirable!' She looked him up and down. 'You should probably shower. That last workout is lingering. I'll see you in the lobby in half an hour.' She waved him towards the door and muttered to herself, 'now, what to wear...' before vanishing into her bedroom, clearly confident that Patrick would play along. *She's right*, he thought; *she'd have been wasted on real life.*

'I... fine,' he called out. 'But only for a little while, OK?'

Audra's head reappeared from behind the door. 'Great! And who knows,' she said. 'Maybe I'll go absolutely wild and get a haircut while we're at it.'

2

Will Wright was halfway through transforming into a woman when his sister called. Upstairs at the Village Inn, the area designated for the drag queens' toilette was a former utility cupboard that had been colonised by the bar's coterie of performers. Dressing tables and vanity mirrors had been installed against one wall, but metal filing cabinets and mouldering cardboard boxes still lined the opposite side, and its occupants wasted no time in enforcing a pecking order. Spots at 'the High Table', as the queens had dubbed the well-lit vanity, were intensely coveted. According to local lore, those chairs were reserved for the more seasoned *artistes* – although, more often than not they were claimed by whoever got there first on a Friday night.

Three drag queens – Faye Runaway, Gaia Gender, Raina Shine – were sitting there now like Macbeth's witches, titivating between sips of gin and tonic. Tammy, the emcee for the evening, was already downstairs at the DJ booth. Julie Madly Deeply wasn't due to join them until after midnight.

Will, who was both the new girl and incapable of showing up on time (according to everyone who knew him), had no chance of a seat at the High Table tonight – or even a proper mirror. As a result, he was sitting cross-legged on the floor and applying his makeup while peering down at the front-facing camera of his phone, which he had propped up against the skirting board. At one point, Gaia left her post to go smoke outside, but Will resisted the urge to take her place and stayed his own licentious hand: stealing such a spot once it had been claimed was a sin akin to sleeping with somebody's husband. Come to think of it, most queens were less territorial over men than they were favourable lighting.

When Will first began experimenting with drag, doing amateurish, clown-like makeup in his bedroom during lockdown, he had daydreamed about being invited behind the curtain at a real club even more than he had thought about performing. He imagined gossiping with the other queens in the dressing room, sharing stories and lipstick, the glamour and the camaraderie. Admittedly, the reality was markedly less 'backstage at the Hippodrome' than Will had once hoped, instead giving the overall impression that they were all preparing to put on a particularly baroque school play.

Faye, at least, had welcomed Will with open arms: he was the latest in a long line of fledglings to be taken under her sequinned wing. But the queen of the runaways had more to offer by way of advice than she did tutelage, deadheading Will's ingénue-like expectations with a French-tipped talon.

'Most of these novices you see on Instagram wouldn't even make a half-decent chorus girl,' Faye had told him. 'It's not a matter of talent. It's that other thing. The ineffable. *Je ne sais quoi*. Not to be confused with Jenny Sais Quoi,' she added, who had recently moved to Bristol to be with a man she had met at the Renaissance tour.

Beat nearly done, Will swore under his breath as his own image vanished from the screen, replaced by his sister's name and a picture from last New Year's Eve in which they were, for once, *both* smiling. He answered the call, dusting foundation from the surface of his phone at the same time, before opening the camera again.

'Thief,' Margo declared. Behind him, Will heard Raina tut indelicately at the tinny sound of the speakerphone.

'Am not,' Will said. This was not a video call, and so Margo could not see the oversized white blouse he was wearing, purloined from her wardrobe on his last visit and tied into a cute little knot at the waist.

'I'm going out with The Girls tonight,' Margo admonished, 'and I was going to wear that top. You are so annoying.'

'The Girls' consisted of Claire and Fiona, women Margo had known since school and who had become very fond of peppering Will with all kinds of questions since they got hip to *Drag Race UK* on the BBC. 'Do you tuck?' Fiona had asked him last Christmas Eve. 'Are you a look queen or a comedy queen? When are you going to go on *RuPaul*?'

'You should wear that top from Reiss,' Will told Margo. 'It's smarter.'

'That top is brand new,' she accused. 'How do *you* know about it?'

'Brotherly intuition.'

'I swear to God, Will.'

He and his sister had been sharing clothes since their late teens, when their wardrobes had consisted solely of oversized hoodies and band T-shirts. As the years went on, they discovered that Will's taste and Margo's income were a match made in heaven, and every quarter or so, without fail, Margo would show up at Will's flat unannounced with a tote bag and a scowl, demanding her stuff back.

'Very *Twelfth Night*,' he murmured to nobody, as he executed a pleasing (if not perfect) cat-eye flick.

Will and Margo were far from twins. In fact they weren't blood relatives at all, just a pair of former tearaways brought together by Will's father and his ever-roving eye. Still, with Will's dark Irish hair and lashes, and the thick black mane Margo inherited from her

Italian mother (not to mention the savage shorthand in which they communicated), you'd be forgiven for thinking otherwise.

'Did you hear who's in Brum right now?' Margo asked, her annoyance giving way under the urge to spill tea.

'Who?' Will asked, owl-like, his mouth a perfect 'O' as he applied lipstick.

'Patrick Lake.'

Will froze, lipstick tube held mid-air. 'Are you serious? I thought that was just a rumour.'

'A bunch of people saw him outside the Grand on Church Street. It's been all over Instagram today.'

'I'm so over social media,' Will said, with a superior air. 'And I've been... busy.'

This was not a lie, exactly. Between his two part-time jobs – drag and bookselling – Will certainly *was* always busy. And he had deleted Instagram and TikTok from his phone a week ago in a bid to improve his mental health, reasoning that any events of significance would make their way to him via WhatsApp, or, if he got bored enough, a newspaper. Mainly, though, he was trying to avoid crossing timelines with his latest ex-boyfriend, Ry. Also, a handful of soul-destroying videos from his most recent ill-fated gig were still in circulation. Better to wait things out. At least, until sufficient time had elapsed that he could gracefully re-join polite society, not unlike a literary heroine whose reputation gets absolutely beasted after she is seen taking a stroll with a scoundrel. (During his self-imposed digital exile, he may have also read half of a Henry James novel from the nineteenth-century section at the bookshop where he worked.)

'It's so surreal to think of a big celebrity just wandering around Birmingham,' said Will.

'I know, right?' said Margo. 'Can't you just picture him popping into the Oasis Market to pick up a bong and get something pierced?'

'Then going to Snobs for a warm alcopop and an STI,' added Faye from behind Will, having determined that any conversation happening via speakerphone was one she could invite herself to join without compunction.

'You might be telling on yourself there, love,' said Will.

'Oh, please,' Faye said derisively. 'I wouldn't be seen dead in that new hole. I remember *old* Snobs, before they moved it.'

'Snobs is straight culture,' announced a self-important voice from behind Will. He scooted around and looked up to see Jordan entering the dressing room, a full drinks tray in hand. Jordan was one of life's main characters, fond of entering rooms with a grand proclamation, pausing in the doorway to give everybody time to take in his words – and his outfit. Tonight, he wore a fitted tank top, high-waisted jeans and a pair of platform heels, all the better to tower imperiously over the twinks who reported to him downstairs. Jordan ostensibly held the title of bar manager at the Village, but in all their years of friendship, the only thing Will had ever witnessed him manage was to make an entire hen party cry. He didn't so much run the place as hold court, like a viceroy or governor installed by the powers-that-be who owned the bar.

Jordan Thomas believed his own hype to the point of egomania, which Will blamed on him having two first names. He also happened to be Will's best friend in the entire world.

'Marg, I have to go,' he said. 'Duty calls.'

'Hi, Margo!' Jordan called out as he set down his tray.

Margo made a noncommittal noise on the other end and hung up.

'Patrick Lake,' Jordan purred. 'What a slice.'

'I thought fancying straight men was against your politics?' Will challenged.

'It is. But I'm only human, Will, and the man's fit as fuck. As *if* he's in Birmingham.' Jordan bit his lip. 'Maybe I could find a way into his hotel. Do some investigative journalism.'

'Firstly, that is not investigative journalism, it is stalking,' said Will. 'And secondly, you are not a journalist. You're a homosexual with an iPhone.'

'How hard could it be to finesse my way onto a film set?' Jordan continued, ignoring him. 'You know, I've always had this theory that gays make the best spies.'

Jordan had plenty of theories about life, the universe, and everything, but Will was quite fond of this one. After all, who could be better equipped for espionage than somebody who had grown up learning to decode the subtleties of body language, read any room for signs of imminent danger, and assume a completely alien identity when the occasion called for it?

'Is one of those for me?' Will asked, nodding to the tray of drinks. Technically, he was reporting to Jordan this evening, but if he were to assume even the slightest deferential tone, the man's ego would tumesce to the point of no return. Better to act like any other drag performer, haughty and superior, even if tonight he would not be on stage, instead functioning as a glorified shot girl. It was a humiliating part of the job, but necessary if he wanted to buy those boots he'd had his eye on. Every spare penny, of which there were precious few, went towards his costuming. Meanwhile, his 'boy drag', as he now fondly referred to his everyday apparel, consisted of bulky work trousers – Dickies and Carhartt when he was on a particularly good charity shop haul – and the aforementioned, gender-neutral loot from Margo's closet.

'Off-brand gin for my best girl,' Jordan said, handing over a large glass before picking up one himself. 'Bottoms up.'

'And down with tops!' Will replied in unison with the other queens, giggling and taking a generous swig. 'Now go, go, I need to get into my dress.'

'Something slutty?' Jordan asked.

'Have you ever seen me in any other kind?'

Once Jordan had returned to his domain downstairs, Will carefully attached his wig, which he had christened Ariel, and stepped into his dress, a sleek black vintage number he loved like a favourite child (if one he'd bought online at a high discount).

'Could somebody zip me up, please?' he asked, but Faye was nowhere to be seen, and the other witches were suddenly so fixated on their own magic mirrors that they didn't seem to hear him. 'Never mind,' he said, 'I'll figure it out.' Will awkwardly reached behind his own back and, with a few small jumps that made his padding jiggle comically, managed to tug the zipper upwards. Crouching as delicately as was possible under the circumstances, he retrieved his phone to give his reflection one final examination.

He grunted in exasperation as his image onscreen was once again obscured by an incoming notification. This time, it was a text from Jordan downstairs:

You will NEVER believe who just walked in.

3

Patrick followed Audra from the foyer of the Grand Hotel onto the street, where their driver Mo waited. The Grand was a beautiful place to stay at first, but even after a couple of days, it was hard not to feel like zoo animals with very enriched enclosures. Sometimes you just had to give in to the call of the wild.

As they climbed into the back seat, Mo asked, 'Where to?'

Patrick was slamming the door behind him when from outside, they heard a faint: 'Hold up!'

He rolled down the window to find Hector on the sidewalk outside the hotel. It was maybe the first time he'd ever seen him wearing something other than fitted gym gear; the buttons of a crisp Ralph Lauren shirt strained to conceal his sculpted chest.

'I heard y'all were going out,' Hector said.

'Where did you hear that, exactly?' Audra asked, her eyes narrowing. Patrick felt a vicarious chill as her gaze passed him on its way to Hector. *I bet even her teachers in high school were terrified of her*, he thought.

'My bad!' Corey gambolled into view. 'So I may have told Hector that we were going dancing.'

'Who told *you*?' Audra demanded. The studio was able to keep every single thing that happened on a Wonderverse set secret from the rest of the world, but inside the bubble, it was a different matter entirely. Gossip travelled faster than light when you had nothing else to do all day.

'And I figured,' Hector said, 'that if Patrick is hitting the town, risking being late for tomorrow's workout—'

'Don't forget the macros,' Corey interjected.

'Not to mention throwing off your macros *and* intermittent fasting,' Hector continued, 'then I should probably come along to make sure you don't irreparably undo all of that progress we've made on Captain Kismet's physique.'

Patrick felt a pang of guilt. His body, he had to remember, didn't exactly belong to him. At least, not for as long as they were filming. The shooting schedule, not to mention both Hector and Corey's livelihoods, depended on his ability to stay disciplined and consistent.

'I'm sorry,' he said. 'Maybe I should go back upstairs.' He'd been Mr Sensible for the last six months of training. What was one more night? A dozen more nights?

'No fucking way,' Audra barked, at the same time that Hector said, more measuredly: 'Well, there's no need to be *too* restrictive...'

He stared intently at Patrick, as if even glancing at Audra would turn him to stone, and it clicked. The poor man, Patrick realised, was down bad.

'Oh, for God's sake,' Audra huffed. 'If you guys wanted to come along, all you had to do was ask.' Patrick opened the door, and Hector and Corey piled into the SUV.

'And you don't have to worry,' Patrick added. 'I'm not planning on drinking tonight.'

'Loser,' Audra remarked, then threw her head back and crowed like a bird, prompting much whooping and woohooing from her compatriots in the back seat, until Mo asked them again for their destination, and they realised they had no idea where to go.

'Downtown?' Corey ventured.

'Dancing,' Audra asserted. 'Take us to the dancing.'

'You got it,' said Mo, and they were on their way. Just ten minutes later – Patrick would never get over what passed for 'traffic' in this town – they pulled up somewhere called Broad Street.

'I don't believe it,' Audra said, pointing out the window at the glittering signage of Coyote Ugly. 'That was my favourite movie as a kid. We have *got* to go in.'

'I'm not so sure,' Patrick countered, reaching over and adjusting Audra's head slightly, so that she was now looking at the two women attempting to scalp one another on the pavement outside.

'OK, fine.' Audra huffed as Mo performed a U-turn. 'What about that place?' They all looked to the right, where through the open doors of Popworld, Robyn demanded somebody show her love. Patrick was about to concede, when a woman was forcibly ejected from the very same doors by a bouncer, vomit visible on her shirt.

'It's eight thirty,' Corey said in something akin to wonder.

'This city is a horror show,' Audra finally agreed. 'Excuse me, sir? Is there anywhere else you could take us? You know, that's less… *This*?'

'One moment,' Mo said, and with patience that bordered on the saintly, he parked in a layby and took out his phone. Several minutes later, after consulting with his younger cousin over WhatsApp, he restarted the engine and they were on their way again.

'This is grody as shit,' Audra muttered, taking in the chipped paint of the building that Mo deposited them outside. 'The Village Inn? It's giving *Wicker Man*.' The uncertainty on her face looked like it might teeter over into outright disgust, but then the unmistakable opening melody of 'We Found Love' issued like a clarion call from inside.

'Rihanna!' Audra squealed, and before Patrick could protest, she had grabbed his hand and started pulling him into the bar after her. 'It's a sign,' she said. 'Let's go, boys.'

As he crossed the threshold, Patrick registered the rainbow flag over the door, by which time it was too late to object. Neither Hector nor Corey seemed to have a problem being in a gay bar, and Audra had already taken to their new environs with zest.

'Gays love me,' she informed them. 'Can you blame them?'

Patrick could not claim the same ease, and so while Audra sauntered to the front of the line at the bar, he stuck to the wall, practically hiding behind Corey and Hector to avoid anyone recognising him. It didn't take long for him to see the flaw in his strategy: People kept looking over anyway, because while Corey and Hector weren't technically famous, being tall, muscular, and conventionally handsome in a gay bar was tantamount to the same thing.

Maybe he was just being paranoid. The simple act of being physically inside a gay bar didn't mean anything. He was here with Audra and Hector and Corey, after all. He was, arguably, playing wingman to his trainer, whose crush on the actress had become painfully obvious. And his companions seemed to be having a great time, swigging beers, not bothered at all by what their presence here might mean. In fact, Audra seemed to be very much enjoying the attention *she* was getting from a group of young men who were 'just *obsessed*' with her last film, in which she had played an exotic dancer who vows to solve the murder of her best friend while battling an opioid addiction.

'You were phenomenal,' one of them told her.

'Iconic,' said another.

'So *raw* and *real*,' added their friend.

Audra grinned. 'My tits looked insane, right?'

'Oh my God, so good!' the first replied. 'Did you—'

'I'm bored!' Audra interrupted. 'Let's dance!' And like the Pied Piper of Hamelin, she led the three men over to the cramped dance floor.

Corey waggled his empty beer bottle. 'Another?'

'I'll take another water,' replied Patrick.

'Careful now,' said Corey. 'You wouldn't want to accidentally enjoy yourself.'

'You know what? I'll take a sparkling water.'

'You're *crazy*,' said Hector, throwing one arm around Patrick's shoulder. 'Corey, mine's a tequila soda.'

'Ah, screw it,' said Patrick. 'I'll have a beer.'

Corey pumped his fist in the air, as if Patrick's acquiescence to hops was a victory for all Australia, and lumbered towards the bar. Before Patrick knew it, one beer turned to two, and then a third, and it was occurring to him just how long it had been since he'd allowed himself to let loose when Audra returned, without her new companions, and pulled in all three of them with her back towards the dance floor, singing along word-perfectly to Dua Lipa.

'How do you know all the words?' Patrick asked, marvelling.

Audra looked at him, stunned. 'How do you *not*?'

Patrick was not intimately familiar with the song currently playing. He didn't even think he *liked* the song. But God, to be three beers deep with your closest friends! Or at least, the closest things you had to friends when you spent your life travelling from set to set.

'I love you guys!' he yelled. Audra laughed, and replied: 'Of course you do, you precious thing,' while Corey nearly crushed him in a headlock. 'We should do this every night,' Patrick said, at the same time as Hector bellowed: 'Shots!'

Some indeterminate time later, the music stopped. All four of them began to protest – surely it was too early for this place to be closing? – until it became clear the dance floor was getting *more* crowded, not less. Patrick followed the direction of everyone else's gaze as a spotlight fell on the raised area that Audra's twinks had been using as a podium just moments before, and which he now realised was a stage.

'Theydies and gentlethems,' uttered a voice over the sound system, 'please welcome to the stage, your hostess for the night, the beast from the East, she of the gaysian persuasion, the wanker from Sri Lanka, Birmingham's very own Messy Desi... Tamil Nitrate!'

A vision in red and gold took to the stage, spinning and waving so enthusiastically that it took Patrick a moment to notice her full, lush dark beard.

'Yes!' Audra squealed next to him. 'Fucking yes! I love drag queens!'

'And we love you right back,' the queen responded via her mic, pointing in Audra's direction. 'Hello, lovely lushes of the Village, my name is Tamil Nitrate but you can call me Tammy. How are we all doing tonight?' When met with assorted shrieks and hoots in response, Tammy nodded her approval. She spoke with the same voice that'd come through the speakers a moment ago, and Patrick found it somehow all the more charming that Tammy had been announcing herself.

'Now,' she said. 'We have got a fantastic show for you tonight, and some amazing queens lined up. But before we begin... I have a little tradition that I like to start each show with.'

She patted herself down in an exaggeratedly lewd manner, eventually retrieving a tiny bottle from her hairy cleavage. 'It's poppers o'clock!' she proclaimed, waving the vial triumphantly in the air.

'Poppers o'clock!' the crowd chanted, clearly composed of regulars. 'Poppers o'clock! Poppers o'clock!'

'What are poppers?' asked Hector. Patrick didn't dare look him in the eye.

'You all know the drill by now,' Tammy continued. 'I'm in need of a strapping young volunteer!'

Patrick felt rather than saw the audience's eyes all turn on him, Hector, and Corey.

'We're strapping,' Corey beamed, revelling in the attention and – Jesus, had Patrick had too much to drink or did Corey just make his pecs dance under his shirt?

'Eeny, meeny, miny, moe...' the queen sang, pointing at each of the men in turn. 'Catch a himbo by his toe... Once he comes, let him go, eeny, meeny, miny... moe!' Her smoky stare settled on Patrick, and turned hungry.

'Yes, you,' she grinned. 'Come on up!'

'Oh my God,' said Audra. 'I am so jealous.'

'I think she likes you,' Hector snickered in his ear.

'I'm waiting!' The queen tapped an imaginary watch.

'Oh, just do it,' said Audra, pushing him forward. 'I dare you!'

After a moment's hesitation, Patrick moved through the crowd and stepped up onto the stage to join the queen, who was holding the mic out to him.

'Um,' he said. 'Hi.'

'Hmm.' She looked him up and down. 'I think I prefer when it doesn't speak.' A murmur of laughter drifted up from the crowd.

'Wait a minute,' the queen said, examining him further. 'Hold the bloody phone just one second.'

Here it comes, Patrick thought, and he adopted the aw-gee-shucks smile that he kept in his back pocket at all times, like a condom or an EpiPen.

'You're him! Off of those films!'

'Yeah,' he said, turning his smile towards the audience, who were now beginning to coo in recognition.

'Well I never.' Tammy leaned forward, as if she had been physically winded by this new knowledge. She jolted upright a second later, and Patrick could see the devil in her eyes. 'You know, folks,' she said, 'I don't think we've ever had a celebrity join us for poppers o'clock. Unless you count Joe Lycett, and I don't, because he's always bloody in here.'

'I'm happy to be here,' said Patrick, uncertainly. And there was the devil again.

'I'm glad to hear you say that.' Tammy sidled closer, unscrewing the bottle as she did so. 'Here we go then, just like jumping in a pool: deeeep breath!' She closed a finger over one of his nostrils and placed the bottle under the other. And Patrick didn't know if it was the disorienting lights in his face, or the beers, or the fact that tonight was the most fun he'd had in weeks, but for a single second he forgot about every single rule that went into maintaining his perfectly crafted image, and breathed in.

'Wahey!' Tammy cheered, and the crowd cheered with her. 'He's off the deep end, boys and girls! Now watch as I dive in!' She sniffed the bottle with practised ease, and as the music started again, the entire club began to swim.

'You're a good sport,' Tammy whispered in his ear, holding his hand so he could step back down off the stage.

'I am?' Patrick giggled as his cheeks flushed and a half-remembered giddiness rushed in. 'I am!'

'Hey, buddy,' he felt Corey take him by the arm. 'I think it's time to go.' Patrick looked around, and saw Hector folded protectively around Audra while more people surged onto the tiny dancing area, shouting her name. Shouting *his* name. *Shit*, Patrick thought, his mind clearing a little. This was what he'd been worried would happen when they came out tonight. Well, not specifically *this* – he hadn't exactly predicted getting just lit enough to do poppers on stage like an absolute idiot (Simone was going to kill him).

'Hey, man,' Corey yelped, after an over-enthusiastic stranger cupped his bottom with both hands. 'Listen, I'm an ally, but that is not cool.'

'Alright, that's enough,' came a new voice from somewhere above Patrick's right shoulder. He turned and looked up into a pair of dazzling green eyes, winged with black eyeliner and framed by a red wig.

'Come this way,' the queen told Patrick, sweeping the others along with a wave of her arm. She led them through the chaos to the DJ booth at the side of the stage, and then through a door behind it. Once they were all ensconced in the tiny passageway, she closed the door before opening another one leading out onto the side street behind the bar.

Patrick staggered as he departed the venue, his warm face tingling in the cool night air.

'What's in poppers again?' he asked, eyes closed, savouring the breeze.

'They're a muscle relaxant, bab,' their rescuer said. 'And you're not short in that regard, but I reckon you'll be fine in a minute.'

Mo's SUV squeezed into the alleyway from around the corner, presumably summoned by one of the others, and Patrick felt the tension between his shoulders detract a little. He took a few deep, greedy lungfuls of air, then said: 'You're a life-saver.'

'Oh, it's no bother. And besides, I think your friend probably needs to go home.' The queen nodded towards Audra, who was doing a clumsy two-step on the pavement, clutching her purse in one hand and a slice of pizza in the other. 'I don't even know where she got that,' they added. 'The nearest pizza place is all the way up the street.'

'I'm not done dancing,' Audra protested around a mouthful of cheese. 'Let's go back inside!'

'You can go back inside,' the queen said, 'if you can tell me where your shoes are right now.'

Audra looked down at her bare feet, took another bite of pizza, and with a shrug of defeat, allowed Hector to direct her towards the car.

'Thank you,' Patrick said, turning back to his unlikely saviour.

'All in a night's work for your friendly neighbourhood drag queen,' she said, dipping into some curious mix of bow and curtsey.

'I'm sorry I won't get to see you perform.'

The queen laughed. 'You ain't missing much, love!'

'Well. Thanks anyway.' Patrick gave a lame wave and headed towards the car. At the last moment, he turned back and asked: 'What's your name?'

'Grace.' She put a hand on her hip and drew herself up to her not-inconsiderable full height. 'Grace Anatomy.'

Patrick grinned. 'That is superb.'

'I know,' she said. 'Now fly, my pretties! Fly!'

4

Will watched the car turn off Hurst Street and took a moment to collect himself.

Patrick Lake and Audra Kelly. He couldn't wait to tell Margo. And April, his shift bestie at the bookshop, would simply die. An encounter with a celebrity felt auspicious. But an encounter with two? He wondered idly whether it was a full moon, or if Mercury was in whatever the opposite of retrograde might be.

He took a long drag on his vape, tucked the pen back into his bra, and went inside, emerging from the door next to the DJ booth just as Kylie Minogue's 'On a Night Like This' began to play. Will grinned, and didn't even stop when Jordan appeared to place a tray of shots on his outstretched, upturned hand.

'Skittle-bombs, three quid each or four for a tenner,' Jordan instructed. Usually, the task of hawking these vile things would make Will dry-heave: neither Cointreau nor Red Bull had passed his lips since an emetic house party several years ago, and already the sickly aroma threatened to turn his stomach. But tonight, he decided, was different.

'Three quid each, four for a tenner,' he repeated, and now that official business was dispensed with, he and Jordan shared an agog look at what had just transpired.

'Patrick Lake!' Jordan squealed. 'In my bar!'

'Doing *poppers*?'

'I know! I *know*.' Jordan waved his phone in the air, shaman-like. 'It's already on our socials. Just think. The Village Inn, Patrick Lake's local pub.' His eyes misted over. 'This could be great for us.'

The Village, like lots of gay bars up and down the country, was under near-constant threat of closure. Covid shutdowns had almost been the death of the place, and then there were the ever-encroaching property developers in shiny suits who wanted to bulldoze all of Hurst Street and build luxury apartments and co-working spaces. Each time the vultures swooped in, the Village managed to beat them back, but the incursions were becoming more frequent.

Jordan had taken it upon himself to make a case for the cultural significance of queer spaces, which so far had consisted largely of him ranting to camera on TikTok wearing a tank top and smoky eye. A photo of movie star Patrick Lake enjoying himself in the venue would certainly help their cause, but Will was surprised by how uneasy the thought made him. People came here to have fun, to shed their self-consciousness and be truly themselves, without fear of being surveilled or harassed. Shouldn't that right extend to all their patrons, even the straight ones?

The clamour caused by Patrick Lake and Audra Kelly's appearance rapidly subsided into the usual buzz of the hive, tonight's punters already seeking new entertainment. Up on stage, Tammy introduced Gaia, and in between peddling his pungent wares, Will watched longingly as she undulated her way through a lip-sync to 'Whip My Hair' by Willow Smith, intercut with a seamless lip-sync to Reese Witherspoon's perm monologue from the climactic courtroom scene in *Legally Blonde*. It was stupid, and genius, and Will yearned to be up there with her.

He wasn't the kind of person who considered himself above slinging shots. There were rules here, a hierarchy, and dues to be paid. Drag queens had been eating shit since the days of Divine. It was just that Will had finally thought he was beginning to make progress with his stage presence. The last couple of times he had been up there, he understood fully that the transcendent sensation he got from performing was being experienced by the crowd too. *This is it*, he had told himself. *This is where I am supposed to be.*

And then he actually ate shit. He'd decided not to lip-sync, but to sing live, like the greatest dames did. It had started so well; gay audiences loved a power ballad, and an expertly executed rendition of 'Alone' by Heart lit up the pleasure centres in their drama-loving brains. But then came that big note in the final chorus, the moment where Ann Wilson channelled every ounce of euphoric longing into her voice.

Maybe he hadn't warmed up properly. Maybe it was simply out of his range. Either way, even Will had been shocked by the flat caterwaul coming from his own mouth. Not since the crowning of Camilla had sentiment so rapidly turned against a queen, and Will plummeted back to the bottom of the pyramid.

Will sold another round of stomach aches to a trio of twinks – who insisted on showing him the selfie they had taken with their new bestie, Audra Kelly – and willed himself to not dwell on defeat. Onwards and upwards and all that. *Tonight was auspicious*, he reminded himself. There were portents.

And then who should emerge from the throng, as if summoned by the universe in that very instant to challenge his resolve, than his all-too-recent ex, Ry? And who should be clinging onto Ry's arm than a new beau, a handsome specimen seemingly acquired sometime in the last two and a half weeks? It appeared that the early bird had caught the worm *and* feelings.

'Oh. Will. Hi,' Ry said, even though at that moment, Will looked nothing like his usual self at all, and was in fact doing his best to embody a flame-haired femme fatale from the golden age of Hollywood.

'Hello, Ry.' Will broke out a smile which he hoped was dazzling but casual. 'Who's your friend?'

'Hi, I'm—,' said Ry's companion, his name lost to the noise of the crowd. He looked strikingly similar to Ry, which was to say, not unlike Will himself – tall, dark, and on the verge of ageing out of twinkdom; never let it be said Ry didn't have a type – but with a thicker neck and deeper voice.

'So…' said Ry. 'I see you're still doing this.' He tilted his chin towards Will's frock.

'Doing drag? Oh yes. Our Lady Grace is still very much at large.' Will adopted a carefree tone, as if his penchant for putting on ladies' clothes and dancing for homosexuals had not been a leading cause of his breakup with Ry.

Ry had seemed to find it amusing at first, as if Will had a silly but ultimately harmless hobby, like colouring books for adults. But it didn't take long for that amusement to sour, for Will to get the distinct impression that Ry was tired of humouring him. And so two months into the relationship, Will stopped talking about it in front of him, refrained from showing Ry sketches for his latest outfit or lip-sync ideas. His boyfriend seemed to like drag queens just fine when they were lined up on a stage being judged on TV. In his own life, though? Not so much.

Ry worked in financial law and spent every other weekend visiting his parents at their farmhouse in Kent, where he would post photos in his wellies with the family dog Luna. Will was never invited to accompany Ry on those weekends, of course. So he hadn't even been very surprised when Jordan forwarded him a screengrab of one such picture – a handsome, wholesome shot of Ry and Luna out for a Sunday walk – that he had found on Tinder.

Ry had denied it for all of five minutes.

'Can you blame me?' he'd asked. 'I mean, I want to buy a house and build a life with somebody, maybe even start a family. I can't do that with someone who's out every night on the scene.'

'Out every night?' Will's voice had reached a pitch never achieved on stage before. 'I'm working!'

'No, Will. *I* work,' Ry had said, shaking his head like a disappointed teacher. '*You* play dress-up and call it work, and frankly it's not funny anymore. It's just… too much.'

Those words, Will liked to believe, were chosen in haste, in anger. Because while he and Ry had only dated for a short time, it was long enough for Ry to know how that would hurt him. *It's too much. You're too much.*

Margo, needless to say, had never liked Ry. She didn't like many people, admittedly, but it had still eased the sting a little when Will called her post-breakup and her response had been: 'He looks like a thumb. Pick up ice on your way over.'

And here Ry stood now, less than a month later, holding hands with a less effeminate facsimile. Will glanced downwards and blanched at the sight of their matching pairs of New Balance trainers. Things must be getting serious.

'How've you been?' Will asked Ry over the din of the bar. 'Bought a house yet?' Then, with a dash of sarcasm, 'Had any kids in the last month?'

Ry's smile faltered. *Shit.* They had split because Ry thought Will wasn't enough of a grown-up, and here he was, proving him right.

'Nice to meet you,' said his replacement, as Ry led him away. 'By the way, your boobs are wonky.'

Will pretended not to have heard him, then as soon as they were both out of sight, he turned on his chunky heel, barged through the crowd, dumped the tray of skittle-bombs at the bar, and hurried upstairs to the queens' dressing room, where Raina was *still* primping.

'Blast, bollocks, and buggeration,' he hissed when he saw his lopsided chest in the mirror.

'Oh, honey,' Raina intoned, but the sympathy in her voice, Will knew, was just a top note. Right underneath it, like the flavour profile of a complex wine, was the tannin of mockery.

'It's fine, I'm fine,' he said, fiddling with his breastplate.

So much for his auspicious night. The planets really needed to get their act together.

5

The call from Patrick's manager came at 6:30 a.m. Simone was in Los Angeles, eight hours behind the UK, which meant she had watched the clock long into her evening to ensure he would be awake when she rang.

'I'm going to assume you know why I'm calling,' she said.

He did. He had been sitting up in bed since five, scrolling through pictures of himself on-stage in the Village, grinning like an idiot as Tammy shoved a bottle of 'room odouriser' under his nose. The images were mostly blurry, hurriedly captured on smartphones by drunk people, but not nearly enough to obscure what he was doing.

'I can explain,' he said.

'I'm sure it's quite a story, and I'd love to hear it,' Simone replied, 'but I'm rather busy at present guaranteeing your continued employment.'

'What?' Patrick frowned. It had been a little bit embarrassing, sure, but people more famous than him had been caught doing a lot worse.

'There is a morality clause in your contract,' Simone reminded him.

'There's nothing immoral about a night out.'

'There is when it's in a gay bar and you're on stage holding hands with a Middle Eastern drag queen,' Simone countered, 'which is how the studio heads see it. Not to mention sniffing *amyl fucking nitrite*.'

'Sri Lankan.'

'Excuse me?'

'Tammy,' Patrick said. 'She's not Middle Eastern, she's from Sri Lanka.'

'Good for her. Now what we're going to do is a short, simple statement to clear all of this up. A single line on your socials should suffice, we don't want to make it a whole thing. Just tell the world that you accompanied the crew to a bar while you're on location filming, things got out of hand, and you're sorry and will aim to set a better example in future. And you can't wait for everyone to see the movie. Can you manage that?'

Back in the heyday of Hollywood, Henry Willson had kept any number of unseemly rumours about his client, one Rock Hudson, from sticking. Simone's dedication to keeping Patrick's private life private – safeguarding their mutual livelihood in the process – could put old Henry to shame.

Patrick said nothing for a moment, embarrassment giving way to sullen rage. He was thirty-one years old. He thought back to Audra's tirade the night before, about how ridiculous it was to be denied a haircut whenever you wanted. And it was. But Audra was different in at least one regard: a secret which only Patrick and Simone knew.

Audra was straight, and Patrick wasn't.

Of *course* last night had felt good, had even felt worth risking everything he'd built in that moment. It was the first time in ages he'd acknowledged that side of himself, so no wonder he'd got carried away. But this was the agreement he and Simone had made when he became her client: Come out and work in mid-tier TV for the rest of his career, or keep quiet and get everything he'd ever wanted.

Well. Almost everything.

They'd come too far now. The first *Kismet* had been a hit, but it was this movie everyone would judge him on. *Can he do it again? Can he lead a franchise?* This sequel was the gateway to the wider Wonderverse on the big screen, to his pick of scripts, maybe even to directing someday. There would come a time when Patrick could hang out in any bar he wanted, be beholden to nobody. But that day was a way off yet.

'Consider it done,' he told Simone.

'Send me a draft before you post it,' she said. 'And it goes without saying, but…'

'I know.' Something inside Patrick tightened and ossified. 'No more gay bars. Goodnight, Simone.'

Seemingly satisfied, Simone hung up, and Patrick collapsed onto his pillow. He would have liked nothing more than to roll over and go back to sleep, but 6:30 a.m. meant a training session with Hector. He had to start getting ready now if he didn't want to miss his call time.

When the knock at his hotel room door came ten minutes later, it wasn't Hector laden with dumbbells and an alarmingly bright demeanour for so early in the morning, but instead a production assistant bearing a sheaf of new sides.

'More rewrites?' he asked. She looked terrified. 'More rewrites. Cool. Thank you. Have a nice day!' he called after her as she fled down the corridor, having already delivered the new script to Audra, who stood in her doorway flapping the pages in the air.

'Can you believe this?' she called across the hall to him. 'He can't be serious.'

Lucas Grant, their new director, had been railroading the writing team into adding whole new sequences to 'make it more dynamic' and 'simplify the story', a tall order considering this movie was intended to launch a cohesive new continuity of interconnected sequels and spinoffs. At this rate, Patrick reckoned the extant cut of *Kismet 2* was already five hours long and in need of a good edit – or an intermission.

'It's wild,' he said.

'Lunch later?' Audra asked. 'Sources close to me say I'm hungover.'

'Sure,' Patrick murmured, only half looking at the pages in front of him as he reached for the door handle, 'but we should probably do our homework first.' He gave her an absentminded wave and turned back into his room, but not before hearing Audra sing, tunelessly yet still sweetly: 'Last night a drag queen saved my life…'

6

1949

When the Office for the Mission to Explore the Galaxy headed by Professor Orson Oswald completed its top-secret project — an aircraft capable of travelling to the stars — there was only ever one person who could be trusted to man the test flight. Captain Richard Ranger had proven his skills as a pilot during the war, not to mention his bravery and valour. Ranger succeeded in flying this experimental craft, nicknamed the Kismet, up into the Earth's orbit — but before he could make his descent, the Kismet was pulled into a wormhole, propelling Ranger light years across the cosmos, where he crash-landed on a distant world known as Zalia. This planet is under siege by a merciless invading force called the Prox, but the Zalians continue to resist, led by their mighty, beautiful princess, Sura. When we last left Ranger, he was preparing to defend the capital alongside Sura in a battle that will determine the fate of Zalia — and all life in the universe.

But passing through the wormhole changed Ranger on an atomic level, causing a transformation he is only beginning to understand and bestowing gifts beyond imagining. Enhanced strength, rapid healing, the ability to breathe in any atmosphere, and even the power to fly. A scientific freak? A miracle? Or the next stage in human evolution? The only thing that's certain is in order to defeat the Prox, save Zalia, and have any hope of returning home, Ranger will have to embody the indomitable strength of the human spirit. He must become…

CAPTAIN KISMET!

'This is really quite good,' said Charles, laying the recap page down on his desk.

'I'm a hack,' said his wife, Iris, over his shoulder. 'But I am having the most marvellous fun.'

'So what happens next?' The first Captain Kismet story had gone down a storm with their editor at the magazine, and Charles had jumped on his offer to commission more short, serialised comic adventures featuring their new hero.

'Captain Kismet defeats the Prox, of course.' She circled the small desk to face Charles. 'But not before Princess Sura is tragically killed in battle.'

'Oh no!' Charles looked genuinely wounded. 'But she has such gumption.'

'I know, I like her too. But Ranger needs to return to Earth, and he can't do that with a purple-skinned sweetheart tagging along.'

'Why does he have to go home?' Charles asked. 'Why can't he stay on Zalia?'

'Because,' Iris said, a wicked glint in her eye, 'the real enemy has yet to reveal himself.'

'Go on.' Charles propped his elbow on the desk and rested his chin on his hand.

'Do you remember how Sura helped Ranger climb that mountain so he could use Zalian science to send a message back through the wormhole and let his superior officers know that he was still alive?'

'Of course.'

'Well, Professor Oswald intercepted that message before Ranger's loyal friend Penny Haven or anybody else back home could hear it. So he alone knows of the wormhole and its uncanny effects. And now, unbeknownst to Ranger, back on Earth, Oswald is attempting to recreate the flight of the Kismet, to give himself the same powers.'

'And will he succeed?' Charles was aware he sounded like a little boy at bedtime, begging for another story. *And then what? And then what?*

'After a fashion,' said Iris. 'But it changes him in different ways. His abilities are all mental, and Oswald becomes malformed so that his body can no longer support his engorged head. He must wear a special mechanised exoskeleton and helmet at all times. Something quite monstrous.' Charles made a note of this, as Iris adopted a reedy, pantomime-ish tone: 'If Ranger represents the next stage of humankind, I am its apotheosis! Let them hail Ranger as the Alpha… for I am the Omega!' She smiled and returned to her usual speaking voice. 'A being of pure, terrifying intellect, unburdened by conscience, who is able to anticipate Ranger's every move. He is to be Captain Kismet's ultimate nemesis moving forward. A hero is nothing without a good villain, after all.'

She paced as she spoke, although there was not exactly very far for her to go. The Ambroses' apartment, a walk-up in Flatbush, consisted of a bedroom, a narrow bathroom that was always freezing, and a living area they had converted into a shared studio, with Iris's typewriter on one side of the room, Charles's drawing desk on the other, and a beaten-up old sofa in between. It was just short of a flophouse – far less than Charles would have liked to offer his new bride – and Iris was in a constant war of attrition with the mouse that had taken up residence behind the stove, but it was theirs.

'This is all excellent,' said Charles, already jotting down ideas for how best to visually accompany the wild fruit of his wife's imagination. 'Haywood will love it.'

'Do you think he'll love it enough to let me put my name on it?' Iris asked. The way she said it was offhand, but Charles knew she resented being forced to publish her contributions under a male pseudonym. It was unfair, he knew it was: the entire story was hers, after all! But Charles knew that if Iris kept insisting on bringing it up to Walter Haywood, the editor would soon be less receptive to publishing their work. And at present, his drawings and Iris's writing were what kept this pock-marked, mouse-ridden roof over their heads.

'I know, I know,' Iris said, seemingly reading his mind. She shook her hands in the air as if to waft away a bad odour and continued her circuit of the living room. 'Anyway,' she added, 'I have been ruminating on something else.'

'Oh?'

'In addition to a villain, there is something else every hero needs,' she said.

'And what's that?' Charles enquired.

'A faithful sidekick, of course.'

7

Will was in the screaming cupboard for less than a minute before he heard the bell chime over the front door of the shop. The screaming cupboard at Gilroy & Son's Rare & Second-hand Books long predated Will's employment there, as integral to the smooth running of the place as the stacks of musty volumes on its cramped, crowded shelves. On his first day, April had even pointed it out during the 'grand tour' of the narrow, single-floor space, as if giving him directions to the loo: 'stockroom on the left, little fridge and kettle at the back (we take it in turns buying milk), and then we've got the screaming cupboard next to the sink.'

'Sorry,' Will cut in. 'Screaming cupboard?'

April had just given him a bright smile and said: 'You'll see.'

At the time, he thought she was joking – after all, how stressful could selling second-hand books possibly *be* – but gamely ate his words after having his first customer-related meltdown, making full use of the shop's screaming facilities within a week of starting.

It wasn't that the job came with a particularly heavy workload, or even that Yvonne Gilroy, widow to one of the '& Son's, was a bad boss: she mostly left Will and April to their own devices. But he had underestimated the challenges of dealing with the more finickity collectors, and the painstaking work of verifying provenance before they would even *consider* making a purchase, not to mention the chancers who would come in with their childhood copies of *The Famous Five*, complete with Crayola scrawls and missing pages, expecting a windfall and kicking up a fuss when none was forthcoming. Bookselling was still retail, after all, and the average customer seemed to still be under the impression that they were always right.

Aside from inventory, these fruitless, maddening conversations took up the lion's share of Will's working day. But rarely was he ever truly rushed off his feet: in between the occasional 'decompression session' in the screaming cupboard, he was still able to spend hours behind the counter reading some doorstopper or surreptitiously planning his next gig. Frankly, he wasn't sure how the Gilroy family made any money at all and was nursing a suspicion that rare books were simply a less conspicuous front for money-laundering than vape shops and bubble tea.

Today's visit to the screaming cupboard was a combination of hangover – Will started each of his nights at the Village with the intent to stay sober, but like any family, the local gays were easier to love with a drink inside him – and lingering embarrassment from his run-in with Ry.

The chime of the door that drew Will back to the present signalled the arrival of April, who was placing two coffees and a bag of pastries on the counter as Will emerged.

'My hero,' he whispered, as much to the coffee as to April.

'I got you, girl,' she said, brushing imaginary dust off the shoulder of what looked like the latest addition to her collection of X-Men T-shirts. *Storm!* it proclaimed. *Mistress of the Elements!* Paired with April's 'Black Girl Magic' choker, it gave the overall impression of somebody who enjoyed making pathetic white men cry on the internet. Which Will happened to know was her second favourite pastime, after ranking comic-book superheroes by their bums. It was a list with ever-changing criteria, from size to pertness to number of appearances on the page, with a whole separate appendix detailing how well the artist seemed to understand the mechanics of the human body. April regularly sent him posts from her blog, and because Will was a good friend, he would always dutifully contribute a click towards her traffic. And while he didn't always read the entire thing, he certainly enjoyed the pictures.

Between sips of an Americano, Will regaled April with the story of last night.

'I can't believe I met Patrick Lake and Audra Kelly with a skew-whiff tit,' he moaned around a mouthful of pain au chocolat. Because yes, seeing his ex had been awkward, perhaps even a tiny bit painful, but the thing he kept going back to about last night wasn't Ry and his unexamined shame around engaging in queer culture. It wasn't the parallel universe version of Will that Ry had plucked out of a Planet Fitness to be his new boo. It wasn't even the crooked breastplate, although that last detail did still smart a bit.

It was the look Patrick Lake had given him, for just a second, before turning to get into the car. A movie star smile was all well and good, but Will had spent enough time performing in his own little corner of the world to know that they never quite reached the eyes. Patrick Lake had smiled at him as if he really saw him and, even more, was pleased by what he saw.

Or maybe that had just been the poppers. Either way, it didn't matter. Small-town drag queens and big-time actors didn't make the most natural bedfellows, and even if Will *was* a little bit lonely, and Patrick Lake looked like the platonic ideal of masculinity as sketched by da Vinci, it was also evident that he was a Big Straight. And that was a game Will refused to play, because nobody won. A crush on a straight guy was permissible in the very early and confusing years of figuring yourself out and no later, he reasoned. In fact, fancying a straight man was much like fancying a celebrity: unlikely to get you anywhere. So why couldn't he stop thinking about that smile?

'Think of it this way,' said April. 'Wonky boobs or not, you saved the day. Stopped a couple of superstars from being mobbed by a horde of drunk gays. Give yourself some credit.'

'Hmm,' Will said, going through the short stack of messages Yvonne had left on Post-its next to the phone. Somebody enquiring as to whether their grandfather's Jeffrey Archer collection might be worth 'a bob or two', the window cleaner calling to reschedule, and a request for something called…

'The Omega Issue?' he said it as a question, picking up the scrap of paper and turning to April. 'Why do I feel like I've heard of that before?'

April's face lit up. 'You actually do read my blog!"

'Huh?'

'That thing is like the Holy Grail for nerds,' April explained. 'It's said to contain the original ending to Captain Kismet's first twelve-issue storyline, before *Wonder* Magazine decided the character was worth keeping around and rebooted his origin story. Can you believe that? They almost didn't realise what they had on their hands. Without Captain Kismet, none of the Wonderverse would even exist.'

'You mean we almost *didn't* live in a world where the only thing at the cinema every summer is a three-hour showcase of CGI that exists solely as a marketing ploy for the post-credit scene that teases the next three-hour origin story?'

'Don't be such a cynic, it'll give you crow's feet.' April slid a miniature Danish to her side of the counter in admonishment. 'These stories mean a lot to people, Will. When Walter Haywood first came up with the character of Richard Ranger, the Second World War was barely in the rear view mirror. All that pain and loss... Captain Kismet was like a beacon of hope. A reminder that standing up for what's right is always worth it, no matter the cost.'

'In other words, propaganda.'

'You really can be such a grumpy wretch, you know that?' April took a sip of coffee. 'All of that was seventy years and a couple of billion ago, of course. Before Wonder Comics stripped back all the nuance and turned him into this hypermasculine power fantasy. There was one storyline last year where he basically acted like a police officer, protecting the status quo and the property of his millionaire friend when aliens invaded. There are a whole bunch of fascists who treat him like a mascot for the American dream. By which they mean, a straight cis dude's right to do whatever the hell he likes without reproach. Of course, these are the same people who think Jesus was a white guy.'

Everybody had their respective areas of passionate research. Will's were *Project Runway* – discounting the newer seasons – and Taylor Swift. Margo claimed to know so much about wine that he often suspected her of faking it, although she *could* clock a corked Shiraz at twenty paces. Jordan was a walking encyclopaedia when it came to LGBTQ+ history, frequently using that knowledge to bolster or rationalise his more outlandish pronouncements. For April, it was all things superhero. She lived and breathed this stuff, could deliver a TED talk at the drop of a hat on how depictions of people of colour in Wonderverse comics had evolved alongside shifting social attitudes in the twentieth century. The glee with which she spoke about alternate timelines and heroic archetypes was one of the many things that Will loved about her. And it was this love that softened his ire as April devoured the last remaining pastry, maintaining eye contact with him the entire time.

'Reparations,' she quipped, with her mouth full. It was a joke she liked to make often, and the first time she'd said it to Will he had nearly choked to death on white guilt.

'So you don't think there's much chance of us tracking down this Omega Issue, then?'

April shrugged. 'There's no proof that there was even an official printing, let alone that any copies made it over here from the States. If we did manage to find one, it'd probably be out of this client's price range.'

'In other words...?'

'A lot of work, for which Yvonne would be very unlikely to reimburse us,' April summarised.

'Message received,' Will said, screwing up the paper along with the empty pastry bag and tossing both into the bin under the counter.

After work, Will made the short walk down to the Bullring outdoor market, where Margo still insisted on buying all of her vegetables before going to the M&S Food Hall her 'nicer bits'.

'I knew it! Thief!' she shouted as Will approached, because he had not done any washing in a while and had simply picked up her pilfered shirt from his bedroom floor that morning, given it a cursory sniff, and put it back on.

'I only steal from the best,' Will said, grinning with what he hoped was sufficient charm.

'You look tired.' This came not from Margo, but from her teenager. Dylan loitered slightly behind Margo, swathed in black, at a carefully gauged distance so nobody would dare presume they were here helping his mum shop. Dylan had been so sweet, a mere matter of months ago. Now they wore all black and spent most of their time mangling chords with their mates in a band called The War on Christmas.

'Hey, Dylan, nice to see you can venture out of your room from time to time,' Will said loudly. 'I was beginning to think you were a vampire.'

'Sun ages the skin,' said Dylan. 'I figured you'd know that by now.'

Little bitch, Will thought proudly. Ever since declaring over a game of Monopoly that they were exploring their nonbinary identity, Dylan had stepped up their shade game. Will liked to think he could take some credit for that, but every now and then Dylan would remind him just how ruthless a disaffected teen could be.

'My skin is more snatched than the Lindbergh baby,' Will replied.

'What's that?' Dylan asked, tilting their head. 'How old *are* you again?'

'Dylan, be nice to your uncle,' said Margo. 'He doesn't live with us anymore; his natural immunity to your barbs is diminishing.' She kissed Will on the temple and held up a basket of tomatoes. 'Do these piccolos look like they'll last the week?'

'They look so ready to go the distance I might buy a ring.'

'You're in a good mood.'

'I *am*. I fought my hangover and I won. Also, you are going to freak when I tell you who I met last night.'

He trailed behind his sister, launching into the tale. Margo barely looked up from the aubergines she was examining when he mentioned Patrick Lake. Will wondered at first if she was really listening, or if last night did not make as good a story as he thought.

Margo, it turned out, was listening; she just wasn't impressed. Which was in keeping with her entire personality.

'The first *Kismet* movie was awful,' she said. 'Me and Dylan watched it on our last film night.'

'Aww, you guys still have film night?' Will teased.

'Barely *ever*!' Dylan protested, clearly mortified by the idea that anyone would know they still spent Sunday nights curled up on the sofa under a blanket with their mother.

'I never saw it.' Will shrugged.

'He was quite good in that other thing, though,' said Margo, holding up a punnet of mushrooms in each hand for scrutiny. 'I forget what it's called. You know, the action thing.'

'You could quite literally be describing anything.'

'She means the spy thriller,' said Dylan, tone exhausted. '*The Bullet Journal.*'

'Do you have dinner plans?' Margo asked, handing her tote bag to Dylan, which was now brimming with fresh produce.

Will thought of his empty fridge and his near-empty bank account.

'I was thinking I might grab myself some sushi,' he said.

'Nice. Ten Ichi?'

'Tesco.'

'Absolutely not.' Margo gagged. 'Supermarket sushi is the pits, Will. You don't get to eat like a poor student when you never actually went to uni.'

'The reduced-to-clear aisle is actually a very happening spot this time of day,' said Will. 'Lots of eligible divorced dads. Come with me. You never know, you might meet someone.'

Just as he had hoped, Margo grabbed Will by the shoulder and steered him towards the indoor fish market. 'There's a great place here where you eat at the counter,' she said. 'We'll all go. My treat. I've decided I can't be arsed to cook.'

'Yes!' Dylan pumped their fist, then immediately acted like they hadn't. Will smiled.

'You don't have to do that,' he said, not even bothering to try to sound genuine.

Margo just shook her head. 'Supermarket sushi. Honestly, Will. You need to want more for yourself.'

Will allowed himself to be led into the hall, stomach already rumbling at the thought of a dragon roll. Maybe some seaweed.

Ooh, and that tasty fried pumpkin thing he liked. Perhaps afterwards, he would go back outside to the rag market and eye up some fabric for his next costume.

Who needs movie stars, he thought, *when you've got a sister who'll pay for dinner?*

8

Interior. Zalian Palace. KISMET and SURA stand over a holo-display of the HYPERIOSPHERE, the ancient device capable of channelling the power of a star.

KISMET
We need to get to the Hyperiosphere before the Prox decipher its activation code. If we don't, they could use its laser to cut through this planet like a bagel.

SURA
I will not allow my world to become a bagel.

KISMET
swipes at the holo-display, which now shows the tallest mountain on Zalia.

KISMET
Looks like they're keeping the sphere at Prophet's Peak. I'll fly up there, disarm the Hyperiosphere, or die trying.

SURA

Listen, flyboy, I don't know about that Earth place of yours, but around here the women call the shots. This is my planet, and if anybody is going to die to save it, it'll be me.

KISMET

You're too important. This world will need you once the war is over. To rebuild.

SURA

There won't *be* anything to rebuild if we don't get to the Hypersphere on time.

KISMET

Hyperiosphere.

SURA

That's what I said.

KISMET

You said Hypersphere. It's Hyperiosphere.

SURA

Hyperiodsphere.

KISMET

Hyperiosphere.

SURA

Fuck's sake!

Audra threw down her script and grabbed a bottle of water from the coffee table in Patrick's suite.

'Hardly Chekhov, is it?' she said, taking a sip. 'Red leather, yellow leather. Red leather, yellow leather. Hyperiosphere. There! God. Why is this so hard?'

'Maybe if it were Dua Lipa you'd get the hang of it,' said Patrick.

'And if I don't, I will never live it down,' she said. 'I swear to God, the only thing worse than comic book movies are comic book movie *fans*.'

'They're not so bad.'

'Really?' She gave him a particularly withering look, and pointed to her phone. 'Why don't you take a scroll through my DMs.'

Audra didn't quite connect with the source material in the same way Patrick did. She had come to the first *Kismet* movie fresh from a messy breakup and a DUI, eager to clean up her image. A big studio project was needed to get her career back on track – it almost didn't matter which one. Her management had settled on this franchise for two reasons. Firstly, Wonder Studios' morality clause would keep her out of trouble, which meant once she could prove she wasn't an insurance liability she'd have her pick of roles. And secondly, what embodied 'America's sweetheart' more than playing a superhero who was also a princess?

'Do you ever find yourself wondering,' Audra said, fanning the script pages out in front of her, 'if this movie might be… you know.' She leaned forward and whispered: '*Bad?*'

'What?' Patrick frowned. 'No. It's… meta.'

'Meta.'

'Sure. Like, we're going back to the pulpy origins of these stories, these characters, and looking at them through twenty-first-century eyes.'

'That would certainly explain why my character, the ruler of a technologically and philosophically advanced matriarchal civilisation...' Audra checked her pages. 'Has *one* scene where she talks to another woman. This script fails the Bechdel test so hard it should be sent to summer school.'

'Well, yeah, but this is all just setting up the universe. Your character will probably get her own movie at some point.'

Audra scowled. 'I *die* at the end.'

'This is comics!' Patrick spread his hands like a showman. 'Anything is possible!'

'Your pep is disgusting,' she informed him.

'I just got really into the lore when I was researching the first movie.'

'This conversation makes me miss Percocet.' Audra stood up and headed for the door, then remarked over her shoulder, 'Please get a hobby.'

'Your script,' said Patrick, pointing to her discarded pages.

'I'll learn it on the day,' she said. 'I don't trust them not to rewrite it in the time it takes for me to get into makeup.' She left the door to swing slowly closed behind her.

She had a point. At this rate their elongated shoot would just keep going and going. It was one of the mantras of showbusiness: hurry up and wait.

Except Patrick had never been good at waiting. To stand still was to let things catch up with you. Better, he thought, to keep moving. He passed a lot of time exercising with Hector and Corey, punishing his body (despite already having shot the movie's single prerequisite shirtless scene) so that the exhaustion would help him sleep. But that solution, like a slain hydra, spawned new problems.

It was impossible to work out with guys like Corey Drummer and Hector Ramirez without noticing how, well, *hot* they were. Patrick could expend as much time and effort as he liked trying to ignore it, but the truth was, he loved men. Their stubble, their body hair, the way they smelled, the fluid ripple of muscle in their backs as they lifted and stretched.

Patrick usually succeeded in keeping these thoughts at a comfortable distance, burying himself in work and going on long, long runs. He was unsure why it felt more difficult now. Nothing had changed, after all. The gay bar had been a blip, that was all.

It was safer to retreat into the comics, he decided. To commit to the role that thousands of fans and millions of dollars were counting on him to get right. To understand Captain Kismet as well as he knew himself, so that in spite of the chaos of this production, he might be able to deliver a performance that he could be proud of. Patrick had faith, at least, in his ability to do that. He'd been acting his whole life.

9

The second time Will Wright met Patrick Lake, his body parts were all exactly where they belonged. Will was perched behind the counter in Gilroy's, reading a reprint of *Maurice* from 1987 when the actor walked in. Even more so than at the gay bar the other night, seeing Patrick here, in his bookshop, caught Will completely off guard, like looking up and seeing the moon in the middle of the day.

Holy shit, he thought, *he's even more gorgeous in daylight*. The sun seemed to bounce off his short sandy hair as Patrick removed his cap and sunglasses, and Will couldn't detect so much as a pore on his clean-shaven, inconsiderately handsome face.

April was currently out buying sandwiches for lunch. She was going to be furious.

'Hello there,' said Will. 'Welcome.'

Patrick smiled, revealing a dimple to the left of his mouth, a single concession to asymmetry. Did Patrick recognise him, he wondered?

'Hi,' he said. 'I'm hoping you can help me.' He placed his hands on the counter and leaned forward slightly, as if about to confide something private to Will. Will, for his part, couldn't help but notice the sheer size of the hands laid flat on the wood, their eyes at exactly the same level now that Will wasn't looming over him in heels. Patrick's eyes were the palest blue he'd ever seen.

'I'm looking for a comic book,' Patrick said.

'Oh. Hmm. We're really more in the business of, you know, *book* books,' Will replied. 'But there's a Forbidden Planet just up the street—'

'What I'm after is pretty rare. Not the kind of thing I could just pick up in a comic book store. And you guys specialise in rare, right?'

'That we do,' Will affirmed, wondering if this rich, almost certainly entitled celebrity was about to become his latest nightmare customer. 'And we do, occasionally, deal with old magazines and comics,' he admitted. 'Why don't you tell me a few more specifics.'

'It's the twelfth and final instalment of the first run of *The Adventures of Captain Kismet*,' Patrick replied. 'It was supposed to be published in the May 1950 issue of *Wonder* Magazine. But there's all kinds of confusion on whether it actually ran or not.'

'Doing some additional character research?' Will asked.

Patrick smiled again, no doubt used to strangers being familiar with the ins and outs of his working life. 'Exactly.' He retrieved his phone from his pocket, scrolling through what appeared to be a list of details in his Notes app. 'It's sometimes known as the Omega Issue,' he added, reading aloud now, 'and features the first defeat of the villain Omega Man.'

Will had been so preoccupied with wondering if he should mention '*oh hey, by the way, I'm the bloke in a dress from the other night*', that it took a moment to register what Patrick had said.

'The Omega Issue,' he repeated.

'That's right,' said Patrick. 'Do you have it?'

Will scanned the countertop, moving his copy of *Maurice* and rifling through the various loose sheets of paper, before remembering he had binned the Post-it bearing exactly those words. Patrick had called ahead and left a message, then dropped by in person when he received no reply. Somebody more naïve than Will, a romantic perhaps, might have interpreted this as a sign that events, circumstances, fate, were conspiring to bring the two of them together.

Will knew better.

'That *is* pretty rare, if I remember correctly,' he said. 'Let me just check anyway...'

He entered the details Patrick had given him into the database that he had spent several painstaking weeks digitising for Yvonne, ninety-nine per cent sure by now that Patrick didn't know he was Grace Anatomy. Will might not have been serving flawless female illusion with his sinewy arms and unshaven legs, but the transformative powers of a wig and half-decent beat were not to be underestimated.

'Don't take this the wrong way,' he said as he typed, 'but don't actors usually do their research earlier on?'

Patrick shrugged with one shoulder, which only served to draw Will's attention to how broad they were, and once again how tightly his T-shirt hugged his bicep. Will's own arms, of which he was quite proud on an average day, were toned but lacked the sheer size of this guy's. And he certainly didn't have anything remotely resembling that barrel chest. All the better to squeeze into a sequinned gown.

Still, Will liked to think he had a better-than-average relationship with his own body. Until somebody who looked like this walked into his shop, because self-esteem had as many laws of relativity as physics; everything existed in comparison to everything else. A vein in Patrick's arm pulsed, and Will felt a familiar pang of desire tinged with envy, or maybe it was the other way around. *Do I want you? Do I want to be you? How might it feel to walk down the street as you? How safe does it feel in your body?*

Will averted his eyes, turning his attention back to the screen in front of him.

'Sorry,' he said. 'It doesn't look like we have what you're looking for.'

'Darn,' Patrick muttered, and Will was taken aback by how adorable it sounded, because even in America, who said 'darn' anymore?

'Well, thank you for trying,' Patrick said, turning to leave.

'Wait!' *God, Will, are you that starved for male attention? I mean, sure, this man is the kind of stunning that would all-but-guarantee him a gruesome fate in Greek mythology. But you need to get a grip.*

'Tell you what,' he said. 'I can ask around, if you like? I know a couple of collectors and dealers who might be able to help. And my colleague April lives for tracking down this kind of thing. Maybe she'll have a lead. Although your best bet is probably—'

'eBay, I know. Trust me, I've been trawling like crazy.'

'If we do find what we're looking for, approaching sellers privately is also likely to end up being quite expensive.'

'That won't be a problem,' was the reply. 'And hey, listen. I really appreciate you offering to help. Here's my number.' Patrick grabbed a pen from a jar next to the till and jotted down his information. 'Give me a call if you find anything. Thanks again.' He put his hat and shades back on, the uniform of a celebrity incognito. 'I'm Patrick, by the way.'

Will laughed. 'I know.'

'And your name is…?' Patrick asked.

'Will.' He cleared his throat. 'Will Wright.'

'Nice to meet you, Will.' And he flashed that smile again, causing a bubble of air to halt in Will's throat.

This, he thought, *will be how I die.*

It wasn't until Patrick was gone, seeming to take at least half the air in the room with him, and Will had vigorously cleared his throat, that he looked down and realised this handsome stranger had written on the closest thing to hand. Meaning he had just defaced a copy of *Maurice* that would now be coming out of Will's pay.

At least it wasn't a first edition.

He was contemplating another sojourn in the screaming cupboard when the bell rang again: It was April. She approached the counter with care, a smoothie in each hand, brown paper bag clutched carefully between her forearm and left boob like she was nursing an infant, but her eyes blazed.

'You will not believe who I just saw,' she said breathlessly.

Will laughed. So much for the hat and sunglasses.

'I could take a very good guess,' he said.

'Shut *up*. He was here? Patrick Lake was here?' April set their lunch down on the counter and slapped Will on the arm. 'And I missed it because you insisted it was my turn to go out for food?'

'You wanted to get your steps in.'

'As if Patrick Lake was in Gilroy's,' April said. 'What was he doing here? Oh! Did he come in to thank you for helping during that whole debacle on Friday?'

'No,' said Will. 'I don't actually think he knew that was me.'

'And you didn't tell him?'

Will dodged the question.

'He's the one who rang about the Omega Issue,' he told her, knowing it would pique her interest. 'I said it could be a tall order, but that we'd ask around for him. I thought maybe it might be a project that's perfect for the expertise of someone who is, let's say, not me?'

The fire returned to April's eyes.

'Absolutely,' she said. 'Oh my God. Patrick Lake, our client. Patrick Lake, *my* client.' She tore the sandwich bags open with abandon. 'What is going *on* in Birmingham right now?'

'I know, right?' said Will, grinning along with her but also turning over April's unanswered question in his mind. Why hadn't he told Patrick who he was, that they'd already met? He wasn't sure exactly, only that it had something to do with the flushed red cheeks of the man he'd met that first night, and the unguarded way Patrick had looked right at him. The more he dwelled on it – and dwell on it he did – the more it seemed to Will that he'd got a glimpse of something that night too. A version of Patrick Lake that few people in the world ever saw.

It was silly, he knew, but for all the swooning he'd felt when Patrick walked into Gilroy's like a cowboy from an old advert, Will thought he preferred that initial red-faced, clumsy grin. So he wouldn't embarrass the man by bringing it up. He would file it away like he had with so many other fleeting glances and secret crushes over the years, and that way he would be able to keep the moment separate and safe, all to himself.

10

Patrick returned to the second-hand bookstore on Bull Street a couple of days later, for reasons he could not entirely explain. He had given the guy who worked there, Will, his contact details, and he knew from his own attempts at finding the Omega Issue that locating a copy would likely take some time. Checking in personally was unnecessary.

And contrary to his wishful thinking, that guy in the bookstore, the one with the dark hair and the cute snub nose, had not been flirting with him. He just worked in customer service. He probably smiled like that at everybody. Patrick still cringed at the eagerness with which he'd written down his number. What a putz!

Maybe I'll pick up some reading material while I'm here, he thought. *Maybe Audra and I can start a book club to pass the time while we're sitting around waiting for Lucas Grant to decide what the hell he wants this movie to be.*

Besides, it was only a short walk to Gilroy's: out of the hotel, across the square where the cathedral looked plastered over the bright spring sky like a decal, and around the corner. You could almost follow the chiming sound of the tram as it slid to a stop opposite the bookshop's front window. Patrick wondered if maybe he needed to soften his earlier appraisal of Birmingham. There was a beauty to the city that took its time in revealing itself; like a dowdy girl in an old movie, she needed to let down her hair and take off her glasses before you could really see it.

Patrick felt strangely nervous as he pushed the door to the shop open and stepped inside. Will stood behind the counter, chatting with a woman in a *Hellfire Gala* T-shirt. Was this the co-worker Will had mentioned? Another young man with bleached hair sat on the counter with his legs crossed and an iced latte dangling from his left hand. His right hand was entwined with Will's, and Patrick was surprised to feel a pang of jealousy. Although he wasn't sure if it was because of the handholding with Will specifically, or merely the casual, almost-unthinking care these two men displayed for each other. To Patrick, being so physically at ease with another man was practically unimaginable.

The bell over the door rang, and all three people at the counter turned in unison, pausing in a comical tableau when they saw him.

'Hi, again,' he said.

'Hello,' said Will, his face blooming into a wide smile. 'Again.' He withdrew his hand from his companion's to swipe a stray lock of hair from his eyes.

'Sorry to bother you,' Patrick continued, 'I just had some time to spare today, and I... I felt bad. I didn't buy anything the last time I was in here.'

'Oh, you don't have to—' Will began, but he was interrupted by his friend.

'We have a wide-ranging collection of fiction, memoir, and history,' she said, 'along with stationery and postcards.'

'Sounds good,' said Patrick, taking a couple more steps into the store. 'I love your shirt, by the way.'

'Thanks!' she beamed. 'I'm a big X-Men fan. I love Captain Kismet too,' she quickly added. 'I'm April – Will filled me in on your Omega Issue assignment. Quite the challenge, I have to say.

I've been emailing with some seriously eccentric collectors, plumbed the depths of forums that would turn your hair white...'

'I appreciate it, truly,' said Patrick. 'Who's your favourite mutant, though?' He rarely got to talk about this stuff; even his co-workers on the movie had superhero fatigue. 'Mine's Emma Frost.'

'She slays.' April nodded in respect. 'But I'm a Storm girl. Always have been.'

'A-*hem*.' The blond sprang off the counter and extended his hand. 'Jordan Thomas,' he said. 'Your forehead is a masterpiece. Botox? No judgements.'

'Jordan!' Will exclaimed.

'I said *no judgements*,' Jordan said.

'No Botox,' Patrick laughed. 'Just lucky, I guess.' The compliment had been genuine, and based on appearances it seemed Jordan knew what he was talking about. Patrick had worked in Hollywood long enough to recognise good cosmetic work when he saw it. Kudos to the aesthetician who had tended to Jordan's lips and brow: his facial fillers were probably the most subtle thing about him.

'It's nice to meet you.' Patrick shook the offered hand.

'We met the other night,' Jordan said. 'Kind of. You were at my bar? The Village. I served you and your friends.'

'Oh! Right!' Patrick withdrew his palm before it could begin to sweat, and immediately hated that his first instinct was to be embarrassed; to grow flustered when all he'd really done was allow his meticulously constructed persona to slip for a few moments. And Grace had stepped in before things got too bad. Grace with the green eyes.

'Jordan actually wanted to apologise for something,' said Will.

Patrick raised an eyebrow. Jordan did too. Or rather, he tried.

'I do?' Jordan asked.

'Yes.' Will prodded him. 'Jordan here, in what I wish I could say was a rare lapse in judgement, took a photo of you.' He closed his hand into a fist, brought it to his nose, and mimed taking a big breath.

'Oh.' Patrick said again, his diminishing cheer now crumpling like tissue paper. 'I see.'

Jordan pursed his sculpted cupid's bow.

'Yeah, sorry about that,' he said. 'Hope you didn't get any flack for it. I mean, it would be corporate cowardice at its most craven if your career were to suffer. Anyway, it's gone now. Will said I should delete it. At first I was like, why? That would be like saying you were doing something wrong, right? You weren't hurting anyone, and it's not like having a good time in a gay bar is a crime. Not since the 1960s. But then I thought, it's a bit vulgar, you know? To post pictures of someone without their permission. Not hot girl shit at all. So... Sorry. Again.'

Jordan was clearly unaccustomed to delivering apologies, but as artless and rambling as it was, Patrick was touched. The smooth running of the entire entertainment industry depended on bland statements, pretty words arranged neatly so as to conceal their emptiness.

He couldn't blame Jordan for his own secrets, or the fact that his contract with Wonder Studios held archaic ideas of what constituted 'family-friendly'. In the first *Kismet* movie, he had punched a bad guy so hard he went through the side of a mountain. Family-friendly bone-crunching violence, apparently. His was a world full of such idiotic rules and contradictions, and he did not begrudge outsiders their insouciance.

'It's forgotten,' he said. Then, eager to move the conversation along, he asked: 'So how long have you guys been together?'

Will and Jordan frowned for a second – or at least, Will frowned, and Jordan's energy grew perplexed – and then they both burst out laughing.

'We're besties,' said Will, and Jordan added: 'I like to think that I can do a lot better than *him*, thank you very much.'

Patrick instantly liked Jordan a little more. The rush of affection tasted like relief, and no, he was not going to interrogate that emotional response right now.

'My mistake. I'm just going to...' He gestured vaguely at their surroundings.

'Yes! Browse!' April said. 'Let us know if you have any questions.'

He turned away and began to examine the spines on the shelves, picking up the occasional book to read the cover, but all the while he could feel three stares burning into the back of his head, so much so that he couldn't concentrate on anything he read and started just pretending to peruse the dust jackets. He experienced a similar feeling exploring art galleries, unsure how long to stand in front of one piece before moving on to the next.

When what felt like an appropriate amount of time had passed, he grabbed three volumes at random: a collection of poetry by Wordsworth, *The Blind Assassin* by Margaret Atwood, and a dog-eared beginner's guide to Feng Shui from the Nineties, which he hoped might give him the inspiration to contact his decorator in LA. When he returned with them to the counter, Will glanced at each title as he rang them up, and Patrick tried to analyse them through those green eyes. His choices were probably basic, pedestrian. He watched Will carefully for the slightest hint of a smirk or eye-roll, but all Will did was say:

'Bag?'

'I'm good, thanks,' Patrick said.

Will shrugged. 'Alright.' And then: 'I think you'll really like that one.'

'Pardon?'

'The Atwood,' Will clarified. 'It's probably my fave of hers.'

'Is that so.' Patrick grabbed his purchases. Will smiled back at him, and then he was finally out of excuses to stay. He held the books in the crook of his arm as he left the store and made the leisurely walk back to the hotel.

Patrick's line of work did not often call for him to look outward, and he couldn't quite remember the last time he had been so curious about another person. When Patrick had walked into Gilroy's, Will had smiled like he wasn't even surprised to see him there, like he was any other returning customer. He had made Patrick feel just for a second that he wasn't a stranger in this town, like he already had a friend.

There was also the dusting of black hair peeking out from under the collar and sleeves of his shirt, the slight flourish of the wrist as he had typed Patrick's request, the little details that Patrick rarely allowed himself to notice in other men. And something about those green eyes made him almost certain that he and Will had met before, but try as he might, he couldn't put his finger on it. He must have been in the crowd at the bar that night, he decided. That was almost certainly it.

Or possibly, it wasn't that at all. It was the other thing, that glimmer of recognition he always did his best to ignore, that said: *you too?*

Fine, so what if he *had* wanted to see him again, however briefly? It had been a while. Longer than a while. He was allowed to look, as long as that was all he did, and discreetly at that. It wasn't about Will-from-the-charming-second-hand-bookstore at all, really. He could be anyone.

Although, as Patrick strolled back across the square in the shade of the cathedral, he could momentarily admit to himself that Will's quick, bright smile alone had been worth the visit.

11

'He is so weird,' Jordan remarked the moment Patrick had left.

'He's just a bit awkward,' Will said, unexpectedly defensive.

'I think he's gay,' said April, and both Will and Jordan spun to her in unison.

'Say more?'

She shrugged. 'Far be it for me to speculate about other people's private lives,' she said, 'but Emma Frost is his favourite mutant.'

'I don't know what that *means*,' Will said.

April shrugged again and sauntered into the back. She would often do this; volunteer to go make a round of tea or pretend to have some kind of admin-related task in the screaming cupboard. She would then sit there for half an hour at a time, writing her fanfiction on FicFix dot com. Will had read snippets. She was quite good. Her stories were evocative, well-plotted, and smutty as hell. She'd amassed a considerable following. Will harboured a suspicion that April was fanfic famous.

'As *if* he thought we were dating,' Jordan marvelled. 'Wait. Unless. Do you think he was coming onto one of us? *Both* of us? Did he think we saw him from across the bookshop and really liked his vibe?'

'Less iced coffee for you,' Will said, sliding the remnants of Jordan's latte off the counter and into the bin. 'And I thought you weren't into threesomes?'

'Correct.' Jordan nodded. 'I do not share the spotlight.'

To be fair to Patrick, this was far from the first time somebody had assumed he and Jordan were a couple. They were physically affectionate with each other, for sure, and had been known to bicker like people who'd been married for years. But most of the time, it was a simple case of a drunk straight woman seeing two men standing next to each other in a gay bar and being overcome by the urge to make them kiss like a child playing with an Action Man and Ken.

The truth was, he and Jordan *had* originally met on Grindr and even gone on a date. They'd talked non-stop over G&Ts about their favourite books, films, *Real Housewives* cast members and Madonna eras, ending the evening by falling into bed together, a decision made largely as a result of said G&Ts and the fact that Uber was surge-pricing at the time. The sex, from what little Will could remember, had been perfunctory at best, and when they both awoke the next morning, they had cackled like hyenas and agreed to never do it again.

The two of them had been best friends ever since, inseparable to the point of co-dependency, and if more than a day or two went by without one of them texting, it was immediately assumed by the other they were dead.

'Anyway, did you hear about the latest nonsense?' Jordan asked.

'I am always here for nonsense. Proceed.'

'Well.' Jordan's tone grew clipped, efficient: what he liked to call his Business Bitch voice. 'The council are trying to limit the opening hours of the bars on Hurst Street again. Noise complaints. Turns out the people who moved into the brand-new block of flats next to the busiest gay bar in the heart of the gay quarter didn't think that they might actually have to deal with real gay people coming and going.'

'For God's sake,' said Will. 'Don't they try this every couple of years?'

'Yep. It's textbook. Try and force the bars to close earlier, which means fewer people end up going, meaning they make less money, meaning they close down, and some wanker in a grey suit can snap up the empty buildings and turn them into flats, or' – he wrinkled his nose – 'a Joe & The Juice.'

'Perish the thought.'

'Capitalism and homophobia are cousins,' said Jordan, with the kind of finality that Will knew meant he would neither explain nor elaborate on what this actually meant.

It was worrying. Gay bars were on the brink of extinction, with old venues closing down all the time, and precious few new ones opening. Will couldn't picture a version of Birmingham without the Village, and he didn't like the thought of having to.

On the surface, the place was nothing special. A run-down watering hole with lights kept intentionally low so punters couldn't see the scars. But people still flocked to the Village every weekend, and Will wasn't alone in harbouring a soft spot for the old girl. If there was one thing gay men were drawn to, it was the shabby glamour of a diva past her prime.

'What are you going to do?' Will asked.

Jordan drummed his fingers on the countertop. 'Something fabulous, I'm sure,' he said. 'I just need to figure out what.'

'Let me know when you do,' said Will. 'We'll fight it together.'

'Thanks, boo.' Jordan kissed him on the cheek, and headed for the exit, no doubt returning home for an outfit change before his shift at the bar. Will pottered around behind the counter for a while longer, enjoying the quiet that descended whenever Jordan vacated a room, a silence permeated only by the comforting sound of April humming in the back. He had half a mind to go back there and probe that theory of hers about their celebrity customer.

Three. This made three meetings with Patrick. (He wasn't sure when he started thinking of Patrick Lake as just 'Patrick', like they were old chums or something, but here he was.) Could April be right? Surely not.

'Emma Frost, my foot,' he muttered, reaching to pick up his vibrating phone. It took him a moment to recognise the voice on the other end: separated from her arched brows and fake lashes, Faye Runaway sounded a little like Ozzy Osbourne.

'I might have a gig for you, babygirl,' she said. 'Olivia Lyfe was supposed to do it, but she just got doxed.'

'Doxed? Sounds painful.'

'Don't be cute, dear. Some bigoted mouth-breathers leaked all her information online. Her phone number, her private accounts. People are sending pictures of her all dolled up to her grandparents in Jamaica.'

'Shit.' Will instantly regretted his flippant tone. 'That's awful.'

'She wasn't out to them,' Faye said. 'She's in bits. She's even talking about giving up drag.'

'She's upset, needs a bit of time,' Will said. 'You're not a real queen until you've threatened to give up drag, even I know that.'

'True. But she's really left me in the lurch, so I think she means it, at least for now.'

'What's the gig?'

'Drag queen story hour at the library. Saturdays at noon. I don't know how you are with kids, but you have that bookshop job, so I reasoned there is a pretty good chance you're at least semi-literate.'

'Tee hee,' Will sang. 'You said "semi".'

He was fairly certain he could hear Faye pinch the bridge of her nose.

'Just don't be late,' she warned. Then, to somebody else as she hung up: 'Never have kids.'

12

A bump in the road jolted Patrick awake, and for one deeply confusing moment he had no idea where he was. It happened from time to time, usually during a press tour, when he would wake up each day in a new time zone. Now, though, he was on the way to Manchester with Will, the guy from the bookstore, who had texted him that morning to let him know he was heading up North after work that afternoon to meet a collector of rare memorabilia and hopefully they'd have some luck.

Will had seemed surprised when Patrick offered to accompany him. Patrick knew that it wasn't exactly normal for clients to tag along, but filming was suspended for the day while the director and the studio hashed out some crucial creative difference that neither Patrick nor Audra were privy to – they were only the meat puppets who had to do as they were told, why would they need to know anything as inconsequential as *story* or *character*? – and so he had been at a loose end.

But this, he reminded himself, was *for* work. Richard Ranger's character seemed to shift with every new version of the script they received. How was he expected to build a performance on foundations that kept shaking? He'd decided he would go back to the beginning, the original run, except those early issues had turned out to be shrouded in mystery. With nothing but time on his hands, Patrick had gone deep down the rabbit hole of online fandom, the fabled Omega Issue evoking first curiosity, then obsession.

His privilege was showing, he figured. He could request whatever he wanted at any hour of the day. Of course he would fixate on one of the few things he couldn't have.

It might even be fun, he had thought, to try and track down this piece of apocrypha. A real-life quest. And time away from the set, the hotel, the cast, was its own reward. Time instead spent with Will, who sat smirking at him in puckish amusement from the opposite side of the spacious back seat.

'Did you enjoy your nap?' Will asked, sweetly.

'Sorry about that,' said Patrick hoarsely, reaching for the bottle of water in the armrest. 'I always fall asleep in cars. On trains. Planes. Can't help it.'

'A handy skill,' said Will. 'Being able to nod off anywhere. Also, adorable.'

'I... what?'

'You're like a baby.'

'I am not.'

'A baby whose mum has to take him for a drive to lull him to sleep.'

'I am a grown man.'

'I hope all the supervillains out there don't find out that the unbeatable Captain Kismet can be thwarted by the slightest rhythmic motion.'

Will's use of the words 'rhythmic motion' was, of course, entirely incidental. But now that he was fully awake, and those green eyes were looking at him so intently, Patrick was painfully aware that he'd become somewhat... excited in his sleep. He shifted in his seat, hoping against hope that Will hadn't noticed. Jesus, it really had been too long.

'You're not going to tell all my enemies, are you?' he asked, adopting the same irreverent tone.

'Your secret's safe with me,' Will told him. He winked, and Patrick nearly choked on his water.

The collector in Manchester was, Will told him, a quintessential crypto bro. 'I mean that in the most derogatory way you could possibly interpret,' he'd said, but Patrick hadn't really known what he meant – still didn't fully understand what crypto *was* – until they were being welcomed into the front hall of a new-build mansion just outside a place called Altrincham.

'Patrick Lake, a pleasure.' Their host clasped Patrick's hand between both of his own, shaking it in some studied display of dominance. His skin bore the kind of tan that did not occur in nature, and the blinding white of his pressed shirt was only outshone by his veneers. 'Harley Manning. And you are…?' He turned to Will, scanning his denim jacket and black jeans as if he could visually ascertain his value.

'I'm Mr Lake's broker,' said Will, his voice comically deep, thrusting his own hand out. 'We spoke on the phone.' Patrick suppressed a giggle.

'Of course, of course,' said Harley Manning. 'Come through to my office, both of you, please. I really think you'll appreciate my collection, Paddy,' he said, appearing not to notice the twitch in Patrick's temple at this presumptuous nickname.

'That's an original Ronan McCann,' Harley said, gesturing to an ugly painting en route to the study as if answering a query. Neither Patrick nor Will had asked. 'It's expected to double in value by this time next year.'

Harley's 'office' was a large white room with a marble floor looking out onto an expanse of lawn through plastic double-glazed patio doors. A pool table dominated one end of the space, while a giant sofa took up the other. The walls were dotted with framed movie posters, comic pages, magazine covers, and cabinets displaying various action figures, vintage toys, and other collectibles.

'Mr Manning,' Will began. 'I never told you Mr Lake was my client. How did you know to expect him?'

Manning shrugged. 'Educated guess,' he told them. 'I know our leading man here has a thing for obscure memorabilia, and I know he's filming in Birmingham. Then out of the blue comes a query from a Birmingham dealer asking about something only the real fans have ever heard of. I took a punt! Not to brag, and I haven't had this like officially verified or anything,' he continued, 'but I'm pretty certain that I have the biggest collection of Captain Kismet merch in the country.'

'Really?' asked Patrick, curiosity piqued.

'Yeah man!' Harley gurned. 'I get that the character didn't go down as well over here because he's such an all-American hero and that, but he was my favourite. The way he just kicks arse and takes no shit, man, you know?'

'I like to think he's a little bit more nuanced than that,' said Patrick.

'And the women! He was *swimming* in it, wasn't he?' Harley laughed. 'Sura, Penny, that Russian spy lady who could do the splits...'

'The Eighties were a weird time for comics,' said Will. 'April did a whole thread on it,' he added as an aside to Patrick.

'Check this out,' Harley continued, taking a frame down from the wall and handing it to Patrick. The cover illustration showed a man in a blue flight suit, blonde hair jutting out from behind a pair of goggles, standing with his hands on his hips, surveying an alien landscape. An aviator turned spaceman turned hero.

The Adventures of Captain Kismet, #3.

'It's a first printing,' said Harley.

'That's awesome,' said Patrick, adopting the same tone as he did when meeting fans under ten. 'These are pretty rare, right?'

'Exactly!' Harley enthused. 'I was so excited! It was like, here are all these opportunities to create whole new original NFTs based on content in the book... Not to mention using AI to autogenerate whole new IP projects! Then my lawyer told me that I only bought this issue and not the 'copyright' and that's not how NFTs work. And I was like, so why did I spend so much of my coin on a few old sheets of paper? But it turns out the issue itself is rare enough to qualify as an investment piece, so it all worked out in the end.'

He pulled a Sharpie out of his jeans pocket.

'Would you sign it?' he asked. 'On the glass, obviously, not the issue itself.'

'Sure,' said Patrick, taking the proffered marker and scrawling his autograph across the lower half of the frame.

'Sweet!' Harley pumped his fist. 'That just doubled in value,' he added, either to himself or to the frame, but seemingly not to either Patrick or Will.

'Mr Manning,' Will interjected, still forcing his melodic voice into a pantomime baritone. 'The Omega Issue?'

'Hmm?' Harley looked up at them, as if he had genuinely forgotten their presence. 'Oh. That. I thought you were kidding! The thing's a total myth. But I knew Paddy here was a bit of a connoisseur, like myself.' He nudged Patrick in the ribs. 'I figured you'd want to see this. Pretty impressive, right?' He used his free hand to take out his phone and snap a rapid selfie of the two of them.

'OK, that's enough,' said Will. 'Let's go.'

'Before you do,' said Harley, putting an arm around Patrick's shoulder. 'I've got an investment opportunity ...'

'*Nope*,' Will barked, stepping between the two, chest puffed out, his performance of butchness somehow still more convincing than Harley's alpha male façade. 'Mr Manning,' he continued, 'you'll be hearing from Mr Lake's lawyer about the delay you caused to production by dragging him away from set today. Not to mention the subterfuge of getting him here under false pretences.' He steered Patrick towards the door of the office with a single wiry arm, and

Patrick went along with the charade. Will made a face like he was doing mental math, then gave Harley a verbal estimate of how much he was going to end up being sued for.

'Come on, now,' said Harley. 'That's not exactly necessary, is it? Paddy, mate…'

'My client's name is not Paddy,' Will said. 'And if I were you, I'd start liquidating assets. Mr Lake's attorneys don't accept payment in the form of NFTs.'

'You make a very good handler,' Patrick told Will in the car, once they were back on the road and had finally stopped laughing.

Will clutched his own chest. 'I hardly ever use my Top Voice,' he said. 'But that was pretty convincing, no? I was kind of *hot*.'

'Top Voice?' asked Patrick, sensing Will's use of capitals.

'Oh, you know. The voice you use for talking to, like, plumbers. When you need to perform manhood.' Will glanced over at him. 'I suppose you don't know, actually, do you? Your Top Voice is just your… voice.'

Patrick laughed. 'I guess.'

'Must be a gay thing,' said Will, turning to look out of the window.

'If you say so,' Patrick replied, his heart thudding a little faster at the confirmation of his pretty robust hunch that Will, the person fast becoming a recurring character in his life, was in fact gay. 'Hey, what was up with that guy's office? It was halfway between a child's bedroom and a sports bar.'

'A *man cave*,' said Will, shuddering even as he said the words. Then, more sincerely, he added: 'I'm sorry, Patrick. What a waste of time. I just…' He huffed in frustration. 'I can't believe he let us come all the way up here when he didn't have what we were looking for, just for a photo and an autograph. That takes some serious brass neck.'

'Dudes like that love to show off,' Patrick told him with a shrug. 'He who dies with the most toys wins.'

'And you're one of the toys?' Will asked.

Patrick shrugged again and smiled. 'A highly collectible action figure,' he said.

They continued in silence for a little while, and Patrick, so used to sitting around doing nothing until somebody cried 'action', suddenly found himself fidgeting, reaching uselessly for things to say.

'Are you hungry?' he asked. 'I'm hungry. We should stop somewhere. To eat. Could you eat? I could eat.'

'Uh, sure,' said Will.

'Great,' said Patrick. 'Why don't you pick somewhere when we get back. My treat, obviously. To say thank you.'

'You don't have to thank me. Today was a flop.'

'Still. To say thank you for trying. I insist.'

Will gave him a confused smile and nodded. 'Sounds good to me.'

'Great,' Patrick said. The silence that followed was a little more comfortable, Patrick gazing out the window at the unfamiliar grey stretch of highway, Will absorbed in his phone, until he heard a mumbled: 'Bugger.'

'Sorry?' Patrick turned back to him.

'I have this thing tonight,' said Will. 'Family dinner. I completely forgot about it until just now.'

'Oh.' *You don't have to lie*, Patrick thought. *I get it. I've taken up enough of your time, and now you want to get back to your own life.*

'My sister is texting asking what time I'm going to be there,' Will continued, reading his mind. 'I'm sorry, I—'

'You don't have to apologise,' Patrick said, forcing a smile. 'I totally understand.'

Will frowned and screwed up his mouth, then said: 'You could... come?'

'Oh, I don't know.'

'Right. I mean, it's not fancy or anything. Lasagne at my sister's house, maybe some wine.'

'I wouldn't want to intrude. I mean, if it's just family...'

'That's kind of an elastic term,' Will said. 'Margo, her kid, April and Jordan. Really more of a free-for-all. You wouldn't be intruding, honest. You're more than welcome.' Will paused, clearly calculating whether or not to say what he was about to say. 'I just thought you might want a night off from being... you know.' He flapped his hand in the air, like that explained everything.

Patrick did know. But how did *this* guy know? That no matter how grateful he was for where he'd got to in life, and even though being recognised in the street by little kids who thought he was a real superhero filled up some empty part of him, there were days when he just wanted to go back to being Patrick Carmichael from South Amboy. To walk into a bar unremarked upon. To hold any hand he pleased. To eat lasagne.

'I'd love to,' he said.

'Late! Again!' Margo yelled as she opened the door. 'What's your excuse this ti—'

'Hi Mags,' said Will. 'I brought a friend, hope you don't mind. Margo, this is Patrick. Patrick Lake.'

'I *know* who he *is*,' Margo hissed, stepping aside to let them both in.

'It's nice to meet you,' said Patrick. 'This is for you.' He held out the bottle of Fleurie he'd picked up on the way, insisting that he could not show up to dinner at Will's sister's house empty-handed.

'What kind of guest would that make me,' he'd said, 'to show up without a gift?'

'Sir,' Will had said archly. '*You're* the gift. Margo and Dylan will be so excited to meet you, it won't even occur to them that you didn't bring something.'

But Patrick had insisted, and so upon returning to Birmingham, they had taken a detour to a wine merchant in the Jewellery Quarter where Patrick had quizzed Will on what kinds of reds Margo preferred. He didn't know why it suddenly felt so important that Will's sister like him, other than he was an actor, so it was in his nature to want *everyone* to like him.

'Thank you,' she said, accepting the bottle and guiding them through to the kitchen where April and Jordan were setting the table and squabbling over what might be a suitable playlist to put on while they ate.

'Room for one more?' he asked self-consciously, like he might have to audition for a seat at the table. April and Jordan ceased their bickering and stared in stunned unison. Because seeing him at a bookstore or a nightclub, sure, they were both public places of business. But he suspected that showing up to an intimate family dinner was a different matter altogether.

'We're a little short on chairs,' Margo interrupted. 'So you might have to carry in a spare from the living room, Patrick. Put those lovely big arms of yours to good use.'

'Sure thing.' By the time he reached the living room, Patrick heard the kitchen fall almost silent. He could picture their faces, asking Will what the hell was going on in incredulous whispers.

He gave it a full minute before returning to the kitchen, depositing the smallest armchair from the living room at the end of the table, where the lasagne had been laid out next to a large bowl of salad, focaccia, and the wine he had brought.

'You don't have to sit there,' said Will, 'take mine.'

'No, no,' he said. 'I'm the one who showed up last minute, unannounced.'

'Exactly,' said Margo. 'That's how it works.' She poked her head out into the hallway and yelled: 'Dylan! Dinner!'

A moment later, Dylan slumped down the stairs and into the kitchen, so engrossed in their phone that they didn't even notice Patrick until they were sitting across from him, a steaming, bubbling tray of pasta between them.

'Erm. Hi,' they said, face unmoving, before turning to Margo. 'Is one of us dying or something?'

Everybody laughed, like they had been given permission to acknowledge how unusual this situation was, and Patrick relaxed into his (comically low) seat.

'Your uncle Will tells me you're in a band,' he said to Dylan, while Margo hacked into the lasagne with a spatula. 'What are you guys called?'

'Right now we're The Duvet Ghosts,' said Dylan.

'Whatever happened to The War on Christmas?' Will frowned.

Dylan shrugged. 'Christmas won.'

And slowly, Patrick felt everyone around him remember why they were really here. Jordan opened the bottle of wine, April tore off a chunk of bread, and to his left, Will held out his plate. Patrick looked to him briefly and they held each other's gaze for just a moment, almost like a private joke, and then it was Patrick's turn to offer up his plate to Margo and be fed.

13

'I really think Margo is coming around,' said Jordan. 'She only gave me one withering look last night, and it barely even chilled my bones at all.'

They were sitting upright on opposite ends of Will's sofa, Jordan's legs resting on top of his, sharing the packet of Frazzles torn open between them.

'Sure,' said Will, opting not to mention that Margo still hadn't forgiven Jordan for spilling Rioja on her sofa the year before. 'And I think you've got a fan in Dylan. They watch your videos.'

'Oh my God, a Gen-Z likes my content.' Jordan laughed. 'What an honour!'

'I keep getting lectures on radical LGBTQ+ politics every time I go over for tea,' Will continued. 'They're at this hilarious age where they think they invented being queer.'

'Precious. Remember being sixteen and thinking you were the only gay in the village?'

'Only one in the *world*,' said Will. 'When I started going to bars and realised there were more, I felt this incredible sense of belonging, but also...'

'You were annoyed you weren't as special as you thought you were?' Jordan asked, reading his mind as was his wont. 'Me too!'

'Are we the worst?'

'Yes. But we're the best at it, so it's alright.' Jordan picked up a crisp and examined it. 'Speaking of,' he said, 'what's going on with your new best friend? Should I be jealous?'

It was the first mention Jordan had made of the movie star Will had brought to dinner, and Will had started to think he wasn't going to bring it up, that maybe he'd slipped into a fugue state last night and Patrick's presence at the table, praising Margo's cooking and joking with April about Captain Kismet and seeming like he was genuinely having a good time, had all been a dream.

'Patrick?' Will snorted. 'I wouldn't worry just yet.'

'He does seem to like you,' said Jordan. 'Not to imply that you're not endlessly fascinating, but... what's that all about, I wonder?'

'I get the impression that he's just a bit lonely,' said Will. 'It must be a strange life, when you think about it. Spending months on end away from home.'

'Travelling the world, being paid millions of dollars to be filmed in the most flattering light imaginable,' said Jordan. 'My heart bleeds for the man.'

'Why would a movie star want to hang out with *us*?' Will continued.

'Who wouldn't? We're great.'

'Maybe it's some kind of rich person game, where he slums it so he can see how normal folk live.'

'Oh! Like a hidden camera kind of situation?' Jordan's eyes lit up. 'Do you think it could be part of some new TV show?'

'I don't know. I keep thinking...'

'That you expected him to be taller? So did I. But that's the thing they never tell you about movie stars. They're not these giants of Olympus, they're just regular sized.'

'That's not what I was going to say.'

'Go on then.'

'I just get – and I know you're going to call me an idiot, so don't bother – but…' Will squinted and then rushed: 'a flirty vibe?'

'Straight guys do love to flirt with gay men,' Jordan said, appearing to give Will's theory serious consideration. 'It grants them the validation they need, and they get to pretend they're being evolved at the same time.'

'He's probably being friendly, and I'm overthinking it,' said Will, feeling foolish for even voicing the idea. 'I mean, *could* he be gay? Surely not, right? Just… nice?'

'Life is full of such conundrums,' said Jordan. 'Is he handsome, or does he just smell really good?'

Will smiled. They played this game often. 'Do you actually like him, or is he just a doctor?'

'Does he have his life together, or does he just own a bedframe?'

'Is he obsessed with you, or does he just text back?'

'Is he the one, or is he just wearing one of those denim jackets with the fleece collar?'

'Oh God, I *love* those.' Will pressed his hand to his forehead in a mock swoon.

'Everybody does,' said Jordan. 'Any man looks hot in one of those. Put Patrick Lake in a borg collar and you'd be a goner.' A moment passed in silence as both men conjured and savoured that particular image.

'Maybe he's bi,' said Will. 'Or pan.'

'If that were the case, it would make him the first bisexual in the universe who doesn't mention it all the bloody time,' Jordan retorted. 'Have you been on TikTok lately? For a group of people who are constantly complaining about being erased, they really don't shut up.'

'Not *you* practising your tight five while I'm trying to have a conversation,' said Will. 'What's next, a joke about vegans?'

'The meat industry is killing the planet and there is absolutely nothing funny about that, William.' Jordan popped a Frazzle into his mouth. 'OK fine, do you want to know what I really think?'

'Rarely, but go on.'

'If Patrick is into men, and that's a big if... I don't think he'd be into you specifically.'

'I take it back. I *never* want to know what you think.'

'I'm being serious. There's a reason that muscular, straight-acting, white gay men tend to only date other muscular, straight-acting, white gay men, not fruity little F-words like us.'

Will sighed and nodded in reluctant agreement. Because Jordan was right, of course. How many times had a guy seemed enamoured of Will's looks on an app, his tall lean frame and dark body hair, only to drastically change his tune as soon as they met in person and heard his loud, reedy voice? Even Ry had gone and found a deeper-voiced version of him, one without all the flouncy extras. He felt stupid for entertaining this train of thought. He should know better by now.

But Jordan wasn't finished.

'There's a reason,' he repeated, and he reached out to touch Will's hand. 'I think they're jealous of us.'

Will scoffed, nearly choking to death on his Frazzle in the process. Jordan sat patiently until he was finished spluttering, then continued.

'It takes a lot of time and hard work to put on muscle,' he said. 'But ultimately, most of us are capable of that, given the inclination. It takes even more work, even more practice and constant self-policing, to make sure your voice is never too high or soft, your wrist never too limp. That sounds like quite an exhausting way to live, doesn't it? Then there's the likes of us. I truly believe that it takes greater strength and genuine guts to be like us. To live as freely and faggily as we do, even though we know it might get us killed if we sashay down the wrong street at night. I don't care how square someone's jaw is, or how well he catches a ball or throws a punch. I'd rather risk a beating than hate who I am, or have women be afraid of me. We're the real men, Will. Never forget that.'

Will sat for a moment absorbing this.

'Do you really believe that?' he asked.

'I never say a single thing I don't wholeheartedly believe,' Jordan replied, hand placed beatifically on his chest. 'By the way, your hair is looking a bit frizzy. What conditioner are you using? You know curls need extra moisture, I've told you this.'

Will stuck up his middle finger and snatched away the last remaining Frazzle. Loving Jordan was akin to loving a housecat – just when you thought they'd finally shown you their soft underbelly, they swiped at you with their claws to remind you who was boss.

The buzzer rang. Will disentangled himself from Jordan, playfully batting at his friend before walking over to the front door and peering at the little screen.

'Speak of the devil,' he said.

'No way,' said Jordan. 'Superman is downstairs? How does he even know where you live?'

'He insisted on dropping me off after dinner last night.' Will hit the intercom button. 'Hi, come on up,' he said, frantically swiping at the pungent, starchy dust that he could now see was all over his T-shirt and jeans. 'What is he doing here?' he yelped in Jordan's general direction.

'No idea,' said Jordan, not stirring from the sofa. 'I bet you're wishing you'd hoovered better.'

'Shit. Do you think I have time now? Real quick, like?'

'For God's sake, calm down. He knows he's in Birmingham, not Beverly Hills. I'm sure he'll find your little hovel quite darling.'

'Says the man who still lives with his mother,' shot back Will.

'Don't bring Diane into this!'

Will hastily gathered up the magazines that were strewn all over the living room floor, attempting to arrange them on the coffee table in a manner that was both artful and would cover up the ring-stains from coffee mugs. Why didn't he use coasters? Why didn't he *own* coasters?

A knock at the door. Will cast a final, desperate look around the room, and opened the front door.

It struck him anew, as it did each time he saw Patrick, just how handsome the man was. The stubble from the day before was gone, and his clean-shaven cheekbones seemed to almost shine in the same hallway light that always made Will look sallow. It was getting dark outside, and so Patrick had eschewed his usual cap and shades; he wore a white T-shirt and black khakis.

'Sorry to drop by unannounced,' he said, holding out a case of beers. 'I was wondering if you might want to… hang out?'

What a Billy-no-mates, Will thought. *Poor guy*.

'Sure, come on in.' He pressed himself back against the open door to let Patrick slide past him. He smelled fresh and woody, like he had just showered in a waterfall in the middle of a rainforest.

'Hello, Patrick,' Jordan said from behind him, regally. He slowly rose from the sofa. 'What are we having, then?'

'Why don't I take those into the kitchen,' said Will, but Patrick shook his head.

'That's cool, I'll do it,' he said, heading out of the room. 'You got glasses?'

'We're not fancy here!' said Jordan. 'Will doesn't mind raw-dogging it, do you, Will?' This was followed by a wheezy '*fuck*' after Will elbowed him furiously in the ribs. He recovered quickly, grabbing Will and pulling him closer.

'I don't say this often,' he whispered, 'but I may have been wrong.'

'What do you mean?' Will asked in the same hushed tone. Jordan regarded him with even more condescension than usual.

'He dropped by your place unannounced,' he said slowly. 'And look. He carries beers like a bisexual.'

Will snuck a surreptitious glance at the way Patrick was carrying the three bottles back from the kitchen, clutching them from the bottom.

'Is that a thing?' he asked.

'Emma Frost,' Jordan hissed. 'The boy's a big old Emma Frost.' In a louder voice, he announced: 'I'm off. Need to go home and make myself presentable for church.'

'Church?' Patrick asked.

'Sunday service,' said Jordan. 'It's a tradition, isn't it, Will?'

'Oh,' said Patrick. 'I didn't realise—'

'He's winding you up,' said Will. 'That's just what everyone calls it.'

'Calls what?'

'Getting drunk on a Sunday,' Will explained. 'Sunday night is cabaret night. We go most weeks. It's a laugh.'

'Sounds fun,' said Patrick. 'And that's at…?'

'My bar, remember? The Village,' said Jordan. He pursed his lips, eyes darting in Will's direction for just a second, then added: 'You should totally come, Patrick.'

'Huh? I don't know about that,' Patrick began, but Jordan cut him off again.

'Like I said, I need to go improve on perfection,' he said. 'I'll take one of these for the road, thanks so much.' He relieved Patrick of one of the beers and blew Will a kiss. 'Love you! Mean it!' he called from the doorway, shooting another urgent, not-at-all-subtle look at Will, and then it was just the two of them.

Will and Patrick each took a seat on the settee, sipping their beers side by side in silence while Will inwardly berated himself for not owning more furniture. He felt at once both too close and miles away from his unexpected guest and resolved to spirit an armchair away from Margo's spare room at the first opportunity.

'It really *is* a laugh,' said Will. 'If you wanted to join us?'

'I don't think that's a good idea,' Patrick said. 'You didn't see me the last time I was there.'

Will bit his tongue. *But I did*.

'It was fun,' Patrick added. 'Until the whole… you know.'

'Poppers o'clock.'

'Yeah.' Patrick smiled ruefully into his beer, then his expression became more serious. His next words felt carefully chosen. 'On second thoughts, I would like, I think,' he said, 'to go back.'

'To the Village?'

'Yes. It was fun. Different, I guess.' Patrick's eyes were fixed on his bottle, and his thumb restlessly rubbed at the neck like he was trying to free a genie. 'That's not the kind of place I usually go to,' he said, '…anymore.'

The word hung in the air between them, a balloon ready to fly away or pop at any moment.

'Was it once?' Will asked.

'A long time ago.'

'Big fan of cheap drinks and Lady Gaga, were you?'

'Yes,' said Patrick. 'I was.' He looked up at Will. 'Am.'

I knew it, Will thought, even though he hadn't, not really. He had suspected. Hoped, even. But you never knew these things until you knew them, and now, as he sat with it, he figured it didn't make much of a difference. This wasn't Jordan or Ry or any other gay man Will had met. Patrick Lake being gay didn't stop him being Patrick Lake. It didn't mean he necessarily fancied Will just because they had this one basic thing in common. You wouldn't put a Great Dane and a chihuahua together just because they were both dogs, would you? If anything, it just lent credence to one of Will's many theories: Patrick wanted friendship. Community. And that, he could provide.

'Come with me,' he said, standing up. He waved for Patrick to follow him into the next room: his bedroom. 'Relax, I'm not going to jump you,' he laughed, maybe a little too loudly. 'I just want to show you something.'

Patrick, brows creased either in bafflement or curiosity, trailed him into the bedroom. There were two wardrobes: a mirrored one with sliding doors built into the wall, and a free-standing, decades-old IKEA monstrosity shoved next to the bed. Will walked up to that one and, with a dramatic flourish, threw the doors open.

Patrick peered in at its contents, probably anticipating the dreadful sight of a superfan's shrine or creepy doll collection, and Will imagined he could see the relief wash over his face, followed by sudden understanding, as he took in the gowns on wooden hangers and, along the bottom of the wardrobe, wigs placed meticulously on polystyrene heads – including a gorgeous red one that Will was exceptionally proud of as it brought out his eyes, and which he thought Patrick might just recognise.

'Grace,' said Patrick in astonishment. 'Grace Anatomy. That was *you*.'

'The very same.' Will dipped into an abbreviated curtsey. 'In the flesh.'

Patrick erupted in laughter, and an instantaneous chill trickled down Will's spine, but there was no cruelty or derision in the sound. It was the gasping, gleeful sound of an audience member who had just witnessed an inexplicable magic trick.

'Why didn't you *say* anything?' Patrick asked him. 'All this time!' He reached out and pulled Will into a sideways embrace, still staring at the treasure trove inside the wardrobe. Will tensed instinctively as Patrick casually slipped his arm around his waist, straightening his posture, contracting every muscle in his body, breath frozen in his chest. It was hard not to stand next to a literal superhero without admonishing yourself for not going to the gym more.

'I don't know,' he said. 'I didn't think you'd remember me. We spoke for all of ten seconds.'

'And you saved my ass.'

'From a gaggle of drunk gays. Hardly Captain Kismet stuff.'

'Hey, not all heroes wear capes. Some wear...' Patrick craned his neck to examine one of the garments hanging from the back of the wardrobe door. 'Kaftans?'

'That's just for lounging. Only hussies wear kaftans out of the house.'

'Good to know,' said Patrick, continuing his fascinated inspection.

'Another?' Will asked, gesturing with his own beer at the bottle in Patrick's hand.

'Sure.'

When he returned a minute later, Patrick was perched on the end of the bed, a breastplate in his hands. He turned it this way and that, tilting his head as he did so, as if trying to comprehend the physics of the thing.

'I'm sorry,' he exclaimed when he caught Will watching him in amusement. 'This is probably some major faux pas. Touching a queen's fake boobs. Like going through your underwear or something.'

'At least they're not wonky this time,' Will said, handing him a second beer.

'Sorry?'

'Never mind.' Will sat down next to him on the bed. 'It's a shame you can't come out tonight. The drag on a Sunday is usually all kinds of wonderful. And weird. And occasionally grotesque.'

'I wish I could,' said Patrick wistfully. 'The closest I get to live drag back home is watching *RuPaul's Drag Race* in my apartment with takeout.'

'So you can't even go to a drag show because you're not... out?'

'Pretty much.' Patrick shrugged. 'Captain Kismet doesn't go to gay bars, and according to my contract, neither do I.'

'That's shit.'

'Don't get me wrong. I know I'm lucky. *So* lucky. To have this career, these opportunities. I'm not playing the violin, you know?'

'I know,' said Will. 'But?'

'Yeah.' Patrick sighed. 'But.'

Patrick held up his beer, and Will clinked their bottles together. He'd seen the fiasco with his own eyes last week, the way people forgot how to behave the minute they spotted a celebrity, and figured that Patrick had good reason to steer clear of situations like that. It hadn't occurred to him that the choice wasn't entirely his own. As somebody whose living was largely made in gay bars, Will found it hard to wrap his head around the idea that being seen in such a place could affect somebody else's.

Of course, being seen was one thing. Being recognised, on the other hand…

Patrick took another swig of beer, then noticed the way Will was staring at him askance, head pulled back to take all of him in. 'What?'

'Nothing, just…' Will looked him up and down. 'Out of interest: what size shoe do you wear?'

14

'And I thought the Captain Kismet costume was tight,' Patrick wheezed. He had no regrets about the second serving of lasagne he'd eaten at Margo's the night before, but even with an extra forty minutes of cardio this morning, he was feeling it. And being squeezed into drag – drag! – only made him more aware of his own body's every last bulge and bump.

'Don't be such a baby,' said Will, before signalling to the taxi driver that he could drop them off just here, thank you. 'Pain is beauty, and you look great.'

'Thank you,' said Patrick. He tried batting his eyes coyly, still growing accustomed to the heavy false lashes, and was rewarded with a burst of laughter.

He still couldn't believe how quickly he had agreed to the idea, why he had agreed at all: to let Will dress him in Grace's clothes, to disguise himself beyond all recognition, so that it wasn't Patrick Lake going to a gay bar, but someone else entirely.

'Nervous?' Will asked.

'Terrified.' An understatement. He was risking everything. If he was found out, it would be game over. The star of *Kismet* caught in full drag in a gay bar. What the hell was he thinking? How had he allowed Will to talk him into this?

Except Will hadn't needed to. Patrick had jumped at the suggestion, enticed by the prospect of being able to go out incognito, but also by something else: the way Will's closet had beckoned like a kid's dressing-up box, promising that same sense of magic and possibility that had made him want to be an actor in the first place. The chance to step into a character, to be someone else entirely, even if just for a little while. To step into Will's world and see life through his eyes.

Damn, those eyes.

Patrick took a deep breath, and then before he could change his mind, threw the car door open. 'Come on, then. Take me to church.'

Will led him through the pub and towards the packed garden, where at least fifty people sat on benches drinking and smoking, facing a small stage that had been set up against the back wall. A twink in a crop top went from table to table selling bright pink shots from a tray, while a young woman with a high ponytail stalked through the rabble holding a bucket for cash donations to a local LGBTQ+ charity.

He followed Will slowly, unsteadily into the crowd, ankles trembling in the uncomfortable, precarious heels, keenly aware that a single wrong move would send him sprawling across the floor like Bambi.

'Racy Gracie!' a queen called out to Will, even though he wasn't presently in drag. Patrick was still unclear on the etiquette.

'Faye!' Will air-kissed the queen, then turned to introduce her to Patrick. 'This is Faye Runaway.'

'Charmed,' said Faye. 'And you must be Gracie's drag daughter. I'd recognise that shoddy contouring anywhere.'

'I'm far too young to be a mother,' said Will. 'Unlike some of us.'

'I took Gracie under my wing when she first started out,' Faye told Patrick. 'She'd been doing godawful drag on Instagram and needed a guiding hand. I'm like her drag stepmother. Which would make you my granddaughter, after a fashion. Do you have a name, love? Do you speak at all?'

Patrick cleared his throat, about to respond, then paused. One word out of his mouth would surely give him away, his American drawl easily attributed to his trademark superhero role. No. If he was going to do this, he needed to go full Stanislavski.

'Infamy,' he said breathily, barely above a whisper, drawing deep on his dialect training from that short-lived tour of *An Inspector Calls* eight years ago.

Faye howled. '*Infamy! Infamy! They've all got it in for me!* That's a good one.'

Patrick let out a silent sigh of relief. Maybe he would get away with this after all.

Faye tottered away, and Will turned to Patrick.

'Infamy?' he said.

Patrick waggled his eyebrows provocatively. The fact that they were currently drawn a full inch and a half above their usual position probably made him look ridiculous, but he was thrilled to realise he didn't care. Was this what Will loved about drag, he wondered? This feeling of absolute freedom from yourself?

'Not bad, right?' he said, in what he thought was a passable English accent.

'You're a better actor than I gave you credit for,' said Will.

'Ouch,' said Patrick, then adding with a snigger: 'You cow!'

Will threw back his head and cackled. 'I should watch my back!' he said. 'You'll be coming for my gig next.'

'I don't know about all *that*,' said Patrick. 'I mean, obviously I look stunning, but I think you probably make a better lady than me.'

Patrick's drag was a little on the butch side. Will had remarked earlier, while picking out clothes for him, that there was no getting away from those shoulders, those arms, that chest, although he had done an admirable job of trying. Patrick's waist was cinched under a loose black playsuit, Will had draped a biker jacket over his shoulders, and he'd squeezed his size tens into a red pair of what Will lovingly called his 'fuck-me pumps'. He had felt absurd, clownlike, while Will did his makeup – a lengthy and intimate process during which Patrick had observed that Will had a slight bump on the bridge of his nose and bit his bottom lip when he was concentrating – but the moment he'd put on the blown-out blonde wig, it was like somebody somewhere had waved a wand. The overall effect was a little like Sandy at the end of *Grease*, if she happened to be a powerlifter.

'I can't believe people aren't staring more,' said Patrick.

'Look around, love. There are flashier sights in tonight.'

'Still. I thought for sure I'd have been clocked by now.'

Will smirked, and Patrick knew he'd used the term wrong.

'Sweetie,' said Will. 'Nobody here thinks you're a real woman. I doubt there are many who'd even call you a decent drag queen, not with the way you're tottering around in those shoes.'

'They hurt my feet.'

'Welcome to the club. The point is, though... nobody *cares*. You're not the first fledgling to come through here, and you won't be the last.' He pointed to the stage. 'I've seen some truly shit performance art go on there. Properly abominable stuff. And the weakest lip-syncs you can imagine. But I've also seen kings and queens and in-betweens step up there and blow everyone away. Real queer genius. And the beauty of a place like this is, there's room for all of it.'

'So which one were you?' Patrick asked.

Will laughed. 'Somewhere in the middle. Come on, let's find a seat. Looks like the show is about to begin.'

What followed was a carousel of some of the most bizarre visuals Patrick had ever seen. A nonbinary performer decked out in a jumpsuit and bubble perm like Sigourney Weaver in *Alien* performed a lip-sync to 'E.T.' by Katy Perry, tearing open their overalls at the first chorus to reveal a creature bursting forth from their chest, a puppet cleverly operated by their left arm under the clothes. A queen in a bright yellow raincoat sang 'Don't Rain on My Parade' while shooting the audience with a water pistol from waist height ('golden showers are a running theme with her,' Will informed him). But his favourite performance of the night, not that he could ever be biased, was the artist who had transformed themselves into Captain Kismet on one half of their body and Princess Sura on the other, flipping back and forth between personas like Julie Andrews in *Victor/Victoria* while miming along to 'Holding Out for a Hero'.

I can't wait to tell Audra, Patrick thought, *she'll get such a kick out of this*. A second later he remembered he couldn't tell anyone he'd been here, that this was the whole point of his disguise. What did the teleporting bank robber Jumpin' Jacques always say right before he vanished from the scene of his latest crime in the comics? *J'étais jamais ici: I was never here.*

Secret or no, though, Patrick wouldn't have changed a thing. He sat in a dazed silence in the car back from the pub, thinking of the people he'd seen not just on the stage, but in the audience – trans kids who couldn't be older than nineteen or twenty, laughing and woohooing along to the cabaret next to gay men in their fifties, safe and at ease in this tiny garden with its high walls and glittering priestesses. He hadn't fully grasped what he had been distancing himself from, until now. Not just the tans, traps and tank tops he'd come to associate with the WeHo bars he'd frequented when he first moved to LA, but that feeling of belonging. Of being entirely, unquestionably at home among strangers.

Patrick removed the red shoes before exiting the taxi, walking barefoot to Will's front door with a heel dangling from either hand, revelling in the way the cool night air and rough pavement felt on his tender feet. Pain, pleasure – when was the last time he had been so present in his own body?

Will helped him out of the wig, Patrick unaware of just how much weight he had been carrying on top of his head until the very moment it was lifted, and unzipped the jumpsuit. His touch was precise and impersonal, like a doctor giving an exam, his focus on removing the clothes without bunching or tearing them. Patrick was used to standing still, mentally detached while costumers dressed and undressed him like a mannequin, and had long since shed any notion of modesty. And yet he felt exposed now, stripped to his underwear, face still painted for the gods, a mermaid caught between sea and land.

He pulled his pants and T-shirt back on, then followed Will into the bathroom, where he was handed a packet of wipes and set about removing the last traces of his new alter ego, Infamy.

'Thank you,' he said, once he could begin to see himself again. 'Tonight was... I'll never forget it.' Will smiled at him in the bathroom mirror.

'Don't mention it,' he replied. 'I'm of the opinion that everybody should do drag at least once in their life.'

'I don't just mean that. Although it was incredible. But also, just... letting me into your world. Meeting your friends, your sister. It's been a long time since I've felt this...' He tried to think of how to put it. 'Connected, I guess.'

He pulled Will into a hug, his body acting on instinct to fill the gap where his words seemed to be failing him. *I am so grateful for this*, he wanted to say. *I am grateful for you.*

'That lot?' Will tutted. 'Oh, you're welcome to them.' But he said it gently, and Patrick could hear the smile in his voice. He drew away and saw that he'd left a trace of makeup on Will's cheek. Without thinking, he reached out and wiped it off with his thumb. He let himself pause like that just for a second, cupping Will's jaw in his hand, then dropped it.

'I should go,' he said.

'OK,' Will said instantly, nodding rapidly, and Patrick realised just how exhausted he must be after putting him in and out of drag and taking him out for the night, how ready for his needy new American acquaintance to leave so he could get some sleep. He remembered the way Will had tensed when he had put his arm around him earlier tonight and decided he had definitely misread things.

It was enough, he told himself, to have this funny, strange, kind person as a friend in this unfamiliar place. It had to be enough.

Will walked him to the door, and they paused there on the threshold. Patrick didn't want this night to end, wanted more than anything to stay here, to go back inside, to grab Will's hand and do what a braver man might.

'Goodnight,' he said, instead. 'I'll... call you tomorrow.'

'OK,' Will repeated, and Patrick watched as he closed the door, seemingly nothing left to say now that they were both men again.

15

Jordan called the next morning while Will was making coffee. That, in itself, was strange: the two of them tended to communicate entirely via text messages, voice notes, and memes. That was their love language. What made it even odder was that Jordan tended not to surface until at least 11 a.m. It was 9.

'Who died?' Will asked when he picked up, at the exact same moment that Jordan demanded: 'What happened last night?'

'I could ask you the same thing,' said Will. 'Where *were* you?'

'Turns out I wasn't on the rota last night, so I went for a curry with April.'

'Wow. Thanks for cluing me in.'

'Well, I kind of got the feeling that you and your new bestie might want to hang out just one-on-one,' Jordan replied. 'Was I incorrect?'

'What do you mean?'

'Just. You know. A vibe I may or may not have picked up on. I'm very intuitive. So?'

Will considered the question. It would be a lie to say he didn't like spending time with Patrick just the two of them. And last night had taken such a wild direction that he had to admit, he hadn't even really noticed Jordan and April's absence. The trust Patrick had placed in him, his game willingness, had been thrilling. But did that constitute a vibe?

It wasn't his business to tell Jordan that he knew, for certain, that Patrick was gay. Or that he had given him a drag makeover, that there had been a split second when Patrick had wiped away a smudge of paint from his face and their eyes had met and Will's heart had threatened to pack up shop and retire for good.

'I don't know,' he said, finally. 'We had a good time, then things got awkward and he left.'

'Awkward how?'

'Awkward like...' Will's phone vibrated in his hand before he could finish the thought. 'One second.' He drew the phone from his ear and looked at the screen: it was a text from Patrick.

'That was him. He wants to know if I feel like showing him around the city today.'

'Right,' said Jordan. 'You need to douche.'

'Oh God, shut up.'

'And wear your best underwear. Calvins. None of that H&M shite.'

'You're deranged, Jordan. He wants to go for a walk, not get in my pants.'

'I'm not deranged, I'm bloody psychic. Do not fuck this up, William,' Jordan insisted. 'If you do, I will never forgive you.' And he hung up.

Will texted Patrick back, saying sure, a walk sounded good, and an hour later they met in Pigeon Park. Patrick admired the cathedral, ducked just in time to avoid one of the eponymous birds colliding with his head, and followed Will down the street to Victoria Square, past the nymphlike sculpture lovingly known as the Floozie, then around the corner to where the art museum opened out onto a wishing fountain that looked like something out of *La Dolce Vita*.

'People love to joke about Birmingham being a dump, but she's always been good to me,' said Will. 'Not to brag, but we have a Dishoom now and everything. Come on. I want to show you something.' He marched on, explaining to Patrick as they went exactly what a Dishoom was.

The Library of Birmingham sat in Centenary Square like an enormous stack of Christmas presents, shining gold in the late morning sun. 'I was here when they did the grand opening,' said Will. 'Malala spoke all about the power of words. I cried. Margo called me a wetter and then we got pizza.'

'It's beautiful,' said Patrick.

'That's not what I want to show you,' said Will, shooing him inside, up a series of escalators and then into the lift. It pleased him, seeing Patrick taking in the library's vast interior, the look on his face as they reached the very top of the building.

'This way,' he said, leading him through a narrow door into a small room that felt even smaller on account of the stacked walls, curlicued brass fixtures, and ornate dark wooden panelling. Birds and flowers bloomed and flitted between the neatly shelved volumes and framed printings situated under glass. On the way to meet Patrick, Will had asked himself what he could show him that would, well, not impress him exactly – this was the midlands, not Malibu – but at least convey how much Will loved this place.

'You're an actor,' said Will. 'I thought you might get a kick out of the Shakespeare Library.'

'A heaven on earth I have won by wooing thee,' Patrick murmured, rapt as he gazed around the room.

'Come again?'

Patrick turned to him, eyes bright. 'I love it,' he said. 'Thank you for bringing me here.'

'Shakespeare's first folio is kept here,' Will said. 'Comedies, tragedies, histories. So many boys dressed as girls.'

'Men in dresses?' Patrick pretended to clutch his pearls. 'Scandalous.'

Will laughed, then beckoned Patrick out of the room and continued with the tour, taking him out onto the secret garden on the library's roof. There was nobody else up here, and Will fancied he could see Patrick's back straighten as they walked between trees and bushes all flush with the bounty of spring, errant petals circling on the breeze that was actually quite brisk.

'There's one more thing I want to show you,' Will shouted to him over the wind, after they had circled the roof and taken in the panoramic view of the city that, he had to admit, was probably more impressive from street level. Birmingham was the opposite of a Monet; she looked far better in close-up.

The Rainbow Room was on the lowest level of the library, in the children's section. This, Will explained as they walked around the colourful, classroom-like space, was where he and Faye Runaway would read to kids as part of drag queen story hour.

'How many jobs do you have, exactly?' asked Patrick.

'Just the two. Bookseller, drag artist. A normal amount. I mean, you know. The economy.' Will waved a hand to convey the financial precarity that had been the background noise of his entire adult life. 'Necessity is the mother of invention and all that. It's like how every single air stewardess has a side hustle selling her worn tights on the internet.'

Patrick grimaced. 'I have a cousin who works for Delta. I may never be able to go to Thanksgiving dinner ever again.'

'Oh, don't be such a prude.' Will punched his arm playfully. 'We all do what we have to, to get by. You must have had your fair share of demeaning jobs before you got famous.'

'I guess. I've been very lucky.'

'I have, too.'

'Oh yeah?

'Lucky to have figured out what I love to do.'

'We have that in common,' said Patrick, holding the door open for Will as they left the Rainbow Room.

'I'd show you my other place of work, but you've already seen the sights of Gilroy's,' said Will. 'The till, the exceptionally charming staff.' He gestured at himself. 'The only thing left is the screaming cupboard.'

'The what now?'

'A contemplative space that April and I use for decompression purposes. It's less dramatic than it sounds, don't worry. I'm not much of a screamer myself. I prefer quiet reflection. You know. Mindfulness and such. I'm actually very chill.'

'You definitely give off a way chill vibe.' Patrick adopted a surfer-esque tone, and Will laughed.

'You just think I'm not chill because you're from LA,' he said. 'I bet everybody there and their *dog* has reiki sessions and a prescription for Xanax.'

'I don't have a dog,' was all Patrick said in response. 'I travel for work too much.'

'But you would otherwise, right? You seem like *such* a dog person.'

'I guess I am. What about you? Let me guess. Cats.'

'I am currently focusing a lot of my energy on keeping a peace lily named Cordelia alive. I'm not quite ready to graduate to sapient mammals.'

From there they walked through to the Rep theatre, then out onto Broad Street, which Patrick remarked looked much improved during daylight. They strolled slowly down Birmingham's very own walk of fame, the stars commemorating some of the city's best-loved sons and daughters. Patrick kept his eyes fixed on the ground as they strolled, proudly pointing to a paving stone from time to time when he recognised one of the names underfoot. Ozzy Osbourne. Julie Walters. Joan Armatrading.

'The Weakness in Me,' he said. 'What a song.'

'Right?' Will stopped and grabbed his arm. 'Not to mention featured in one of the best Shakespeare adaptations of all time.'

'*10 Things I Hate About You*!' Patrick practically yelled back, and held up his hand for a high five. He could have been the good-natured jock in a high school movie in that moment, an all-American himbo prom king who got the girl after learning some valuable lesson or other. Will gamely slapped his palm and then kept on walking.

'We should go see a movie,' said Patrick, catching up with him.

'Now, you mean?'

'Sure.'

'That's so weird,' said Will. 'I have never thought about actors just, like, going to the cinema. Which is entirely stupid, because of course you would. It probably counts as work. I bet all of your cinema tickets are tax-deductible.'

'Plus I really, really like popcorn,' said Patrick.

'I mean, who doesn't?'

'Do you know where has the best popcorn in the world?' Patrick turned so he was walking backwards and facing Will at the same time. 'The Chinese Theatre in Hollywood.' He glanced down at his feet, currently obscuring one of the Moody Blues. 'It's on the *other* Walk of Fame.'

'Well, we probably can't compete with that,' said Will, 'but I am pretty sure I can hook you up with some popcorn.' He got out his phone to check nearby listings, and they settled on a screening of an action movie with some variety of plane in the title. Or maybe it was a boat. Will supposed they would find out.

Click, click, click.

'What's that sound?' he asked, looking around. 'I hate to sound a hundred years old, but kids who don't have their phones set to silent drive me insane. I was on a bus the other day and all I could hear was someone clickity-clacking away on their screen. And then they took a video call. *Without headphones*. Tell me that's not serial killer behaviour.'

'It's not,' said Patrick, smile fading. 'Not kids, that is.' Will followed his eyeline to where a middle-aged man in all-black denim stood a hundred or so yards away, photographing Patrick from behind a transparent bus shelter. It was such a stupid place to hide that Will almost laughed. Instead, seeing the way Patrick's entire body language was changing, becoming all closed off, he whipped out his phone again and opened a different app.

'This way,' he said, playing tour guide once again and hurriedly directing Patrick around a corner, where his phone informed him an available electric scooter was sitting idle.

'What's this?'

'It's like a Boris bike,' said Will, stepping onto it and scanning his phone across the handlebars.

'That sounds made up,' said Patrick.

'Welcome to England,' said Will. 'Now hop on and hold tight. I'll get us out of here before that pap can catch up.'

Will had never learned to ride a bike. His mom had never been very outdoorsy, and his dad had never been, well, present. But one of his favourite ever birthday presents as a kid had been his scooter. It was a glorious shade of electric blue that Will had been convinced made it go faster somehow, and he'd lost count of the number of times he'd pushed it to the top of a nearby hill and then whooped and hollered all the way down, wind stinging his eyes, feeling for just a second like he was flying.

The public scooters did not go that fast, and they were an ugly shade of orange, but still, Will felt almost the same way as the two of them raced through the city, Patrick laughing in his ear, arms firmly around his waist. Like he was capable of anything. After a while, he felt Patrick carefully remove his arms, and he looked back just for a second to see him, hands outstretched, eyes closed. And if anybody walking through Birmingham city centre that day saw a tall, blonde blur whizz past and had time to ask themselves, 'Was that Patrick Lake?', he was already gone.

The New Street Odeon was run-down and in dire need of an update compared to the other cinemas in the city, which boasted reclining chairs and IMAX screens, but that was exactly why Will settled on it. This place was all but empty on weekdays, meaning Patrick could walk in unbothered.

Will had already bought the tickets online en route, and he made small-talk with the anaemic-looking teenager at admissions while she scanned the QR code on his phone, keeping her attention on him and not the guy next to him, whose face was casually turned away. He told himself he had chosen a practically abandoned picture house to make life easier for Patrick, and not so that he would have him all to himself, and he got halfway to convinced before the memory of Patrick's thumb on his cheekbone came back to him.

Knowing that Patrick was gay didn't change a thing, in theory. Nor did knowing that he had a far more flamboyant side than his exterior indicated. But as with all knowledge, it did beget more questions. Or at least, one question in particular that Will didn't dare ask.

Do I have a shot with you?

The theatre was already dark by the time they had bought popcorn and drinks, and so they slipped into the first couple of seats on the back row.

'Are we late?' Patrick asked.

'Barely.'

'You're just feeding the stereotype at this point,' Patrick teased. 'About gay men always being late.'

'I object to that. We're right on time. It's not our fault if everybody else shows up early.'

'All I know is that if I turned up late to an audition, I wouldn't book many gigs.'

'You do realise that the screening time they tell you is a lie,' Will said. 'The trick is to rock up half an hour after that, and they'll only just be dimming the lights then.'

'But then you miss the trailers,' Patrick countered. 'I like the trailers.'

'The same trailers that have been all over the internet for weeks?' Will asked, throwing a fistful of popcorn into his mouth.

'It's all part of the experience,' said Patrick. 'I just love going to the movies. Always have. I went as often as I could when I was a kid.'

As they continued to talk over the trailers Patrick claimed he wanted to see, their voices lowered and lowered so as not to disturb the dozen or so other moviegoers scattered around the room. By the time the film began, they were whispering; each remark necessitated a turn of the head, a slight lean inward. Patrick was just a dark outline next to him, and Will found himself teasing the actor for his corny earnestness, his Americanisms.

'You guys have amazing foreign policy,' he told Patrick in a hushed tone as they watched a helicopter launch a missile.

'We learned from watching you,' Patrick fired back.

Will wasn't even fully aware of the fact that they had been flirting until he felt the slightest nudge of Patrick's little finger against his on the armrest between their seats. As an experiment, he withdrew his hand, plucked a single piece of popcorn from the bag in his lap, and popped it into his mouth, before returning it to the armrest. Patrick's hand was still there, unmoving.

'I suppose it must come in handy now too,' whispered Will.

'What must?'

'Going to the movies.' Will nodded to the rest of the theatre, and said quietly: 'In the dark, nobody knows you're you.'

'You're right,' said Patrick.

'We could be anybody right now,' Will continued. 'A couple of complete strangers.' *What are you saying?* he screamed inwardly. *What are you doing?*

'True,' said Patrick. 'But all the same.' Was it Will's imagination or was Patrick's finger moving against his? 'I'm glad that I'm here with you.'

'Me too,' said Will, lifting his pinkie ever so slowly in response.

Patrick shook slightly next to him, and it took Will a second to realise he was laughing gently.

'You're going to make me do it, aren't you?'

'Do what?' Will asked.

'You know what.'

'I don't!' Will whispered. 'Honestly, I haven't a clue what you're talking about.' Reasonably, he didn't. Such a thing was so far outside the realm of things that happened in the real world, least of all to him. But at the same time, some part of him thought that he might know. But fear had taught him the best thing to do with that secret knowledge was bury it.

Those instincts had kept him safe. Kept him alive, on nights when he had the sudden, urgent intuition that a man he had got too close to could turn on him, that somebody who hated himself would channel that rage outward. Survival first. Happiness second.

What if, though? He thought. Good God, what *if?*

And once that question is uttered, it demands an answer.

'I'm asking you,' said Will, 'to do it.'

Patrick inched closer. 'Do what?' he asked, feigning innocence this time.

Oh no, Will thought. *This man.*

'Do,' he whispered, 'the,' he leaned in, 'thing.' When Patrick didn't move away, he inclined even further, their faces a breath away from each other. A second passed, just long enough for Will to think he had made a terrible mistake, and panic began to bubble up inside him. 'Wait—' he began, before Patrick's mouth closed on his, and whatever words that may have been on his lips were gently brushed away.

Intermission

In 1855, an inventor in Birmingham by the name of Alexander Parkes sought to create a form of plastic capable of waterproofing his coat. Following his death, Parkes's work was spirited away to America by another inventor, John Wesley Hyatt, where it would become known as celluloid, the basis for photographic film and a building block for the movie industry. Thousands of stories, billions of dollars, an incalculable number of hopes and dreams and broken hearts on either side of the screen, countless first kisses shared in the back row of a shadowy cinema, ideas begetting ideas like timelines branching in a multiverse, all tracing back to a workshop in a smoky industrial town on the other side of the planet.

One hundred and sixty years after a man created a substance capable of capturing the moving image, seventy years after a husband and wife dreamed of a man who could fly, two boys sit in a darkened room, hands reaching for each other in the shadows. On the screen, explosions and embraces play out via plastic and projected light, shadow puppets on the wall of a cave.

Fortune favours the brave, Patrick thinks, a common refrain of Captain Kismet, as he cups the back of Will's neck to pull him closer.

This isn't actually happening, thinks Will, feeling his body surrender under the other man's touch.

Kissing in the back of a cinema, each tasting sugar and salt on the other's lips, they could be anybody, any pair who walked in expecting one kind of story and ended up starting their own.

ACT TWO:
A SPY IN THE HOUSE OF LOVE

'There are easier things in life than being a drag queen, but I ain't got no choice. Try as I may, I just can't walk in flats.'
Harvey Fierstein, Torch Song

16

1949

It is an uncommonly quiet night in Park City, cloudless and serene, when the young man falls from the sky. He plunges like a comet towards the waiting earth, aglow in burning atmosphere — or is that strange vermillion light something else entirely?

'I love it,' said Charles, grabbing a pencil and beginning to sketch this new hero's meteoric trajectory. Iris stood in the doorway, reading aloud from a sheaf of hastily typed pages, which she had already crisscrossed with notes and amendments.

*Penny sees it through her telescope, all the way out at her father's house in the country, and immediately telephones the one man she knows can be trusted to investigate this strange phenomenon. Richard Ranger, the pilot and war hero known to millions as Captain Kismet, jumps in his car and sets off in pursuit of the light, following its wake through the night sky. Whether this is a falling star or an invasion of some kind, he has vowed to keep the people of this city, of this country, of this **planet**, safe from harm. He tracks it all the way to a canyon just outside the city, where it plummets straight through a highway bridge and crash-lands fast and deep into the rock with a flash of blinding light.*

'Are we sure this isn't a little... Christ-like?' Charles enquired. 'He might as well be announced by a star.'

Iris shrugged. 'This is America, Charles. People love Jesus. Not necessarily *our* people, but still. They're mad for him.'

'True enough. Continue.'

Ranger approaches the crater with caution, and calls out:

'Greetings, stranger! If you be a friend, then welcome to Earth. If you be an enemy, allow me to introduce myself: I am the one they call Kismet. I am the protector of this world.'

'Trite, but dashing. I could positively swoon.'

'Will you just draw?'

'Fine. Go on.'

A head appears through the rubble and red smoke; a swoop of dark wavy hair, bright eyes, a broad smile, a strong jaw and a mischievous chin—

'A mischievous chin?' Charles interjected. 'How exactly do you propose I imbue a chin with a sense of mischief?'

Iris ignored him.

'Hello, friend!' the newcomer exclaims. Forgive me so rude an entrance, your planet's exosphere gave me a touch of trouble. I'm usually gentler on the way down.'

'Walter will never print that kind of innuendo.'

'He's an alien, he doesn't know it's innuendo.'

'If you say so. Does our extra-terrestrial friend have a name?'

'I'm getting to that part.'

'Allow me to reciprocate your introduction,' says the stranger, dusting himself off and holding out his hand in what is recognised across the universe as a symbol of friendship. 'I am Prince Axilon P'Shar the Brave of Ko-Fon-Thet, Son of the Star King Vixus, Steward of the Lesser Worlds.' He pauses for a second, then adds: 'That includes this charming place.'

'Lesser world?' Ranger sputters. 'In all my days—'

'I mean no insult,' says the prince. 'I only mean, the planets with civilised societies that have not yet mastered intergalactic travel.'

'Well, there have been a few setbacks in that regard,' says Ranger, remembering his own adversity while traversing the wormhole, the war on

Zalia, and the loss of his beloved Sura, all trials that stemmed directly from Man's quest to the stars. 'But what brings you to our world?'

'It is a tradition among my people,' the prince explains. 'The second-born son of the Star King will travel out into the galaxy, offering assistance and friendship to any and all he encounters. It is my sworn and sacred duty.'

'Your offer of help is much appreciated,' says Ranger, 'but unnecessary. This planet already has a bodyguard.' (He is unaware that even now, at this very moment, the man formerly known as Professor Oswald is undergoing a transformation which will place the Earth in grave danger.)

The alien tilts his head.

'How curious,' he muses.

'What?' Ranger asks.

'That you believe yourself capable of guarding the front door as well as the back, at the same time.'

'What is **that** supposed to mean?'

'Only that a wise man takes the hand of friendship. Until I have aided this planet in some way, I am bound by the ancient code of my people to remain.'

'And... how long might that be?'

'You would have to consult the Seers at the great caves of Elsor,' the prince says, 'for precognition is not one of my gifts.'

'What **are** your gifts, exactly?'

At that moment, they both hear an engine approaching above them, nearing the bridge which Axilon destroyed on his descent. A moment later, Ranger's enhanced eyesight can make out headlights.

'They must not be able to see the hole in the road!' he says, readying himself to scale the ravine should he need to catch the vehicle as it falls. Before he can move, the air around him begins to swirl with scarlet energy, and he watches in dumbstruck wonder as the ruined stones of the bridge float back up above them to form a new makeshift bridge. The car passes over it and vanishes into the trees on the other side of the valley. When Ranger turns to the prince, he is resplendent in a crimson glow.

'One of my gifts,' he says.
Ranger smiles and extends his hand.
'What did you say your name is again?'
'Prince Axilon,' he says. 'But please. Call me Axel.'

Iris placed the final sheet of notepaper on the desk next to Charles and took a sip of his coffee, grimacing upon realising it was cold, and putting it down again.

'Iris.' Charles's voice was low and careful. His wife rarely spoke of her family, had very few charitable words to spare for many of them. The sole person she had ever mentioned fondly, and even then only once or twice, was a younger brother who had died in the war. A brother named Axel.

'I know,' she said. 'The prince is too earnest. I think a sidekick should have more of a sense of humour, don't you agree?'

'I think he's perfect,' said Charles, reaching out to place his hand on hers.

Iris did not meet his eye, but did not pull away immediately either.

'This coffee tastes dreadful,' she said eventually. 'I'll make some more, shall I?'

Later that evening, Charles crossed the river by train and took the subway to Washington Square. He slowly circled the park twice, making sure he hadn't been followed, before proceeding to his destination. Old habits died hard, and tradecraft was the habit of a lifetime. He didn't think he was under any kind of suspicion, and his record of service to his country afforded him a certain amount of favour, but this McCarthy was starting to get a little overzealous and Charles wore his caution like an undershirt.

He walked into Mona's like it was any other gin joint in the world, and he was just here for a casual drink after a long day at the office. And as a matter of fact, he was, but none of the patrons of this establishment frequented it because of the quality of the liquor. They were all looking for something else, something far harder to find than a stiff Rob Roy — now *there* was a thought — and this was one of the safer places in the city you might stand a chance of finding it. Sure, cruising the pier had its thrills, an adult game of hide and seek, but it also wasn't without its dangers. Not to mention it was nearly November, and it was hard to feel anything out there other than the chill coming in off the Hudson, like Lady Liberty herself could see what they were up to from her vantage point on the horizon and did not care for it one bit.

Charles ordered a whiskey and leaned with one elbow against the bar, surveying the rest of the room. He did so nonchalantly, although around the place he saw much more brazen stares, men young and old shooting lustful come-hithers through the air like Cupid's arrows. One especially brave or stupid boy was *en femme*; Charles could tell with a single look that those were a woman's silk blouse and slacks. If there was a raid tonight, the poor fairy was toast. And yet Charles couldn't help but feel a pang of… what? Not envy. He'd never felt the slightest inclination towards women's clothing, outside of trying on his mother's shoes as a boy and nearly breaking an ankle. Admiration then, perhaps, for the sheer pig-headed gall. Charles knew a little about what it cost to be truly fearless. Plenty of young men he'd known had claimed to be just that. Then half of them got blown up, and the other half learned the value of fear. Fear kept you sharp. Fear kept you alive. Even now, four years and change since he came back, Charles kept his fear as close as an old friend. The war was over, but for men like him that just meant the danger was far closer to home.

'I say,' came a voice from right behind him. 'That's never Charles Ambrose.'

He recognised the voice instantly. It was rich and deep, as English as croquet and colonialism.

'Dickie,' he said, turning to shake the other man's hand. *I must have conjured you*, he thought. 'Dickie Oswin, as I live and breathe.'

'You could have fooled me,' said Dickie, a twitch of a smile on his lips. He looked exactly the same, right down to that impeccably kept moustache. Charles could still remember how it felt. 'You don't call, you don't write...' Dickie laughed. 'Only having you on. Join me for a drink, won't you?'

Charles nodded and slid onto the barstool next to Dickie.

'It's good to see you,' he said. 'How long do you suppose it's been?' He knew precisely how long it had been since their last encounter. Their one and only. It was a memory he returned to often, taking it out and turning it over and over in his hands, a miser with his most prized possession.

'Five years,' said Dickie. 'Istanbul.'

Istanbul. A city that bridged continents and, crucially, transcended alliances. Officially, Charles had been an American working legally as a bank clerk in a neutral city. Truthfully, he had been stationed under MacFarland at the OSS. When the veracity of the intelligence they were mining from the Dogwood chain had come under question, he was partnered with a British liaison. Captain Dickie Oswin, dispatched to Istanbul by the SOE (and, rumour had it, Churchill himself).

They had worked together well, efficiently if not particularly closely. Oswin, as Charles had called him then, was cordial but professional, focused entirely on the task at hand and forgoing any of the idle chatter that permeated some of the other desks at the OSS. If at times that came across as cold, well, Charles put it down to the man's Englishness. And there *was* a war on.

Charles, too, liked to keep his head down and get on with the work, and it was only ever against his own will that he would occasionally find himself thinking that Oswin was a good-looking fellow, dashing like a young Errol Flynn. He had known, by then, that he was never going to desire women the way he did other men: the hands and mouth of a young GI on a boat from New York to Belfast had put paid to any lingering doubts Charles may have had. But strangely enough it was easier to maintain the lie here, where the other men were all separated from their sweethearts and far more eager to talk about their own girls back home than ask Charles about his. To carry on like he was not keenly aware of how Oswin smelled when he leaned over his shoulder (shaving foam, peppermint, something with spice) or how it felt to have those grey eyes on him (nervous as a schoolboy), wasn't as easy.

He respected Oswin. Maybe even liked him, inasmuch as it was possible to befriend anyone with whom you spent hours deciphering and translating in silence. And the work they were doing mattered, so much more than any childish infatuation.

That was much how it continued, for weeks. Until one night when they had both stayed late poring over some scrap of information that was found later to be of absolutely no import, and Oswin did two things he had never done before. He loosened his tie and unfastened the top button of his shirt, although that evening was no warmer than any other, and he reached into his desk for a bottle of Scotch and invited Charles to join him in a drink.

'You've been holding out on us,' said Charles. Oswin procured two glasses from the recesses of his desk and said, as if he hadn't heard him: 'We've earned it.'

They didn't speak much more than that, just sipped their Scotch, but Charles felt an easing between them, another loosening of the proverbial tie. When he stood and announced that he was going to retire for the night, Oswin surprised him by standing too and saying he would walk with him awhile.

'My lodgings are not that far from yours,' he said. Nothing in his choice of words or enunciation gave him away, or would have aroused suspicion in a bystander, but Charles instantly understood. Half the tongues of Europe were spoken under this roof, but this was a language precious few could interpret. Meaning conveyed not through speech but a look, a gesture, the slow intention with which a man unfastened his top button. An invitation, to those who knew enough to accept.

'Alright,' said Charles, holding Oswin's eye for just an instant longer than he would usually allow himself. 'I don't see why not.'

They walked in silence through the streets, unease dwarfed by the sounds and smells of a city that brimmed with life at any hour. A city that had stood for millennia and gone by more names than any spy, which had no interest in the idle fancies of two foreigners.

Oswin did not even pause at the door when Charles unlocked the entrance to his rooms. He walked right in with the air of a man who had been there a hundred times before. Charles locked the door behind them and then turned to Oswin, who had approached him from behind and now stood dangerously near.

Where did this boldness materialise from? Charles had time to think, before Oswin's fingers circled around his wrists. His grip tightened until he was holding Charles's arms firm by his sides, not painfully. Only then did he bring his face closer. *It's so I don't strike him*, Charles realised with remarkable clarity. *Clever man.*

When their lips touched, he thought momentarily that Oswin's moustache tickled rather pleasantly, and then he didn't have it in him to think at all.

'What brings you to New York?' Charles asked him now, surrounded by the jazz and fairies of West 3rd Street.

'It would be violating the Official Secrets Act if I were to tell you that,' said Dickie with a wry smile.

Charles scoffed. They had been through a war together, they each knew how the other tasted, any secret Dickie had to keep now felt absurd and insignificant. But that was the way of things for the likes of them. You gave yourself, and then you politely took it back, folded it up neatly and hid it away again.

'What *can* you tell me?' he asked.

Dickie Oswin considered the question, his fingers tracing the rim of his glass, and said: 'That I would be lying if I said I hadn't hoped I might run into you.'

'A cute line,' said Charles once he had parsed the double negative. 'How could you ever know I might be here?'

'Optimism,' said Dickie, with that smile again.

'You're different from before,' said Charles. It was true; the proper Englishman he had met in Turkey had lost some of his impenetrable stiffness. He looked, Charles thought, like a man who had taken a long hot bath. 'These last five years must have been interesting.'

Dickie placed some cash on the bar.

'Come for a walk with me,' he said, 'and I'll tell you all about it. Or what I can, at least.'

Charles almost said no. He tried to persuade himself he had only come out tonight to drink watered-down bourbon and watch the boys go by, but he failed. And how often did the past reach out to you and beckon you back into its warm embrace?

'One moment,' he said. 'I need to use the honeypot.'

Dickie smiled and rose from his stool when Charles did, like he might for a lady. It was not half as insulting a move as Charles might have thought.

'I'll be right here,' Dickie said.

When Charles had pissed and washed his hands, he inspected his own reflection briefly. How different did he look now? How much had *he* changed since then? Five years might as well be an eternity, and he hadn't been what you might call 'dashing' to begin with. Too slight of build, an expansive forehead topped with what was clearly now a widow's peak. He looked old, and suddenly he felt it too. The weight of everything hidden and lost pulled on him now. No. He would go home. To the apartment. To Iris. No good could come from chasing a boy's foolish dream.

He walked back out into the bar, and there Dickie was, standing, ready to leave. Charles walked over to him, breath faltering, grasping for the words to say this was not going to happen. Dickie picked up Charles's coat from the bar stool where he had left it, and held it out with both hands, again, like he might for a lady. Charles turned around, allowing Dickie to assist him in sliding his arms through the sleeves.

'What a gentleman,' he said. He had meant it to undercut the moment, but it came out almost a whisper. He was so aware of Dickie right behind him, hands heavy and warm on his shoulders, then his upper arms, then gliding down, grazing the backs of his hands, until their fingers were entangled.

'Come on then, darling,' Dickie whispered in his ear. Absurdly, a line from a film popped into Charles's mind; something long and overwrought with Bette Davis.

No one ever called me darling before.

He followed Dickie out of the bar to the hotel where he was staying while he was in the city. It was not far, but they meandered and circled the streets of Greenwich Village to get there, arms crossed against the bracing autumn wind, that old craft seemingly rooted just as deeply in both of them. Finally, safe in the knowledge they were alone, Dickie led Charles in from the cold and locked the door behind them, one spy ready to share his secret with another.

17

Simone looked as pristine as ever when she answered Patrick's video call, makeup subtle but expensive, hair blown out and glossy in her sun-drenched office, like the beautiful-but-severe host of a morning show.

'Thanks for making time,' said Patrick. 'How's your better half?'

'Ugh.' Simone rolled her eyes. 'You know I hate that expression. You can just say girlfriend.'

'I could,' Patrick said, 'but in this case, she definitely *is* the better half.'

'You've got me there. I had to send her an edible arrangement to apologise for missing our first-month-of-living-together anniversary.'

'What did you go for?' Patrick asked. 'Fruit? Chocolates? Those tiny muffins where you need to eat at least four to equal a normal-sized one?'

Simone looked at him like he was stupid. 'Edibles,' she said.

It was hard for an outsider to tell, but ever since meeting Harper on a yoga retreat three months ago, Patrick had never seen Simone so happy. She had claimed to be spending her weekend at Shangri-LA to re-centre herself and achieve enlightenment, but in reality she had followed indie darling Bella Grey there in the hopes of poaching her from a rival agency. While Simone may have ended up leaving on Monday no closer to personal enlightenment *or* a new client, she did have a budding romance on her hands. She and Harper had struck up a conversation about the current state of lesbian representation in cinema ('Why are they always set so far in the past?' 'I know, right? Let the poor girls have some electricity along with all that pining.') and had become almost immediately inseparable. It was the first and only time Patrick had ever known his agent to get distracted from her work. Having met Harper he could see why and was glad of it. Simone never forgot a mission for long, though: she locked down Bella a week later, after cornering the poor girl in the ladies' room at Soho Warehouse.

'So what can I do for my favourite client?' Simone asked.

Patrick's attention snapped back to the task at hand. As delightful as Harper was, he had brought her up for a reason. He was hoping that appealing to Simone's romantic side — such as it was — would make the following conversation easier.

'I've met someone,' he said.

'I thought you might have,' she replied.

'What do you mean?'

'Well for one, you haven't been sending me quite as many emails complaining about the changes to the script. And I know the production is still very much a mess, so I assumed your attention was elsewhere. But anyway. I'm assuming that this "someone" you've started seeing is…?'

'A man.' He decided to keep '*and a drag queen*' to himself for the time being.

'OK.' Simone said nothing for a moment, didn't even move, and Patrick began to wonder if the call had frozen. Then: 'How serious is it?'

'I don't know.' Patrick shrugged. It was the truth. He was almost certainly jumping the gun entirely by telling Simone about Will.

They'd kissed. Once. Well, technically a *lot* of times, but only the one time, and Patrick had been eager for more, but the encounter had been frustratingly abbreviated.

The credits had long rolled when Patrick and Will walked out of the theatre, giddy and breathless. Patrick could not bring a single detail of the movie to mind. They smiled shyly at each other as they adjusted clothing that had grown tight and uncomfortable, bashful all of a sudden under the artificial foyer light. The darkness had freed something in them both, and Patrick's cheeks flushed again at the memory of Will's lips on his, the warmth of his tongue, the way he'd moaned softly into Patrick's mouth as he pulled him closer.

Acting on instinct, Patrick reached for Will again and then hesitated as a couple of teenagers walked past them so that his knuckles knocked clumsily against Will's wrist. He saw it in Will's face too: the harsh, unflattering glare of reality chasing away their wonderful shadows. An almost physical pain jabbed at Patrick, a stitch in muscles that had been allowed to atrophy. His arms hung at his sides, useless, and then he got a call from Audra with some crisis or other that required his presence back at the hotel. Rather than say no, provoking questions about his absence, Patrick had acquiesced. He had made his pathetic apologies to Will, who looked understandably hurt and confused, and left. And the entire time he had stood in Audra's room – it turned out all she really wanted was for somebody to be present while she ranted about the terrible table she had been given at the Ivy across the square – he had checked and rechecked his phone, but of course Will hadn't messaged him. He wouldn't have messaged either, after that abrupt departure. The next move had to be his. And so here he was.

'It's serious enough that I'm telling you,' he said to Simone now. 'Serious enough that I'd like some time to see where it might go.'

'OK,' she said again. 'Is he discreet?'

'You sound like a closeted guy on Grindr.'

'And I've told you never to go on Grindr because your phone can be traced. I'll ask again: Can you trust him to be discreet?'

'I think so. I mean, yes.'

'You don't sound so sure.'

'I am. I just...' He sighed. 'I hate this part. It's why I don't date. Any time I meet somebody, I don't even get a chance to figure out if I really like them before we start talking about NDAs and lawsuits.'

'It's the way of the world,' Simone told him.

'Should it be, though?' Patrick asked. 'I wish I could just spend time with Will like a normal guy. Take him on a real date. Maybe even think about having a boyfriend.'

'If you wanted normal, you chose the wrong career,' Simone said, her tone light. 'And I'm sorry to remind you, but you're *America's* boyfriend.'

'And if I don't want to be?'

Simone laughed, as if he couldn't possibly be serious.

'Do you remember the conversation we had when I first agreed to represent you?'

'You said if I had a thing for pills I should head back to Buttfuck, Indiana right then and there because you're an agent, not a fixer or a babysitter. And I told you I was actually from New Jersey, and you said "same difference".'

'Right,' Simone said unwaveringly. 'Do you remember what *else* I said?'

Patrick sucked air through his teeth.

'That if I wanted to publicly date men, I might become a gay role model, but only for about five people, because I'd never get booked for anything bigger than network.'

'And what did you say to me?'

Patrick sighed, frustrated by this exercise, but Simone's stare remained casual, as if she were between thoughts at a nail appointment. He was the one to look away first.

'I said...' He folded his arms. 'I came here to be a leading man.'

'Not quite.' Simone leaned forward in her chair. 'You said you wanted to be *the* leading man. And I believed you. I saw that for you, and I still do.' Her gaze softened into something that might pass for affection, before reclining again. 'The question is, do you still want that for yourself?'

'Of course I do.'

'Then what's changed?'

'I think I like him, Simone. And... he might like me.' It felt like a betrayal to be saying this to Simone before he and Will had even had a proper conversation. Things were so fragile and new. He stopped himself from saying '*we haven't even slept together*'. He didn't need to tell Simone that. She already knew. And before he and Will took that step, Patrick needed assurance. Simone had coached him well.

'If that's the case,' she said, 'then...' She raised an eyebrow.

'Will.'

'Then *Will* is going to have to get on board. If he really cares about you, and not just sleeping with a celebrity, then he'll understand.'

'That's easy for you to say.' Patrick knew how petulant he sounded, but he couldn't help himself.

'Sweetie, I'm just as queer as you are. But I'm also a realist. I know what kind of industry we're in, and let me tell you, it's not one that's particularly fond of change. We work with what we have. You want to tell the world their favourite superhero knows what dick tastes like? I'll support you, and I'll do my best to get you work on Ryan Murphy's next project. But if you want longevity in the Richard Ranger movies, a five-year contract, freedom to choose any project you like after that, have a *legacy*? All the things we said we were going to make happen? Then this is simply the cost of doing business.'

There were monsters in the Captain Kismet comics called the Ravagions, a race of semi-giants with long, claw-like fingers they used to wrap around entire torsos and squeeze the life out of people. Patrick felt like he was in the grip of those talons right now. The tightness in his chest, the quivering uncertainty in his stomach.

He had no idea how to broach this with Will, how to possibly ask so much of somebody he had just met. But if he didn't...

He thought of every phone number he'd been given by a man and then thrown away, every smile in a bar he hadn't returned for fear of what it might lead to, the risk it might bring. All of it in pursuit of a single goal, an opportunity like the career he was building. Choosing to be alone for the last ten years, even when it felt like it might kill him? It had to be *worth* something.

If word got out about Patrick before filming on *Kismet 2* wrapped, if the studio decided to recast him while they still had time, to bury it in streaming, then what was all of that for? All that sacrifice, all that loneliness?

It was another compromise, he knew. But something had changed these last few weeks. A part of Patrick that had lain dormant and undernourished for so long was now wide awake and ravenous. He thought back to the almost painful gentleness of Will's touch as he'd dressed Patrick, those soft moans of desire he had made in the cinema. The sweetness and the salt of him. Patrick wanted more. He wanted to see how far the hair on those arms and legs went, to feel Will quiver under his touch, to take those whimpers and coax them into screams.

If he had to sign a piece of paper to ensure all of those things remained a secret, that was an easy compromise. He only hoped that Will would see it the same way.

'Fine,' he said.

Simone nodded. 'Send me his full name. I'll draw up the paperwork.' She ended the call without another word.

18

Axel limps into Ranger's quarters, still sore from their battle against Omega's automatons that afternoon. They'd been unable to capture Omega himself, who'd absconded while his mechanical minions kept the two of them busy, but Axel knows it is only a matter of time before they'll see that psychopath again. There are three things he is learning you can count on in this part of the universe: death, taxes, and assholes who call themselves geniuses refusing to leave well enough alone.

I'm going to feel this for a week, he thinks, rubbing his sore shoulder, before he is jolted from his reverie by the sight of Ranger's muscular back. His comrade sits stripped to the waist on the edge of the couch, doing his best to clean and bandage his own wounds, occasionally muttering a pained 'ouch' or 'dang it'.

Axel can't help but smile. He has revelled in learning every curse word this planet has to offer, in as many of its gorgeous languages that he can comprehend. He has collected profanities from across the galaxy, luxuriated in their foulness, savoured how they feel in his mouth. Ranger's strict adherence to propriety, in contrast, baffles him. But he also finds it charming and a comfort. Ranger is the physically strongest man on this planet: he could crush his enemies like insects if he so wished. His constant gentleness, then, is a choice.

And to choose kindness, in the face of the countless horrors and injustices the two of them have witnessed together, to lead continually and defiantly with love, takes real strength.

'Here,' he says softly, although he is sure Ranger heard him approach. 'Let me help.'

Ranger turns gingerly to face him, and Axel steps forward to tend to the many cuts and scrapes that mar his torso. They will heal quickly, and in all likelihood be gone by morning, but in this moment, they look like they smart.

'Thanks,' says Ranger.

Axel tries not to notice the warmth of Ranger's chest beneath his fingers as he swabs the disinfectant, or the way his muscles tighten and harden as Ranger winces in discomfort while he dresses the worst of the cuts.

'All done,' he says, and is about to pull away when Ranger's hand closes around his own.

'Thank you,' Ranger says again.

'It was nothing,' Axel replies.

'I don't mean this,' says Ranger, shaking his head. 'I meant, thank you for being with me. Today. And so many other days like it.'

'That's the job,' says Axel, smiling lopsidedly. 'Sworn and sacred duty, remember?'

'Don't give me that,' Ranger huffs. 'Whatever obligation you may have once had towards the people of Earth, you have more than fulfilled it. There are doubtless other planets out there in need of saving, other perils...'

'This crazy planet keeps me more than occupied,' Axel protests.

'Don't I know it. I guess what I'm trying to say is, I'm glad you stuck around.'

Ranger laughs ruefully.

Ranger's hand, Axel realises, is still on his: grip firm, hot, unyielding.

'Ask me,' he says, almost choking, as if, after all this time, he has just learned he is unable to breathe in Earth's atmosphere.

'Ask you what?' Ranger says. Is it Axel's imagination, or does he sound breathless too?

'Why I stay,' says Axel, edging forward slightly.

'So many bad guys,' Ranger murmurs. 'So many people in need of saving.'

'One,' Axel whispers. 'One person.'

Ranger's lips are on his before he can finish the thought, and he responds hungrily, kissing him with every ounce of the fervour he has repressed since he first laid eyes on him in that crater in the valley. How strong and brave he had looked. Axel had fallen twice that night.

'Richard,' he whispers into his friend's cheek.

'Axel,' Ranger whispers back. With one hand, he reaches under Axel's shirt, ghosting his fingertips along the grooves of his abs. With the other, he deftly unbuckles Axel's belt. 'Axilon P'Shar.' His hand reaches into Axel's underwear, closing around him with such assuredness that all Axel can do is gasp into the crook of Ranger's neck. 'Axilon the Brave,' Ranger says, pushing Axel backwards onto the couch and sinking to his knees.

'My prince,' he whispers, keeping his gaze fixed up on Axel while lowering his mouth onto—

'April.'

April slammed the laptop shut at the sound of her name, neck snapping up to face Will, who stood in the doorway to the screaming cupboard.

'What's up?' she asked.

'Anything good?' he asked, gesturing at the computer. 'Let me see.'

'It's not done yet.'

Will knew enough not to push. He had come straight to the shop after Patrick had left him at the cinema, mind and pulse racing. His first instinct had been to find April and Jordan and debrief them in giddy detail like they were all adolescents giggling at the back of a school bus. But as he made his way up Corporation Street, the specifics of what had happened began to blur in his mind – Who had initiated the kiss? Had it really felt as exhilarating as he was remembering? Could things like this even happen to a person like him? – until the entire thing felt like a daydream. And then, of course, there was the way Patrick had practically bolted afterwards. By the time Will walked into Gilroy's, nodding to Yvonne behind the counter, and found April busy typing away in the cupboard, his burning impulse to tell her everything had faltered. He doubted that Patrick would appreciate Will spilling his private business. And this was just so typically him, getting carried away prematurely.

So they'd kissed. So what? People kissed all the time. For a lot of gay men, kissing was like talking about the weather or playing cards: something they did to pass the time until a better option came along. Only somebody truly naïve would go running to gush to his friends about snogging a man at the grand age of twenty-nine.

He was too excitable, he knew. Too intense, according to some guys.

Too much.

'Why are you even here?' April asked, slipping her laptop under her arm and shimmying past him in the cramped back room to flick on the kettle next to the sink. 'You don't work Mondays.'

'I... forgot.' He stood there awkwardly, knowing exactly how odd he was being. 'I should go! And enjoy my day off. So. That's...' he made a big deal of pivoting towards the front of the shop. 'That's what I'm going to do.'

'OK,' said April, expertly uncapping the tin of teabags, placing one in a mug, and filling it with hot water, all one-handed. 'See you later. Weirdo.' She placed her laptop on the small counter while the tea steeped, and as Will left the room, he heard her mumble to herself: 'Now. Where were we...'

How soon was too soon to text somebody after making out in the back of a cinema? Will tutted at himself instinctively even as he silently posed the question. How juvenile. How 2003 of him. How deeply stupid this all was. And yet none of those very true things stopped the question from doing shaky laps of his mind, like a nervous student driver stuck on a roundabout.

The longer Patrick didn't text him, the longer he agonised over whether he should be the first one to reach out. As a rule, Will rejected dating etiquette and did his best to keep game-playing to a minimum. If he wanted to contact somebody, he did. If he liked someone, he told them. But this was far enough removed from his usual playbook that he didn't know. One of the many things he loved about being gay was that both participants were men. And while for some that meant transcribing the stereotypical traits of men and women onto the top and the bottom, that was nonsense he had never trafficked in.

But there *was* a power differential here, and he couldn't pretend otherwise. Patrick wasn't just the usual kind of privileged that came with being white, male, able-bodied, cisgender, and attractive. He was a literal movie star. Money and fame changed things. Didn't they? Patrick was probably used to having people throwing themselves at him, to having secret hook-ups with people he never called again. Will didn't necessarily want to be another notch on what he had no doubt was a very expensive and tastefully designed bedpost.

And so Will didn't get in touch. For days. He composed and deleted countless messages but stuck to his resolution that Patrick might be rich and famous and one of the most talented kissers he had ever encountered (and that wasn't to be discounted because it was actually surprising how many men got to their age without ever mastering the basics), but Will would not give one more inch of ground. If the man who could have it all wanted him, then he would have to bloody well make the next move. For the first time in his life, Will Wright decided that he would play hard to get.

Until the following Thursday.

I'm so sorry for going quiet on you, the message from Patrick read. *We've been shooting crazy hours this week, but that's no excuse. Can I see you tonight?*

Will was finishing up a shift at Gilroy's when the missive came through. He read it three times, and then handed his phone to April.

'Could you hold this for exactly ten minutes, please?' he asked. 'And don't give it back to me a second before then?'

April shrugged, tucked the device into her back pocket without even looking at it, and returned to scrolling through her own phone. Will took a pen and paper from the front counter and recused himself to the back room, where he proceeded to draft a dozen or so responses to Patrick's message, each of which articulated some aspect of what he intended to say. At first he thought he would scold Patrick for going dark all week, but then again, so had he. He thought about telling him it was fine, no worries, he understood, but that didn't feel right either. For a single white-knuckle ride of a moment, he considered not replying at all. That would be one way to retain a shred of mystery after Patrick had rested a warm, heavy hand on Will's upper thigh in the cinema and felt just how keen he really was.

But he knew himself. 'Mysterious' and 'aloof' were right up there with 'mindful' and 'financially stable' in the pantheon of descriptors that applied pretty much exclusively to other people.

You're right, he typed, once April returned his phone to him. *That's no excuse at all. But I am willing to be the bigger man and forgive you.*

It's more than I deserve, Patrick texted back, thankfully leaning into the bit. Then, seconds later: *If you still think I need to be punished, I will understand.*

It was clearly meant in jest, but unaccompanied by emoji or emoticon, it was perhaps the most brazen thing he had ever witnessed Patrick do. It also flew in the face of any expectations Will might have had about their potential dynamic, should things get that far – a scenario he may or may not have speculated about in depth all week.

So... Patrick texted again before Will could reply. *Tonight?*

There was something about walking into a fancy hotel and taking the lift straight up to a man's room that would never not make Will feel like Julia Roberts in *Pretty Woman*. As he knocked on the door of Patrick's room, he looked down at his oversized shirt and ripped jeans and wished for a moment he had worn hotter clothes, then remembered he didn't have any. Not in his boy drag, anyway.

'Hi,' said Patrick, opening the door and ushering him inside. He looked as devastatingly handsome as ever, all-American in blue jeans and a white T-shirt.

'You look nice,' said Will. 'Like, I don't know. Bruce Springsteen for Calvin Klein.'

'Thanks,' said Patrick, rubbing the back of his neck. He couldn't quite look Will in the eye, and for a second Will had the horrid feeling that he was about to be pre-emptively dumped.

'This place is lush,' he said, casting a glance around the suite.

'Yeah, it's cool,' said Patrick, as if just noticing his environment for the first time. 'I've definitely stayed in worse.'

'Living in hotels must lose its shine after a while,' said Will. 'I mean, after a week in Gran Canaria I know I'm desperate to be back in my flat, with my own things.' He paused. 'I just realised. You must have an amazing place.' He tried to picture what kind of dwelling Patrick would call home. A Spanish-style villa in Bel-Air or glass-walled mansion on Mulholland Drive, no doubt.

'I just bought a house, actually,' said Patrick. 'In Studio City. I'm having it decorated while I'm here. I'm about forty emails deep in a chain with an impeccably stylish, devastatingly expensive interior designer named Asa.'

Will scanned the room furtively for clues as to Patrick's taste, but there were no strewn belongings, open suitcases, or homey touches. The entire place looked like it was still waiting for somebody to check in.

'When I moved into my flat, I just had Jordan come round and help me paint in exchange for a bottle of wine,' he said. 'So... what's going on?'

'About the other day,' said Patrick. *Here we go*, thought Will.

'The other day?' he feigned nonchalance.

'The other day,' repeated Patrick. 'When we...'

'When we?' Will tilted his head, intentionally obtuse. *If you're going to ditch me, that's fine, but I'm going to make you say it. It happened. I didn't imagine it.*

'When I kissed you,' said Patrick, finally bringing his gaze up to meet Will's. And in what he would come to think of later as a minor miracle, all of Will's self-doubt fell away. Nobody had ever looked at him the way Patrick was looking at him now; with abject, unfiltered desire, free of guile or condition.

He wants me, Will realised, and he dropped his tote on the floor just in time for Patrick to grab the back of his head and pull him into a kiss. This wasn't the playful, tentative kiss of the cinema. Patrick was forceful, hungry, exploring Will's mouth with his tongue and breathing hard. Will pushed back with equal ardour, running his hand through Patrick's hair, biting his lip and delighting in the groan that elicited.

Who knew how long they stayed that way, pawing at each other's clothes like animals, until Patrick finally tore himself away, as if remembering something important, like he had summoned Will here to fix a leaky tap or replenish his towels.

'I need to talk to you about something,' he said. 'Before we go any further.'

'Ok...?'

'It's... kind of awkward.'

'Oh. *Oh*. If it's a safety thing, I'm on PrEP. And I... not to be presumptuous, but I brought the essentials.' He nodded to the tote bag on the floor, which contained everything he had deemed necessary for the occasion: poppers, lube, condoms, chewing gum, chapstick, as well as a granola bar, bottled water, and a novel for the bus home.

'It's not that,' Patrick said. 'I mean, it *kind of* is. And that's all good to know. Really good to know.' He pulled his phone out of his back pocket. 'Did you get an email this week from somebody at Summers & Chase?'

'I did. It sounded like spam for a new soap brand.'

'Summers & Chase are a talent agency. They're who my manager Simone works for.'

'Your talent reps are emailing me? That's very nice of them, but unless they're planning on opening an office in Brum, I don't really see the point in them wanting to represent me.'

'That's not... Shit. Sorry. No. That's not it. I mean, I'm sure they *would*. You're great! But.' Patrick exhaled deeply. 'I'm not doing this very well. Here.' He walked over to a desk in the corner of the room, picked up a sheaf of official-looking papers, and handed them to Will, who glanced down at them just long enough to see his full name – *William Oliver Wright* – at the bottom of the first page. Had he even told Patrick his middle name?

'If we're going to, you know? Then I need you to sign this.'

'What is it?'

'A gag,' said Patrick.

'Sounds hot.'

'It just means you can't talk about anything that might happen between us. Or anything that already happened. There's a retroactive clause in there that covers what happened at the movies the other day.'

'That sounds considerably less hot.'

'I know. I'm sorry. This is just how these things work where I'm from.'

'Jersey?'

Patrick smiled, as if pleasantly surprised that Will had remembered this biographical detail. Of course, it was easy to remember things about the guy you were into when he had his very own Wikipedia page.

'Hollywood,' said Patrick. 'It's how everything works there. Lawyers, non-disclosure agreements, fake relationships constructed by PR firms and real ones covered up by the same people.' He rubbed his mouth and looked at Will with a sorrowful arc to his brow, as if to say *I wish it didn't have to be this way. I hate asking this of you.*

This was all utter bullshit, of course. What could be sillier, more of an instant mood killer, than doing paperwork before having sex with someone for the first time? Will understood why it was necessary in principle, but to see it in black and white was another thing entirely.

'I can't say it's the most romantic proposition I've ever had,' said Will, walking slowly over to the desk. 'But you're also not the first man to ask me if I can be discreet.'

'It's not that I don't trust you,' said Patrick. 'I truly cannot stress that enough.'

'I haven't told anybody about what happened the other day,' said Will. 'Which is honestly kind of amazing, actually. I've been dodging texts from Jordan about it all week because he already thought you fancied me.'

'He wasn't wrong.'

'He's all but guessed, though. Which means he's probably in a side-chat with April about it. Also, you came to dinner at Margo's, so she almost definitely thinks something is going on. So...' he tapped the documents in front of him. 'It's technically already out there.'

Will felt a warmth rush to his cheeks upon hearing this.

'Hmm.' Patrick looked down to the paper, then back up at Will. That look had not yet fully left his eyes. Will hoped it never did.

'Do you trust them?' he asked.

'With my life,' replied Will.

'Then that's good enough for me,' said Patrick. 'I like them. I hope they like me. I don't think they'd rat us out either.'

'OK then.' Will picked up a pen from the desk. 'Just promise me,' he said, his eyes drifting from the bed behind him to Patrick, 'that it will be worth it.'

Patrick's breathing deepened. He approached Will, towering over him until he backed up into the desk, leaned down, and whispered in his ear: 'I promise.'

His fingers traced down Will's arm, extracted the pen from his fingers, and, still leaning over him, signed his own half of the contract, then handed it back to Will. Will turned to face the desk and wrote his own name at the bottom. He felt the heat of Patrick behind him, the sheer bulk of him, and coyly moved ever so slightly backwards until there it was: unmistakeable hardness. He dropped the pen onto the desk with a satisfying plonk, and they both watched as it rolled backwards towards the wall, vanishing over the edge of the polished wood.

'Signed, sealed, del—'

He felt Patrick's lips against the side of his neck, nuzzling him. Patrick's arms enclosed him from behind, one of them circling around his chest to hold Will tight against him while his other hand lightly caressed his lower stomach through his clothes, drifting up and down between his navel and his jeans, his touch infuriatingly light even as it strayed lower. Will bucked into his hand slightly and was pulled back by Patrick's other arm, a vein bulging visibly in his bicep. Patrick spun him around and hauled him up onto the desk, and Will immediately, instinctively wrapped his legs around Patrick's waist.

Following the same unspoken impulse, Patrick gripped his buttocks firmly and picked him up, making Will gasp in surprise.

'I'm sorry,' Patrick said. 'Is this too much?'

'Not even close,' said Will, pulling Patrick back to him. 'Don't worry,' he added. 'I can handle it.'

Patrick smiled, touching his tongue between his teeth, and something about it made Will even harder. Then he went to carry Will towards the bed, but paused on the way — how *big* was this *room?* — to pin him violently to the wall. Will yelped upon impact, and Patrick paused.

'You'll let me know if I go too far?' Patrick asked. 'I don't want to hurt you.'

'Patrick.' Will pushed him away now, held him at arm's length so Patrick could see the earnestness in his eyes, and told him with every ounce of feeling he had: '*Ruin me.*'

The longer they kissed, the more their hands explored each other, the hungrier Patrick seemed to become, and Will didn't dare even ask how long it had been since this man, this hewn sculpture of a man, was last touched. Last felt the impossible heat of a body on his. Will committed to Patrick's pleasure, to helping him make up for lost time, to remind him just how good this could feel. To reintroduce him to a part of himself that he had kept locked away, to reassure him that his desires were not wrong. To draw that side out, to wrap him in his arms, and to say *you are safe here.*

Hours later, when concepts like 'time' had lost any concrete meaning, Will sat up in bed gingerly, wincing in delicious soreness.

'I should go,' he said.

'You really shouldn't,' retorted Patrick, yanking him back down like a rag doll. Will sighed and consented to being spooned for a little while longer, their breathing finally returned to normal, chests rising and falling in unison.

'I just thought,' he said, 'it would probably be better if I left under cover of darkness, rather than in the harsh light of day?'

'Damn.' Patrick kissed the back of his head softly. 'You're probably right.'

They fell silent again for another minute, then Patrick asked: 'Can I see you tomorrow?'

'Dylan's band are performing downstairs at the Flapper tomorrow,' said Will. 'Margo and I agreed to go, because that's the kind of thing a supportive mother and gay uncle do. They're going to *hate* it.'

'Oh. Well, have fun.'

'Ugh!' Will rolled onto his other side so he could face Patrick. 'The implication was that I wanted you to come with me.'

'Yeah?'

'Obviously. Christ. It could be. I don't know. A date.'

'I'd like to,' said Patrick. 'Really. I want that. To go on a date with you in public. But there's the whole...' He nodded over to the desk, where a document forbidding exactly this lay signed and dated. 'Getting into full drag again to go to a gig un-harassed sounds like it might draw focus.'

'You wouldn't need to get all bitched up this time,' said Will. 'I've thought about it, and it's kind of genius actually.'

'What?'

'It's a teenage band playing to other moody teenagers.'

'And...?'

'And what is more cringeworthy to that kind of crowd than, well, *us*?' Will grinned, and Patrick began to smile too as realisation dawned. 'They won't even *look* at anyone over the age of twenty. They'll think we're the most boring people on the planet. Invisible, almost.'

'So what you're saying is...' Patrick gestured at his own face.

'If we deck you out in the lamest clothes ever, they won't see Patrick Lake, star of the *Kismet* movies. They'll see a normcore guy in a baseball cap and assume you're someone's older brother. If they even see you at all.'

'That... that *is* kind of genius.'

'I know, right?' Will kissed him briefly on the mouth, and it felt like punctuation.

'Is the band any good?'

'If I admit that they're bloody awful, will you still come?'

Patrick pulled him closer, looked into his eyes, and said: 'I can't think of anything I'd rather do this tomorrow evening than see a terrible band play terrible music with you.'

Will kissed him again, a firm and languorous full stop this time.

'Then it's a date,' he said. 'I am going to dress you up *so* ugly.'

'Oh yeah?' Patrick grinned.

'It's going to take all of my considerable talents.' Will nodded. 'You're quite good-looking, I don't know if anybody has ever mentioned that.'

'You're pretty damn gorgeous yourself,' Patrick said.

Will laughed. 'I'm alright.'

'No. Really.' Patrick's gaze grew serious, his voice deeper. He flipped Will onto his back, that strength making quick work, and pinned him to the bed. Will's breathing quickened as Patrick leaned down to growl in his ear: 'Let me show you what I mean.'

19

1949

For the third time in as many weeks, in what was fast becoming an unspoken ongoing arrangement, Charles collapsed on top of Dickie with a wordless, guttural exclamation, robbed of human speech. A moment later, he rolled off him so that they lay side by side, legs entangled in sheets, glistening chests rising and falling in near-unison as they caught their breath.

Dickie lit two cigarettes in his mouth, and then handed one to Charles, the same way Paul Henreid had done for Bette Davis in that picture. Now what was it called? He'd be damned if he could remember. Charles could barely remember his own name at this present moment, he was still so caught up in that devilishly clever thing Dickie had done with his tongue.

'You've learned a new trick or two since Istanbul,' he said.

Dickie laughed. It was a full and throaty sound, and once again Charles could not help but wonder what the last five years had held for Dickie, the ways in which they had changed him from that taciturn captain to this louche dispenser of ungodly pleasures.

'I will admit, I am more experienced than I was,' Dickie said. 'When you and I first met, I was... well, let's not be shy about it. I was a real pill.'

'You were not.'

'I was! I took life so seriously, and we were at war, life *was* a serious business. But since then, I've come to think of it as less of a business entirely, and more like...'

'Play?'

Dickie blew out a cloud of smoke, turned to him, and smiled. 'Play. Precisely.'

'Well in that case,' said Charles, 'I am glad that you disappeared, and even gladder to have found this newly enlightened Dickie Oswin.'

Dickie's smile settled into a thin line.

'I should have written,' he said. 'After that night. When I was reassigned.'

'I could have too,' said Charles. 'When they sent me back.'

The rest was left unsaid between them. They each knew that they had been careful not to be followed that night in Istanbul, but they also knew that even the best spies were sometimes caught with their pants down. Charles doubted that a couple of men spending the night together was viewed as cause for incident given the larger scheme of things, but the timing of their separation had seemed conspicuous. Perhaps the English and the Americans had simply not wanted their operatives getting too close. They might have been on the same side, but that didn't mean they'd ever stopped spying on each other.

But what did it matter, really? Dickie had found a way back to him. It was the kind of luck that Charles hadn't ever dared to dream of. To have survived the war, to have found a friend and ally and partner in Iris, to not have been caught out in one of the bar raids that were happening with alarmingly increasing frequency... was all that not enough? To ask for more would be churlish, arrogant even.

Still, each time that Charles left Dickie's hotel in Manhattan and made the journey back to Brooklyn, he would allow himself to indulge in a daydream of what it might be like if things were different.

To not have to look over his shoulder when they arranged to meet. To be able to sleep in Dickie's arms for more than a single night. To wake up and drink coffee and eat eggs and read the newspapers. To *live*. Together.

It was an idle fantasy, nothing more, but still he found himself giving voice to it.

'Wouldn't it be something,' he said, 'if the world were different for those like us?'

'How do you mean?'

'Well, if a man could kiss a man like he would his sweetheart.'

'I believe I did that mere moments ago.'

'You certainly did. But you know what I mean. If we could do that the way men kiss women. Freely. Openly. Without reprisal. As if it were... oh, I don't know. Ordinary.'

The moment he said it, he felt foolish. The very idea of such a thing was a child's imagining, even further beyond the limits of possibility than his and Iris's flying captain.

'It would be quite the thing,' said Dickie. Charles watched the cigarette burn down until the embers were almost touching Dickie's fingers, and yet the other man didn't move. 'Quite the thing,' he said again, eyes unreadable. A sudden sadness came over Charles, and a pang of guilt that he may have hurt this man – a man whom he held more dearly than even he had realised – by taunting him with the one thing they would never have.

The name of the movie finally came to him. *Now, Voyager*. Paul and Bette standing in the garden, smoking cigarettes and dreaming of what might have been, once upon a time. Charles reached over and took the now-dead cigarette from between Dickie's fingers, placing it next to his own on the ashtray beside the bed.

'Don't let's ask for the moon,' he said. 'We have the stars.'

Richard Ranger, the soldier, pilot, and hero known across the galaxy as Captain Kismet, has faced all kinds of challenges and trials: marauding aliens, robots from another dimension, and of course, the perpetual machinations of his arch-nemesis, Omega Man. But he is about to face his greatest adventure – and danger – yet: LOVE.

Penny Haven, the humble and loyal scientist, has been by his side through thick and thin, and knows his heart and his bravery even better than his friend and companion Axel, the extra-terrestrial prince known also as Kid Crimson. But Penny's inquisitive nature may be her downfall. Ever since Ranger was first imbued with his cosmic gifts in the wormhole, Penny has sought to understand how such things are possible, and her search for knowledge has led to experiments that are beyond even her talents. On her secret moon base, Penny is building a machine capable of tapping into the unfathomable powers of the universe. But what she doesn't know is that the slightest miscalculation could tear open a hole in reality and propel her through time and space, where she will be lost forever. Will her hubris, like Icarus's, lead to her downfall? Or can Captain Kismet reach Penny in time and bring her back from the brink of destruction by finally confessing his true feelings?

And all the while, Omega lurks, ready to strike when Kismet and those around him are at their most vulnerable…

'Are we sure we want to turn Penny into some kind of mad scientist?' asked Charles. 'She's Ranger's girl Friday. The readers seem to really like her.'

'It's a metaphor,' said Iris. 'For how women are constantly being told they're over-reaching whenever they try to pursue their own ambitions.'

'Hmm.' Charles rubbed his stubble. 'I don't know.'

'You don't have to know,' said Iris. 'You just have to make it look good. Eleanor, what do you think?'

Eleanor jumped at being called on, having seemingly given up on trying to follow their conversation from her position on the couch. Charles had been so engrossed in his and Iris's work at the desk that he had almost forgotten she was even there. Eleanor was a rather pretty young thing who had the tendency to giggle like a schoolgirl, and Charles found her mildly irksome, but he knew Iris was fond of her, and so he tried not to let his irritation show.

'I think it's very like a man,' said Eleanor, after a moment's thought, 'to see it as his job to rush in and interrupt a woman's business. To think he knows better.' She looked at Charles pointedly, and Iris smirked.

'I can see I am outnumbered,' said Charles. 'I shall make it look splendid,' he added to Iris, and she blew him a kiss.

Charles knew it had never been Iris's plan for he and Eleanor to be in the same room at the same time, just as he had absolutely no intention of her ever meeting Dickie. But Iris and Eleanor had no other place: Eleanor lived with her husband, and it might raise more suspicion for two women to go to a hotel than two men, so Iris had started inviting her over to the apartment in Brooklyn.

When Charles had walked in a few days earlier to find Eleanor cradled in Iris's lap, girlish face flushed as Iris worked away under her skirt, they had all been mortified. Iris could probably see the surprise flit across his face as the two of them had sprung apart like a couple during a bar raid and she had braced herself. Instead, Charles had simply laughed. It was only after the horror at being caught gave way to relief that they joined him in his mild hysteria, Iris's laughter low and throaty, Eleanor's tinkling like a bell.

After that, Charles had begrudgingly accepted Eleanor's occasional presence, although Iris did her best to keep them separate. They never dined together, for instance, and so later that evening when Charles suggested they go out for dinner to talk more about

Kismet, Iris gave Eleanor a discreet peck on the cheek goodnight and sent her out of the apartment.

'Where are we going?' Iris asked Charles later, holding onto his arm as he led her through a neighbourhood she said she didn't think she had ever visited before.

'You'll see soon,' he replied, and true enough, just a few minutes later they were walking down some stone steps and into a narrow doorway under a small sign marked 'The Vanguard'.

The woman on stage was dressed in a dinner jacket, dark hair slicked back like a man's, every inch the heartbreaker. There was a time not so long ago that such a sight would have scandalised them both, when the notion of a girl dressed as a boy would have been as far-fetched as a masked man taking flight, but they knew now that there were more true things in heaven and earth than could be dreamed up.

They were led by the hostess to their table, Charles pulling out Iris's seat for her before taking his own, and they each ordered a cocktail. Tonight was a celebration of a sort; Captain Kismet was a roaring success, and Walter had hinted that he would commission more from them if he liked the way they concluded the saga of Ranger's feud with Omega... and if they gave Axel a nickname other than Kid Crimson.

'All that red,' he had said, shaking his head. 'It's too Commie. Kid Kismet sounds better.' They had agreed to the change immediately: he was the one signing the checks, after all.

'To princes who fall from the sky,' said Charles, raising his drink, 'and other impossible things!'

Iris touched her glass to his and smiled weakly.

'What is it?' Charles asked. 'You were quiet on the way.'

'It's nothing,' she said, but of course, even a man of Charles's persuasion could deduce that this wasn't true.

'I am sorry for what I said earlier,' Charles continued. 'About the Penny story. I think it's a good idea, I really do. I suppose I just didn't exactly understand where you were coming from.'

'I shouldn't have expected you to,' said Iris. 'I know you and I are franker with each other than a lot of husbands and wives, and you certainly understand how it feels to not quite fit the role you were given, but you are still a man.'

Charles smiled ruefully. 'Yes,' he said. 'I am.'

'For women, it's...' Iris shook her head. 'From the moment we are old enough to walk and talk, there is a set of rules we are expected to follow. A gospel we are all to know by heart, taught to us by our mothers who learned it from their mothers and none of them ever seemed to like it or agree with it, but that's just the way things are. To be a woman is to be confined. But, well, what if I don't feel like a woman all of the time?'

'I see,' said Charles, taken aback. He wasn't sure he saw at all. 'And what do you feel like, then?'

She paused for a sip of her martini, trying to articulate her meaning. For all her talents as a writer, this seemed to be something she didn't quite have the words for, words that Charles imagined may not have even been invented yet.

'I feel like her,' Iris said, nodding over to the sliver of black and white on stage singing 'The Very Thought of You'. 'Trussed up and pretending to be someone else.'

'I could have lent you a suit tonight,' Charles joked. 'Although it might drown you.'

'You're making fun of me.'

'I'm not. I promise, I'm not.' The mirth left Charles's eyes. He had gleaned, from Iris's infrequent remarks, that her brother Axel had been of their same persuasion, and that the two had been close. Charles couldn't help but think he made a rather inadequate confidant by comparison. 'Are you...' He took a sip of his Gibson, for courage. 'Are you saying you would like it if you were free to dress how you pleased?'

He hoped she would hear the question in his question.

Would you rather live as a man?

'Firstly,' she said, 'ask any woman, and I am certain she'd tell you she would like more freedom to dress howsoever she pleases. But... I don't know. I don't think so, at any rate. I enjoy so much of the artistry that goes into being a woman. It makes me feel like I am both Pygmalion and Galatea at the same time. But I like it even more on others.'

She took another steeling sip of her own drink, and Charles was aware that they rarely spoke about these things in such direct terms. Introduced at a mutual friend's dinner due to their shared creative interests, they had each discerned the other for what they truly were, had seen the sense in a marriage of – if not convenience – mutual safety. Their entire arrangement had, up until now, been predicated on an unspoken understanding. But the more she spoke, the more freely words came, far more easily than either could have expected, like they had been brewing inside her all along, waiting for the opportunity to make themselves known.

'When I am with a woman, I feel more of a woman myself,' she said, careful to keep her voice low, even in these friendly surroundings. 'Then there are the instances when I am wearing trousers with my hair pinned up, and I catch sight of myself in a store window or the rear mirror of a cab and I think...' Her eyes tingled with the threat of tears. 'Well, I think: Don't I look handsome?'

Charles said nothing. It struck him then, somewhat incredibly for the first time, that for all of the things they shared, the entire little world she and he had created together, they remained strangers to one another.

'I have been toying with an idea for another character,' Iris said, smoothing away the infinitesimal creases in the tablecloth.

'A shapeshifter. Somebody who can take on the form of anything or anyone they please. Sometimes they may look like a man. Other times, a woman.'

'That sounds like it could be confusing to the reader,' said Charles.

Iris shrugged. 'It was just an idea.'

Charles felt a pang of affection for her, then. He held her so dear, as much as any other husband did his wife. He downed his Gibson, rose from his chair, and extended his hand.

'May I have this dance?' he asked.

Iris looked to the stage, where the crooner was singing 'Blue Moon'. She put her hand in his, and he assisted her to her feet and led her to the small area in front of the band where sweethearts swayed like dandelions in the breeze. He only noticed as he placed his hand on her waist that they were the only man and woman dancing together. He grinned. What a pair of inverts they were!

Charles leaned in closer and whispered in his wife's ear: 'Why don't you lead.'

20

The Flapper stood teetering over the Birmingham canal like a dipsomaniac who could topple into the water at any time. Dusk had not long fallen, strings of artificial lights twinkled over the water, and Patrick felt this city working on his defences again. She was letting her hair down, alright.

'I haven't been here in ages,' Will breathed as he held open the gate for Patrick. 'I practically lived here as a teenager.'

Will wore a battered leather jacket with the collar popped and the sleeves rolled up. He looked, frankly, devastating. By comparison, Patrick felt hopelessly square in his grey hoodie, stone-coloured khakis, blue baseball cap, and trail shoes. He didn't want to think about where Will had procured this 'straight-man drag', whether he had a box somewhere filled with detritus from old boyfriends and one-night stands. But if the object of the evening was camouflage, then mission accomplished: Patrick was dressed so unremarkably, he imagined he could walk straight into traffic and the cars would pass right through him.

He allowed Will to lead him across the narrow walkway over the terrace below into the building itself, and downstairs to the small, packed space where the gig would take place. Margo stood near the front of the crowd, chatting with a dark-haired man who could only be Dylan's father. Will and Patrick found a spot at the back of the room, where they were less likely to be noticed, and squeezed behind a standing table.

'Good for him for showing up,' Patrick said, jerking his head towards the front. From what he had gleaned, Margo and Owen hadn't been together since not long after Dylan was born.

'Good for him?' Will frowned. 'Dylan's his child. Jesus. The bar for straight men is on the floor.'

Patrick flushed, embarrassed by his own remark and uncertain if Will's ire was aimed at him or at the man who had once hurt his sister. Eager to change the subject, he glanced around at the stickers and band posters plastered all over the walls and low ceiling. 'I wouldn't picture you as the kind of guy who'd come to a... rock pub? Is that what we'd call this?' he asked.

'You're adorable,' said Will. 'But, yeah, I used to knock about here all the time.'

'Aren't you full of surprises?'

'Margo had a grunge phase. Which meant I had a grunge phase.'

Almost on cue, as if to illustrate his point exactly, an instantly recognisable electric guitar riff broke out across the sound system, and Will's eyes widened in pleasure. He threw one arm around Patrick's shoulder and another in the air, singing along to the opening verse. 'Oh, make me over!' he belted. 'I'm all I wanna be!'

'Wow. You've got some pipes.'

'Thank you for noticing.' He smiled shyly. 'I was in a band once, you know.'

'Oh yeah?'

'Yep. A million years ago. I was like, seventeen maybe, and spending basically all of my time with this boyfriend who was a year older and knew somebody who knew one of the Scissor Sisters. Which, as I say it now, I realise was probably complete bullshit. But, yeah. We thought it would be a great idea to start our own band. I sang, he played the guitar. We were like if Alex Turner and Jamie Cook from the Arctic Monkeys were *actually* sleeping together. We called ourselves the Nine Bob Notes.'

'I don't get it,' said Patrick, pretending not to feel the rankle of jealousy. He did a pretty good job, he thought. Acting!

'It's an old saying. "As queer as a nine bob note." I don't even think it meant queer in that way, I think it meant you were like, a bent cop or something. Nobody called us on it, though. Mainly because we played exactly one gig, and then we broke up.'

'A short-lived era,' said Patrick. 'But wow, to be one of the people who can say they were in the room when the Nine Bob Notes played their one and only show!'

'I know, right?' Will laughed. 'We were pretty good, too. Are you hungry? They do Korean fried chicken upstairs. It's quite good.'

Patrick shook his head. 'No thanks,' he said. 'How come, if you sound like that, you always lip-sync on stage?'

'You're going to think it's silly.'

'I would never.' Beat. 'OK, I might, but tell me anyway and I'll pretend it's not.'

'I get stage fright.'

'You? *You* get stage fright.'

'Yep.'

'You literally just told me you used to sing in a band.'

'I was a *child*. You don't know to be afraid of anything when you're that young.'

'And now?'

'It's different.'

'I thought Grace was like your suit of armour.'

'She is. But even she has her limits.' Will shrugged. 'I only started doing drag during the pandemic, you know. I was stuck in my flat for months, nothing to do, all this anxious energy that no amount of running could burn off. I'd always thought that I'd write, given that much free time, or get into painting or something. If only I had the right muse. Turns out, I was she. It was Jordan's birthday in lockdown, and we threw him a party over Zoom. I knew it was going to be truly one of the most depressing nights of his life if we didn't do something to make him laugh, so I decided to give him the present of a lifetime.'

'And that was...?'

'A special birthday message from Dolly Parton. Or at least, a close enough approximation.' Will smiled at the memory. 'He laughed his absolute arse off at it. I looked so clapped! A twenty quid wig, some makeup I'd ordered on sale from Superdrug, and chicken cutlets in a chambray shirt. I called myself Dolly Hardon, and Jordan said, "Dolly Hardly, more like." But that was that. It was the most fun I'd had in, well, maybe ever. I started doing it over Instagram, posting different looks – some truly awful stuff to begin with – and making friends with other queens. And the more I learned, and the better I got, the better I felt. More in control. Like, even when the world outside was going to hell, I was making something beautiful in my tiny bedroom. Creating a strange kind of life from glitter and glue, like a very gay Dr Frankenstein.'

'I get that,' said Patrick. 'When we're kids, we all love to retreat into a world of make-believe. But grown-ups need the same outlet.'

'It's very that,' Will said. 'But there's a huge difference between exploring your creativity as a fun Covid hobby and trying to make a living from it.'

'You're talking to an actor here, baby. I did my fair share of off-off-off-Broadway theatre.'

'Right. Where you and a hundred other people exactly like you are all competing for the same gig. That's what it was like when the bars opened up again. I thought I was pretty good by that point, after Faye helped me fix my busted mug, so I started trying to get work performing. And it was fucking *terrifying*.'

'Terrifying?'

'Rabbit in the headlights, life flashing before your eyes terrifying. Because every other queen in this city is an absolute weapon.'

'So you don't sing live because you're worried people will compare you to the other girls?'

'It's not that, exactly. That's part of it, I suppose. *Drag Race* definitely made it easier. I mean, your average basic gay who watches that show only wants you to point and twirl while lip-syncing to Ariana in a high pony, so you might as well just give them that and leave the real hard work to the experts. But it's also. I don't know. Grace is a fun disguise, and she makes me confident. But when I sing, that's *me*, you know? It's hard to feel like a bad bitch when you're showing your soft underbelly.'

Patrick tried hard to suppress every piece of advice his old acting teacher had ever given him about how accessing your own vulnerability could only make you stronger as a performer. Will was simply telling him a story. He didn't need Patrick immediately jumping in with advice and thinking he knew the answer to his problems after knowing him for all of five minutes. Instead, he reached out under the table and placed his hand on Will's knee.

'Well, I think your voice is beautiful,' he said. Then he slid his hand a little further up Will's thigh and lowered his voice. 'Especially when you're about to...'

'Oh my God, stop.'

'Hey, I'm just appreciating you as a vocalist.'

'Patrick!' Will's cheeks reddened, and Patrick hardened at the sight.

'And there you went,' he added, smugly. 'Saying you weren't much of a screamer.' His grip on Will's leg tightened, and even with the music, the sound of Will's staggered exhalation thrilled him. He was about to suggest they get the hell out of here when an ungodly screech from the PA system announced the beginning of the show.

The entire band had taken to the stage without either of them noticing.

Patrick recognised Dylan on bass, standing to the left of the lead singer, a bleach-blonde with a guitar slung over her shoulder.

'Alright,' she said. 'We are Supermarket Sushi.'

Will laughed at the band name, shaking his head as if at some private joke.

'It's so stupid,' he said when Patrick asked him. 'I'll tell you later.' And then the band began to play.

Will's eyes shone, and Patrick was confused for a moment, because he wasn't looking at the stage. He was looking at Margo, who stood stone-still, hands clutched so tightly around her glass it might break, her gaze fixed unblinking on the stage, eyes trained so solely and fiercely on her child she didn't even seem to notice Owen's hand as it came to rest on her shoulder.

Patrick watched Will as he watched Margo, as she watched Dylan, each unaware they were themselves being observed, and something fell into place for him that he had never realised before, at least not consciously. Love was, fundamentally, an act of perception. *I see you. I know you. Don't think I haven't noticed and remembered every last thing about you.*

He thought it would sting, to find himself on the outside, an occasional chair pulled up to the family table. But then he felt a hand find his, and Will turned those eyes on him.

'You love them so much, don't you,' Patrick whispered, although he didn't need to; the music was loud and, as Will had promised, not very good.

'Adore them,' Will said. 'Don't get me wrong, they're a pair of nightmares. But... I really do. It's funny, actually. The gays talk about chosen family all the time, and they mean, like, leaving home and finding other people like themselves. But I chose them, too.' He nodded towards Margo and the stage. 'And she chose me.'

Patrick squeezed his hand.

'Tell me,' he said.

And so he did.

One Wednesday when Will was nine, his father picked him up after school in his Jaguar. This in itself was unusual, as Will couldn't remember the last time he had not walked home from school with the childminder. Also, his dad rarely ever let him anywhere near his prized Jag on account of his 'sticky handprints'. But now Will was on the cusp of double digits, it seemed Eddie Wright saw him as nearly a man, and worthy of being welcomed into his car – and his confidence.

'Where are we going?' Will asked.

'I just need to see a friend about something,' said his dad, pulling up outside a terrace house Will had never seen before. 'Come on!' He flashed his son a wild, white grin and practically leapt from the car, keys jangling in his hand. It struck Will as curious, as he followed his father into the house, that he hadn't knocked.

'Eddie,' said the woman in the living room. 'You're early! Breaking the habit of a lifetime?' Even though Will was nine, and already wondering why he didn't seem as fascinated by girls as his male classmates, he knew this woman was beautiful. Her wild black hair and olive skin made her look like she should be dancing flamenco or singing opera in Italian. But when she spoke, it was with a broad Black Country accent.

'Can you blame me?' Dad took her by the hand, leading her out into the hallway and towards the stairs. 'Will, why don't you go in there,' he said, nodding back to the living room, 'and watch the telly with Margo.'

Will nodded mutely, unsure of what to do other than simply obey. He knew instinctively what was happening here, but the words for it lay, like the adult world at large, just beyond his reach.

A three-seater sofa and large armchair took up almost the entire living room. At the centre of the sofa sat a girl, sixteen or so – he was terrible at guessing people's ages, especially girls, whose makeup and perfume and hair straighteners were like warp engines propelling them into adulthood at a speed with which the boys could not follow.

'Margo?' he asked. She didn't reply. 'I'm Will,' he said. Still no response. He glanced over towards the television. 'What are you watching?' he asked, moving towards the sofa. Margo instantly flopped down and pulled her legs up so that she was lying lengthways across the entire couch. She didn't have to speak, it turned out, to get her message across. Queasy now, Will glumly traipsed over to the armchair and took a seat. *It's fine*, he thought. *It's like detention. I'll just keep my head down until it's time to go home.*

On the screen, a group of startlingly thin women were standing in a line, looking for all intents and purposes like they were waiting to be shot.

'It's *America's Next Top Model*,' said Margo, still horizontal. 'And I'm about to find out who gets eliminated this week, so no talking.'

'Alright,' said Will. She hit him with a pungent glare. 'Sorry,' he mouthed silently.

At nine, he did not yet know the future: that he was gay, that in years to come he would feel more comfortable around women than he did most men. On that day in the mid-two-thousands, all he knew was that teenage girls fucking terrified him. Maybe even more than the abstract idea he had in his head of what was going on between his father and Margo's mother upstairs.

It became the closest thing to a father-son activity Will would ever know. Each week, Dad would pick him up at the school gate and they would make the trip to Carla's house – that was her name, he soon learned, Carla – under the pretext of Will having some after-school club or other. That Will's mother never asked for details of any kind, or even seem to notice that this club never met on the same day from week to week, made the lie easier to uphold, and took up a lot of the afternoons later in life when Will would unpack all of this with his therapist.

The visits blurred together. Each week, he would perch quietly in the corner of the living room and watch whatever reality show Margo had recorded the night before – *America's Next Top Model* and *The Hills* and *The Simple Life* and *Faking It* – then his dad would come downstairs, red-faced and smirking even wider than when he went up, and drive him home.

'Your mum wouldn't understand,' he said the first few times, as they sat in traffic. 'Best not to tell her, ey?'

Will said nothing. Had no idea how to articulate the cauldron of anger and shame bubbling away in his guts.

'A man of few words,' his dad said on one such journey. 'I like that. I respect that. My guy. My little man.' He reached over to ruffle Will's hair, something he had never done before, and which felt so awkward to both parties that he never attempted it again.

If this was what it meant to be a man, Will thought, he wanted no part of it.

And then it happened. The day that changed everything.

A couple of months after his father first brought him to the house, Will walked into the living room to find Margo's dog, an ancient, hideous little thing named Bandit, on the armchair. It growled at him when he approached, and Margo refused to let Will move him, so she reluctantly shifted over and allowed him to take a seat next to her on the sofa. She did, however, still insist on keeping a full cushion between them, and would occasionally glance over at him as if he were the source of a particularly nasty odour. He didn't blame her, really. He was a symptom of the thing they both continued to pretend was *not* happening in the room directly above them, the sound of which was blissfully drowned out by Margo's mother's record collection. A decade from now, all it would take was a few bars from 'Desirée' by Neil Diamond to make Will feel vaguely nauseous.

They were back on *Top Model* this time. By this point, Margo had started to offer up curt context clues so Will could understand an episode even if he had missed the last one. She did this without ever looking at him and in such a way that made it clear follow-up questions were not encouraged. 'She did well in the challenge so the other girls don't like her,' she might say, or 'they made her cut off all her hair this week so she's obviously going home, they always do that.' One time she whispered, Will suspected more to herself than to him: 'Nigel is so fit.'

This week, Tyra was once again lording it over the girls. But something was different. Even through the TV, it was like Will and Margo could both feel a change in the air pressure.

'Be *quiet*,' Tyra snapped. 'Be *quiet*, Tiffany!'

Margo sat bolt upright, eyes fixed on the screen.

'Is she usually like this?' Will asked quietly.

'Shut up!' Margo hissed. Then, a second later: 'No. This is new.'

They sat in rapt silence as what would eventually become one of the most famous moments in reality TV history unfolded before them, and by the time it was over, Margo was wide-eyed and red-faced with excitement. She looked like one of those pictures of girls from the Sixties who are ready to faint at a Beatles concert.

'Did you *see* that?' she gasped, turning to Will and grasping his arm. 'Can you believe that actually *happened*?'

'Poor Tiffany!' Will said.

'Poor Tiffany? Oh, sure. I mean, yeah. But oh my God, Tyra. Tyra! *Learn from this!*' Margo dissolved into giggles at her own impersonation, having seemingly forgotten, for the moment at least, that she considered Will an enemy.

'I'm hungry,' she said then. 'Come on.' She dragged him by the hand into the kitchen, and ten minutes later they were eating cheese toasties with marmite and cups of tea. The warmth of Margo's demeanour faded a little along with the second-hand glow of reality TV exploitation, but she never seemed quite as angry to see him after that. The axis of the world had shifted: their relationship, such as it was, suddenly had room to grow.

Years later, after Will's parents divorced and Eddie moved in with Carla, and then after Carla kicked him out, and then finally when Margo was old enough to move out and get a place of her own, she and Will would still drink tea and watch telly together. When his own mum forgot to do any food shopping, he knew that if he dropped in on Margo, she would begrudgingly make him a toastie. When Bandit finally died after spending his final years half-blind and peeing on the curtains, Will shoplifted a bottle of tequila and joined a tearful Margo in toasting the mangy mutt's memory until they both threw up and swore off the stuff. When Margo got together with Owen, and then Owen got her pregnant, she told Will before anyone else. And when Owen left, Will became Margo's de facto babysitter, reimbursed in dinners and bags of clean washing.

There was no clear point at which Will could say that she became his sister, no event horizon where they transitioned from forced proximity to genuine affection. All he knew was that he couldn't remember the last time he'd spoken to his dad, and his mum spent her life pinballing from one spiritual retreat or pyramid scheme to another, and the only remotely stabilising influence he'd ever had in his life was this mess of tangled dark curls and smoky eyeshadow who might have an even shorter temper and fouler mouth than him.

'That's so sweet,' Patrick said. 'I mean, for a story about trauma bonding.'

'Oh, for heaven's sake.' Will rolled his eyes. 'Could you be any more LA? Not everything is trauma. Sometimes it's just a thing that brought two people together. Obviously, it was far from ideal, but I think I am *remarkably* well adjusted. You know, for a part-time crossdresser with a secret lover.'

'Is that what we are?' Patrick asked. 'Lovers?'

'Oh God. Pretend I never said that. It sounds so cringe.'

'No. I like it. "Lover." It's... continental.'

Will laughed derisively and then looked away. Patrick knew he had said it offhand, as a joke, the way he said most things, but they were veering close to dangerous territory. For all the legal jargon they had both signed their names to, the NDA had not included an actual definition of what they were to each other. It might have been easier if it had.

Supermarket Sushi finished their short set, and the band they had opened for started playing. They were older, better, more polished. Out of a rapidly growing sense of loyalty, Patrick immediately disliked them.

'So anyway, that's my origin story,' said Will, and Patrick was grateful to him for bringing the conversation back onto safer ground. 'What about you?'

'What about me?'

'How does a guy go from South Amboy, New Jersey to Hollywood?'

Patrick folded his arms. 'Well it sounds like you should know, you've clearly been reading up on me.'

Will raised his hands; a tacit admission. 'I *may* have googled you the night we met. But I want to hear it from you.'

'There's not much more to tell,' said Patrick. 'I was an only child, both my parents worked, so they sent me to a lot of after-school clubs at our local church. They weren't super religious, but it meant somebody else would watch me after school.'

'What are they like? Your parents?'

'My parents are nice people,' he said. 'I don't see them as much as I'd like to because of work.' It was a well-rehearsed line, rolled out so many times in interviews it could have left grooves in the carpet. 'But anyway, that's how I got into plays,' he continued. 'Church productions; haunted houses. It was fun, playing pretend. So when I started high school, I joined the drama club. Did every school play. Eventually got into a college theatre program on a partial scholarship. Worked in every diner and drugstore in South Amboy to pay for it. Moved to New York, auditioned for some plays. OK, a lot of plays. *Salesman*, *Streetcar*, *Six Degrees of Separation*. I was almost George in *Our Town*. I understudied for Ricky in *Glengarry Glen Ross*. I was an admittedly shaky Burrs in *The Wild Party*.'

'A sexy clown,' Will mused. 'Not unlike a drag queen.'

Patrick laughed, and nodded. 'I guess. Anyway, I got a lot of bad reviews, then a couple of good ones. Moved out West.'

He sounded, he realised, like he was reading his own biography: the last ten years condensed to a PowerPoint presentation.

Got an agent. Did some small walk-on TV roles. A small part in a reboot of a slasher franchise set in a frat house called *Pledge Week*. Then he met Simone. Started getting better work: a role in an ensemble show on HBO that was critically acclaimed but only ran for one season. A soldier in a war movie, then a gunslinger who fell in love with an indigenous woman in a sweeping Western that was called 'ambitious' and 'problematic'. Got the lead in *The Bullet Journal*, an action movie that caught the attention of a Wonder Studios head, who was on the lookout for the kind of handsome, all-American leading man who could shoulder a reboot of the entire Captain Kismet universe.

'And what about having a life?' asked Will. 'Outside of work, I mean.'

'Getting the work *was* the life,' said Patrick. 'I was friends with other actors who'd moved to LA around the same time as me, who were going up for similar roles. We'd go out, drink, complain about always being passed over on parts we'd've been *perfect* for… But then I started booking bigger gigs, and that momentum really took off, and things changed so quickly. They were happy for me, but I kind of felt weird going to drinks with them and hearing about their shitty auditions when everything was going so great. And they felt the same. Once or twice, one of them would ask me if I could pass on their reel to my agent, and I'd give them her number, but nothing ever came of it. Then one of them asked if I could get him a part in the show I was doing, and I felt weird, but I said sure, I'd see what I could do. Connected him with the right people, he came in to read. He wasn't right for the part, and he blamed me. Seemed to think that I was hoarding all of the success instead of sharing it. After a while, the guys stopped inviting me out to drinks.'

'Must have been lonely.'

'It was.'

'And you never…'

'Never what?'

'Dated?'

'A little. I wasn't, like, a regular at Mickey's or anything. But yeah, I went out. I dated a bit. I'd hook up from time to time, and every now and then one of them would look at me a certain way, like he was trying to figure out where he knew me from. Which happens all the time in LA. Bump into someone with your shopping cart at the market, there's a good chance they played a panty-sniffer on an episode of *CSI*. I once gave head to a guy who was on Netflix's number one show in Canada.'

Will's mouth dropped open in pantomime shock. 'No!'

'I did! And before you ask, yes, he did tell me that particular fact *during*.'

'The glamour. It's almost too much.'

'I know, right?' Patrick paused. 'But then I did *The Bullet Journal*, and I thought at first that I could keep on just having these low-key not-quite-dates, like nothing would really change. Until I met up with a guy from Grindr and the first thing he did when I walked in the door was ask me for a selfie.'

'Wow,' said Will. 'Have some chill, gay!'

'I turned right around and got the hell out of there.'

'And nothing since?'

Patrick shrugged. 'Nothing since.'

Will gazed into the middle distance for a moment, then his eyes snapped back to Patrick's.

'That's four years.'

'What?'

'I may have read your IMDb, don't worry about it. *The Bullet Journal* came out four years ago. You really mean to say I'm the first person you've…?'

Patrick cringed. 'Don't. It's so embarrassing when you say it out loud like that.'

'No. No, it's not.' Will slid his now-empty plastic cup across the table until it nudged against Patrick's water. 'I feel honoured.' He glanced around the room, adding: 'And also like you have got a *lot* of catching up to do. Shall we…?'

'Get the fuck out of here?' Patrick replied, lowering his voice until it was barely even a whisper, and uttering bashfully in Will's ear: 'I thought you'd never ask.'

Will grabbed his jacket and within seconds they were outside, having said goodbye to nobody. Unprompted, Will called an Uber to hail a ride back to his place. Patrick felt a swell of affection and appreciation for Will understanding that there could be no digital evidence of what was about to happen, but something else was happening here too. Will opened the car door for Patrick when the taxi arrived, steering him in and shutting the door behind him before walking around to his own side. He did the same when they arrived at his apartment.

'I told you I was taking you out tonight,' he said when Patrick questioned him, unlocking his front door and gripping Patrick's hand. 'And now I'm taking you home.'

The self-assuredness with which he said this had an effect on Patrick that he didn't fully understand. He knew he was gay, that being attracted to men was kind of the whole deal of that, and he had certainly been drawn to confident, commanding types in the past.

Patrick had bottomed before. A long time ago. Had enjoyed it. Wanted to do it again. There were toys in his house back in Studio City to prove it. He had even thought that he might want to with Will, although he had been uncertain how that would work. He had been attracted to Will's softness, his fey humour. He was a beautiful thing that Patrick wanted to possess, to grip tightly as his own, and that was exactly what he had done the night before. As deeply uncool and heteronormative as it probably was to think so, everything about this fabulous man until now had screamed *fuck me*, at least once quite literally. But to see Will taking control like this, to be marched into the flat and then into the bedroom like *he* was the prey and the prize... Fuck, why did this turn him on even more?

'Will—' he began, unsure even of what he wanted to say.

'Shut up.' Will's voice was different. Not deeper, exactly, but stronger. Authoritative. Patrick complied, felt like a complete sissy for doing so, and was taken aback even further by how hot that was to him. He went to kiss Will, but was pushed back. He stood there dumbly, raising his arms obediently as Will undressed him. There was none of the foreplay here that they had indulged in prior, and yet there was still a romance to Will's efficient movements, the way he folded each item of Patrick's clothing before placing them down. At six foot one and two hundred eighty pounds, Patrick felt delicate for the first time in his adult life.

'I want you to...' he rasped, voice thick with desire, face hot with the opposite of shame. 'I want you to fuck me.'

Will looked him in the eye, and Patrick's gaze fell to the floor. Will forced his chin up to return his gaze.

'Have you...?' Will asked, his meaning clear.

'Yes,' said Patrick. 'Earlier tonight.' Will smiled crookedly, realising now why Patrick had not wanted to eat anything at the gig. Why he had drunk bottled water all evening.

'You little slut,' he whispered, and Patrick's face grew even hotter as he nodded. Yes, he was. For tonight, he would be anything Will said he was.

He stood there naked and hard as a rock, vulnerable, thrillingly so, awaiting further direction. Allowed himself to be pushed onto the bed and flipped onto his stomach. Heard the lowering of a zipper, the creak of leather as Will positioned himself over him, still fully dressed. Felt the bottle of poppers being pushed into his hand, obliged by taking a deep breath of the chemical that had started all this.

He winced and cried out at the initial bite of hurt and discomfort, but his groans soon became louder, less pained. Soon he was crying out in wordless, unadulterated pleasure while Will stretched and filled him, teeth tugging at his earlobe.

'Pull my hair,' he grunted, wondering where the hell *that* had come from and then losing the question as Will grabbed a fistful and yanked his head back to kiss him passionately, then pushed him back down onto the pillow. He moaned again, coming alive under Will's rough care. He spoke in tongues, transcendent and yet at the same time beautifully worthless.

He'd thought he had unleashed all of his desires on Will in the hotel last night, that the weight of all those years of frustration and fear had been lifted. But that loneliness wasn't just a weight to be removed, he knew now. It was a mark, a stain. And as he lay face down, hands pinned behind his back, surrendering entirely to the will of the man above him, Patrick finally felt cleansed.

21

The first coherent thought to enter Will's mind as he woke was that this might be the only time he had ever slept in another man's arms without waking up a sweaty, disoriented goblin. He'd always loved the romance of the idea, but after five minutes of spooning he usually became so hot and irritable that it undercut the purpose. So aside from the very rare occasions when he would wake up with a dreadful hangover being spooned by an unconscious Jordan after crashing at his place, he tended to avoid it. This morning, though, opening his eyes to find himself tucked into the side of Patrick's body, arm draped over his chest, head nestled under his shoulder, he realised it may have been the best night's sleep he'd had in a long time.

The second thought arrived quickly on the heels of the first and announced itself far less gently: He had overslept. The sky outside was a bright, warm blue, and the sun had already moved around to this side of the building, which meant it was noon. At least.

'Shit,' he whispered, carefully extracting himself from Patrick's embrace and leaning over to check his phone on the nightstand. Then, when he saw just how much he had slept in by: 'Shit, shit, shit!'

Will scrambled to exit the bed in such a hurry that he became entangled in the covers and nearly went head-first onto the floor.

Feeling Patrick begin to stir next to him, he finally liberated himself from the sheets and tiptoed out into the bathroom to pee, brush his teeth, and hastily scrub the goop from the corners of his eyes and mouth.

When he returned to the bedroom, Patrick was awake.

'Good morning,' he mumbled happily, stretching.

'No, it is not,' Will informed him, tripping over the shoes he had kicked off the night before in what had felt at the time like erotic abandon, and now struck him as an act of sabotage against his future self. Why did he never pick *up* after himself?

'It's not a good morning?' Patrick asked, squinting in the direction of the window, where a house sparrow had decided to set down at that very moment, like something out of a Disney movie. Except this particular princess would have to dress herself and would deal with the inevitable bird shit on the windowsill later.

'It's not *morning*,' Will said. 'We overslept. No. *I* overslept. It's story hour in the Rainbow Room in… Jesus, in less than an hour.'

Patrick watched, clearly amused at first, as Will floundered around the room, gathering little containers of eyebrow glue, foundation, highlighter, and a dozen other tools of his craft from various drawers and surfaces. It was a curated chaos that might not make sense to an outsider, but Will knew exactly where everything was. Except for when he finally sat down in front of his mirror, then realised he'd forgotten something, swore, and got back up.

'Are you about to get into so called "quick drag"?' asked Patrick, sitting up in bed. The sheet slid down, revealing enough of his chest – those nipples! God, the sounds Patrick had made when he played with them – that Will was momentarily distracted before remembering the task at hand.

'Pretty much, yes,' he said, checking his phone again. 'I need to be ready in, like, twenty minutes. Which is a lot to ask, even for those among us who are already women when they wake up.' He fumbled while trying to open one of the many little tubes in front of him, and he forced himself to take a deep breath.

'I'm sorry,' he said. 'I just really need to focus. I can't believe I've let this happen.'

A strange look passed over Patrick's face, and Will realised how he must have sounded. He'd meant *I can't believe I forgot to set an alarm and I'm late again*. Patrick probably heard *This is your fault*.

'I should go,' said Patrick, rising and pulling on his boxers and jeans.

'OK,' said Will with his back to him, mouth morphed into an exaggerated 'O' as he concentrated on expediting the metamorphosis that would ordinarily have been conducted with a patient, ritualistic reverence. 'I'll call you later,' he added, guiltily. 'I... I had a great time.' Patrick paused before leaving the room to kiss his crown and rest a hand for a second on the back of his neck.

'Break a leg,' he said, his expression in the mirror still odd. Then he grabbed his jacket and let himself out in a hurry, and Will didn't have the time to linger on the stilted goodbye, or to feel like shit for rushing him out of here, especially after last night had taken such an intense turn.

He ignored several text messages and a missed call from Faye Runaway while rushing through the final stages of his makeup, carefully installed his wig, then called a taxi and squeezed into his outfit and heels while he waited.

Daytime drag was a little like daytime drinking: as fun as it was, Will always had a guilty suspicion in the back of his mind that it was something he probably shouldn't be doing, and one of these days suspected it was going to end in an injury. Everybody he knew had a friend who had been beaten up – or worse – for the crime of being too fruity in public; holding hands with their boyfriend, walking with just a little too much sway in their hips or flounce in their wrist. Stepping outside his front door before dark dressed like a conservative Christian's worst nightmare – or more specifically, a cutesy interpretation of Dorothy from *The Wizard of Oz* complete with pigtails, gingham pinafore and sparkly red Mary Janes – was practically a provocation. He'd had taxi drivers refuse to pick him up when they saw him, and he knew that in the wider scheme, that was probably a best case scenario. But needs must when the devil drives, or in Will's case, when the gay never passed his practical test and had to rely on Uber because the only alternative was a bus, and in these shoes? He didn't think so.

Luckily on this specific day the driver offered Will little more than a bemused glance in the rear-view mirror as he scooped up the voluminous tulle of his skirt to prevent it from being trapped in the car door.

'I'll tell you what, Umar,' Will said, strapping himself in. 'There's a five-star rating and a cash tip in it for you if you can get me to the library in under ten minutes.'

'Ten minutes?' Umar considered the proposition as he manoeuvred back onto the main road. 'Easy-peasy.'

'You're my hero,' Will told him. 'Now let's fly.'

They pulled up to Centenary Square with twenty whole seconds to spare, and Will shoved a tenner in Umar's general direction before unspooling himself and his skirt from the vehicle and trotting across the plaza to the Library of Birmingham.

'Sorry! Sorry! Sorry!' he exclaimed as he entered the building and caught the eye of Annie (or was it Amy?), the library staffer who helped them organise the story hours. 'I'm late, I know, feel free to flog me later,' he continued. 'How angry are the parents? Scrap that, how angry is *Faye*?'

'Everything's fine!' said Annie or Amy, beckoning him to follow her to the Rainbow Room. 'I mean, honestly, we were all just so *surprised—*'

'That a drag queen didn't show up on time? It's a sorry fact of life, darling,' said Will. 'Death, taxes, and men in frocks barrelling through the door fashionably late.'

'No, not that,' said the admin, who Will remembered now was actually called Allie. 'The surprise guest. The kids were all *so* excited. So were the parents. I mean, we all are!'

'Surprise guest?' Will paused for a second, then resumed his pace to keep up with Allie. Blessedly, she led him to the lift, having encountered the story hour queens enough times to know that they didn't do exceptionally well on stairs.

'He's a huge hit,' Allie said. 'I've been hearing the kids cheering from across the building for the last ten minutes.'

'*He?*'

The lift doors opened, and a moment later Will was entering the Rainbow Room, where he saw the usual semicircles of young children sitting cross-legged, on tiny stools, or in their parents' laps. And seated before them, reading with impressive projection and enunciation from *The Little Prince*, was Patrick.

Or rather, Captain Kismet. Patrick wore the famous blue bodysuit, red boots, aviator goggles pushed up over his forehead, pushing his hair out of place every which way so that Will's hand twitched at his side with the impulse to smooth it.

'What the...'

Faye spotted him and silently glided to the back of the room to join him, her reproachful glare heightened by her evil queen regalia.

'I see you finally made it,' she whispered.

'Sorry,' said Will.

'I need to be able to count on you, Gracie,' she continued. 'This isn't performing for gays who are so off their faces they don't know what time it is.' She nodded towards the children, who were all still rapt under Patrick's spell. 'They're our most precious audience. And days like this are precarious enough as it is.'

She was right. Will knew she was right. The story hour was about opening up the world to kids, showing them the pure magic of imagination. And even more than any birthday clown or costume-shop Elsa, queens were the embodiment of that imagination; living proof that you could grow up to be whoever and whatever you wanted to be. Children's books were full of orphans and neglected waifs who discovered magic. Faye and Grace – and Patrick, it seemed – held the keys to that world. If Will were more prone to sentimentality, he would call it one of the great privileges of his art.

The children and parents all applauded, signalling the end of Patrick's story. Acknowledging the presence of Captain Kismet for the first time, Faye said: 'I suppose I can't be too miffed, given your stand-in. Watch your back, girl, you could be looking at your replacement. He does better voices than you and he was *on time*.' She widened her eyes dramatically, and then turned back to the room, jumping back into the character of empress-emcee as though Will had just flicked a switch on the back of her dress, effortlessly corralling the families into a queue so that the children could have a picture with their favourite superhero.

Wildly, Will didn't think half the grown-ups in the room even understood that this was really Patrick Lake the movie star; they just saw a guy in a costume and were grateful that it made their child happy.

Allie sidled up to him. 'He's good with kids, isn't he?' she said, seemingly for want of anything else to say. Then: 'I kind of want to get in line for a photo, too. But, oh God, I don't know. Would that be loser behaviour? I kind of think it's almost cooler *not* to ask, don't you?'

'Hmm,' said Will, noncommittally.

'I've got to ask,' she said. 'How on earth did you book Patrick Lake for this? How did you even get in touch with him?'

Will tilted his head sideways in Allie's direction, like he was about to share a secret with her. She leaned in expectantly. He allowed his voice to fall to its deepest and said: 'We go to the same barber.'

'Oh. Oh!' She laughed, and before she could ask for a serious answer, Patrick approached them both.

'Hi,' he said, cheeks flushed, voice slightly hoarse from projecting. Will got a sudden flash of the earnest, enthusiastic theatre major Patrick must have been once, the kind of person who was *always* surrounded by queers and queens before life took him on a different trajectory, and felt a tightness in his chest.

'This is Allie,' he blurted.

'Hi, Allie,' said Patrick, reaching out and shaking her hand, a smile breaking out on his face as if she were exactly the person he had been hoping to run into at exactly this moment. *He's so good at that*, Will thought.

'Allie is too shy to ask herself, but I think she'd really like a picture,' he added, and he felt her feign mortification next to him.

'Of course!' Patrick handed the book he'd been reading from to Will, and Allie excitedly pulled out her phone to take a selfie.

'Thank you!' she trilled. 'OK, I have to get back to the front desk. Thank you!' She scurried away, already frantically tapping at the screen, no doubt disseminating the photo through every group chat in her phone.

'What's going on?' Will finally asked, turning to Patrick. 'What are you doing here?'

'You just seemed so stressed out earlier, I wanted to help,' Patrick said. 'I thought that if you were going to be late, then maybe I could just show up and mug for time a little.'

'So you...' Will's eyes drifted downwards to the costume.

'Before shooting began, I pulled a hamstring, so we did all my costume fittings in my hotel room. I ended up keeping one of them. I'm honestly kind of amazed nobody has asked for it back yet, the studio is usually really strict about that kind of stuff, and this thing would sell like crazy on eBay. Anyway, I rushed back to the hotel, put it on, and came straight here. It's like five minutes on foot.'

Will didn't say anything, could barely wrap his head around what Patrick had done. *This is the part where you say thank you*, he told himself, but the words were somewhere else, in a place he couldn't quite reach them. Narnia maybe, or Oz.

'I'm sorry if I overstepped,' Patrick said, less sure of himself now. 'I wanted to help.'

How did he do that? How did he have the courage to lay himself so bare, show his beating heart like he didn't care about getting hurt? And why was he doing it for *Will* of all people?

Will smiled so widely he was almost certain it would ruin his makeup.

'My hero,' he said, for the second time that day. 'This is honestly the sweetest thing anyone has ever done for me.' Then, under his breath: 'I could kiss you.'

The pink in Patrick's cheeks didn't deepen, but it didn't go away either.

'I could actually do a lot more than kiss you,' Will added.

'Flirt,' Patrick whispered back. 'Listen. About last night...'

An iron vice appeared out of nowhere to crush Will's chest.

'It was... God, I don't even know.'

'Too much?'

'Incredible.' Patrick said breathlessly. 'I never even... You were... Yeah.'

Will smiled again, shyly this time. 'Yeah,' he agreed.

'You look amazing, by the way. Judy would be proud.'

Will waved a hand as if to say *this old thing?* 'Just something I threw together in twenty minutes,' he said. 'I can't believe you got in drag for me *again*.'

Patrick snickered. 'But I should really get going. Before those pictures go online and Simone puts one of those geolocation tags on me.'

'Are you going to get in trouble?'

'If I do, it will have been worth it.' He tapped the chest of his uniform and reiterated: 'I should get this back.'

'Damn, but don't you wear it well.'

He could see Patrick begin to shake his head ruefully, to do the 'aw, shucks' self-deprecating downwards glance and smile that he could see now had become a reflex over the years, the result of doubtlessly rigorous media training – and then he seemed to stop himself.

'Thank you,' he said. 'Though I'll admit, it's not the most comfortable thing in the world.'

'You are talking to somebody wearing six inch heels,' said Will. 'And a girdle.'

'Point taken. I'll see you later.'

'Wait a second.' Will reached out and pulled Captain Kismet's goggles back down over Patrick's eyes. 'In the event of paps,' he said.

'What would I do without you?' Patrick grinned.

It was only after he was gone that Will realised he had not actually thanked him for doing this. For saving the day. For considering Will somebody whose arse was worth saving.

'The little people are getting restless,' Faye said, reappearing. 'Let's give them one more story and then get them out of here.'

'Sure,' Will said, reaching into his bag for his copy of *The Wonderful Wizard of Oz*. He already had the perfect passage picked out: Dorothy meeting the Scarecrow, the Tin Man, and the Cowardly Lion, and encouraging them to join her on her quest. It was what he used to read to Dylan when they were younger, doing his best to create distinct voices for each character. Not to mention that a story about making friends with people who were different from you, who each have their own flaws and goals, felt downright educational.

Except his audience weren't especially receptive to such benevolent messaging. He could feel the children becoming fidgety and irritable while he read aloud, the excitement of Captain Kismet's visit waning along with their attention spans. It was perhaps the most unenviable slot he'd ever performed in. How was one supposed to follow a real-life superhero?

'Cameron, if you bite Lara again then I am going to leave you here,' one exhausted-looking mother hissed at a remorseless toddler, and Will stifled a laugh as he came to the final line of the chapter and closed the book dramatically.

'The End,' he announced, and tried not to take it too personally when the applause sounded a little half-arsed compared to Patrick's ovation.

He hung back as everybody began to filter out of the room, several small children now screaming inconsolably at the indignity of being transported anywhere without their prior approval.

'*The Wizard of Oz*?' Faye remarked from the corner of her mouth. 'Ground-breaking.'

'You're just feeling left out because I stopped before we met the Wicked Witch,' Will retorted, and they both laughed.

'Share a cab?' Faye asked, and Will knew that this meant *share a cab down to Hurst Street, where we can enjoy a drink and not be ogled?*

'Sure,' he said.

'And then you can explain to me why you sent your boyfriend to do your job for you,' Faye added, with the tone of a teacher who has read your assignment and *just knows* you are capable of better.

'What?' Will froze. 'What are you talking about? He's not my—'

Faye raised an eyebrow.

'Oh please, I read enough schlocky celebrity gossip to know that man has never had a real girlfriend,' said Faye. 'And I'd know those shoulders anywhere.' She adopted a higher, Kenneth Williams-esque voice as she straightened the last of the chairs. 'Infamy, Infamy!' she wailed. 'They've all got it infamy!'

'You can't tell anyone,' Will babbled. 'It's a secret. I mean, I can't talk about it. I mean, there's nothing to talk about!'

'Calm down, dear, your secret's safe with me.' Faye looked at Will as if seeing him for the first time. 'Bloody well done, mind!'

Will giggled involuntarily, panic turning to relief. He hadn't said anything, had technically not broken the NDA. He could hardly be blamed for the fact that most queens were like truffle pigs when it came to sniffing out gay gossip. And it felt good, for someone to know that Patrick had been here today for *him*. Even if he couldn't so much as give Will a peck on the cheek in public, he'd still found a way to show he cared.

He was dwelling on this, a giddy smile on his face, eyes down on his sparkly red shoes, when he and Faye exited the building and he first heard the jeers. Looking up, he saw something he hadn't registered properly on his way in, he had been in such a hurry: a small group of protestors. Only a dozen or so, but their boos were vocal, and each of them touted signs that ranged from the innovative – *The Devil Wears Padding* – to the weak – *It's Adam and Eve, Not Adam and Steve* – to the downright inexplicable: *Bibles Not Books.*

'And I thought the kids were a tough crowd,' he remarked.

'Ugh. There's more of them,' Faye said, and her earlier words came back to Will. '*Days like this are precarious enough as it is.*'

'More?' Will asked.

'They were at the last reading too, the one you missed because of that cold. It was only five or six then. Pathetic, really, I almost felt sorry for them.' She jerked her head in the opposite direction. 'Come on, lass. Let's go.'

In the exact same moment that they turned away, Will heard an impact right next to him. A muffled, wet thud. Faye stood still, face stricken, and Will instinctively stepped around her to check something he already knew.

The remains of an eggshell were embedded in Faye's wig, the slime of the yolk already seeping into the fibres. Will wasn't sure if it could be salvaged or if the entire thing was ruined, but he knew instantly, could tell from Faye's wordless stare, that the desired effect had been achieved.

'You should all be ashamed of yourselves!' he yelled at the protestors, scanning the crowd for whichever one was armed with an egg box.

'Not now, Gracie,' Faye whispered. 'Just keep walking.' Will looked at her for a second, and the rage bubbling up inside him subsided into something far worse. Something approaching pity.

'Alright then,' he said, taking Faye by the arm and marching away. The crowd did not follow. Their mission had been accomplished.

Will messaged the driver and requested he meet them around the corner, and he used the waiting time to pick eggshell out of Faye's hair. He suggested first that she remove it, but her silent refusal let him know he needn't ask again.

When the car arrived, Will began to walk around to the other side, but Faye said: 'I think I'll go home now, if it's all the same to you.'

'Of course,' Will said. 'Do you want me to come with you?'

Faye shook her head. She climbed into the car and let Will carefully close the door after her. Then she sat stiffly and silently, looking at the back of the driver's seat as the taxi pulled away, her face stony in profile, head held high in quiet dignity.

22

'I don't remember ever being this angry,' Will said. Patrick was perched on the armchair in Will's living room, watching him pace back and forth with a glass of red wine and listening as he recounted what happened to him and Faye after the story hour. 'I could throttle them. Set them on fire. Walk them over a thousand upturned plugs.'

'I'm so sorry.' Patrick didn't know what else to say. He had come to Will's straight from the set, excited to finally see him after spending all day so distracted it had taken him multiple takes to deliver a single line. But his hopes for the evening had evaporated when Will opened the door, eyes wide with hurt and fury, and Patrick had pulled him into a hug before even thinking to ask what had happened. And now he sat listening, frustratingly helpless. His instinct when a friend was hurting would usually be to leap into solutions-offering mode, but what was the solution here? Fix structural, systemic homophobia singlehandedly?

'It's just so *dumb*,' Will continued, gesticulating with his glass so hard he nearly stained the carpet crimson. 'The whole homophobia thing. Just utterly stupid. It makes no sense. Hating us, attacking us when we've done *nothing*, deciding that we're what's wrong with society, that *we're* the threat to children. All because what? Some absolute wally mistranslated a Bible passage into Greek and fucked us all over. Threw us in jail. Chemically castrated us. Forced us to justify our existence, to beg and scrape for the barest human dignity.' He turned to Patrick. 'And you still can't tell the world you sleep with men in case you lose your job.'

'That's not exactly *how* I would probably put it,' said Patrick, but Will had already resumed his brisk, furious laps of the living room.

'Because heaven forbid the world find out their favourite superhero is a fag.'

Patrick wrinkled his nose. 'I *hate* that word.'

'Oh, grow up.' Will rolled his eyes. 'We're post-reclamation of hate speech now, darling. It's practically a term of endearment.'

'Sorry I'm not as with it as you,' said Patrick, edgy now, and Will paused momentarily, casting him a contrite look.

'Sorry. It's not your fault.'

'It's OK. You're upset. I hate that you're upset.'

'I shouldn't have taken it out on you. I can be such a gobshite sometimes.'

'Excuse me?'

'A gobshite. It means... ugh, never mind.' He looked down into his wine, then added: 'Faye lost most of her friends, you know.'

'She did?' Patrick didn't ask how, or when. Didn't need to.

'Yeah. Saw the world turn against her and everyone she knew. Weathered that. *Survived that*, somehow. Lived long enough to be bestowed with a fraction of the respect she is owed, by us if not the rest of the world. And to be treated so...' His pacing faltered. 'I've never seen her like that, Patrick. She looked so... *old.*'

'What can I do?' Patrick asked.

Will looked at Patrick, and Patrick knew he'd asked the wrong question. There was only one thing he could do, he knew: one thing in his power to affect any kind of change, to move the needle even a fraction of an inch.

Come out. Talk about his personal life. Risk tanking his career and inviting hordes of those same protestors onto his own front lawn.

'There *is* something,' said Will, 'that might make me feel better.'

'What is it?' *Please don't ask me to do that*, he thought. *Anything but that.*

'Right. Don't judge me...' Will said, pausing in front of the coffee table where his laptop lay. He set down his wine, opened the computer and started typing.

Thank God, it's a sex thing, Patrick thought. He leaned forward in his seat to get a better look, prepared to indulge Will in whatever pornographic fantasy he liked. But when Will swivelled the screen around to show him what he had looked up, Patrick was confronted with a streaming site's loading screen for a late Noughties slasher entitled *Pledge Week: New Blood*. The photoshop rush job of a poster showed several up-and-coming actors from that time, including one baby-faced Patrick Lake, superimposed over the front door of a fraternity house.

'They're *dying* to get in,' intoned Will gravely, echoing the movie's tagline.

'What's happening right now?' Patrick asked, aghast. 'Where did you find this?'

'Again, I say, don't judge me.' Will took a gulp of red. 'But I've sort of been watching your back catalogue.'

'You what?'

Will gasped and pointed at him. 'Oh my God. Did you hear yourself? You sounded so English just then!' He screamed with laughter, so clearly the wine was taking effect. '*You what, mate?*'

'You've been watching my movies?' Patrick continued, ignoring him.

'Yeah. It's probably silly. I just...' Will shrugged. 'It felt like another way of getting to know you.'

'That is...'

'Creepy? It's a bit creepy, innit. I knew it was creepy. April told me it was creepy.'

'I was about to say adorable. But then, I have been out of the scene for a long time, as we've already established, so maybe it *is* creepy and I just don't know it.'

'So...?' Will nudged the laptop forward.

'I don't know,' said Patrick. 'I kinda hate watching myself.'

'And I hate scary movies,' said Will. 'So this will be horrible for both of us.'

'*This* is what will make you feel better?'

'I just need to stop thinking about those egg-throwing bastards for a little while and turn my brain off with something mindless.'

'Mindless!' Patrick feigned offence. 'That's my *oeuvre*, I'll have you know.'

'I've seen your oeuvre,' Will said, winking. 'It's fuzzier.'

He scooted around the coffee table and sank onto the sofa, threw a blanket over his lap, then held up one end of the blanket and patted the sofa cushion next to him. Patrick made some light protesting noises before rising from his armchair and moving over to the couch. Will curled into him as Patrick raised his arm to make room in near-synchronicity. There was something about this automatic motion on both their parts that Patrick found deeply pleasing.

'Now if there are any bits that get too tense or gory,' Will began.

'Don't worry,' he said. 'I'll protect you.'

'I was going to say, we can just turn it off. As long as we make it past the first third. I want to see all of your scenes, and your character gets killed off at the start of the second act.'

'How do you know that?'

'Seriously? Am I going to watch a horror film without having read the plot summary on Wikipedia first? Like some kind of madman?'

'Fine,' said Patrick as Will hit 'play', then nestled deeper into the crook of his shoulder. 'Just be warned... I look kinda different in this.'

'Oh, I know. I googled some stills. You are fully in your twink era. You look so cute. Proper murderable.'

'Flatterer.' Patrick kissed the top of Will's head. Barely minutes later, after only one disappointingly bloodless kill (the studio had been keen for a PG-13 rating, which all but killed the movie), he felt Will's breathing slow and deepen. He smirked. He couldn't wait to rub it in his face after that whole 'nodding off in the car' thing.

'Are you asleep?' he whispered.

'No,' Will retorted, eyes closed. 'I am gripped. This is a real *filmé*.'

'If you like, we can switch this off and I can just read the Wikipedia plot summary to you,' offered Patrick.

'Like a bedtime story?'

'A really fucked-up bedtime story.'

Will yawned. 'You're so good to me,' he mumbled. 'Best boyfriend ever.'

Something in Patrick's chest expanded up on Will's use of that word.

'Come on, you,' he said, rubbing Will's shoulder to rouse him. 'Let's go to bed.'

Audra Kelly lay in Patrick's arms, held so close to him that he could feel her heartbeat, and told him: 'I think I love you after all.'

'I thought you said you had no time for love,' he replied. 'That there were other, more important things.'

'That was before,' she said, placing her hand on his chest, feeling his own heart. 'Before you.'

Patrick pressed his forehead against hers, felt her breath on his skin, and kissed her. How strange, he thought, that her mouth should be so much softer than Will's, with none of its strength: she did not push back but gently caressed his lips with her own.

'I never thought I would have this,' she said. 'I am so glad. That I lived long enough to meet someone like you.'

'Don't talk like that. You're going to be fine.'

'You are a terrible liar.' Audra's breath fluttered weakly. 'Looks like I was right, flyboy. I'm going to die for my planet after all.

'I am not afraid, and nor should you be,' she continued. 'When a Zalian's body perishes, their essence lives on. We ascend to a higher plane of existence. A resplendent, perfect dimension. Oh... no tears now. Please. Or at least, let them be tears of joy. How lucky we have been, that the cosmos brought us together. That of all worlds, you crash-landed on mine. What perfect design! What fate!' She stroked his face with a shaking hand. 'What kismet.'

Patrick whimpered in grief, his chest heaving, and then... nothing.

'Shit,' he muttered. 'Sorry.'

'Cut!' yelled Lucas Grant, throwing up his hands in exasperation. 'Patrick, what is so hard about this? Why. Are you not. Fucking crying? Your alien girlfriend is dying in your arms and you look like you're thinking about what to have for dinner. You told me you'd got this.'

'I'm sorry,' said Patrick. 'I really thought I did.'

'It's fine,' the director said, in a way that let Patrick know it was most definitely *not* fine. 'I'm pushing for maximum *cinéma-vérité* here, but whatever. Everybody, take five! Then when we're back, we'll use the god damn menthol, I guess.'

Audra jumped to her feet, and a runner materialised to hand them both bottles of water while the crew redressed the set, which was to say, returning various tennis balls on sticks to their original positions.

'Don't worry,' she told Patrick between delicate sips. 'You'll get it next time.'

'*Cinéma-vérité.*' Patrick rolled his eyes, realising as he did so that it was with more than a touch of the urbane sass he had come to associate with Will. 'We're filming against a green screen on a sound stage in Birmingham, and your character has just been shot by a flying lizard carrying a laser rifle.'

'In the canon of tragic heroine deaths, it's not exactly Ophelian,' Audra agreed.

A small cadre of makeup artists descended to fuss over her, touching up her eyes and lips, ensuring that none of her purple skin tone had rubbed off during the last take, that the spatter of fake indigo blood across one cheek had not smudged and therefore posed a threat to continuity.

'I look pretty good for a dead bitch,' she remarked upon being shown her own reflection in a hand mirror.

'Your turn, Captain Handsome,' said Estelle, the chief makeup artist, lightly gripping Patrick's chin and turning his head first this way and then that, inspecting her handiwork. 'Huh,' she muttered to herself.

'Huh?' Patrick, head still tilted back in her grasp, raised an eyebrow.

'Nothing,' she said. 'You just need some more powder, is all. This way.'

She marched off in the direction of her station, and Patrick obligingly followed, lowering himself into the makeup chair and seeing for the first time what Estelle saw: a mild stubble rash on his nose and chin which looked bright red under the unforgiving lights. Estelle covered it up quickly and easily enough, patting him on the shoulder when he was good to go, and Patrick was painfully grateful for her discretion.

'Two minutes!' yelled the AD 'Places, people!'

Patrick and Audra reconvened on the sound stage, somebody waved a vapour stick under his eyes, Lucas Grant called 'Action!', and Captain Kismet wept for his lost princess.

'Can you really not cry on cue, though?' Audra asked him later, sitting next to him on the sofa in her room, bare feet draped over his legs.

'I don't know what it is!' said Patrick. 'I think of every sad thing I can: poverty, famine...'.

'Those uggos who get made over on *Queer Eye* and realise they have value as people!' Audra interjected with an earnest gasp.

'Sure, that too. And I can *feel* the tears coming. But then something just gets in the way. They never make it out. It's like I'm, I don't know, emotionally constipated or something.'

'I have a guy for that,' said Audra. 'For five hundred dollars he'll make you a green juice that flushes out your entire insides, and then he does energy healing on you while you drink it, so you end up shitting out all your bad vibes too. It's *very* cathartic. Want me to give him a call? See if he's free to fly out?'

'Let's call that a good backup plan,' said Patrick. 'I think I'll just go with the menthol stick for now.'

'As you wish.' Audra shrugged. 'It's your energy.'

'I appreciate it, though,' he added, realising that all this talk of vibes and pooping was Audra's own, LA way of trying to be sweet.

'Does that work for you?' he asked. 'Is that how you're able to cry whenever you want?'

'Do I *shit* so hard that I start sobbing?' Audra looked at him like he was insane. 'Do you have any idea what an awful thing that is to say to a woman?'

'What? No, I just meant...' Patrick felt the ground of the conversation giving way beneath him. 'Because you said...'

'I can't believe you would ask me something like that,' Audra continued, her face crumpling like tissue paper. 'I am a *lady*, Patrick. Why do you want me to feel bad about myself? Do you have any idea how hard it is to be a woman in this industry? The obsession with our bodies? Like we're public property. And you just go asking me about my *butthole*?' She burst into tears, and in an instant her face was soaked, her cheeks flush and smeared with tears. 'God, you must think I'm really *disgusting*,' she bawled, wiping away snot with the back of her hand.

'Jesus,' said Hector from the doorway. 'Did you break Audra?'

'I didn't mean to!' protested Patrick. 'I just... there was this vapour stick, and energy juice, and Audra was telling me about her body, and—'

Hector grinned wolfishly, and Patrick realised Audra's sobs weren't actually sobs. She was cackling. He turned to her, stunned, to see her face transformed once more, smiling sweetly through the oil spill of her mascara.

'And that,' she said, daintily dabbing at her eyes, 'is how you cry on command.'

'You are a sociopath,' said Patrick.

'I am an *actress*.'

'It's one hell of a party trick,' said Hector. 'The first time she did it to me I was horrified. I thought I was gonna be hearing from her lawyer.'

'She's done it to you too?'

'And half the crew.'

'It's a power thing,' she said. 'You would not believe how much easier it is to get things done just because men never want to think they've made a pretty girl cry.'

'Sociopath,' Patrick repeated.

'I'm not proud of it,' she added.

'Really? Because it sounds like you kind of are.'

'Oh, she is,' said Hector.

'Since when have you two been spending that much time together?' asked Patrick.

Audra shrugged. 'Since you never seem to be around for me to tease anymore, and my self-esteem is like a quantum physics experiment. I need a handsome man around at all times to observe me being beautiful, or I cease to exist.'

'Schrödinger's hottie,' said Hector, looking as pleased as punch.

'Oh.' Patrick looked from Hector to Audra. '*Oh.*'

'Hector came looking for you one afternoon, and you were nowhere to be found,' Audra said, 'and I was bored, so I bet him he couldn't lift me.' Hector flexed a bicep as if to illustrate the story. 'Turns out he can. Hector, show him.'

Springing into action like a show dog, Hector scooped Audra up and threw her over his shoulder while she squealed in delight.

'See?' she giggled, tapping Hector's back until he spun her around so she could face Patrick. 'See?'

'I do,' Patrick said, forcing a smile. He saw, alright. Boy meets girl, boy physically lifts girl. He didn't want to resent Audra or Hector. He liked them both. But he couldn't get it out of his head how neither of them thought twice about their display of affection. He hated that it was the kind of thing he wouldn't have even noticed, at least not consciously, until very recently.

'How long has this been going on?' he asked.

Hector shrugged. 'Just a few weeks.'

'I didn't know.'

Audra peered down at him from her perch. 'Well, you *are* a little self-absorbed.'

'Did you tell him yet?' asked Hector.

'Not yet,' she said. 'Now put me down, I'm getting dizzy.' Hector obeyed, and after Audra had fixed her barely-mussed hair, she informed Patrick that the cast were having a little shindig.

'Everyone is sick of these endless reshoots and rewrites and needs to blow off a little steam,' she said. 'So we're doing karaoke in my suite tomorrow night to celebrate this hell nearly being over. BYOB: bring your own bangers.'

'I don't know,' said Patrick, remembering what had happened the *last* time Audra convinced him he needed to let his hair down. 'I'm not really a karaoke kind of guy.'

'Don't be ridiculous. Just do some Bon Jovi or Bruce Springsteen. You'll have fun.' She paused, then added: 'And if you wanted to invite somebody, that would be fine too.'

'Invite somebody?'

Audra glanced sideways at Hector, and Patrick was thrown back in time to the apartment where he grew up. It was the same look his parents would exchange when they had clearly been talking about him when he wasn't in the room.

'You've seemed very... preoccupied lately,' said Hector. 'Going off on your own. Sometimes you're not here in the mornings. We just figured that maybe you'd, you know...'

'We figured you were getting laid,' said Audra. 'And if you wanted to bring them to karaoke night, it could be fun!' She placed a hand on her hip. 'I promise I won't even tell them about how you just made me cry.'

'That's sweet of you,' said Patrick, 'but—'

'I insist, actually!' said Audra. 'Come *on*, Patrick. We've been on a closed set for weeks. I love these people, but at this point the pool is so small we're becoming conversationally inbred. We need new blood. Please. Bring them.'

This was the third time she had used 'them'. Which could just be a figure of speech, but what if it wasn't? Audra could be remarkably perceptive on the rare occasions when she turned her gaze outward. She'd clocked that Estelle was pregnant before Estelle told anyone simply because the makeup artist had changed her morning coffee order.

'I know you value your privacy,' Audra said, gentle but still pushy, 'and you should. The vultures are always circling. But who gets that better than us? Who else can you trust to be discreet?'

She knew. She had to. God, Patrick felt so naïve. This was the woman he'd danced with in a gay bar. Who must have noticed that he started disappearing off someplace almost immediately after that night. She wasn't stupid. She never had been.

'I…' he said, but he choked on whatever he had been about to say next, his face hot, throat thick.

'It's OK, buddy,' said Hector, sitting down beside him, but the impulse to cry was already subsiding, as it always did. Years of practice.

He had become so scared of what might happen if he acted on his feelings, he had not thought any further than that. Had not even realised he wanted this; to bring Will into his life, to share him with others. To introduce his date to his friends, like other people did.

Patrick felt Audra take a seat on his other side and lean her head on his shoulder.

'Bring him,' she whispered. 'Or I will cry again.'

23

'Karaoke is straight culture,' Jordan announced, as they filed into the lift on the ground floor of the Grand.

'Is *not*,' said April.

'You think everything is straight culture,' said Margo, looking up from her phone. 'Some things are just embarrassing no matter what your identity. Karaoke is one of those things.'

'And yet you are a serial murderer of "You've Got the Love",' Will pointed out. 'I'm surprised Florence hasn't sent her machine after you by now.'

Margo shrugged, firing off a text and dropping her phone into her bag. 'I'm a thirty-something single mum. I reserve the right to be embarrassing.'

'Fine,' said Will, 'just please don't be too embarrassing tonight? That goes for all of you.' He was rewarded with a round of shocked, offended stares. 'I just mean…'

'We know what you mean,' said April, rubbing his arm affectionately. 'We're all about to go out with your secret boo and his fancy friends. You're nervous.'

'But there's no need to be a dick about it,' cut in Jordan.

'Fair. I'm sorry.' Will took a deep breath as the lift took them higher and higher. Patrick had been the one to suggest he bring

Margo and his friends tonight. He'd thought it might make the whole evening feel more normal, and as they were all technically in on the secret already, nobody was violating any non-disclosure rules. The gag remained firmly in place.

So to speak.

The sliding doors opened onto the top floor of the hotel, which housed only two suites: one belonging to Patrick – with which Will was already intimately familiar – and the other to Audra Kelly, who appeared in the doorway as they all exited the lift.

'Welcome, welcome!' she shrieked gleefully, tugging Will into an embrace. 'You must be Will. Patrick's told me absolutely nothing about you. Isn't he just the worst? Honestly. Come in, come in, everyone! Help yourself to anything. Liquor, sushi, weed gummies.' She pulled Will by the hand into a suite that was the mirror image of Patrick's and bathed in pink and purple lights.

'Bisexual lighting,' she explained. 'I discovered it while playing a woman called Joy who discovers her husband is trying to frame her for her girlfriend's murder in the erotic thriller *Two for Joy*. Doesn't it just make my hair *pop*?'

'It sure does,' said Jordan, heart emojis practically bursting from his eyes in the presence of TikTok's current favourite actress. 'You were so fabulous in that one.'

'Oh my God, stop!' Audra dropped Will's hand and took Jordan's, leading him over to a sofa where he could continue to praise her filmography.

'We've lost him for the night,' said April, picking up a napkin from the main table. 'Ooh, unagi!'

'Is that The Rock's tequila?' Margo swiftly scooped ice into a glass and poured herself a large blanco on the rocks.

'I thought you were anti-tequila,' said Will.

'I am anti-*cheap* tequila,' said Margo. 'Which heretofore has been the only variety available to me.' She took a sip and closed her eyes in pleasure. 'Still kind of minging, but definitely an improvement. I can work with this.'

'There you are,' said Patrick, emerging from Audra's en suite and sidling up to Will and enveloping him in a hug. He kissed Will on the cheek and Will almost flinched before remembering that this was allowed and they were among trusted friends.

'I know, I guess they'll let anyone in here,' he said, wrapping his arms around Patrick's waist. 'You should really have them tighten up security downstairs.'

'Nah.' Patrick kissed him again, this time on the forehead. It seemed he was savouring the novelty too. 'I told them Grace Anatomy herself was coming and they should roll out the red carpet.'

'*Pour moi*? You shouldn't have.'

Will tried not to grin too idiotically as Patrick took his arm and walked him around the room, introducing him to his stunt double Corey and his trainer Hector, both of whom he had already met, albeit as Grace, and some others he hadn't: makeup artist Estelle, whose beat was so flawless she seemed to literally glow; Audra's stand-in Honor, whose neat blonde ponytail and hoodie put Will in mind of someone who would ruin your life on the hockey field; and a tall, thin Swedish actor who was playing the supervillain Omega in *Kismet* whose name Will didn't quite catch but *sounded* like he might be a minor Skarsgård.

He couldn't get over how good this felt. To be held by his boyfriend, in something approaching public. For the other people in the room to know they were together and treat it like no big deal.

It really *wasn't* a big deal, of course. Will tended to get carried away with these things, but even he knew that a few weeks of hanging out and having admittedly incredible sex did not constitute a world-changing romance. He hadn't even *called* Patrick his boyfriend out loud, apart from that one time when he'd been half-asleep from rage and Rioja.

'Patrick!' Audra barked from across the room. 'You're up.'

Patrick groaned. 'Can't someone else go before me?' he asked.

'You're our leading man,' said Audra. 'I insist.'

'As do I!' added Will, his eyes mischievous. 'What are you going to sing? Oh God, don't choose Joan Armatrading. Please. I'd swoon and everyone else in the room might commit suicide.'

'Laugh it up now,' said Patrick. 'I'm making you go next.'

'Oh, you mean I'm going to be the centre of attention? Don't threaten me with a good time, Mr Lake.' He gave Patrick a playful shove towards Audra. 'I only get stage fright when I'm Grace, remember?'

Audra pushed a microphone into Patrick's hand.

'I've taken the liberty of choosing for you,' she informed him, and seconds later the room was filled with the larger-than-life overture of 'Livin' on a Prayer'.

'Come on, Jersey Boy,' Will crowed. 'Show us what you've got!'

His mockery did not last long. The moment Patrick knew he wasn't getting out of this embarrassing ritual, he committed fully, strutting with a hypermasculine swagger from one end of the room to the next while belting into the microphone, barely even looking at the screen to check the lyrics. It was like looking momentarily into another timeline, Will thought. One where Patrick headlined a Broadway show or movie musical, something where even a fraction of his sheer warmth and charisma could be channelled effectively.

'Woo!' Audra squealed. 'OK, now me!' She snatched the mic from Patrick, having already queued up her own choice, and launched into a straight-faced, deeply sincere cover of 'Lucky.'

She butchered it. Audra's singing voice was flat, nasal, and seemed to change key every other line. It was, quite possibly, the worst thing to happen to Britney Spears since the conservatorship, but

Audra was clearly connecting with the material and having a great time, and Will found himself liking her all the more.

It made her a pretty easy act to follow.

He tried not to overthink his own song choice, ignoring the conversation Jordan and April had been having earlier about how your go-to karaoke song is even more telling than your zodiac sign, and just went for the first pop song that came into his head. He tried not to look directly at Patrick as the song began, but felt his eyes on him, as warming as a spotlight.

'You think I'm pretty without any makeup on…'

They were under a dozen people in a hotel suite, but it was hard not to fall back into performing mode, and by the second half of the song Will was adding riffs and runs. As the final chorus dropped, so did he, right into a split. The crowd – all eleven of them – went wild, and Will stayed on the floor as he finished the song, rolling around until he was entangled in the microphone cable and Patrick had to help him extricate himself.

'You're unbelievable,' Patrick said, once they had moved aside to make room for Jordan and April's 'Elephant Love Medley'. 'I stan you.'

'I should've stretched first!' Will groaned, rubbing a sore adductor. 'Still. Far from my worst gig.'

'And here I am, without a single to tip you.'

'Oh, honey.' Will leaned in closer. 'I want more than just the tip.'

'Harlot.'

'You don't know the half of it.'

'I'm starting to get a pretty good idea.' Patrick pulled him closer. 'I'm low-key obsessed.'

'Careful,' Will whispered. 'You're starting to talk like a little f-word.'

'You're a bad influence. I'm clearly spending too much time with you.'

'Not much time left now,' said Will, focusing all of his attention on a wisp of fluff that had drifted onto Patrick's shirt. 'Two more weeks, right?'

Patrick's expression sobered. 'Yeah,' he said. 'Will, I—'

'Let's not talk about it.' Will forced a smile. 'I don't want to think about you leaving just yet. This is a party. Let's just enjoy each other for as long as you're still here, OK?'

Patrick returned the smile. 'Deal,' he said. 'But how about we ditch these guys and have a party of our own? Say, in my room?'

Will's grin broadened. 'Race you there,' he said.

Sneaking around wasn't so bad, Will thought. It was actually kind of fun, like the two of them were playing some kind of game against the rest of the world and only they understood the rules. For the last week of filming, Patrick procured a key card from the hotel staff that granted Will access to the building from the rear – he was proud of himself for only making one crass joke to that effect – and use of the staff lift, enabling him to reach Patrick's room with little to no interference. When Will raised the idea that this was a pretty big breach in hotel security, Patrick had simply shrugged and said: 'People don't like to say no to me.' Will had thought this an uncharacteristically arrogant thing for him to say. He also found it incredibly hot.

Evading the paparazzi had also become a lot easier now that they had willing accomplices. Corey was a game enough ally: if he wore a large pair of aviators and smoothed his scruffy hair into a side parting, his resemblance to Patrick went from passing to, well, passing. He was more than happy to play decoy for them, donning his Patrick drag and going for public walks around the Jewellery Quarter and Brindley Place, stopping for dumplings in Chinatown, tailed by photographers like he was in a really low-stakes spy thriller.

Once they'd succeeded in their subterfuge, though, Will and Patrick enjoyed relative freedom. The search for the Omega Issue had been called off without either of them actually saying as much, almost as if they both accepted it had only ever been a pretext that they no longer required. Instead they hunted for time: gaps in Patrick's schedule where they could steal half an hour together, nights when Grace wouldn't be missed from the Village and Will could use his misappropriated key card. He feigned illness to Faye to get out of a story hour and eat craft services in Patrick's trailer between takes. Skipped movie night with Jordan and April so he could be waiting in Patrick's room when he finished a night shoot. The end of production loomed ever closer, and Will's old life would still be waiting for him when his time with Patrick inevitably came to a close.

Will never ceased to be surprised by how completely ordinary their time together felt. At some point when he wasn't paying attention, he had stopped being quite so dazzled by Patrick's good looks, and that awe had been replaced by something else, sublimated into a kind of loving familiarity. He smiled at the very thought of Patrick's face, not just because it was so pleasing to look at, but because of the way he jutted out his bottom lip when he was trying to be cute, for the intensity of those blue eyes when he was really *listening*, because now he knew the real man in all his complexity, and that goodness shone brightly through the surface, only making him even more handsome. It was like Will's affection had painted Patrick in newer, richer colours, and that in being so seen and known, he opened up even more, a flower in full sun.

Now Will's favourite pastime was charting the parts of Patrick that the rest of the world didn't see. There was a smattering of freckles across Patrick's shoulders that he hadn't immediately noticed but that he was now obsessed with. He liked to trace over them with his fingers in those moments before sleep. He wondered if he were to take a Sharpie and play connect-the-dots what kind of constellations he might make, what kaleidoscopic patterns would dance out across his lover's skin.

On one such night, fingers tiptoeing from one freckle to another, Will whispered: 'Tell me something the magazines don't know.'

Patrick grunted, an amused kind of hum, which Will had recently learned meant he was on the edge of sleep. He was silent again for long enough that Will assumed he had drifted off, then said: 'I used to have a stutter.'

Will didn't reply, his fingertips' continued exploration of Patrick's freckles confirmation enough that he was listening.

'Not a terrible one,' Patrick continued. 'I mean, I could make it to the end of a sentence fine. But the way I'd trip over certain words, get all flustered and short of breath, made everything I said sound like a question. My dad hated it. A perfectly natural speech impediment, but I knew he thought it meant something more. About me. Or maybe about him, and the kind of son he'd produced.'

'So what changed?' Will asked.

'Performing in plays at school. I sucked at first, obviously. Couldn't muster the breath to project, stumbled on my lines. The more *serious* drama kids found me incredibly frustrating. But this one teacher, Mr Banks, gave me a bunch of reading to take home. Told me to practise by myself, when nobody was around, so I wouldn't feel self-conscious. Monologues from Shakespeare and Chekhov and Williams. And poetry! Something about the way stanzas were ordered, letting you know exactly when to breathe. He said I had to get to grips with the language, live in it, that way I wouldn't be afraid of it. God, I loved it. I'd recite speeches and sonnets over and over and over, tomorrow and tomorrow and tomorrow, and even when I didn't fully understand every single word, I felt like I knew exactly what these people were saying. Like they were talking through me.'

'And that helped? With your stammer?'

'My parents finally shelled out for a speech therapist my senior year of high school. But the confidence to speak? That came from Mr Banks.'

'Well.' Will's fingers ceased their foxtrot, and he laid his palm on Patrick's chest, nestling into the crook of his arm. 'Here's to Mr Banks.'

Two nights before the shoot was due to wrap, Corey, Hector, and Audra all went for a very public dinner at a restaurant on the twenty-fourth floor of a building that was immensely popular among visitors to the city. At the same time Patrick, decked out in a hoodie and baseball cap, used Will's Uber account and took a car to game night at Margo's house.

'I think you're the killer,' Will said, looking Dylan square in the eye.

'Nope,' Dylan said, barely even moving their face. *I should teach them poker*, Will thought. *We'd make a fortune.*

'OK, then I am officially clueless,' he said. 'If it's not Dylan, I don't know who it is.'

'That figures,' scoffed Patrick.

'Excuse you?'

'Come on, Will. I mean this in the nicest way, but… you're not great at reading people.' Patrick reached out and twirled one of Will's curls around his index finger. 'It took you how long to figure out that I liked you?'

'In fairness, it's not every day that a movie star takes a liking to you. And you could have just asked me out,' Will said.

'I *did*!'

'Sending me on a treasure hunt for a mythical comic book and then inviting yourself along is not a date, Patrick. And besides, I thought you were dating Audra.'

'Audra? Are you kidding me?'

'The way you were with her!' Will protested. 'All those photos of you two cosying up behind the scenes on her Instagram Story.'

'I have no idea what you're talking about,' said Patrick. 'But you're starting to sound like a stalker. Maybe you *are* creepy after all.'

'I've figured out what it is,' April announced. 'You've got resting boyfriend face.'

'I've got *what*?'

'Resting boyfriend face!' she continued triumphantly. 'Like, when everyone said you were going out with Emma Roberts because you looked so good on the red carpet together. Or that photo at a pool party with a supermodel on your shoulders. I sometimes click on *Mail Online* links. I know, I'm part of the problem.'

Still met with a roomful of blank looks, April rolled her eyes and steered Margo by the elbow towards where Patrick was seated. 'Here,' she said. 'Perch on the arm of the chair like that. OK… and… Say cheese!' She took out her phone and took a quick picture, then turned the screen around to show everybody. 'See?'

The result was uncanny. Margo, all five-feet-ten of her, looked positively dainty next to Patrick's strapping frame, and the pair of them were smiling serenely, as if they had just announced their engagement.

'Bloody hell,' said Margo. 'I might have to send this to Owen. His head will explode.'

'That's just a fluke,' Will protested.

'Fine.' April shrugged and stooped down right next to Patrick so that the side of her face was squashed against his, and snapped a rapid selfie. When she offered up the phone as evidence once again, the photo looked like it had been taken in the middle of a particularly fantastic date, April's round cheeks dimpled gleefully against Patrick's as if they were sharing a private joke.

'Oh, this is *fun*,' said Jordan. 'Do me next! Move!' He practically shoved April out of the way, plonking himself down next to Patrick and arranging his narrow legs just so. Patrick, for his part, merely smiled and blinked placidly as yet another photo was taken.

'Oh my God.' Jordan's eyes lit up as he saw the picture. He thrust it in Will's face. 'This is beyond. Can't you just imagine the two of us adopting an inbred little Pomeranian together?'

'OK, OK,' Will said. 'Enough now. Jordy, can you please get out of my boyfriend's lap. And for the record, it would never work between you two. An ash blonde and platinum blonde? Gauche.'

Jordan tutted and obliged, swinging his legs off Patrick's and sauntering into the kitchen, presumably to plunder what remained of the wine.

Patrick reached out to Will, who took his hand and allowed himself to be pulled down into an embrace on the sofa.

'You and your slutty face,' he muttered.

'Don't tell me you're jealous.' Patrick grinned.

'I'm not,' Will said with a pout, and Patrick's chest shook with laughter beneath him. 'I'm *not*,' he insisted, his mouth twitching involuntarily, threatening to break into a smile of his own. 'I'll have you know that people mistake me and Jordan for a couple all the time, actually. Come to think of it, so did you. It's just…' The smile vanished. 'Nobody's ever going to see us together and assume we're dating, are they? Not the way they would with you and April, or Margo, or Emma bloody Roberts.'

'Emma is actually really nice when you get to know her,' Patrick began, 'she—'

'I'm never going to be allowed to stand next to you on the red carpet, am I?'

Patrick's grin softened. 'No,' he said. 'Probably not.'

'And even if I were, you'd tell people I'm a good friend, or your flatmate or something. Because we both signed several pieces of paper saying that as far as the rest of the world is concerned, that's all we will ever be to each other.'

Until next week, he thought. *After then, we won't even be that.* Will had done his best to avoid broaching the subject of Patrick leaving, playing the part of someone who was just along for the ride for as long as it lasted. He kept his eyes fixed on an abstract point on the wall behind the armchair, and so he felt but did not see Patrick's hand slip into his.

'Do you regret it?' Patrick asked softly. 'The NDA?'

'I didn't have much of an option, did I?' he said.

'That's not what I asked.'

Will laid his head on Patrick's chest, and Patrick enclosed his free arm around him.

'If the choice is between getting to be with you in secret, or not being with you at all... No. I don't regret it.'

He felt Patrick kiss the top of his head, felt what he said next rustling into his hair.

'I'm glad you feel that way,' said Patrick. 'Because I do too. I know for some people, this wouldn't be enough.'

'It is,' Will said. 'You are.'

It was the right thing to say in the moment. It was what Patrick needed to hear, he knew. Will even thought that he might mean it, at that very second, with the solid warmth of Patrick pressed against him. It was all the other moments that bothered him.

24

1950

'The pot roast is a tad overdone,' Charles remarked, peering over Iris's shoulder at the blackened hunk of meat. 'That cow has seen more heat than I did in the war.'

Iris threw up her hands. 'If you married me expecting somebody who could cook, I have some terrible news for you,' she huffed.

'Some of this is salvageable,' Charles said. 'And there are always the potatoes. Out of the way, dear.' He kissed her on the cheek as she withdrew from the stove, removing her apron and offering it to him.

'We shall just have to keep our guests' glasses full,' Iris said.

Charles put on the apron and tended to what remained of dinner while Iris fixed them both drinks, each of them falling into the dramatis personae of domesticity, only in reverse. He beamed. He had never felt so married. This must be what it was like when little girls played house, he thought.

They had never entertained before: the old apartment had been too small, too cold, too much like an opium eater's garret. Their new place in Crown Heights, though, was large enough to accommodate a dining table – such luxury! – and a liquor cart in the living room. They could even afford bottles for the cart: Captain Kismet was paying his keep nicely. Iris had resisted the increase in comfort at first, claiming she would rather die than live like her parents, but she rapidly became accustomed to the pleasing little ritual of a sidecar and a cigarette after she had finished writing for the day.

And, of course, the second bedroom meant freedom for them both, from each other as much as from the outside world. Eleanor had already visited the new apartment a handful of times. She and Iris would disappear into the first bedroom, and on those occasions, Charles, working on his drawings in the afternoon light, would throw open the window and turn up the radio to give them some privacy.

God only knew where Eleanor's husband thought she was during these visits. Perhaps she had concocted an ailing relative or secretarial lessons. She had a knack for discretion that Charles had come to trust, even admire. He had thought Eleanor unbearably frivolous at first and had judged her harshly for it. But the more often she came around, and the longer she lingered for coffee after she and Iris resurfaced, the more he realised she had a good head on her shoulders. She was not silly, she simply wasn't serious. And who would want to be serious? Certainly not Charles, whose living was made with flights of fancy.

Dickie had not visited the new apartment, just as he had never been to the old one. To this day, they only ever rendezvoused at the hotel near Washington Square where Dickie stayed when he was in town.

That would change tonight, Charles reminded himself. And right then, as if responding to a cue now that the stage of his and Iris's little domestic play was set, there came a knock at the door.

Dickie and Eleanor stood side by side, making such a dashing couple that for one disorienting moment Charles grew confused.

'I hope we're not early!' Eleanor said. 'I just happened to walk into the elevator at the exact same moment as this gentleman here, and he offered to push the button for me, and I said "four please," and he said "what a coincidence, that's where I'm heading too," and I thought, well how many apartments on the fourth floor can be hosting dinner and drinks that start at eight sharp? And how many would have invited such a handsome fellow? So I held out my hand' – here, Eleanor extended her hand, inviting her new companion into the re-enactment, and Dickie gamely took it – 'and I said "I'm Eleanor, pleased to make your acquaintance, might you by any chance be Dickie?" And he said, "well, I'm sure you can guess." Hello, my love.'

She waited for Charles to close the door behind them before delivering a breathless kiss to Iris and surprising him by giving him a peck on the cheek as well.

'It's good to see you, Charles.' She seemed to mean it.

Dickie stood with his hands behind his back, and Charles was suddenly overcome with an odd shyness.

'You need a cocktail,' he informed Eleanor, crossing the room to the cart, where he busied his hands with liquor and ice. Eleanor accepted the drink and took it into the kitchen, where he heard a soft 'oh dear.'

'Don't worry,' said Iris, marching into the kitchen behind her. 'We have potatoes.'

And then he was alone with Dickie, in the home that he shared with his wife, and occasionally with his wife's girlfriend.

'Oswin,' he said.

'Ambrose.'

Dickie brought his hands out from behind his back, smiling bashfully as he held out his offering: a rose-coloured plant. A housewarming gift, Charles realised. The gesture was so quotidian and yet so unexpected that it took him a moment to recognise the bright, latticed petals, initially mistaking it for a carnation before recognising it as the camellia, the flower Bette Davis adored so much in *Now, Voyager*. Charles had recounted the entire plot to Dickie in bed one afternoon upon hearing the other man had not seen it.

'You have a beautiful home,' said Dickie, holding his gaze, the furthest edges of that damned moustache curling in pleasure.

'Oh, how thoughtful!' Iris said, reappearing and extracting the plant from Dickie's hands. 'Charles, don't just stand there, take Dickie's coat and pour his Martini.'

It did not matter, in the end, that the roast was ruined. With Iris's enthusiastic permission, Dickie chopped away at the charred exterior of the beef and carved what remained edible inside. They slathered the dry meat with horseradish and washed down hastily made sandwiches with wine, and lots of it. They sat around the dinner table that was so shiny and new it contained a coppery image of the four of them within its surface, and laughed over how awful a cook Iris was.

It was a quintessentially American activity. McCarthy himself, that grey-faced angel of death, could have peered through their window and passed right over their house. For so many years Charles had wanted to take a match to the linen and lace framing his parents' dinners, and now here they were! Something about having Dickie and Eleanor over like they were one ordinary couple socialising with another felt such a delicious inversion, the cleverest sort of trick. That they had all found each other was remarkable enough: that they sat here now, mirthful doubles suspended in the amber of the table, was nothing short of miraculous. He could, as his darling wife might have said, 'plotz'.

'To Kismet,' Iris said, holding up her glass. She was prone to toasting their child once it reached a certain point in the evening, when her consonants would begin to soften and drip like the candles she always lit for dinner. Charles didn't think his wife especially superstitious, but it was almost as if she felt compelled to thank the fictional superhero for everything he had given them, raising her glass in pagan offering for fear that it would all be taken away.

Charles understood the impulse, even if he did not share it. Privately, he saw their good fortune as a dare. He and Iris had lost so much – her brother to the war, his parents to their unforgiving Christian convictions – that any change in their circumstances felt deserved. They had come by their newfound means through honest work, had carved out a tiny corner of happiness in the world's most indifferent city. He was sometimes overcome by a sensation of snowballing momentum, and the urge to see how much further they could take this, wondering if it were possible to chart the limits to their luck. If they would ever be able, through sheer dogged determination, to live the kind of lives that other people took for granted.

What if nobody stops us? What then? What can't we do?

'To Kismet,' the table echoed, but as Eleanor brought her glass to her lips, she froze and her breathing quickened.

'Excuse me,' she blurted, bolting from the table.

'Poor thing,' said Dickie. 'Not everybody has the stomach for gin.'

'I'll check on her,' said Iris. 'I suspect we've rather led her astray. She was such an innocent when I met her.' She gave them both a devilish wink and left the table.

'It's getting late. I should go,' said Dickie, pushing back in his chair but not yet standing.

'Won't you have one more drink?' Charles asked. The conviviality of dinner was burning down to embers, but he felt the desire to attempt to stoke the flames, all the same. He didn't want this night with Dickie and Iris and Eleanor – yes, even Eleanor! – to end, could almost believe that if they only kept laughing and lighting cigarettes and opening cheaper bottles of wine, it might just go on forever.

'Stay,' he said. 'Just one more.' Pleading shamed him mildly, but his body had developed quite the high tolerance for that particular poison.

Iris and Eleanor returned from the bathroom, Eleanor's face bright and freshly scrubbed, her smile refreshed.

'I don't know what came over me,' she giggled. 'It must have been the beef.'

They all laughed, and Charles realised that everybody he loved was in this room.

'One more,' said Dickie. 'For the road.'

25

'Have you ever been given an atomic wedgie?' Audra asked Patrick as they gingerly left the soundstage. She had good reason to ask: they had both spent the better part of the afternoon and early evening strapped into harnesses and suspended on wires while they performed a portion of the film's final battle against a green screen for endless takes.

'I imagine it must feel something like this,' Patrick said, aware that his bandy-legged walk was giving John Wayne.

'I have been wearing a bra since I was thirteen,' said Audra. 'I have been funnelled into every kind of shapewear you can think of. I know the extent to which the human body can be remoulded. And I wholeheartedly believe that a person's ass should *never* be nestled between their shoulder blades.'

'I can't wait to shower this day off,' said Patrick, 'and go straight to sleep.'

'I am going to make Hector give me a massage,' Audra declared. 'The deep tissue kind that athletes get, you know, where you feel like you've been hit by a car but in a good way. And then I am taking a vodka on the rocks to bed with me.'

'Lucky vodka.' Patrick threw an arm around Audra's shoulder. 'Hey, just think. One more day, and we are officially wrapped.'

Audra tossed back her hair and sang: 'One! More! Day!'

A single scene remained to be filmed that actually required Patrick and Audra's faces; the rest of the more complicated stunts had already been captured using Corey in Patrick's stead, and Audra's own stunt double Honor. There was talk of a post-credit scene, which would tease the introduction of Kid Kismet to the franchise – every bright-eyed 19-year-old in Tinseltown was rumoured to be in talks for the role – but Patrick did not need to be present for that.

They were finally on the verge of having completed something resembling a real movie. At this stage of the process, Patrick was usually filled with that sentimental last-day-of-camp feeling: he would thank every grip, gaffer, camera operator, and runner for their hard work, already heartsick with the sensation of missing the experience before it was even over. Today, he just felt bone-deep fatigue.

Patrick and Audra travelled back to the Grand by car while still in their costumes, too wiped to change, all banter subsiding into exhausted silence. When they reached their floor, Audra retreated to her suite without another word.

'One more day,' he muttered to himself, opening his own door.

Will was waiting for him there, sitting on the floor of the hotel room.

No. Not sitting. Kneeling. In...

'What – what are you *wearing*?' Patrick sputtered.

The bodysuit was a red mirror of his own, albeit made from far cheaper material; the kind that could be bought online for fifty bucks. An eight-pointed star was emblazoned over the chest. It was an image Patrick had seen countless times over the last few years; whizzing, kabooming and zap-powing across panels and pages as Kid Kismet faithfully came to the aid of his companion.

'Hello, Captain,' said Will. His hair was slicked back, unruly black curls tamed into an approximation of Axel's wavy quiff. His lashes looked even darker and thicker under the crimson mask covering his eyes. The scarlet fabric clung to his chest and shoulders, stretched over his muscular quads as he crouched submissively, gathered between his legs in such a way that Patrick knew he was wearing nothing underneath.

'Fuck,' he whispered.

'Captain?' Will asked. He was looking up at him with such wide, eager eyes that Patrick instantly became hard.

'Come here,' he said, the timbre of his voice surprising even him.

'Of course,' said Will. No, said *Axel*. His lips caressed those hard 'R's in a decent imitation of an American accent, and he crawled with slow purpose across the carpet to where Patrick stood. He looked up at him imploringly, and with the slightest of nods from Patrick, reached out and ran his hands up Patrick's calves, then up to his thighs, squeezing his firm quads and adductor muscles, his breathing growing shorter. His hands came together, cupping and fondling the weight of Patrick, and then without being instructed, he began to unzip the fly that had been discreetly sewn into the costume.

Patrick grabbed fistfuls of that dark hair, eyes closed, all exhaustion forgotten as he luxuriated in the feeling of soft locks between his fingers, of Will's warm tongue teasing his head before taking all of him into his mouth.

He grabbed Will by the back of the neck and hauled him up to his feet. Will complied with a soft yelp. Looking into his eyes through the mask, their identical heights had never felt so intimate. Patrick had spent such a long time suppressing his desires, sparing little thought for kink or fantasy, that he wouldn't have even known, if asked, whether the superhero-and-sidekick thing turned him on. Here, though, right now, was the answer.

'Axel,' he whispered, and the sidekick's lips parted in desire. 'Get onto the bed.'

Axel nodded.

'I'll go anywhere you tell me,' he said. 'You know that.'

Patrick shoved him back onto the mattress and crawled on top of him, pinning him down with his forearm across his chest.

'You're mine,' he growled, pulling at the cheap red fabric until the costume stretched and tore under his grip. 'You're mine.'

'I'm yours, Captain,' Axel said, and Patrick felt himself disappear.

When the master entered the servant, it was gently at first, but it wasn't long before his thrusts grew more intense, rapid and forceful as the man beneath him gasped in pained gratification.

The sidekick looked up at his captain like he was his entire world. *I am yours*, that look said. *This is my body, in your hands, to love as harshly or kindly as you choose.* 'Fuck me,' Axel gasped. 'Fuck me, *please.*'

With a single, primal yell, the captain collapsed, covering the sidekick's body with his own. This was the superhero in his purest form, all of that strength and power fuelled by a fierce and primal instinct.

'You're mine. I just want to take care of you,' he whispered, and he saw tears form in the eyes behind Axel's mask.

'I… ' Axel whispered faintly. 'Patrick, I…' Something in the world shifted and it was no longer Axel beneath him, but Will. At the sound of his own name, Patrick came tumbling back down to earth, crash-landing into himself. The soreness and lethargy of earlier returned, and he climbed off Will with a sudden, all-consuming weariness.

He needed to clean up. He padded into the bathroom and stopped cold when passing the mirror. His face was blotchy and red, his costume rumpled and smeared with lube and semen. His cock hung heavy and useless from the fly, and under the harsh overhead lights, the still-forming memory of what had just transpired between them began to wilt. Had it really felt so transcendent? Could it have truly been that much of a thrill, or had he simply been starved for so long that he hadn't been able to control his own basest urges?

Patrick felt a great, unstoppable rush of shame. The panic that had threatened to swoop in earlier arrived now, turning instantly to red-hot anger.

When he returned to the bedroom, he tossed a washcloth to Will on the bed, hating what a porny cliché this was. *Clean yourself up*, says the minister to his acolyte, the doctor to his patient, the sergeant to his subordinate.

'I have an early call tomorrow,' he said.

'Oh yeah,' said Will, swabbing delicately at his wet stomach. 'Big day, innit.'

'Yes. It is.' Patrick reached behind him and grasped at thin air a few times before finally finding the zipper of his costume and tugging at it uncomfortably.

'I can—' said Will, starting to rise from the bed.

'I've got it,' said Patrick, already pulling his arms out of the loosened suit and shoving it down around his waist like a workman's overalls. Cool air massaged his clammy, wretched skin. 'I need to shower,' he announced.

'OK,' said Will, tossing the hand towel onto the floor next to the bed. What was *wrong* with him? Had he always been such a slob, and Patrick just hadn't noticed?

'Could you…?' Patrick let the sentence trail off, hoping he wouldn't have to finish it. Will followed his eyes to the door.

'Oh,' he said, eyes widening almost imperceptibly. 'You want me to—'

'Yeah. Yes. Sorry. It's just… like I said. Early call.'

'Right. OK.' Will stood, retrieved a bag he must have stashed under the bed, and began to extract himself from what remained of his Kid Kismet costume, taking an interminable amount of time to step out of the leggings and put on clean underwear, jeans, T-shirt.

'I'm gonna...' Patrick nodded towards the bathroom.

'Right this second?' Will asked, bent over to tie his shoes. 'Alright.' He rose up and crossed the room to kiss him. Patrick, lips closed, pecked him on the cheek and then went into the bathroom, closing the door behind him. He turned on the shower and stood next to the door listening, waiting for the sound of Will leaving the suite before stepping under the water.

26

When Will got back to his apartment, shredded costume balled up at the bottom of his bag like a dirty PE kit, he immediately ran himself a steaming bath and opened a bottle of Malbec. He could feel the fat, hot tears coming any minute now and figured he might as well lean all the way in, like ritualising the act of crying would somehow lessen how wretched he really felt.

I'm not really upset, he could tell himself. I'm doing a bit.

He thought getting it all out, however dramatically, would be cathartic. But snivelling under the bubbles struck him as merely childish, and as he lay in the long-cold water, fingers wrinkled and eyes puffy, Will felt no cleaner or lighter than before. It was far from the first time he'd been practically marched out the door after a hook-up – knowing when to grant your host a speedy exit was all part of carrying oneself through life with a semblance of dignity – but this was the first time it had happened with someone he was seeing. Even Ry would've had the social grace to make Will a cup of tea or allow him to shower before calling him a taxi.

He had misjudged the idea of the costume, clearly.

Or had he? Patrick had seemed so into it, had thrown himself into the roleplay with vigour, had almost become a different person entirely in the process. Maybe that was it, Will thought. Patrick had stepped so entirely out of himself that when he came back, he hadn't liked what he'd seen.

That must be it. Why Patrick had acted so coldly, so suddenly keen to be alone when the person Will'd first met had been so deprived of touch that he would hold onto Will like a life-raft.

Patrick would call in the morning, Will reasoned. He would apologise.

Or, he countered himself, he wouldn't.

Tomorrow was the last day of filming, after all. What if that had been Patrick's plan all along? To not talk about what might happen after he no longer had a reason to stay in Birmingham, to not even say goodbye, to ghost?

But that was so not Patrick, Will argued back. He was so guileless, did he really have it in him to play such a tacky game? He was too upfront.

Upfront? The other Will parried. From the man who, as far as the entire world is aware, dates women?

Touché.

This battle of Wills continued throughout the night, in which he desperately clawed at sleep in fitful ten-minute spells before snapping awake again, and into the morning, so that by the time he arrived at Gilroy's for his shift, anxiety and exhaustion had teamed up to turn his stomach into a roiling, intricate Celtic knot.

He went through the motions of opening up the shop on autopilot, pulling up the shutters that covered the window display, turning on the till, things he had done hundreds of times before but which felt distant and alien today, performed by somebody else's hands.

He sold a clothbound edition of *Emma* to somebody who thought it was a real find and didn't have the heart to explain that it was actually a reprint that came out three years ago. He took three messages for Yvonne over the phone and then afterwards couldn't make sense of what he had written down. When April arrived at 10 a.m. with their usual coffee order, his tasted both bitter and sickly-sweet. Three sips were enough to give him painful indigestion, and he poured it down the sink when April wasn't looking.

Jordan dropped in at noon as he did semi-frequently, at a loss for lunch plans, and the three of them ordered gyros from the Greek place next to the train station. Will stared into space, picking at a stray piece of onion, until finally Jordan and April ceased their conversation and Jordan asked: 'What the hell is wrong with you today?'

'Nothing,' Will said instantly.

'Bollocks.' Jordan delicately dabbed tzatziki from the corners of his mouth with a serviette. 'You are never this quiet. Ninjas are never this quiet.'

'I'm just tired,' said Will. 'I didn't sleep very well.'

'Oh,' said April. 'I see. You didn't sleep well, because...' She winked.

'Because you were getting dicked down!' Jordan said. 'Dicked all the way down to Chinatown!'

'Yeah,' said Will, weakly. 'I was. I mean, we did.'

'You don't look happy about that,' said April. 'It has been a while for me. I don't know whether it's different for us straights, but I would be happy.'

'I am,' said Will, even less convincingly. 'I mean, that part was good. Great. Top notch. I mean, fucking hell, you have no idea.'

'Then why the long face?' Jordan's eyebrows contracted slightly, doing their best to furrow despite the paralysing agent between them.

'It's nothing.'

'It seems like something.' Jordan leaned closer, as if he might be able to sniff the truth above the onions. 'Was it chemsex?'

'Pardon?'

'Did you two take a load of drugs and shag until dawn and now you're dealing with friction burns and the existential dread of a comedown?'

'Fucking hell, Jordan, no! Patrick doesn't even vape.'

'Then what?' Jordan looked to April, then back at Will. 'Something's up. Our bestie senses are tingling. It's a real thing, it's basically a superpower all of its own, don't question me on that, April knows what I'm talking about. Now spill.'

Will was too tired to protest, and so he told them both what had happened the night before, eliding the more graphic details and focusing on the way it had ended.

'He's under a lot of pressure at work,' he said. 'And maybe I'm being overly sensitive, but... it's not on, is it?'

Neither April nor Jordan spoke for a moment.

'Oh God. Am I making a big deal over nothing?' Will asked.

April reached out and touched his hand.

'We've all been involved with someone who makes us feel like we're overreacting, like we're imagining problems where there are none,' she said. 'It's one of the many downsides of dating men.'

'I hear that,' Will said glumly.

'I like Patrick, you know I do,' she continued. 'But I know what I'm talking about when I say: he is acting like a wasteman.'

'Really?'

'Pure fuckboy behaviour. Not becoming of America's sweetheart at all. I'm very disappointed.' She speared a stray piece of feta with a fork and popped it into her mouth.

'Jordy?' Will asked, turning to his suspiciously silent friend.

'I'm going to kill him,' Jordan said calmly. 'I am going to actually kill him. I'm going to have my own Netflix documentary after I murder Patrick Lake and chop his body into tiny little pieces.'

'You'll do no such thing,' said April.

'How dare he? How dare he!' Jordan's level voice rose to a screech. 'So he fucks you, this man who has been controlling the last month of your life—'

'I wouldn't say controlling,' Will interjected.

'He makes you sign that insane document and basically frog-marches you back into the closet, forces you to sneak around like thieves in the night—'

'Again, he didn't force me.'

'And then when you do this thing for him, something special and secret and just for the two of you, in other words exactly what he wanted, something that sounded bloody hot, by the way—'

'It really was.'

'He has the audacity to go cold, kick you out afterwards? No.' Jordan began to shake his head vehemently, the gold cross that dangled from his left ear swinging like a blade. 'Nope. I do not think so.'

'I think he was just stressed,' said Will, suddenly regretting saying anything. Sharing this kind of intimate information, even with his two closest friends, was technically violating the NDA. God, why couldn't he do anything right?

'Don't you dare start making excuses for him,' Jordan snapped. 'I don't care that he's famous, or a superhero, or that he has a dick like a draught excluder. He's your boyfriend, and he made you feel like shit.'

'I don't even know that he is my boyfriend,' said Will. 'We haven't exactly defined the relationship.'

'Are you joking?' Jordan huffed. 'You've been spending every available minute together.'

'He's met your sister,' April pointed out.

'He's been chasing you ever since he first saw you as a redhead in a black cocktail dress, for heaven's sake,' Jordan added, slapping the counter. 'And he hurt you.'

'I...' Will paused, as if considering crucial new evidence. 'You're right. You're totally right!'

'As per.' Jordan blinked slowly, as if tired by the burden of always being right.

'He made me feel really shit right after having sex with me. That's so not OK.'

'Literally what I just said.'

'So... what do I do?'

'Talk to him about it,' said April.

'Hmm.' Will nodded noncommittally.

'What have his messages been like since last night?' she asked.

'Hmm.'

'He hasn't even texted you?' Jordan animatedly began gathering his phone and his keys from where he had discarded them on the countertop earlier. 'Right. April, hold down the fort. Will, you are coming with me.'

Jordan insisted on driving him across town to the set to confront Patrick there and then. It all felt very empowering and get-up-and-go until they ended up getting caught in traffic on Digbeth High Street because they forgot that half the city was in a perpetual state of being dug up and repaved.

Will would have thought that sitting still behind a car blaring 'Despacito' would kill any sense of momentum his outrage had acquired, but instead his anger simmered in the passenger seat, poisoning the air.

'Go,' said Jordan eventually. 'We'll be here ages. You go and have it out, and I'll catch up with you when I find somewhere to park.'

Will thanked him, got out of the car, and walked with a fiery urgency, cutting through increasingly quiet side streets until he reached the vast warehouse that had been turned into a sound stage. He had been here only once before, accompanying Patrick to work one morning behind the blacked out windows of a car. This time, he marched straight towards the gate.

'Can I help you, buddy?' A security guard the approximate size of a telephone box stepped into his view, obstructing his path.

'Jesus,' said Will. 'Where did you come from? You're enormous.'

The guard, an American presumably flown in along with the rest of the production, did not look amused.

'Can I help you, buddy?' he repeated, tone so empty that Will wasn't entirely sure he understood the meaning of the word 'buddy'.

'Yes, please,' he said. 'I…'

Fuck. He had not thought this far ahead. He'd simply envisioned storming onto the set, flinging open the door to Patrick's trailer, and letting him have it. Except of *course* he wouldn't be allowed on set. Will wondered how many random fans had made their way down here over the last several weeks, hoping for a glimpse of their favourite actor. He couldn't exactly say, 'I'm here to see my boyfriend, we're about to have a massive row and I think you'd take my side if you heard all the gory details.'

'I have an appointment,' he said, finally.

The guard looked him up and down, probably wondering who he could possibly have business with, and then asked: 'What kind of appointment?'

'The really important kind?' said Will, defeat already creeping into his voice. This was humiliating. He was losing before he even got a chance to *have* the fight.

'Will? Is that you?' A familiar voice called across the lot. Will saw the Captain Kismet suit, and the snakes in his stomach began to squirm once again before the figure removed the flight goggles, and he saw that it was Corey.

'It's OK,' Corey said to the guard. 'You can let him in. He's with me.'

'You're a stuntman?' the guard asked, appraising Will once again.

'What, like it's hard?' Will said, indignantly, swanning through the gate.

Corey waved him inside and pointed him towards Patrick's trailer.

'Gotta run, mate,' he said. 'Big day for the ol' crash test dummy here. Good to see you!'

'Thanks,' said Will. 'Good luck with your... erm... crashing!'

He entered the trailer, planning to sit and wait and plan how to carefully explain his feelings to Patrick. But sitting was beyond him, and so he paced, taking in the script pages and bottled water and tastefully packaged black tubs of creatine and whey and collagen and God only knew what else, trying to calm down, until he heard the door open behind him.

'What are you doing here?' Patrick asked. He wasn't wearing his costume, but rather a black bodysuit covered in neon green dots, which Will guessed would later act as a canvas for all manner of CGI wizardry. Right now, however, Patrick looked mildly ridiculous.

Will suppressed a laugh. 'It's nice to see you too.'

'You can't be here.' Patrick's voice was steady and cold. 'You know you can't be here.'

'I needed to talk to you.' Will put his hands on his hips in what he hoped was a power stance, and not a pose that made him look like a little teapot.

'We'll talk later.' Patrick turned to go.

'I think the everloving fuck *not*,' said Will. 'We are going to talk now, because I am your boyfriend and I am upset.'

'Will.' Patrick pinched the bridge of his nose and drew in a sharp breath. 'I am at *work*. This is my job. You can't just show up here. Every minute we get held up costs a lot of money.'

Will was being spoken to like a petulant child, and he wondered now if that's how he was behaving.

'I'm sorry,' he began. 'I should have thought...' The words died on his lips. 'No. I'm *not* sorry, actually. I want to talk now.'

Patrick sighed. 'Fine,' he said. 'What about?'

'Are you serious?' Will frowned. 'About last night.'

Patrick pursed his lips and folded his arms.

'No, don't do that,' said Will. 'Don't act like you're above talking about sex.'

'Now is not the time or place.'

'You're right. The time and place to talk was last night, in your hotel, but you kicked me out. You made me feel so used, Patrick. It was horrible.'

'I made *you* feel that way?' Patrick's lip curled up. 'There was fucking cum on my work stuff, Will. Do you have any idea how inappropriate that is? All of it? What were you thinking?'

'I was thinking that I wanted to make you happy,' said Will. 'And I'm pretty sure I did. And then you just shut down. Froze me out. I thought we were beyond that. I don't know, I thought that you'd—'

'God, you're so convinced you know everything, aren't you? So sure you know me better than I know myself. It's condescending. It's annoying. Because the truth is' – Patrick pointed at him, jabbing the air furiously – 'you don't *listen*. Not really. I tell you, over and over, I have to keep my work separate from the rest of my life, and you show up. I set a boundary, and you come prancing right over it.'

'That is bollocks,' said Will, 'and you know it. I have done nothing but try to respect your boundaries. This entire relationship has been on your terms. Your bloody lawyers made sure of that.'

'You don't get to throw that in my face. You knew the score when we started seeing each other. You agreed to it.'

Will felt a lump in his throat at Patrick's cold words. 'I did. But you should have known how unfair you were being. How impossible it is to be with someone when you can't really *be* with them.'

'I *am* with you! I am with you *all the time!*' Patrick yelled. 'I met your family, I brought you to Audra's party, I even put on a fucking dress and a wig so we could go out together. I have given more of myself to you than anyone else in my life, Will, and God, it's never enough! You need so much! I can't handle it!'

The words hit too familiar, fresh and sharp.

'If I'm so difficult to be with, then why are you even bothering?' Will asked.

'I'm starting to ask myself the same thing,' Patrick said it calmly, which was worse somehow. It was a sad fact, like he had just noticed it had begun to rain.

'You don't get to treat me like an inconvenience, Patrick.'

'You've always known exactly what I was able to offer. It's not my fault if you thought that would change.'

'I can't help it. I want more. I deserve more. We both do.'

'Then I don't know what to tell you.' Patrick cleared his throat. 'I should have known you wouldn't be able to handle it.'

'You act like things are the same for us. They're not. How you move through the world is very different from the way I do.'

'I know my work comes with some advantages—'

'I'm not talking about your work,' said Will. 'I'm talking about how nobody takes issue with your sexuality, because you keep it private. And that is your choice. I don't know that I ever *had* a choice. The first person to call me gay was my PE teacher. I was eight. He knew before I had even figured it out for myself.' He flapped a wrist pointedly. 'I've never been able to hide anything.'

Patrick looked down, then back to the trailer door. Will could feel the seconds he had left with Patrick slipping away, knew that this was maybe the last time they would ever be in the same room together, his last chance to get Patrick to understand how he felt.

'I—' he began.

'You really need to go,' Patrick said.

There were no magic words, Will realised. No spell he could cast that would reverse the flow of time or change the reality of their lives. This was it. This was all they would ever get.

'Fine,' he said. 'Bye, Patrick.'

He walked numbly out of the trailer and back out across the lot towards the exit. Digbeth looked the same as ever, which felt incorrect. The graffiti and cigarette butts and broken bottles from overturned bins had not changed. But hadn't everything changed?

'Will?' He felt a hand on his shoulder.

'I finally found a place to park,' Jordan said when he turned around. 'Are you OK? What happened? What did he say?'

'It's over,' said Will, almost flinching as he heard his own voice. 'It's over,' he repeated, and Jordan pulled him into a tight hug.

'I'm so sorry,' he said, rubbing Will's back. 'That bastard.'

'I don't understand what happened,' he mumbled into the side of Jordan's bleached buzzcut. 'I went to talk. I just wanted to talk...'

'Bastard. The absolute bastard.'

'Jordan. I... I think I...'

'It's OK. It's going to be alright.' Jordan's hand made a soothing circular motion on his back. 'You're better off without him. Good riddance.'

'What?' Will lurched away from Jordan. 'What do you mean?'

'I mean, he really upset you,' said Jordan. 'It's probably for the best that it's over.'

Will *had* been upset. But he hadn't intended to go to the set and start a huge argument. He'd wanted to wait for Patrick to cool off so they could talk properly. That had been his plan. Until.

'Why did you make me come here?' he asked. 'You always think a big, dramatic confrontation is the right thing to do.' The more he thought about it, the more this felt like typical Jordan, inserting himself into everything. 'I can't believe I let you talk me into this.' He turned to walk away, hearing Jordan's footsteps following soon after.

'OK, first of all, I didn't talk you into anything,' said Jordan, catching up to him again, 'other than standing up for yourself.'

Will stopped in his tracks and turned to face him. 'You don't understand what's at stake.'

'Some cishet wet dream's reputation? Who *cares*, Will? He's leaving anyway.'

'Were you trying to sabotage me?'

'What?'

'It makes sense,' said Will. 'You've always been the little star. Lording it over everyone at the bar. And you love how people recognise you from your videos. I wondered, when I started doing drag, if you might get a little sour at me getting attention.'

'You sound crazy.'

'I didn't want to think it,' Will continued, taking a step towards Jordan, his rage gathering momentum and his thoughts racing to keep up, 'but you're *jealous*. Aren't you.' He brought his face right up to Jordan's. 'That my world suddenly got so much bigger than yours? That I'm the one getting us into parties with movie stars?'

Jordan took a step back. 'Parties that you're not legally allowed to talk about because your boo is a massive closet case. I'm not jealous, Will, I feel *sorry* for you.'

'It's none of your business, Jordan! It's *my* relationship.'

'Oh, sure, and when you get treated like shit, I'm supposed to just not say anything. That's not how this works, doll.'

Will paused. 'Are you in love with me? Is that it?'

'I was wrong before. *Now* you sound mental.'

'Then why can't you stand to see me happy with someone else?'

'You're not happy, Will! You've been fucking miserable, and too dickmatised to see it!'

'How the hell do you know?'

'You've been changing, Will. Don't tell me you don't know what I'm talking about, because I won't believe you. You've been dimming your shine. Making yourself smaller, quieter. To fit in with *him*.'

'That's ridiculous.'

'Is it? I'm not the only one who's noticed, you know. April has, too. I bet even Margo has. And as for everyone else…'

'What do you mean, everyone else?' Will could hear his voice getting higher and higher, but he couldn't stop it. 'You've been talking about me? Who have you been talking to? This is a *secret*, Jordan.'

Jordan flicked his wrist scornfully. 'Oh, calm down, nobody has mentioned Patrick by name. It's not about him. It's about *you*. You've been taking fewer gigs. Not showing up for the story hour. Faye is worried about you. All the girls are. It's like now you've found your straight-acting fantasy, you don't care about your community anymore.'

Will bristled. 'Maybe you want to ask yourself why,' he said coolly, 'after all these years of being such a beloved hero in our *community*, you still haven't found anyone to love you.'

He knew he'd gone too far before the words even left his mouth, but out they tumbled, and he saw the hurt blossom like a bruise across Jordan's beautiful face, a wound that had already been right under the surface. A pain Will had known was there.

'Fuck you, Will,' said Jordan. 'And fuck your coward of a boyfriend, too.'

He turned and walked away, and Will let him go, too ashamed to even try to apologise. His tendency to shoot from the hip was nothing new. Unfortunately, he'd always had terrible aim.

27

1950

The headquarters of *Wonder* Magazine consisted of two rooms above a deli on the Lower East Side. Walter Haywood welcomed Charles and ushered him through the first room, where his secretary Sheila sat hammering away at a typewriter, into the second, much larger room, his office.

'Sit, sit,' he said, circling the large desk and taking his own seat opposite Charles.

'What's this about, Walter?' Charles asked.

Walter's fingers drummed over some papers on the desk, and Charles recognised them immediately. It was the final Captain Kismet story he and Iris had been commissioned to deliver. An open ending to the current saga, leaving opportunity for further adventures in the future, just as had been requested.

'I like you, Charles,' said Walter. 'Your work is decent, you do it on time, and you make me money.'

'Thank you,' said Charles. 'I really think there are so many exciting directions for Captain Kismet to go. So many more stories—'

'I agree,' Walter interrupted. 'But this?' He picked up the pages that Charles had mailed over the day before. '*This*, Charles, is pornography. We are a *family* magazine.'

'Pornography?' Charles frowned. 'I don't understand.'

Walter sighed and flipped to one of the last pages of the story. Penny Haven's experiment had torn open a vortex in time and space, and she was on the very brink of being pulled in when at the very last minute, Ranger and Axel had arrived to grab hold of her. Or at least, one version of her. For every instance where Penny was rescued, there were other possible realities where she had fallen into the rift, causing her body and mind to scatter across the omniverse, atomised. Iris had been especially pleased with that twist: the reader got the satisfying moral ending of seeing Penny saved from the dangers of her own boundless ambition, but now there were countless versions of the same woman out there in the ether, primed to show up as heroines, villainesses, or whatever else future stories might require. One woman's multitudes.

But what's this? While Penny, restored to her senses, is busy shutting down her machine and closing the vortex, who should appear from nowhere but Omega Man! He has been plotting for months now to destroy Captain Kismet, not by fighting him one-on-one, but by taking what he holds most dearly. Kismet sees Omega materialise, wielding an energy gun, and leaps in front of Penny to once again protect her... but Omega's dark aim falls on Axel, his most trusted friend. Omega has time to fire off just one deadly shot before, with a terrible 'NO!', Kismet punches him so hard that the monstrous being is propelled out of the moon's gravity, condemned to float endlessly in the void of space for as long as his shattered exo-suit can provide air.

Kismet rushes to Axel's side, cradling his friend's broken body, and begins to weep. He has fought so hard to protect the people of the Earth and has been able to do so only because of Kid Kismet, the boy who fell from the stars and pledged to be his ally.

'His wounds are too severe,' cries Penny. 'There... there is nothing we can do.'

'How lucky I have been,' says Axel softly. 'That of all possible planets, I crash-landed on yours...'

Ranger frowns. These words! They are so familiar. On a distant world, he held a woman in his arms as the life bled from her and she thanked the universe for bringing them together.

'Sura?' he asked.

'I told you,' the voice of the princess comes from Axel's lips, 'that when the people of Zalia die, they do not perish, but ascend to a higher dimension. I have been watching you, my dear captain, all these years. It was my hand that guided Axilon to you, to be your friend, to save you from your own loneliness.'

'Sura.' Ranger sobbed. 'I already lost you. I cannot lose another.'

'You never lost me,' Sura spoke through Axel. 'And there is still time. An ancient Zalian magic that might yet revive your fallen prince.'

'What is it?' Ranger asked. 'Anything.'

'We must reach across planes,' Sura told him. 'My life force in this new dimension is strong. I can lend Axilon some of my own energy, to heal his broken body.'

'How?'

'To bridge our worlds, I need a conduit,' she said. 'My energy must pour through somebody else into him.'

Axel's hand rose up to meet Ranger's cheek.

'One last kiss?' she asked. 'To save a life?'

The final panel of the page depicted Ranger lowering his head over Axel's, their lips barely touching, a golden, life-saving light flowing from one man's mouth into another, while the Earth glowed like a jewel in the black sky above them.

'This is obscene,' said Walter.

'I think it's beautiful,' said Charles. 'Ranger got to speak with his lost love again. That love helped to save his friend.'

'You can try to bamboozle me with your mumbo jumbo, Ambrose, but all I see is Captain Kismet kissing a boy. And it sickens me.'

'He wasn't really kissing him!' protested Charles. 'He was kissing *her*!'

'I don't care,' Walter said, his patience waning like the cigarette in his hand. 'I am not putting this filth in my magazine.'

'Alright,' said Charles. 'Give me and the writer a little more time, and we can come up with an alternative ending. Something less… controversial.' He had known, of course, that Walter would almost certainly hate this final issue, that even with the pretext of Sura's ghost and Ranger's sweetheart Penny standing mere steps away, the image of Ranger cradling Axel would be too much. But when Iris had told him how the story ended, how Captain Kismet's truest and greatest strength was his love, Charles had been so excited that he'd insisted they at least try.

So often an act of creation was an act of dilution, of compromise: grabbing at the soft purity of an idea, squeezing it so hard to hold it still that it became dented and bruised beyond all recognition. Every early sketch felt like a crude blasphemy, a child's mural daubed on a temple wall. In this story, Iris had captured exactly what she wanted to say, and his drawings had brought that to life, given it meaning. He could not have been prouder if the pages had come to life and called him 'father'.

'You're not hearing me, Charles,' said Walter. 'When I say that I will not publish this filth, I am also referring to you.'

'Me?'

'You and your kind.' Walter stubbed out his cigarette, any goodwill he had been feigning towards Charles evaporating along with the smoke. 'This is a family business, Charles. My son comes in here and helps out after school. Did you really expect that I would allow you to keep on coming around?'

Charles was so horrified by Walter's implication that he could not formulate a response, which Walter seemed to interpret as confirmation that his suspicions were correct.

'I want you out of my office and out of my magazine, Charles,' he said. 'Now.'

'Fine,' said Charles, the rage finally coming. 'We'll take Captain Kismet elsewhere. People love him, not your cheap rag, Walter. The readers will follow their hero.' His cheeks spiked with red heat, and he could only imagine he was glowing scarlet like Axel.

'That's where you're wrong again.' Walter lit another cigarette. 'The adventures of Captain Kismet and his assorted companions will very much continue, here at *Wonder* Magazine.'

'What?'

'Didn't you read your contract?'

'My contract?'

'I own Captain Kismet.' Walter blew smoke across his desk, directly into Charles's eyes. 'I always have.'

Charles could tell with a sick certainty that Walter was not bluffing. He and Iris had both been so swept up in the thrill of the story they were telling and the money they were being paid to do so that they had taken Walter at his word. What utter fools they were.

'But he is not your invention,' he said, weakly. 'You're stealing him.'

'This is America,' said Walter, shrugging. 'It's not stealing if we both signed that piece of paper.'

'It's not right.' To his own indignant fury, Charles's eyes were watering from the smoke. 'We'll... we'll take you to court.'

'This is *America*,' Walter repeated. 'I don't think either of you are going to want to draw any more attention to yourselves than you already have, do you?'

The threat wasn't even veiled. Walter could report Charles and Iris as any number of things. Pornographers. Predators. Communists. And he would be believed.

Charles wanted to tell Walter Haywood so much. That Captain Kismet's costume was as inspired by the leather men he saw in the bars as it was by an actual pilot's uniform. That he'd modelled Sura's appearance on a working girl he'd known in the war. That Axel was Iris's tribute to her beloved, fey brother. That Penny Haven was almost entirely their old friend Joey, who much like one of Tolkien's grand elves, had gone far into the West where Joey could be short for Joanne. That this world they'd created, the world currently making *Wonder* Magazine such a hit, was built and populated by inverts.

But it didn't matter. Because *this* world had its own rules, and Charles and Iris had broken them all.

'Now get out of my office.' Walter grinned, and it was the ugliest sight Charles had ever seen outside of wartime.

'He can't do that,' said Iris for the third or fourth time. 'He just can't.'

'He can.' Charles took another swig of brandy and massaged his temples, while Iris stood still, hands fixed to her hips, vibrating with anger.

'I should go down there,' she continued. 'Give that schmuck a piece of my mind.'

'All you'll give him is an excuse to inform on us to the Un-American Activities Committee,' Charles snapped.

'Well we have to do something!'

'No, we don't,' said Charles. 'We lost, Iris.'

A knock sounded. Charles and Iris shared a wordless look – *Are you expecting company? No, are you? No.* – before Charles rose and walked to the door.

Eleanor stood in the hallway wrapped in a man's coat, her fashionably short hair dishevelled, an enormous pair of sunglasses obscuring her eyes. Once Charles had opened the door, she removed them, and he heard Iris gasp behind him as they both took in her black eye.

'Come inside,' he said immediately, leading her in by the hand. He felt a rush of protectiveness over her, standing in their draughty hallway, looking so small and frail in that oversized coat. He realised, for the first time, that she couldn't be much older than twenty-five.

'What happened?' Iris asked, enveloping Eleanor in her arms. 'Oh, darling, what happened?'

'He gets like this sometimes,' Eleanor said, her voice stuffy with snot and tears. 'I thought it was getting better. I thought I could manage it.' Iris led her to the couch and eased her down onto the seat. 'It was bad this time,' she continued, her gaze unfocused. 'The worst he has ever been. He only stopped because I told him…'

Her hands moved instinctively to her stomach, and Charles swore under his breath.

'Oh, sweetheart,' Iris whispered.

'I don't know what to do,' Eleanor said, her breathing bubbling up into tiny sobs once more. 'I can't leave him. He works for my father.'

'Yes, you can,' said Charles. 'You will.'

Iris looked over to him gratefully.

'I can't,' Eleanor said, eyes streaming again. 'The baby.'

'I shall kill him,' said Iris. 'Truly. That man. That damn man, I am going to kill him.'

Charles could tell she meant it. The fury in her eyes, it was not hot, the kind that burns itself out like a candle. It was cold. Icy. Dangerous.

'Iris, stop,' he said as she made her way to the door. She ignored him. 'Iris,' he repeated, 'stop right there.' She froze, and he could tell it was sheer surprise more than anything else. He rarely ever spoke to her that way; like he was the man and she his wife. He didn't much like the sound of it in his own mouth even now, but he couldn't have Iris marching across town all gung-ho, causing even more trouble when their situation was already so precarious.

'We have to be careful,' he said, more measured now. 'We have to *think*.'

Iris lingered in the doorway, as if considering ignoring his counsel and carrying on with whatever half-baked revenge she wanted. Then her eyes drifted back to the couch, where Eleanor's weeping had subsided into the occasional pained sniffle, and she begrudgingly relented. She returned to the couch, where Eleanor immediately clung to her.

What are we going to do? he thought. *What the hell are we going to do?*

'Iris,' he said, halting at her baleful glare. 'What…'

'Yes?' she asked, obstinacy softening.

He felt ridiculous asking out loud, but forged ahead: 'What would Captain Kismet do?'

Iris did not laugh, as he had thought she might. She gave the question thought, and when she answered, it felt immediately correct. The captain was her own invention, after all. She was the closest thing anyone in this room had to a real hero.

'Don't attack or avenge when you can protect,' she said. 'Don't destroy what you can't rebuild.'

He looked over at Eleanor, who had curled up on the sofa with her head in Iris's lap, then to his wife, who was tenderly stroking Eleanor's hair, and said: 'Alright, I have an idea.'

The journey into Manhattan took long enough for Charles to question his plan, abandon it entirely, and then recommit several times over. By the time he reached the hotel off Washington Square, he was certain that he was doing the right thing.

He knew Walter Haywood's influence and was sure that he and Iris would be unable to get their stories published anywhere else of note in New York. He could picture already how the rumours would start to spread about them, beginning with nasty little inferences and eventually turning outright ugly. Doors would be slammed shut, calls would go unreturned. Charles had seen it happen to others, had thought himself lucky, had even congratulated himself on being clever enough to avoid such trouble. Until he invited it with his own damned hubris.

The city was off limits now. Their only options were to choose escape or wait for exile.

The door to Dickie's room was ajar when Charles reached his floor, and for a single dreadful moment he thought that he'd disappeared, as he had in Istanbul, that fate had conspired to separate them. But when he pushed the door fully open, there was Dickie Oswin in his shirtsleeves, suitcase open on the bed.

'What good timing,' said Dickie, pushing the door closed behind Charles before giving him a kiss. 'I was just about to call you.'

'You were?' asked Charles, glancing over Dickie's shoulder at the suitcase.

'I've been summoned home.' Dickie said, resuming his packing. 'Back to Blighty, I go.'

Charles watched as Dickie rapidly, efficiently folded clothes, retrieved his shaving kit and comb from the tiny bathroom, and put on his jacket. Charles could have sworn there had been more belongings scattered everywhere, more signs of life, but in mere minutes the room had become bare.

'I would not have left without saying goodbye,' said Dickie, catching the slightly lost look in Charles's eyes. 'Not this time.'

'What if it didn't have to be goodbye?' Charles asked, snapping back to the moment. 'I came here to tell you about a plan.'

'A plan?' Dickie said, amused. 'Do tell.'

Charles stepped forward and took Dickie's hands in his.

'We're going away,' he said. 'Iris and me. And Eleanor. All of us, we're leaving. Tonight.'

'Leaving?' Dickie asked. 'Where exactly do you plan to go?'

'Into the West!' Charles grinned. 'We will find a place to live, and any work we can, and Eleanor is going to have a baby, and we will raise it together. Think of it, Richard. What a grand adventure.' He squeezed Dickie's fingers. 'You could come with us.'

'Charles.' Dickie pulled his fingers away. 'This is madness.'

'Maybe so.' Charles shrugged. 'Perhaps it is all a childish fantasy. They are my stock in trade. Am I so silly, to want one to be real? To want more than a life where we have to hide and sneak and lie, like crooks? A life free to be ourselves?'

The mirth drained from Dickie's eyes, and he looked at Charles with genuine sorrow.

'It would be quite a thing,' he said. 'But you know I can't do that.'

Charles felt a sharp pang in his heart, and nodded. He did know. Had known all the way over here. But he would have regretted it for the rest of his life if he did not at least ask, and in asking the question, let Dickie Oswin know the depth of his feeling.

What chance did he have of ever being a half-decent father, if he couldn't muster up enough courage for that?

He cupped Dickie's chin in his hand and kissed him softly, savouring the tickle of that moustache one final time. His Errol Flynn. His matinee idol. His secret and only darling.

'Then I think this is goodbye,' he said, finally. 'My love.'

ACT THREE:
KISMET

'Someone, I tell you, will remember us, even in another time.'
Sappho

28

While the rest of the cast and crew caught a connecting flight from JFK to LAX, Patrick hired a car and drove to his parents' house in New Jersey. He called them en route to let them know he was coming, and an hour later parked up outside the four-bedroom he'd bought them in a neighbourhood his dad had used to make fun of.

'Patrick!' His mother stood on the porch and watched him walk up the driveway. He gave her a hug, breathing in the smell of her, a combination that hadn't changed in thirty years: hairspray, cold cream, and a heady cloud of Elizabeth Arden perfume that masked the lingering whiff of cigarette smoke, because as far as Janet Carmichael told anyone, she hadn't touched those filthy things since the Bush administration.

'I'm making potato salad,' she announced, extricating herself from his arms. Patrick realised he had no idea how long he had been clinging onto her. 'Your dad is out in the yard grilling up dinner. Oh, he is so good on that thing. What is it about men and fire, you're all a bunch of cavemen when it comes down to it.'

Patrick followed her into the kitchen, letting his mother's words wash over him like a white noise machine as she asked him would he mind setting the table, and telling him about what his various cousins were up to, and wasn't it just wonderful that Melissa was pregnant again, weren't babies such a blessing, and no that *wasn't* a hint but when *was* Patrick going to make her a grandmother? It all came out like a monologue from some kind of domestic drama, requiring no response or input from Patrick other than the occasional nod and hum. This was the way it had always been. Her chatter was a fortress of defence against awkward silence, or even worse, the possibility of having a real conversation. That was how things went in the Carmichael family. Patrick's father rarely spoke, his mother spoke enough for both of them, and nobody ever actually *said* anything.

'Frank,' she called out of the open kitchen door into the yard, 'unless you want me to serve those steaks in an ashtray, I think it's safe to bring them inside now. Come say hi to your son.' She turned back to Patrick. 'He is so good on that thing.'

A moment later, Patrick's father entered holding the heralded steaks on a plate.

'Pat.' He nodded in Patrick's direction, laying the steaks at the centre of the table, in pride of place, surrounded by the potato salad, mac and cheese, greens, and rolls his mother had prepared and which had undoubtedly taken more effort than a few slabs of meat on a barbecue.

'Hey, Dad,' he said in return, hardly expecting any more fanfare than that. It wasn't like he'd been across the Atlantic working for the last few months. Or that he lived on the other side of the country and only made it home for Christmas or the occasional birthday.

'Eat! Eat!' his mother commanded, and they each took a seat. The kitchen was large, airy, and full of light – a real selling point when Patrick had brought them both to view it after signing his ten-year contract with Wonder Studios – but as they sat slicing and chewing in near-silence, he couldn't help but think longingly of a more cramped kitchen table in Birmingham, where everyone talked over each other so badly it was amazing they had time to eat anything.

'This is all really good, Mom,' he said. 'The steak's great, Dad.'

'Lucky we had enough to go around,' his dad said, not looking up from his plate.

'You gave us no notice!' Patrick's mother tapped his arm playfully.

'Sorry for just dropping in unannounced,' he said.

He waited for one of them to ask why he was here, but all he heard was the light scraping of knives on plates, and then, eventually dinner was over. His mother got the men each a fresh beer and made herself a cup of coffee, and then they all went and sat in the living room, a whole new space in which to not talk.

'Did I tell you cousin Melissa is having another baby?' she asked.

'Yes, Mom, you told me.'

'Isn't it wonderful?'

'So wonderful. I'll have to send her a present.'

'Oh, that would be nice!' She sipped her coffee. 'So nice.'

'I'm really happy for her,' said Patrick. 'Happy she's happy.' He paused. 'I don't think *I'm* happy.'

'For Melissa?'

'No, Mom. I mean. I'm not happy. I thought I was, for a long time. I loved my job.'

'We're all very proud of you,' his mother said, almost automatically.

'I thought that was enough,' he said, 'but it's not. Work. It's just... work. You know?'

'Hard work isn't supposed to be fun,' his dad said. 'Not that I'd call your job *hard*.'

'I know, Dad,' said Patrick, skipping right on past the dig. 'But it's my job, and I enjoy doing it, and I guess I'm just realising you need more to build a life on.'

His mother looked at him expectantly.

Here goes nothing, he thought. 'I was seeing someone. His name is Will.'

Patrick's mother took another sip of coffee, looking mildly disappointed, and Patrick wondered what it was she had wanted to hear. His dad gave no indication he had heard him at all.

'You'd have liked him,' Patrick said. He paused and laughed. 'Actually, you'd probably have hated him. But I liked him. God, I liked him so much. He wasn't like anyone I'd ever met. I don't think I'd ever even *met* a drag queen in person before the night I met him.' He felt the air pressure in the room shift, but he couldn't stop. 'He was so funny and weird, and he danced like the world was ending, and he had such a beautiful singing voice.' Patrick's throat thickened. 'I fucked up,' he said. 'I ruined it all.'

'Language, Patrick, please,' his mother sighed.

'I think I loved him, Mom.' His voice cracked, and his eyes began to sting. 'I wasn't sure. I mean, I've never been in love before. How can you tell for sure? How did you know, with Dad?'

'You know what,' his mother blurted, jumping up from the couch. 'I bought a key lime pie yesterday and forgot all about it!'

'I don't want dessert, Mom—'

'You boys sit right here, I'll be back in a jiff.' She vanished back into the kitchen, and Patrick was left alone with his father. The two of them sat in silence, and would have continued to, but Patrick's sinuses suddenly stung, and a single sob erupted from him with such violence he feared for the commemorative Niagara Falls plates on the wall. He pressed the heels of his hands into his eyes, ineptly trying to stem the coming tears.

'Sorry,' he said, sniffing. 'This is embarrassing.'

'What are you doing, son?' his dad asked, looking at him now. 'Crying over some fag?'

'Jesus, Dad. You can't say that.'

His dad shook his head and shrugged. 'You know what I mean,' he said. 'You're gay, but you're still a man about it. Just look at you. This other guy, though. All that… wearing girls' clothes… I don't like it. It's weird. If you wanna be a woman just be a woman. They can do that now, right? No need to put on a big song and dance and make us all watch.'

'That's not… He isn't…' Patrick felt the sting of tears again, but he refused to let them come this time.

'I'm not homophobic or nothing,' his dad continued, as if that was in *any* way his call to make. 'I just don't understand why everything has to be such a big deal these days. You do you, just don't do it in my face.'

Any threat of tears was now gone. Patrick felt suddenly still and cool. Water you could drown in.

'I never rubbed anything in your face,' he said curtly.

'I know you didn't,' his father replied. 'That's what I was just talking about.'

'Maybe I should have a bit more.' Patrick's jaw clicked. 'I knew you loved me, but that you didn't have any idea how to talk about me being gay, so I kept my love life completely private. The guys I dated, the experiences I had.' His dad grimaced, but Patrick forged on. 'The time I was sixteen and I met a guy off the internet, but when I got in his car he was ten years older than he said he was, and so I jumped out when we stopped at a red light and ran all the way home. I was really freaked out, and I wanted to tell someone what had happened. I wanted to tell you or Mom, but that felt impossible.'

'There's a lot of pervs out there,' his dad said, taking a swig of beer, avoiding his eye. 'That's for sure.'

'That's not what I'm saying, Dad.' Patrick clasped his hands together. 'Then when I was eighteen, I was best friends with Mickey Callahan, remember him? We used to make out after football practice. I thought I loved him. I was *so* sure he loved me back. And then he took Sarah Costello to prom, and my heart was fucking *broken*, and again, I didn't say a word. Because no matter how much pain I was in, my top priority was not making you uncomfortable.' He let out a short, flat laugh. 'That's *wild*, right? You're my dad. You were always the toughest guy I knew, but I thought you couldn't handle a simple conversation.

'I wonder why I felt that way,' he continued. 'I mean, I could've come to you, right?'

His dad said nothing.

'*My parents are nice people*,' Patrick told anyone when they asked. What a detestable word that was. *Nice*. A free coffee in exchange for a fully stamped loyalty card was nice. A stranger giving you their seat on the bus was nice. Couldn't he expect more from the people who were supposed to love him? Wasn't that allowed?

'Because you *knew* I was gay,' Patrick said to his father. 'I came out to you when I was a teenager, and that's not the kind of thing you forget about your son. Right?'

His dad's mouth tightened. Never a good sign. The kind of storm warning Patrick had spent his childhood attuned to.

'But,' he said, 'it felt like the moment I told you, it was like it never happened. We never talked about it. If I brought it up, Mom would smile and nod and ask zero questions, and you would grit your teeth like you did when I was six and I'd tell you all about my imaginary friend.'

'What did you want us to say?' his dad asked. 'You told us you were gay, we were fine with it, end of story. It's not like we kicked you out or anything.'

'No, you didn't. Thanks so much for that, by the way.' Patrick shook his head. 'Jesus. Will was right. The bar really is in hell.'

'What's that supposed to mean?'

Patrick didn't know how to say it in a way that would make his father understand. How coming out wasn't something you just did once. That every time he met someone new, every time he took a new job, he had to decide: *Am I safe here?* Queer people came out every day, or they didn't, and either way it sucked, but that was just a part of life.

'I guess I just never thought I'd have to keep on coming out to my parents,' he said, 'or that it would be too much for them to be remotely interested in what's going on in my life.'

'Now that's not fair,' his dad snapped. 'You're making out like your mother and I are monsters. We fed you, we clothed you, we encouraged you with your acting even though there was a next-to-zero chance you were ever going to make a living from it.'

'You told me at eighteen that if I failed out of college, I shouldn't bother coming home at all.'

'I said no such thing.'

Patrick could have screamed. Laughed. Punched himself in the face. His father appeared to have gotten hold of the same complex contraption Penny Haven had used to tear a hole in space-time and was now living in a parallel universe where the events of his childhood had unfolded in an entirely different manner. Which made sense, he figured. Nobody wanted to cast themselves as the villain of the story.

'I just wish it was easier for me to talk to you guys about things,' he said. 'I mean, look at Mom. She legged it the minute I brought up Will.' As if conjured by the mere mention of his name, Patrick heard Will's voice in his head. *Legged it? You've gone native, mate.*

'Now, I won't have that in this house,' his father said, standing. 'I won't hear a word said against your mother. How dare you!'

'I'm not talking bad about Mom, I p-promise.' Patrick's cheeks grew hot, and he felt that awful, familiar shortness of breath. This was how interactions with his dad always devolved. He became that scared, stammering kid again. 'I just. I don't know,' he forced himself to carry on. 'I... I... I was hurting, and I just wanted to come home, and I'm realising now maybe I shouldn't have.'

'What is *that* supposed to mean?'

Patrick paused for a moment, to let his father know that the next words out of his mouth weren't being said in anger. He reminded himself of Mr Banks's advice, to know when to breathe and when to speak. Those hours spent in his room pacing and reciting. *This above all: to thine own self be true.* Polonius had been right about that. Even if he ended up dead.

'It means... It means...'

'What? It means what?' His father asked, that familiar impatience all over his face.

'It means I'm a f... I'm a fag, Dad,' he said. His father flinched. 'And just so you know, I'm the o-o-only person in this room who can use that word.'

'Hey now.' His dad prodded thin air with his finger. 'I won't be told what I can and can't do in my own house, Patrick. You're not in LA now!'

'You're right, I'm not. But I really should be. In fact, I think I'm g-g-g-gonna get going right now.' He stood up and walked towards the front door. 'See you at Christmas, Mom!' he yelled down towards the kitchen, then turned back to his father.

Breathe in. Hold. And release.

'Enjoy your house that your fag son paid for,' he said.

When Patrick got into the rental car outside, he turned on the ignition and then almost immediately turned it off, too angry to drive. He flicked on the stereo, dialled the volume all the way up, and screamed into his open palm.

Captain Kismet had, in total, six different origin stories. They all included the same basic ingredients: the test flight, the wormhole, the princess of a far-off planet. But each version differed in key ways. Sometimes Kismet was stoic and stern, other times he fell instantly in love with Sura. She was both a pulpy, anatomically improbable collection of scantily clad curves, and a sensibly attired general. The brutality of the conflict varied wildly.

Retcons were a fact of life in comics, stories were rebooted time and time again, the lore of previous tales overwritten and imagined anew. The next time Patrick Lake spoke to either of his parents, all memory of this unpleasant conversation would have been purged. Previously, that thought might have been a comfort; there would be no consequences for speaking to his father so bluntly.

But now, Patrick found himself wishing for consequences. If he could tell the truth and it was never spoken of again, how could it mean anything?

He shouldn't have come here. He felt so stupid now, wasn't even sure what he had hoped to find but knew that it had been a mistake to look for it in his parents.

Patrick dialled Simone as he bore left onto the turnpike. She answered after just one ring.

'Where are you?' she asked.

'On my way to Newark,' he told her. 'I'm coming home.'

Simone said she would have her assistant arrange his flight back to Los Angeles and email him the details. He would be in his own bed that night.

He rolled down all of the windows and hit the gas until the sounds of the wind and engine roared in his ears, drowning everything else out.

'I'm a fucking fag!' he yelled at the top of his lungs.

The only response he got was the honk of a horn as he veered into a different lane.

29

When Will showed up at Margo's house the day after Patrick left, with a bag in each hand and one under each eye, she didn't ask any questions. He got the impression she had heard about what happened one way or the other and knew better than to press him for more information, and she had left him to see himself up to the spare bedroom alone.

Will dropped his things just inside the door, kicked off his shoes, and got into bed, pulling the covers over his face and breathing in the scent of clean linen. He wasn't sure how long he stayed there, leaving only to attend to urgent bodily functions, just that at some point the sheets were no longer quite so fragrant. At first Margo would bring up cups of tea and plates of sandwiches, then she began to send Dylan to make the deliveries. Will would drink the tea but found that even a few small bites were all he could manage, resulting in the sandwiches he'd leave on the landing outside his door looking like a family of mice had nibbled them. Every day Margo would march in and noisily gather the collection of mugs that had accumulated around the bed like votive offerings, huffing and clanking them together, occasionally yanking back the curtains to let in a few harsh streaks of daylight, and Will would pretend to sleep through it.

He knew he couldn't stay like this forever. Knew his sister's patience was wearing thin. Knew that at some point April would be unable to keep covering for him at the bookshop, that Faye would need him at the library, that his life couldn't just *stop* because yet another man had decided he was too much trouble. He knew all of this practically, consciously, rationally. But the thought of showering and putting on clean clothes and going to work filled him with a bone-deep sense of fatigue. He felt like he had been stricken by some terrible virus that sapped him of all energy, rendering him as helpless as one of those bed-bound invalids featured in Victorian novels. That's what he was, he decided. An emotional haemophiliac. A consumptive downer whose sensitive disposition had been stricken by ill humours.

He would have been well-suited to that lifestyle. The swishy, fey, mildly sinister cousin who dispensed witty bon mots and ominous warnings to a virtuous heroine from his ambulatory chair.

There you go again, he thought. *Casting yourself as the side character. That man really did a number on you.* The voice, he realised, sounded rather a lot like Jordan. The knowledge came with a pang of guilt that twisted his empty stomach into a facsimile of indigestion. Each time he thought back to that awful fight, the things he had said, he inched closer to the possibility that he had been wrong. But this was a notion he was unwilling to explore further at present, and so he turned his pillow over and buried his face in the cool side until he drifted off once more.

Will was vaguely aware of the sound of the door to the bedroom opening, but then there was nothing. It was only when Margo spoke, jolting him fully into consciousness, that he knew she had been watching him from the doorway.

'Have you eaten today?' she asked.

'Not hungry,' he mumbled.

'Oh. That's a shame.'

Silence.

'I was just thinking I might make rarebit.'

More silence. Then:

'With the...'

'Gruyere and truffle? Yes. But on reflection, it's probably a bit heavy. Not to mention excessive, making it just for myself. Perhaps I'll just make do with a teacake.'

Will's head lifted ever so slightly from the pillow, an ordnance map of creases running river-like down his cheek.

'I might actually be a bit hungry,' he said, realising even as he made the pronouncement just how true it was.

'OK.' Margo didn't stray from the door.

'And rarebit might help.'

'Fine,' she said. 'But I expect you to shower before you come downstairs. The smell in here is threatening to ruin *my* appetite.'

Will stood under scalding water until he was certain he had scrubbed away every inch of the sweaty film he had acquired, then stood there some more for good measure. Once he was lobster-red and had shed at least one layer of skin, he threw on a clean hoodie and sweats and ventured downstairs, where he wolfed down lunch with a hunger that he hadn't felt in what seemed like forever.

Afterwards, he curled up on the sofa with his phone, watching YouTube videos and taking occasional sips from a pint of water. Margo looked like she was about to say something but then didn't, probably having decided that having him downstairs, showered and fed, was better than leaving him upstairs to fester.

Some time around four, the doorbell rang, and a moment later April walked into the living room, lunging forward and trapping

Will in a fierce embrace. Will returned the hug, patting April's back appreciatively, until it became apparent she was in no rush to release him from her asphyxiating affection, and he was forced to extricate himself with a heaving backwards push.

'That was from Jordan,' she said solemnly.

'Oh. Right. Well, thanks,' said Will, still catching his breath and suppressing the by-now-familiar clench in his gut at the sound of that name. 'And well done on a successful delivery.' He did not believe for one minute that Jordan had told her to give him a hug. It was peak April to try her best to smooth things over, but she couldn't *Parent Trap* Will and Jordan into coming to terms.

'What are we watching?'

'Brandy. The beagle. She's an amputee. Brandy the amputee beagle.'

'That sounds... super healthy for you,' April clambered onto the sofa next to him and after a few seconds of staring blankly at the screen, relented and dug into her pocket for her glasses. 'This video is from 2009?'

'Yeah.'

'And it looks like it was aggregated from an earlier source. That's how these things work, you know? None of the videos on *ImportantAnimalNews* are actually "news". They're clips that have been reappropriated and packaged more neatly.'

'So?' Will asked impatiently, irked at his attention being drawn away from his new dear friend Brandy.

'Nothing,' April said. 'It's just that... That dog is probably dead by now.'

'What?' Will felt a tightening in his chest, and April's eyes widened as she realised just how gravely she had erred.

'No! Oh, no, no!' She rubbed his shoulder. 'I'm sure Brandy is fine! I bet she's thriving, actually!'

But it was too late. Having replenished his body's moisture reserves, Will found himself crying again. Brandy had been through so much. She'd had such spirit. Such *pluck*. What a life.

'Brandy,' he wailed.

April cast a helpless glance around the room as if some whisperer of grief-stricken homosexuals might appear *ex nihilo* to console Will, but when none were forthcoming, she did the next best thing: grabbed the glass of water from the coffee table and tossed a good half of it in his face.

Will froze, more from shock than from the cold. The glass had been sitting there for nearly an hour, and was room temperature at best.

'I can't believe you did that,' he said.

April, seemingly just as stunned by her own actions, replied: 'Me neither.'

Neither of them spoke for a moment, both seemingly uncertain how to proceed. Then Will raised a hand to wipe the dripping water from his chin and began to laugh. Not because it was funny, necessarily, but because it seemed better than any alternative. After a few seconds, April started to laugh too, albeit nervously, like somebody who had just stepped off a rollercoaster. Once their awkward giggles had subsided, she re-joined him on the sofa, avoiding the growing damp patch surrounding Will.

'So,' she said. 'Patrick?'

'Gone.' Will placed a cushion in his lap and hugged it for comfort, even though Margo would be far from thrilled he was making it soggy in the process

'I know. But... are we talking *gone* gone? Or more like, he just needs to cool off and then he'll be back on a private jet with a bunch of flowers and an Oscar-worthy apology speech?'

'He's not that good an actor.' Will sank further into the sofa. 'And the first *Kismet* movie wasn't that great either.'

'You watched it?'

'I watched the trailer on YouTube. And a deeply off-putting video essay about what it did and didn't "get right" by a man with a patchy beard and vocal fry. I much prefer when you're the one giving TED talks on this stuff.'

April smiled. 'Thanks. Actually, on that subject...'

'Yeah?'

'Never mind.'

'April, what.'

'I finally found a half-decent lead on the Omega Issue.'

Will, whose face had all but buried itself behind the cushion, emerged, groundhog-like, at this revelation.

'You did?'

'Yeah. An old lady in California got in touch after I put out all those feelers online. Seemed a bit kooky, but sound.'

'Kooky but sound,' Will echoed. 'We know a thing or two about that.'

'I was going to put her in touch with Patrick,' said April. 'But if we hate him, I won't. I mean, obviously we hate him, he's a pillock of the highest order, but...'

'We don't hate him,' said Will. 'Not really. Or at least, not *fully*. He's just let a load of bullshit get inside his head and he shouldn't be with anyone until he's got that sorted out.'

'That's very mature of you.'

'I would also not be morally opposed to him getting just a tiny bit run over.'

'Yeah?'

'Nothing huge. A Nissan Micra or something. Just to wake him up a bit.'

'That sounds proportionate,' April said.

'You should give that lady Simone's number,' said Will. 'She'll be able to sniff out if she's legit or just a weirdo.'

April pursed her lips. 'Nah,' she said.

'No?'

'Nah. I can't hit the man with my car, on account of I don't have a car, or a licence, and because he is presently about five thousand miles away. But I can make sure he doesn't get everything he wants.'

'It's your decision,' said Will. 'Honestly.'

'Filming has finished now anyway,' said April. 'I doubt it would make any difference. I just don't think he deserves this.'

'Thank you.'

'You're welcome.' April stood up. 'I'm off to write some fanfic in which a series of increasingly painful and humiliating things happen to Captain Kismet.'

No sooner had Will heard the front door close behind April than Margo returned to the living room, a wine glass in each hand and a bottle of Pinot Noir under one arm. He realised that he was being watched in shifts, and felt a touch of petulance at the idea, but reached out for a glass as Margo filled it all the same.

'So,' she said. 'Patrick.'

'I don't want to talk about him.'

'Fair.' She sat down on the dry side of the settee and took a contemplative sip of wine. 'Jordan?'

'Him neither.'

'Fine.'

'He was such a *bitch* to me,' said Will, immediately changing his mind. 'He just gets so high and mighty, you have no idea.'

'Oh, trust me, I get it,' said Margo, tucking her feet underneath her and getting comfortable for the venting portion of the breakup ritual. 'Remember when I came on a night out to the Village with you guys, and he acted like you'd brought your *mum* out with you? Telling that story about railing some twink and then being all "Oh sorry, Margo, didn't mean to shock you." Like I was some kind of bumpkin! I've given birth, it takes a *lot* to shock me.'

'I'm sure.'

'The *smell*, Will.'

'I get the picture!'

'I'm just saying, I'm not brand new. I am very aware that gender and sexuality are a vast and rich spectrum. I'm raising a nonbinary teenager, am I not? And sure, I'm doing the whole suburban motherhood thing, and the only person I ever loved happened to be a man, but that doesn't mean I've been shipped off to Stafford.'

'Do you mean Stepford?'

'Shut up.'

'I never knew Owen was the only person you loved,' Will said.

'Who else would there have been?' Margo asked.

Will shrugged.

'I suppose I just assumed all those nights you used to go out when we were younger, you were having all kinds of outrageous love affairs.'

'Oh, I was.' Margo's face was deadpan. 'The quickest way out of my teen angst was in the back seat of an older boy's car. But love had very little to do with any of that. And then...' She placed her hands on her stomach and made a *boom* gesture. 'Baby.'

'Baby,' Will repeated. He remembered when Margo had called him to tell him she was pregnant. Her tone had been characteristically neutral, and he'd had to ask her whether she was phoning him to tell him he was about to be an uncle, or because she needed a lift to the clinic. '*I'm keeping it*,' she'd said. '*If only to see the look on Mum's face.*'

'Just Owen, then?' Will asked.

She let out a little *pfft* sound, and repeated Will's own words: 'I don't want to talk about him.'

Margo never wanted to talk about Owen. Ever since Owen left, taking a decent chunk of Margo's heart with him, Will suspected her stony demeanour was becoming less of an act and more of a default. Not that he would ever dare say that to her face. He wasn't stupid.

'He's not the worst dad in the world,' Margo said, unprompted.

'No,' Will countered. 'That particular honour goes to mine.' Margo didn't argue; she just elbowed him and topped up their glasses.

30

The driver carried his luggage to the front step of his house in Coldwater Canyon while Patrick fiddled with his keys, and when he unlocked and threw open the front door, he almost accused the driver of bringing him to the wrong address. That could be the only explanation, Patrick thought as he rolled the suitcases into the hallway of the newly decorated hillside lot, for whatever the hell he was walking into.

He grabbed his phone and pulled up the last email from Asa, the decorator.

> *Hey P-Man!*
> *Your casa is ready and waiting. I had so much fun with this brief! Your taste is sublime, my guy. I think it's fair to say I understood the assignment here. This home just SCREAMS 'Patrick Lake'. I can't wait to hear what you think.*
> *A.*

Patrick wandered from room to room, feet echoing on the tiled floors, blinking against the light streaming in from the wall-to-ceiling glass that lined the side of the house looking out over the treetops. He recognised certain things that he had, for certain, requested. The sectional couch, the giant abstract painting in the living room by an artist that he had been assured would only increase in value. If this house did, as Asa promised, scream 'Patrick Lake,' it begged the question: Who the fuck was Patrick Lake?

Los Angeles was a desert, and this house was fitted with technology that enabled him to command any temperature. Still, the whole thing felt cold. Maybe it was the severe lines, the multitude of greys that he had thought chic but seemed lifeless now. Even the furniture looked bare, unfinished. No old, pummelled cushions, no throws or blankets, none of the colour or texture he'd grown accustomed to in Birmingham.

He couldn't even say he hated it. He had *asked* for this. Instead, he felt nothing but the awkwardness one always felt when they were alone in somebody else's home. Somehow, it even *smelled* like a hotel.

'I need a shower,' Patrick announced to no one, his voice reverberating around the angular structure. He dragged a suitcase into the bathroom, a vast spartan cube, and scrubbed away the last twenty-four hours under the rain shower. He had just pulled on a T-shirt and sweats when the doorbell rang, echoing ominously throughout the entire building, and he padded barefoot to the front hallway.

'Patrick, hi!' An attractive woman with auburn hair and glasses held out her hand. 'I'm Tabby.'

'Tabby?' Patrick shook her hand, more muscle memory than manners. Behind her, what looked like a full camera crew were unloading equipment from the back of a van.

'Tabby Glazer,' she said. Then, seeing his blank look: 'From *Architectural Digest*?'

Right. Shit. Right. They were here to shoot the house. He was supposed to give a video tour of the place. This had been in the books for months, painstakingly timed to coincide with Patrick's return to the States and the commencement of the promotional campaign for *Kismet 2*. It had seemed like a perfect idea when he left for England.

Another vehicle rolled onto the driveway, and Simone disembarked before it had even come to a complete stop, trailed by somebody Patrick vaguely recognised, an assistant from the agency.

'Tabby, hi,' she said. 'Patrick, welcome back.' She gave his casual attire the briefest of glances, and he could see the equations taking place behind her eyes. *He looks scruffy, but maybe that works better. Authentic. Un-staged. He's at home, he's relaxed. Let him welcome you inside and get you a beer. He's America's boyfriend.*

He felt ill.

Once they were all set, half of the crew stayed inside, just out of sight, while Tabby knocked on the front door again and Patrick answered, smiling to the camera.

'Hello, *AD*,' he said. 'I'm Patrick Lake. Welcome to my home!' He held the door open, and the camera followed him into the house, panning down to a pair of Captain Kismet's boots, which were lined up carefully next to Patrick's Nikes in the hallway. They had not been there a moment ago, and Patrick once again felt like he had glitched into a different reality, the way a bone might pop out of a socket. He realised that while Simone kept Tabby talking, her assistant had run through the house with a gym bag full of 'finishing touches' ready to be spotted by eagle-eyed Easter-egg hunting fans on YouTube.

In the living room, the coffee table sported a neatly arranged stack of pages, the top sheet of which bore the title: *Kismet 3*.

'Uh-oh, that wasn't supposed to be there!' Patrick said, mugging stiltedly for the camera. 'Pretend you didn't see that,' he winked. 'It's top secret.'

The truth was, beneath that title page lay a pile of blank paper. A script for the third Kismet movie didn't even exist yet. It would be a miracle if post-production on *Kismet 2* was done in time for the premiere.

'And this is the kitchen,' he continued, gesturing to the gleaming steel appliances. 'Obviously.' He was one of those sham realtors, doing his best to show a house he had never set foot in.

You can do this, he thought. *You might not be able to cry on cue but if there is one thing you can do, it is sell the hell out of whatever piece of shit you have been given. Just commit.*

With renewed conviction, he showed Tabby and the cameramen the admittedly stunning view of the canyon from the living room – 'this is where I like to read, meditate, just *be*,' he lied – and waxed lyrically and falsely about the gigantic painting over the couch, which he now realised, after looking at it for longer than two seconds, that he hated.

This was all going a lot better than it could have, and as they climbed the stairs to the master bedroom, Patrick found faith in his own acting skills once again. *I convinced the world I'm straight*, he thought, *I can convince a magazine I like my own house.*

In the corner, an expensive-looking guitar sat propped against the wall next to the bed. How the hell had Simone's assistant snuck that thing in here? And for *why*? Patrick almost cracked up at the thought of himself picking it up to serenade some poor soul who had ended up in his room. '*Thanks for the sex, now here's "Hey There, Delilah"*.'

'Care to play something for us?' Tabby asked.

'Sure,' said Patrick, the people-pleaser in him speaking out before he could remind himself that he did not, in fact, play the guitar. Simone must have seen the mounting panic in his eyes, holding her phone out in front of her like a pistol.

'I'm so sorry, but something has just come up and Patrick is needed elsewhere,' she said. 'I hope you got everything you needed!' she added, guiding Tabby and the videographer out of the room.

'Actually, we didn't—' said Tabby.

'Fantastic!' Simone exclaimed. 'We can't wait to see how it turns out. Can we, Patrick?'

'Sure can,' said Patrick. 'Thank you, everybody.' And then he was clapping. Oh God, why was he clapping? Somewhere along the way of promising himself he would never take anyone or anything for granted in this industry, he had become the corniest, most condescending mook in the business.

Tabby, visibly bewildered to realise she and her camera crew had allowed themselves to be herded out onto the driveway, raised a hand as if to ask a question. Simone closed the door on them.

'How are you?' she asked. 'We haven't caught up in a while. Not in the flesh.'

'I'm good. How's Harper?'

'Infuriating. Messy. I'm obsessed with her.'

Patrick smiled. 'Good.'

'What about William?' Simone asked.

'Who? Oh. *Will.*' Patrick wasn't sure he had heard anybody use Will's full name the whole time he had been in Birmingham. But Simone would only know him as a signatory on a piece of paper, swearing on his government name to never tell the world what he meant to Patrick Lake.

'That's over,' he told Simone. 'You don't need to worry about him anymore.'

Simone simply nodded.

'It's good that you had some fun,' she said. 'While you were away. Because you've got a packed summer of press ahead of you.'

'That's fine. I'm ready to work.'

'Great.' Simone adjusted her necklace and cleared her throat. 'Well. I've taken up enough of your time.' She turned towards the door and paused. 'You should come over for dinner sometime. Harper told me to tell you.'

'I'd like that.'

'Alright.' She nodded once more and opened the door. The *AD* team were gone. Patrick suddenly, desperately didn't want her to go.

'Simone—'

'Welcome home, Patrick. The place looks great.' She closed the door quietly behind her, and Patrick was left with nobody to talk to but the idea of the man who lived in this house. He strolled back into the lounge, stood in front of the huge painting, and after a moment's consideration, clambered up onto the couch and lifted it off the wall, carefully manoeuvring it down and placing it in the vast window, facing outwards. The tourists and dog walkers could appreciate it while he figured out what to do with it.

Patrick perched on the edge of the sofa next to the coffee table and the script that didn't exist until the sky outside had dimmed and he had lost almost all feeling in his lower body. Finally, too tired to go upstairs to bed, he stretched his legs out on the cushions and closed his eyes, telling himself that first thing in the morning he would order a blanket online.

31

Two Months Later

It was a Friday night in Birmingham, and as had become a norm for Will in the months since moving back in with Margo and Dylan, everybody had plans but him. He lay on Margo's bed, watching her do her hair, and for just a moment he could almost imagine that the last twenty years hadn't happened yet, that he was a little boy watching this difficult, impossibly glamorous creature getting dolled up for a night out. He had once gazed so longingly, so transparently, at Margo's makeup that she had groaned and tossed him an eyeliner.

'You should try a cat eye,' she'd told him. 'You've the colouring for it. Just don't go mad or you'll end up looking like Amy Winehouse.'

In retrospect, Margo was probably to thank for him falling in love with drag. Or to blame, depending on how you looked at it.

'You look nice,' he said now, somewhat pitifully. 'Where are you going, again?'

'Just dinner with The Girls,' she said.

Margo still thought that Will believed her when she said she was going out with The Girls, but he knew she found them basic and boring, and had simply been using them as an alibi: by Will's count, she had been out with Owen three times in the last two weeks. (If

Margo really wanted to cover her tracks, she'd have insisted Owen drop her off around the corner and not right outside the house, where they could be observed from the landing window.)

At first, Will had been uncertain how he felt about this apparent rekindling: he had been witness to the first theatrical run of their relationship and it had ended in a nine-hour labour and lots of foul language. But Owen seemed to have gotten his shit together in the years since. God knows Margo was a different woman now. An incredible one. She'd raised a headstrong, annoying, weird and brilliant kid. She'd practically raised Will too. *Good for her*, he reckoned. *At least one person in this family deserved to be happy.*

'Mind if I tag along?' he asked, curious to know if he could call her bluff.

'And have you dripping your misery all over my evening?' Margo tsked. 'Absolutely not.'

'Ouch.'

'I already have one moody teenager to contend with, and *they* are at a mate's house. Which means it is my night off. If you want company, call one of your friends.'

'April's busy.'

'You might be at a low ebb right now, but I know even *you* have more than one friend.'

'I'm not talking to him,' said Will.

'*I'm not talking to him*,' Margo parroted in a high-pitched, petulant tone. 'Honestly, Will, it's knackering enough parenting Dylan. Grow up.'

'I...' Will fidgeted with one of the many tasselled cushions on Margo's bed. 'I was really harsh to him. What if he doesn't want to talk to me?'

'He might not.'

'So—'

'But you'll never know if you don't cowgirl up and reach out.' Margo finally turned away from her reflection to face Will fully. 'Jordan might be a pretty-boy twerp with more followers than sense, but real friends are a rarity, Will. And far, far more important than whatever men might come in and out of your life. You know I know what I'm talking about.'

Will fidgeted with the pillow in his lap. 'I do,' he said.

'Right. So, are you going to be a big boy and call your friend? Or are you going to lie in bed reading *The Song of Achilles* for the sixth time?'

Will grimaced. 'Patroclus is a nause. I should really call Jordan.'

Margo smiled. 'Good. Anyway. I'm off.' She gave her hair one more playful ruffle in the mirror for good measure, picked up a glittery clutch, and headed for the door.

'Don't wait up,' she said. 'Oh, and Will?'

'Yeah?'

'Get out of my room.'

Will was certain that he *would* have worked up the courage to contact Jordan eventually. But the little bitch called him first.

'Are you coming?' he said as soon as Will picked up.

'Jordan?' Will asked, and he could practically *hear* him rolling his eyes.

'No, it's the tooth fairy,' came the reply. 'Now are you coming or not?'

'Coming where?' Will asked. 'Jordan, I've been meaning to call you. I just want to say—'

'No time for that now,' Jordan said, his voice brisk. 'I've just texted you the details.'

Will's phone chirped, and he glanced down at what Jordan had just sent him:

```
Anti-Anti-Drag Gathering.

Starts outside the Village. Saturday 12pm.

Category is: Dressed to protest.
```

'I'll be there,' he said.

'Good,' said Jordan. 'Don't be late.' He hung up before Will could say anything else.

The next day, Will arrived at the Village at twenty to twelve to find half of Birmingham's queens already lining the pavement. Faye Runaway and Tamil Nitrate were among them, along with Sadie Chatterley, Elle Fire, Lexa Kimbo, Paris Social, Izzy Uno, Hennessy Williams, Auntie Dot, Evelyn Carnate, Julie Madly Deeply, Alicia Tried, Raina Shine, and Gaia Gender, all seemingly dressed up with nowhere to go.

Will spotted other familiar faces: punters he recognised from the Village, a handful of bartenders from other gay venues on Hurst Street, some guys he only identified from their profiles on Grindr. Ry waved awkwardly from the crowd. There was no sign of his new boyfriend, and Will determined that it was a sign of personal growth that he felt nothing, not even the slightest pang of Schadenfreude, at this observation.

'Well there's a bloody turn-up for the books,' somebody commented beside Will. Somebody whose platinum blonde hair and Bleu de Chanel scent, even in his wig and lash-obscured peripheral vision, were instantly familiar.

'Jordan,' he said, turning. 'I'm glad to see you.'

'I think this might be the first time you've ever been on time for anything,' Jordan remarked. 'Let alone early. I suppose we should be honoured.'

He wasn't forgiven, then. Will wasn't surprised. Had not expected to be.

'This is a good turnout,' he said, nodding to the growing mass outside the bar.

'Well, it's important,' said Jordan. 'People care. This idea that drag queens aren't safe to be around children, that they're predators... it's the same shit they used to say in the Eighties. When you see history repeating itself, you have to do something.'

'Safe for children.' Will tsked. 'What does that even mean? We're reading them *Peter Pan*, not *American Psycho*. It drives me mad. The number of straight comedians who've been absolutely filthy in their stand-up, have been known and *celebrated* for it, then gone on to voice an animated bunny or play the dad in some Disney film, it's fucking infuriating.' He clutched his vape tightly, thumb worrying over the button like a rosary.

'It's absolutely *clapped*,' Jordan agreed, seemingly forgetting that he was yet to absolve Will. They shared a look, and Will found himself momentarily grateful for the bigoted little shits who had brought them back together.

'I am still very angry with you,' said Jordan, reading his mind. 'Don't think I'm just going to let you off the hook. You said some really fucked up things to me.'

'I know, and I'm so—'

'But I still fucking love you and that won't change just because you've been a heinous idiot. So you will simply have to make it up to me later.'

'I know. I will, I promise. But just for the record...'

'Yeah?'

'There's nobody else I'd rather ride into battle with.'

Jordan pouted.

'I mean, obviously *same*,' he said, just as Faye stepped onto an upturned beer crate, which was, both at her age and in those heels, probably an unwise thing to do.

'Oh my days,' Will whispered. 'Who gave Faye a megaphone?'

'She brought it from home,' said Jordan. 'You know these old girls come prepared.'

'Thank God for her, honestly,' Will said, but Jordan was already shushing him, holding up his phone ready to stream Faye's address.

'Raise your hand, clack your fan, make some noise,' she began, 'if you have ever been called a name, some disgusting word, for no reason other than simply being who you are.'

The crowd around Will and Jordan clicked, clacked, snapped, stamped, and whooped around them.

'Let's hear some of those names,' said Faye.

'Puff,' somebody called out.

'Bender,' said another.

'Bummer!'

'Dyke!'

'Fag!'

'Fudgepacker!' This one elicited a few awkward laughs, and precipitated a cacophony of the silliest, stupidest slang that Will had been hearing since primary school.

Shirtlifter! Nancy boy! Pansy! Limp wrist! Flamer! Willy woofter! Fairy!

'Fairy!' At Faye's interjection, the crowd fell silent again. 'Imagine thinking that calling somebody a "fairy" was an insult,' she said. 'Fairies used to be feared and revered. People would make offerings to them to appease their moods, and heaven forbid if you were to meet one at a crossroads. The word "homophobia" supposedly means they're afraid of us, but I think they've forgotten who they're dealing with. They're trying to push us back into the margins, throwing grains of rice on the ground so the fae will be distracted and forget what we're owed. Talking about us like we're not real, so we waste our precious time on this earth arguing for our own existence, proving how good and meek and mild we can be.

'I have spent the better part of fifty years being the bigger person,' Faye continued. 'And let me tell you something: I am bloody sick and tired of it. Going high when they go low. Trying to fool myself into thinking that if we're nice enough, and quiet enough, and don't rub it in people's faces too much, contort our gay asses into knots so that *they* are not made remotely uncomfortable, then maybe, just maybe, they'll stop hating us. So that something as simple as holding hands won't be the reason I end up in hospital or on a slab. Or worse: with *eggshell* in my *wig*.'

'You've got to lead with love,' said Gaia.

'I don't love those cunts!' yelled Will. 'I love *us*.'

'Yes, bitch!' Tammy howled, waggling ten dangerously pointy nails in hearty agreement.

'Too bloody right, sweetheart,' Faye boomed into the megaphone. 'Now we're going to make our way through this city and share our fabulousness with the world. We're going to prove that no matter how much they try, they can't scare us into hiding. We're going to march, or should I say *mince*, right up to those ugly little souls and let them know that the library is now, and will forever stay, OPEN!'

'Yes!' Will screamed, and he heard everyone around him do the same. 'Yes!!'

Tammy mounted a portable speaker onto her broad shoulder, and with a yell of 'Let's go, girls!', they departed.

Will would later wonder what the rest of Birmingham thought when they saw this small army of goddesses stomping and sashaying from Hurst Street all the way up to Centenary Square, stopping traffic as they went. 'I Am What I Am' blared from Tammy's speaker; it could just as well have been 'Flight of the Valkyries.'

They arrived in front of the library a little before one, and Will didn't recognise any of the homophobic protestors individually — how could he, the sea of ill-fitting jeans and waterproof jackets that they were — but the awkward phrasing of the placards was proof enough. This was the same group of people who had been staging that horrible display the last time. The ones who had tried to humiliate Faye.

The queens shimmied in single file between the protestors and the library, then Julie Madly Deeply and Auntie Dot split off from the group and headed inside for that day's story time. The rest of them would stay here, a sequinned line of defence between the Rainbow Room and the hatred outside.

'You make me sick,' one of the sign-holders shouted.

'You should be ashamed of yourselves,' another sneered.

'Guys, guys, calm down, it's alright!' Tammy called out to them. 'All is well!'

'Why is she trying to reason with them?' Jordan asked, but Will, who had got ready for many a Pride brunch with Tammy before, broke into a grin.

'Have you heard the good news?' Tammy bellowed. 'Praise be! The Vengabus! It cometh!'

Right on cue, the sound of honking blared from the speaker at such a volume that Will wondered how many of them would have full use of their ears by the end of the day.

'We. Like. To party,' the queens all chanted in unison, and Will joined in like a knight pledging allegiance to crown and country. Some of the protestors still wore that generic mask of outrage and disgust, but as the queens broke out one Nineties banger after another — with accompanying dance routines — more and more of them began to look, well, baffled.

That was the thing about queer joy. So much of it was so inherently, deeply *silly*. Will pranced and jumped around to '5, 6, 7, 8' and 'Wannabe' with Faye and Tammy and Gaia and so many others and felt impossibly grateful for this unhinged sisterhood he had been welcomed into. And sad for anyone who didn't have this, either because they couldn't reach it, or because they'd rejected it outright. This was their community, their family, at its dumbest and its mightiest, and Will's heart could almost burst at the glory of being right here in the middle of it all. It was the best time he could remember having since a certain actor left town, and Will could tell he wasn't the only one having fun: Some of the kids arriving at the library with their parents were so enraptured by the pantomime taking place outside that they didn't want to go inside for story time.

Leave it to the far right to get all book-burny about the concept of 'fun'. Frankly, Will thought, anybody who felt even remotely threatened by a bunch of gays doing the 'YMCA' was a fucking idiot.

Story time was almost over by the time the cops showed up. Whoever called them had probably been hoping they'd show up in riot gear with batons and water cannons to disperse the deviants. As it was, Will almost pitied the pair of bobbies who approached the queens mid-cancan.

'Hello, officers,' Tammy purred. 'What can we do you for?'

'We received word that there was a violent protest occurring in the square,' one of them said.

'Violent?' Will looked to his left and then his right. 'Does any of this look violent to you, sir?'

The policeman cast a slightly baffled look around the gathering, and before he could answer Will continued: '*They* are staging a protest.' He pointed to the crowd of beige facing them, then gestured at himself and the other queens. '*This*... is a flash mob.'

'A flash mob.' The second officer did not appear convinced.

'You might want to go and investigate some of the hate speech on those placards, though,' Jordan said, a helpful smile on his face.

'I'd be careful,' said Faye. 'They may be carrying.'

'Carrying?'

'Eggs. Concealed cholesterol. Probably not even free range. In fact, talking of *violence*, officer…' Faye stepped just close enough that she towered over the pair of them, but not so close that it might be deemed intimidating. 'I reported being harassed and assaulted by this very group of people several weeks ago, and as far as I am aware, sweet diddly squat has been done about it.'

'Oh, that's a shame,' said Jordan, holding up his phone. 'That's a bad look indeed, officer… I'm so sorry, I didn't catch your names?'

The two policemen exchanged a glance, and then the first one spoke again.

'You're going to need to wrap this up soon,' he said. 'It's Saturday, Broad Street is going to be full of drunks soon enough, and we don't want any of them harassing you ladies.'

'No bother,' said Faye sweetly. 'Story hour is almost over.' She cast a cold look over the cop's shoulder at the protestors. 'I'm more than happy to close the book on this.'

'Thank you for your assistance, gentlemen,' said Jordan, still filming. 'You both look very dashing, by the way. Not everyone could pull off those neon vest thingies.'

The officers gave them a cursory nod, and ambled slowly over to the protestors, presumably to give them the same marching orders. It was hardly a barnstorming triumph, Will thought. The war, if that's what they were calling it, was not won.

But this felt enough like a victory that he couldn't stop smiling.

The queens did not, in fact, disperse as requested, so much as funnel their numbers back the way they came, Faye leading the way, the others following their fairy queen home towards the gay quarter.

'Oh my days, did you see their reaction when we started doing the Macarena?' Jordan cackled. 'Their faces!'

'What is the Macarena,' said Will, 'if not voguing on the lowest difficulty setting?'

'Voguing for beginners,' Jordan agreed. 'And you still fumbled the moves once or twice, don't think I didn't see you.'

'I'm sorry.'

'Save it for Los del Rio.'

'No, Jordan, I'm *sorry*.' Will touched his wrist and they both stopped, moving aside as Faye marshalled the other girls into the Village. 'All of those things I said, I didn't mean them. I was angry and upset at Patrick, and I took it out on you because you were there. Which is the story of my life, isn't it. You're always there, and I take it for granted, *especially* lately. I'm sorry.'

'Good,' Jordan said, expressionless. 'I'm glad you're aware of what a bitch you were being.'

'I am, trust me.'

'Fine.' Jordan pouted. 'And I *suppose* I could have been a bit more understanding. You were in an impossible situation, and I expected you to act like you weren't. It's easy to have all kinds of principles when you're preaching into the front-facing camera. Bit harder when you're in love.'

'You ended up being right, though. I know how much you enjoy that.'

'I didn't want to be, Will. I wanted Patrick to do right by you. I was rooting for that fucker.'

Will smiled weakly. 'Me too.'

'I guess we're the lucky ones,' said Jordan. 'We stopped wasting time resenting ourselves for being different a long time ago.'

'Exactly.' Will nodded. 'If I could step through a portal into any strand of the multiverse, another life where I would be straight, I don't think I could do it. What would that life even look like?'

'The most clapped timeline.'

'I wouldn't have met you. Can you imagine! My best friend, erased, just like that,' Will continued, caught up in his own thought experiment. 'I wouldn't have found drag either. Who would I even *be*?'

'I can see straight you now,' said Jordan. 'All tribal tattoos and missionary.' He shuddered emphatically.

'Couldn't be me,' said Will. 'I would always choose this life. The frocks and glitter and poppers and Kylie and yes, the crying and the fighting too. I'd choose all of it. I love all of it. Why rob myself of that? I like myself enough to know I deserve that much.'

'It's the least of what you deserve,' said Jordan. 'Everyone makes out like being queer makes your life harder. What are they on about? It makes it *better*. I'm just going to say it. *We're* better.'

Jordan took the vape from Will's hand and inhaled on it deeply. It was a small, intimate act, but when he released the cloud from his mouth, it felt like all of the tension between them dissipated with it. Will pulled him into a hug, ignoring Jordan's protests about his hair, and marvelled at the simple joy he felt in holding his friend. No wonder people were always mistaking them for a couple. They were soulmates, in their own way.

'I love you,' he said. 'I've missed you so much.'

'Bit dramatic,' Jordan sniffed.

'I'm a drag queen. I reserve the right to be dramatic.'

He felt Jordan relax into him, like a spring uncurling, and Will thought: *Maybe this is enough. A good man loves me after all.*

'Just think,' said Jordan, still mid-embrace. 'If you hadn't been such a crap shag all those years ago, we never would have become best friends.'

'*You* were just as crap, my love,' Will laughed. 'And yes, we would. Some things are written in the stars.'

They stayed like that for who even knew how long, the tallest woman and the prettiest boy, clutching each other in the doorway to a gay bar like sweethearts on a dance floor who didn't ever want the night to end.

32

Patrick had seen his fair share of soulless conference hotels doing press tours and junkets over the years, but the venue for this year's LGBTQIA VIP Awards, a Ramada near the airport, was one of the sadder contenders.

'I'm still not entirely sure what I'm doing here,' he said, trailing Simone into the ballroom, a vast white space that had been spruced up with a handful of potted plants and rainbow banners. 'Isn't this just going to start even more rumours?'

'Think about it,' said Simone. 'Would a guy who's in the closet attend such a high-profile LGBTQ+ event? No, of course he wouldn't, it would draw way too much attention. But a straight guy who's comfortable with his sexuality and believes all people deserve love and respect?' She patted him on the back. '*That* guy buys a plate.'

'So I can't walk down the street with another man,' Patrick said slowly, trying to follow Simone's logic, 'but I can attend a queer awards ceremony?'

'We're playing 4D chess here,' Simone told him. 'Here! This is our table.'

Simone waved a hand and took a glass of champagne from a passing tray while Patrick poured them each a glass of water from the bottles on the table.

'I usually wouldn't dream of putting you in the same room as this many Netflix-tier celebrities,' she said, disdainfully side-eying the table next to them. 'But you've been so down lately, I thought it would do you good to get out of the house. Be around the community.'

'That's... sweet,' said Patrick. He understood that Simone meant well. And even if nobody else here knew the real him, being in the room was enough to make him feel just a little less isolated. He took a sip of water and grabbed a program from the table.

'Wait a minute.' He frowned. 'It says here I'm up for an award.'

'Hmm?' His manager's lack of a reaction was, in itself, a reaction.

'Simone. What did you do.'

'I *may* have put you forward for something.'

'Simone.' Patrick prodded the piece of paper in front of him. 'You have nominated me for Ally of the Year.'

'And?'

'And... I didn't *do* anything!'

'You're hot, and you haven't tweeted that you hate gay people.' Simone shrugged. 'Apparently that's enough.'

'Simone, this is so fucked up!' He leaned in to whisper in her ear: 'I can't win an award for being a gay ally when I'm actually gay but not *doing* anything to make life better for other gay people. It's perverse.'

'Well, if it makes you feel any better, you probably won't win anyway,' Simone replied. She took a tiny sip of champagne. Patrick didn't see a single smudge of lipstick on the rim of her glass.

'I won't?'

'Unfortunately, you have some rather stiff competition,' she said, pointing to the name below his on the program. It was a singer whose second album had recently been released, the lead single of which had been a ballad accompanied by a music video featuring couples of all gender configurations embracing on a beach. His fanbase, comprised largely of the same young women that Patrick's team had been courting, were just this side of feral.

'I swear that guy can't stand on a stage longer than five seconds without draping himself in a pride flag,' Simone continued. 'His manager is Adrienne Schmidt. She's a genius. And you should see her *legs*, Patrick.'

'I need a drink. Excuse me.'

'Nothing with bubbles,' said Simone. 'That photoshoot with *Esquire* tomorrow, remember? You'll bloat.'

'I... Fine.' Patrick left the table, fists clenched at his side. Simone was, he reminded himself, in many ways, one of the best things to ever happen to him. She had seen his potential, taken his career to an entirely new level. They enjoyed a close working relationship, and he sometimes forgot that it was a relationship predicated on her feeling free to comment on any aspect of his life, including his body. As if there weren't enough people doing that already.

It was a strange thing, to know without a doubt that you were handsome, because the world told you so. On the one hand, Patrick's looks were a matter of genetics that he could neither change nor take credit for. On the other, his appearance was a part of his livelihood. The greater the scrutiny upon him from all angles, the more he felt like an insect being watched through a magnifying glass until it inevitably burst into flames. Every pimple that broke out on his trademark jaw, every starchy carb he ate, every unflattering photo angle captured by an asshole paparazzo, took on inordinate significance in his mind, the tiniest detail a potential thread that could unravel his entire image.

There had been a story that did the rounds a year or so ago, during the press tour for the first *Kismet* movie. Patrick had been wearing a fitted off-white T-shirt, doing interviews on a voluminous sofa that seemed to sink a little more each time he moved, enveloping him until he was practically horizontal. The footage, while not terrible, did him no favors, either. And nor did the headlines, which speculated that his weight was spiralling out of control, as if a few rumples and a visible tummy were the end of the world.

'I wasn't fat,' Patrick had told Will while recounting the story. 'I was *hydrated!*'

The thought of Will made him want to pick up the phone. Or failing that, a bottle of vodka. Maybe a cheeseburger. He settled for a tequila on the rocks at the bar and lingered there for a moment, reluctant to return to Simone.

'Don't you just hate these things?' The voice next to him was gravelly and familiar. It was the voice of a bodyguard who had taken a bullet for the first female President of the United States after falling in love with her in the romantic action drama *These United Fates*. A grizzled former Marine in the Netflix movie *Attrition*. An American everyman fighting to keep his family safe during an alien invasion in *Ultra-Terrestrial*. All projects Patrick had auditioned for and for which he had been ultimately deemed too 'boyish'.

Reece Mackenzie. If Patrick were the sort of person inclined to make vision boards, Reece Mackenzie would be at the very centre. He'd used that career trajectory as a blueprint for his own, and now Reece Mackenzie stood just feet away from him sipping a Modelo in this place where corporate activism went to die. Patrick had been in the same room as him on a few previous occasions – a *Vanity Fair* party and a SAG lunch – but had never gotten close enough to take in just how handsome he was in the flesh: russet hair that had been combed back but that was now springing down in a fetching swoop over thick eyebrows; slightly unkempt stubble flecked with white; that trademark scar on his chin that lent verisimilitude to his many action roles.

'Um… Hi.' Patrick laughed self-consciously. 'Wow. It's been a while since I got starstruck.'

Reece frowned and smiled at the same time and shook his head. 'Way I see it,' Reece said, 'we're all just clowns in the same circus.'

'Circus is damn right,' said Patrick.

'To the clown show,' said Reece, holding up his beer. Patrick raised his glass, and they both drank in silence.

'There you are!' A beautiful woman with beachy mermaid waves in a tiny blue dress under a blazer approached them both. Patrick had loved her on her season of *The Bachelor* and had thought that she should have gone further in the competition (a sentiment he had expressed to precisely nobody), but clearly Cupid had had other plans: She'd met Reece shortly after the reunion aired, and the two had gotten hitched the following summer.

'Has he been complaining that he had to come?' Brianna Schlesinger, now Brianna Mackenzie, said to Patrick. 'He always does this! Says yes to the invitation, then spends the whole evening sulking by the bar or the coat check. I swear, he's this close to taking up smoking just so he has an excuse to go loiter outside.'

'Not at all,' said Patrick. 'Although I have to say, I didn't expect to see you both here.' An action star and reality dating show sweetheart power couple tended to appeal, Patrick had learned, to a very large segment of the population – just not necessarily one that cared much for queer people.

'LGBTQ+ issues are very close to our hearts,' said Brianna, earnestly sounding out the acronym in a staccato, like a kid at a spelling bee.

'Oh?'

'I have a cousin who's bi,' she said, by way of explanation. 'Or is it pan? I forget. Anyway. We're huge allies, aren't we, baby?'

'Huge,' said Reece, and Patrick couldn't tell if his smirk was one of amusement or derision.

'Well, it's so nice to meet you both,' he said. 'Would you please excuse me?'

Patrick swiftly abandoned the Mackenzies at the bar as the opening speeches began. Rather than returning to his table, he opted to take a lap of the room, walking with intention and pausing only occasionally to take a thoughtful sip of his tequila, doing his best to look like a man who was on his way somewhere, or otherwise preoccupied and not to be approached or interrupted.

He passed the majority of the ceremony this way, circling the venue with more pitstops at the bar. Drinking in America, he decided, was nowhere near as fun as drinking in England. The quality of the booze at this event was undeniably superior, but the resulting feeling was one of woozy light-headedness, with none of the giddy pleasure he so missed.

When a brand ambassador for a Palm Springs luxury resort took to the stage to talk about the importance of vocal allies in the fight for queer rights, Patrick ducked into a semi-private bathroom. He thought for a moment that he might throw up, but after leaning against the sink and splashing water in his face, the worst of the fog passed. What was he *doing* here? He had no right, had done nothing to deserve being welcomed like this. His people deserved better heroes.

He didn't hear the door to the bathroom open and was only made aware that there was someone else in here by the sound of the lock being turned. He looked up. In the mirror, Reece Mackenzie was approaching him.

'Hi,' said Patrick. 'I should get be getting ba—'

Reece grabbed him by the shoulder and spun him around, and for one wild instant Patrick thought he was going to hit him, that Reece had somehow figured out what he really was and it had made him sick with anger. Patrick's fingers were curling into a fist when Reece pulled him forward and kissed him forcefully, almost violently, his tongue hungrily prising apart Patrick's lips.

Patrick did not resist, or shove him away. He simply marvelled at what was happening, and it was like reliving his first excruciatingly nerve-wracking visit to a gay bar, when a delicious, terrifying possibility finally entered his head for the first time: *Am I not the only one?*

And then he began to kiss Reece back, bringing one hand up to caress his rugged jaw, using his other to pull him closer. The longer the kiss went on, the more they grabbed at each other, desire fuelling desire. You never really knew how hungry you were until your first bite.

Finally Reece drew away, just long enough to guide Patrick by the hand into the nearest stall and shut the door behind them.

'I've wanted to do this ever since I first saw you at that *Vanity Fair* party,' he said.

If Patrick's face hadn't been flushed already, it would be now.

'You're kidding,' he said. 'But you're... *you*.'

'Shut up,' Reece leered, and kissed him again. Reece's breath was hot in his mouth, slightly sour from the beer, and Patrick didn't realise the pants of his suit had been unzipped until he felt Reece's hand sliding inside his briefs.

'Fuck, you're big,' Reece breathed. 'I knew you would be.'

Reece shoved him back against the wall, cupping his face firmly with both hands. He kissed him even harder, forcing his mouth open with his fingers. It was rough, needful, and Patrick recognised that fervor. Had felt it in a hotel room in Birmingham when he signed a piece of paper finally allowing him to crack open the door of his own cage.

Reece understood him. Reece *was* him. Maybe—

Metal clanged against Patrick's teeth, an unpleasant jolt.

'What—' he began, at the same time that Reece said: 'Sorry, I usually take it off—'

Oh. Of course. Reece was wearing a wedding ring.

'One sec,' said Reece, pulling at the platinum band on his finger.

'No, hold on,' said Patrick. What had felt outrageously hot just seconds ago now struck him as... What *was* the word for hooking up with a married man in a bathroom stall while his wife was in the next room? He imagined Will would call it something like *clapped* or *minging*. Never mind the word for the plummeting sensation Patrick felt right now.

'Brianna,' he said. 'She's next door.'

'Don't worry about that,' said Reece, closing in again.

'No,' said Patrick, reaching down to pull up his pants. 'Your wife is next door, I'm not OK with that.'

'Fine,' said Reece. 'Let's get a room. We're in a hotel.'

He was wilfully missing the point, Patrick thought, and it suddenly made him a lot less attractive.

'What would your wife say,' he asked Reece, 'if she knew about this?'

Reece shrugged. 'Probably that she'll take the car and expect me home in an Uber later.'

'What?'

'Well I can hardly ask *her* to take the cab, can I?'

'You mean... She knows?'

Reece looked at Patrick like he was brand new. 'I love Brianna, she's my partner, but... well, she's a business partner. Our brands work well together, we respect each other, and we've built pretty great lives and careers as a team.' He frowned. 'I thought you *got* that. Simone said—'

'Hold up.' Patrick felt like a glass of ice-cold water had just been thrown in his face. '*Simone* said? Simone said *what*?'

'That you'd be open to something...' said Reece. 'Discreet, mutually beneficial.' His fingers began to inch along the waistline of Patrick's pants again. Patrick squirmed away, opening the stall door.

'I'm sorry,' he said. 'There has been a pretty major misunderstanding.'

'Oh. *Oh.*' Reece's eyes widened in alarm. 'I... shit...'

Again, so like looking in the mirror. The rage Patrick felt building towards Simone was tempered by a deep sadness.

'Don't worry,' he said. 'I won't tell anyone.'

He tucked his shirt in, took a deep breath, and unlocked the door to the bathroom, heading out into the ballroom just in time to hear the silver-haired exec on stage reach the climax of his address.

'Nothing says "Gay rights!" like doing poppers with a drag queen,' he laughed. 'Which is why I am thrilled to announce that this year's LGBTQIA VIP Ally of the Year, in association with Hulu and Absolut Vodka, is Captain Kismet himself, Patrick Lake!'

33

'You look good as a blonde,' Jordan remarked as Will straightened his wig in the bedroom mirror. 'It doesn't wash you out at all.'

'Thanks, doll,' said Will, keeping his voice purposely monotonous because the only thing Jordan liked more than a compliment was a reaction. 'Whatever did I do all those weeks without you?'

'Ignore him,' said April from her perch on the bed. 'It's fierce. Sarah Michelle Gellar found shaking.'

'I'm the one who's shaking,' said Will. 'Look at these hands. It's taken me twice as long to do my makeup.'

'Have you decided on a number yet?' Jordan asked.

Will shook his head. He had been so emboldened by their victory on Centenary Square and his reunion with Jordan, that he'd decided to keep moving forward, to – in Jordan's words – 'get over himself' and sign up to sing live that Sunday night at the Village. As much as it still stung, he was learning that there was a strength to be found in vulnerability, in letting yourself be known. He had Patrick to thank for that, at least. He had finally found his voice.

'Not yet,' he said. 'I've been listening to so much Taylor Swift and Joni Mitchell, I'm amazed the Spotify algorithm hasn't arranged for someone to come over and do a welfare check.'

'Don't worry,' April told Jordan. 'I blocked all of Patrick's social media on Will's phone, so he can't obsessively scroll while crying to "Both Sides Now".'

'That would have been my first move too,' said Jordan. 'Well done. But what about the pictures in his camera roll?'

April winced. 'He technically wasn't allowed to take any,' she whispered. 'It was part of that NDA.'

'Fucking *hell*.' Jordan whistled.

'It's even more pathetic than that,' said Will, reminding them he was still in the room and had heard every word. 'I keep going through receipts on my phone. The taxi rides. That stupid scooter hire. The routes we took. Just to remind myself that it was real, that it happened.'

'Oh, babe.' April sighed.

'Even more proof that Patrick Lake is a waste of a haircut,' said Jordan. 'If he kept you as his dirty little secret, he should have at least made it worth your while with gifts. Something expensive and sparkly that you could sell for a boatload of cash to pay for a trip to Mykonos.'

'Huh. You're right. He's *rich*.' Will tutted at himself. 'I kept forgetting that part.'

'Still,' Jordan added. 'Maybe it's for the best that a five-star Uber rating is all you have to remember him by.'

'Not quite all.' Will pointed to the copy of *Maurice*, which hadn't left his nightstand since that day in the bookshop, when Patrick had blithely defaced it.

Jordan picked up the book and it fell open to the bookmarked page where Patrick's phone number was scrawled across the scene where Alec climbed up to Maurice's bedroom window on a ladder. He had that entire passage memorised by now. *Sir, was you calling out for me?*

'I'd have preferred jewellery,' Jordan said, snapping the volume shut and replacing it on the bedside table.

'Anyway!' April clapped her hands like she could reset the room. 'Song choice. Madonna? Cher? Kylie? You love a bit of Kylie.'

'Hardly ground-breaking,' said Jordan. 'Why not lean into the heartache? It works for Adele.'

'And *she's* a national treasure,' added April.

'Isn't she!' agreed Jordan. 'Adele era?' April nodded, and he turned to Will. 'Adele era?'

'It's my first time singing live,' said Will, 'and I am still bricking it just a smidge. So if you could please stop comparing me to *Adele*, that would be great.'

'Fine,' said Jordan. 'But just so you know… you're a national treasure, too.'

Will paused mid-lip-liner, unsure if he had heard him correctly.

'Jordan,' he said. 'That is quite possibly the nicest thing you have ever said to me. Are you feeling alright?'

Jordan cleared his throat. 'So anyway, I posted something online a little while ago, just trying to raise awareness of what was happening at the Village, how the council keeps trying to shut it down.'

Will simply nodded, uncomfortably aware that this was something he would have only too gladly helped Jordan with if they had been speaking at the time.

'Anyway,' Jordan continued, 'it's picked up a little bit of attention.'

He turned his screen around for Will to see. Thousands of likes and shares, which in itself was great. Then Will started to scroll through the comments.

Hundreds of people had responded to Jordan's post, sharing stories of their own experiences at the bar. Some were just a line or two, but others went on for paragraphs, spilling over into replies and whole separate threads spinning out under Jordan's message.

So many firsts. First rebellious teen nights out, awed at finding a place where they could be themselves. First crushes. First kisses.

First loves, first fights, first heartbreaks. First nights feeling brave enough to go out wearing women's clothes. Firsts, seconds, thirds, the maps of entire lives unfolding within four walls and a smoking area, a safe place to tell each other love stories.

'This is amazing,' Will said, tearing his gaze away from the phone and up to the ceiling, because he was *not* going to cry on this fresh beat. 'You're amazing.'

'No need to sound so surprised,' said Jordan. 'And anyway, April has something to show you too.'

April looked up at Jordan from her perch on the bed, eyes suddenly wide like a rabbit in the headlights.

'I do?' she asked.

'Yes. On your phone. Remember?'

'Oh. *That.*' April shrugged. 'It's nothing.'

'It is not nothing.' Jordan turned to Will. 'April has a new job.'

'What?' Will gasped. 'You're leaving Gilroy's?'

'Well… yeah.' April held out her arms. 'You actually happen to be looking at the new Digital Editor for *FanFam*.'

'*FanFam*? Well, that's fun to say. Isn't that the…'

'The biggest online destination in the world dedicated to pop culture from the perspectives of people of colour? Sure is.' April grinned. 'I get to write about comic books *for. a. living.*'

'Oh my God, you superstar!' Will fanned his face. 'Why would you tell me this *now*? I'm going to have to redo this!'

April cackled. 'I love you too,' she said.

'You need to finish getting ready if you don't want to be late again,' said Jordan.

Will blanched. 'I *am* ready.'

Jordan blinked. 'Well, alright then. I shall hail us a carriage.'

When the car arrived, Jordan called shotgun, and began immediately issuing instructions to the driver.

'I'm going to need you to avoid the Bristol Road,' he said, as Will and April ensconced themselves in the back. 'Go the long way, past the uni.'

The driver shrugged, happy to accept the higher fare, and Will smiled. Jordan had just requested a route that would avoid passing any of the billboards advertising the impending release of *Kismet 2*. The first time Will had glanced out of the tram window to Patrick's face looking back from the side of a building, he'd had to breathe into a paper bag.

'Right, Miss Grace,' Jordan said, swiping down playlists on his phone. 'We are choosing you a song by the time we get to the bar.'

'"Since U Been Gone"?' suggested April. '"Thank U, Next"?'

'I don't think so,' said Will.

'"Breakup Song"? "*Potential* Breakup Song"?'

'Too on the nose.'

'"Don't Speak"? "All Too Well"? "Someone Like You"?'

'No, no, and no.' On and on came the heartbreak anthem suggestions, until finally Will took the device out of Jordan's hands and started conducting his own search. 'I think,' he murmured, 'I know what I want to say.'

Jordan grabbed the phone back and peered down at the screen. 'J'approve,' he said. 'And look! Perfect timing.' The car pulled up outside the Village, and Jordan jumped out immediately, marching inside to give the sound guy (also known as Dave in the DJ booth) instructions.

'Drink?' April asked.

'Absolutely.' Will nodded. 'I'll be right in.'

All those stories in Jordan's phone. They started right here. And the more time that went by, the more Will began to feel that another story that began here, the unlikeliest one of all, remained unfinished. Even if it wasn't happily ever after, didn't Will deserve to know how it ended? Weren't they *both* owed that?

He reached into the jacket he'd put on over his dress because it was September in the UK, which meant summer had left the building, and drew out his phone.

'Time to be brave,' he muttered, and dialled. Nothing happened at first, and he began to wonder if he'd forgotten to enter the international dialling code again.

'Hello?' came a voice on the other end of the line, crisp and clear. Funny. Will had expected the voice to sound further away.

'Hello, Simone,' he said.

34

The day before the premiere of the first *Kismet* movie, Patrick, Corey, and Hector had hiked Runyon Canyon. It had been a pivotal moment in each of their careers: the biggest movie Corey had ever worked on as a stuntman, marking Patrick's ascent as a leading man with a body built by Hector. They had all been more nervous than any of them had wanted to admit, and walking up a big hill had felt like a good way to burn off some of that anxious energy.

The day before the premiere of *Kismet 2*, in what Patrick hoped would now be a tradition of theirs, the three of them met at the bottom of Runyon again.

'And he tried to do it with you right there? In the *bathroom*?' Corey whistled. 'That seems risky. And retro, sort of.'

Patrick had given Hector and Corey an abridged version of the events at the gala, taking great care to obfuscate Reece's identity.

'What did Simone say?' asked Hector.

'Oh, get this.' Patrick jutted his chin out and recited: '"This is how it's done, Patrick. You don't want to come all the way out? Fine. This is the middle ground." I told her it felt grubby, and she said: "Compromise always is."'

'Maybe Simone has a point,' said Hector. 'Not that you should be having your management team pimp you out like that,' he added, seeing Patrick's mortified expression, 'but come on, man. You've got to figure out *some* way of meeting guys.'

'I don't know,' said Patrick. 'This town makes things kind of impossible.'

'And you and Will are definitely...' Corey ventured.

'Over? Yes. Me and Will are one hundred per cent over. It's for the best, for both of us. For him especially. I asked too much of him. It wasn't fair.' Some people simply weren't supposed to hide away. Patrick understood that now. Will was born to shine. It would have been a crime, to let that light flicker out in a closet.

'That's a shame,' said Corey. 'I really liked him.'

Patrick turned to look at him. 'Really?'

'Sure! He was funny. He has, like, that dry English sense of humour where I feel like I'm constantly being called an idiot, but in a nice way, plus a little something extra.'

'He's got spice,' added Hector.

'You guys surprise me,' said Patrick.

'Why?' they both asked.

'I don't know. Will is just so different from...' He didn't know how to finish that sentence.

'From guys like us?' Corey offered.

'Yeah. I guess that's what I meant.'

'That's fucked up,' said Hector. 'That you would think that. About your boyfriend.'

'It really is.' Patrick nodded, the knot of shame he'd been carrying around in his stomach for years tightening. Only this time it wasn't shame about who he was, or who he wanted. He knew nothing about those desires was wrong. He couldn't say the same of the way he'd behaved. The things he'd said and done. The restrictions and rules he had laid down that made it impossible for Will to ever really get close to him, or at least as close as Patrick truly wanted.

'I'm going to die alone,' he announced to the vast sky above them. 'Alone, in a big empty house, surrounded by supplement pills and magazines with me on the cover.' He laughed, but it came out all wrong, a warped and ugly sound. 'That's showbiz, baby!'

'I don't know what's messed with your head more,' said Hector. 'Being gay, or being an actor.'

'Yeah,' Corey echoed. 'Sure, Will is a li'l zesty, but I mean, so are you, at least these last few months. And you've been a lot more fun to hang out with.'

'I have?' Patrick looked at Corey quizzically.

'*So* much more fun than you were on the first *Kismet* movie,' Corey confirms.

'And yeah, Will might not be addicted to the gym and eat elk every day,' Hector continued, 'but didn't you see his death drop into a split? Do you know how much strength and flexibility that takes? I mean it, man. Those queens are *athletes*. The stuff they do is like the Olympics, but they do all of it backwards and in heels.'

'Ginger Rogers!' Corey blurted out, clearly thinking he was helping.

'Which season of *RuPaul* did she win?' Hector asked.

'*You* watch *Drag Race*?' Patrick asked, incredulous.

Hector fixed him with the kind of stare he usually reserved for when Patrick crapped out on his tenth burpee.

'Pat.' He squeezed his shoulder. 'I am a whole bisexual.'

'Oh.' Patrick stopped in his tracks. 'I… I didn't know.'

Hector simply shrugged. 'You never asked.'

He was right, Patrick realised. These two men, these generous, patient, fantastic men, were probably two of the only real friends he had in the world, and he knew next to nothing about them. He'd succeeded in becoming exactly the kind of self-centred asshole he'd always bragged he'd never be.

'I am starting to think,' he said slowly, 'that I may have been very stupid.'

'Yes,' said Hector.

'A real dark-sided dumbass,' concurred Corey.

'An absolute gobshite,' Patrick continued.

'I don't know what that is,' said Corey, 'but... sounds like it, yeah.'

'The question now is,' Hector continued, 'what are you going to do about it?'

'I don't know what I *can* do,' Patrick said. 'It's over. It's too late.'

Corey shook his head determinedly.

'What am I always saying?' he asked.

'That only idiots skip leg day.'

'Well, yes. But what else? The trick to doing stunts safely?'

Patrick gave him a blank look.

'You've fallen,' Corey said. 'But there's still time for you to figure out where you want to land.'

The real world was waiting for Patrick when he left the canyon. He had purposely left his phone in the car and avoided wearing the smartwatch that told him how close he was to meeting his fitness goals for the day. When he was in movie-prepping mode he was essentially paid every time he moved his body. After weeks of doing press for *Kismet 2*, he wanted to hike with the guys however he damn well pleased.

Patrick scrolled through notifications as he sipped water and wiped sweat and sunscreen from the back of his neck with a towel. Most were updates from Simone and the publicist she had hired about the premiere tomorrow, the logistics of where he would be and when, details that had been ironed out, balled up and ironed again so many times that he knew them by heart. The Chinese Theatre on Hollywood at 7 o'clock tomorrow.

Patrick deleted all incoming alerts, except two which had piqued his curiosity.

The first was from a number he didn't recognise.

I got your number from Maurice. I thought you should see this.

Patrick had no idea who Maurice might be, but as soon as he opened the attached video, he realised it could only be from Jordan, and the terse tone made sense.

The footage was shaky, with a lot of background noise, but Patrick almost immediately recognised the location: the Village. The camera was trained on the stage, where Faye Runaway stood in a floor-length gown and turban à la Norma Desmond.

'Our next act is familiar to some of you,' she said over tipsy whoops and cheers. 'And no, not because she can be found in the third stall of the gents during the interval. That would be me.' She delicately pretended to wipe the corner of her mouth, and Patrick let out a brief snort of laughter. 'No, this next queen is very near and dear to my heart and yours. She's a lady, she's a tramp, she's an absolute bastard... Let's hear it for Grace Anatomy!'

Patrick's stomach tightened, and he almost stopped the video. Even on a tiny screen, the prospect of seeing Will made the hairs on his arms stand on end.

Grace wore an ivory gown and a blonde wig, with a leather jacket hanging delicately over her shoulders, like a girl whose boyfriend had just noticed she was cold. Patrick instantly recognised the visual reference – Buffy Summers, all dressed up to fight to the death on the night of her first school dance – a split second before he recognised the jacket. It was the one Will wore that night at the Flapper. The one he'd worn while Patrick came undone.

Grace stepped up to the microphone stand.

'He said let's get out of this town,' Will sang. 'Drive out of the city, away from the crowds...'

It was a song Patrick knew, a song he happened to know Will loved, but right now he felt like he was hearing it for the first time. Oh God, Will was singing, singing *live* and so beautifully, the audience in thrall to this wildest dream. Until he reached the chorus, and his voice came close to cracking, his face wracked with emotion.

The knowledge that Patrick was behind that pain shattered him inside, but the pride he felt for Will in that moment rebuilt him. How he wished he could have been there, to tell anybody who would listen 'See that person there? See her in all of her glory? She is the queen of my heart!' To rush the stage and kiss the hem of Grace's gown. To throw roses. To scream and clap until his throat and hands bled. To hold Will afterwards, to tell him over and over again how special and important and precious and dear he was.

He reached the end of the video and started it again, taking in this time the pride in Faye's voice as she introduced her protégé, the whistles and whoops as Grace took the stage, the crowd singing along when she reached the final chorus.

He drove back to his apartment and watched it again. Then once more after taking a shower. He was on his sixth or seventh viewing when he remembered he still had one more outstanding message: a voicemail. Patrick tapped the Play button and left the phone on his bed as he pulled on a pair of sweats.

'Hello, I am trying to reach Mr Lake.' The voice that came through was female, smoky, and if Patrick had to hazard a guess, middle-aged. 'You don't know me, my name is Ellie Hoffman. I've been given your information by Simone Toussaint. A charming woman, I have to say. She seemed quite protective of you but agreed that you would probably want to hear this.'

Ellie Hoffman paused to clear her throat. Whether this was for dramatic tension or incidental, Patrick was practically hunched over the phone by the time she finished her message:

'I have the Omega Issue.'

35

Will had been out on such a limb when asking Simone this favour, he hadn't been fully prepared for her to actually say yes. What would have taken all of Will's rainy-day money and Margo exhausting every last one of her precious credit card points to achieve, Simone did in a matter of seconds. She was not forthcoming about why she was using agency resources to help Will out, but he got the feeling that she had her own reasons.

And so a three-hour coach journey, two-hour wait at Heathrow, eleven-hour flight and fifty-five-minute cab ride later, Will arrived at the Chateau Marmont in Los Angeles.

Despite Patrick's stories, Will had been unsure of what to expect from LA It was the city of dreams, or at least purported to be, yet most of what he saw of Sunset Boulevard from the back of the taxi had been drugstores and coffee shops and, he was pretty sure, the nightclub where River Phoenix died.

Will got out of the car and into the lobby, instantly grateful for America's love affair with air conditioning: he'd left an island shrouded in damp fog and landed in a desert. He approached the front desk and the concierge – who looked as much like a movie star as anyone Will had ever met – gave him a look with which he was becoming familiar. It was the once-over that asked: *Are you famous? Are you worth my time? How nice do I need to be to you?*

'Hi,' he said, and bloody hell, why was he waving awkwardly at this well-groomed, chicly dressed, not-at-all sweaty gentleman? 'I'm here to see Patrick Lake?' he continued. 'Erm... Simone should have let you know I was coming? Simone Toussaint?' He hated the way everything he was saying came out as a question, like he knew deep down that he wasn't supposed to be here, and any moment the man on the other side of the desk would sense it too. But after a few hushed words into an earpiece that gave him the look of a backing dancer for Janet Jackson, the concierge nodded briskly and directed him towards the elevator.

Simone – he assumed – was standing there waiting when the doors slid open on the third floor, immaculate in a Gucci suit and Louboutins.

'Hello, Will,' she said. 'It's so good to finally meet in person.' Her face gave no indication that it was, indeed, good to meet him. Perhaps she was as partial to Botox as Jordan. Or, she simply didn't see this bedraggled stray from England as worth the risk of wrinkles.

Here she is, he thought. *The woman who has held my fate in her hands all this time.*

Will felt about Simone the way he felt about every other powerful woman he had ever met: as fascinated as he was cowed. Heels like that were powerful but, he knew from experience, hurt like hell after longer than a few minutes. He wondered if she kept a pair of sneakers under her desk for when nobody was around to intimidate. If she tucked a napkin into the collar of her ivory blouse while she was eating lunch. Not that Simone was the kind of woman who looked like she spilled things. Or ate, for that matter. And God, her makeup! That winged eyeliner could cut a bitch.

Enough! He told himself. *We're not here to stan.*

'Hi, Simone,' he said. 'Thank you for the flight. Honestly. I'll pay you back.'

Simone exhaled impatiently at the notion that the price of his air fare might be remotely consequential. When Will had phoned her, he hadn't had much of a clue what he wanted to say, other than to try and arrange a face-to-face with her client. He'd reasoned that, understanding now how Patrick's world worked, he should show that he was willing to follow the rules, and check with his 'people' that he was open to talking. More truthfully, coward that he was, he'd been too afraid to call Patrick himself.

His best-case scenario had been that Simone would facilitate a Zoom. Instead, after hearing him out, she had simply said 'leave it with me,' and five minutes later a British Airways reservation had landed in his inbox. He had no idea why she'd done it – she certainly didn't seem the type prone to sudden bouts of generosity – but he wasn't one to look a gift horse in the impeccably lined mouth either. He was just glad his passport was still in date.

'If the niceties are out of the way?' Simone took off at a brisk pace down the hallway. 'Everybody is getting ready through here.'

'Everybody? Meaning...'

'Patrick will be here soon. He and a few of the others are attending the premiere together.' Simone paused in the last doorway at the end of the corridor. 'Will, listen. I wouldn't usually dream of distracting my client right before a premiere by flying in his secret ex-boyfriend. It is, frankly, amateurish behaviour.' She examined her flawless manicure. 'But after an unfortunate misunderstanding, I happen to have some making up to do to Patrick. And I know that he has not been the same since he came back from England. So. Here we are.'

'Here we are,' Will echoed, still not understanding fully.

'I will permit you to be here,' Simone said, 'on the proviso that you wait for Patrick in the last bedroom on the right in the suite, do not interact with any other members of the cast, and when they all leave to attend the premiere, you stay behind. Do we have a deal?'

Will wondered how many other lives had been sent on a new trajectory by a verbal covenant in a hotel corridor. *So this is Hollywood*, he thought.

He thrust his hands in his pockets and said: 'Deal.' He crossed his fingers, unseen, and followed Simone into the suite.

'Remember,' Simone said. 'Go straight to that far room and don't talk to anyb—'

'Will!' The entire room seemed to call his name at the same time in various levels of surprise: Audra was here, as were Hector and Corey, and a handful of other faintly recognisable and pleasingly symmetrical faces.

'Will!' Audra sprang up from the chair, where Estelle was applying the last flourishes to her makeup, running over to hug him and thinking better of it at the last minute, air kissing him so that her face remained untouched.

'It's so good to see you!' she said. 'You look terrible!'

Will couldn't disagree, and confronted with a roomful of some of the most beautiful people on this coast, he suddenly felt completely out of his element. This was Patrick's utterly bizarre world, not his. He couldn't confront the man he maybe-loved and maybe-always-had in the painter's trousers and tank top he'd sat sweating in for eleven hours. Maybe this entire enterprise had been a mistake.

'Bro!' Hector and Corey both said, almost in unison, and without a single jot of the homophobia Will had come to expect from that simple word.

'Hi guys!' he replied, overcome with relief that they were both huggers and no embarrassing manshake was required.

'Are you here to see Patrick?' asked Corey.

'That's kind of the idea, yeah.'

'Well thank God, Goddess and all the others for that,' said Audra. 'He has been a total bummer these last few months. Have you ever done a press tour while lumbered with a sulking, broken-hearted sadsack? Not fun, let me tell you.'

Will decided to let all the ways in which the word 'bummer' got lost in translation to an English homosexual go uncommented upon.

'It's good to see you, man,' said Hector, clapping Will on the shoulder, nearly sending him through a wall in the process.

'Yeah, dude,' said Hector. 'The gobshitery has been off the charts around here.' He paused. 'Did I use that right?'

Will seesawed his hand. 'Close enough,' he said. 'You guys look... Bloody hell.'

Hector and Corey each wore suits that lovingly hugged their physiques, and Will reminded himself once again that looking that way was their full-time job. He resisted the urge to ask them both to turn around (because was there a greater sight in the world, outside of a sunset or a baby's first steps, than a man's bottom in tailored trousers?), and instead turned to Audra.

'I can't see Patrick looking like this,' he said. 'Is there somewhere I can freshen up?'

Audra was already rifling through the duffel bag he'd brought with him, tutting at its contents.

'And there goes the myth about gay men having style,' she said, taking him by the hand. 'I suppose there's nothing for it. You need a makeover.'

'A makeover?' Will asked.

'Well, sure!' Audra's eyes sparkled. 'You've just arrived in Hollywood. Time to change everything about yourself. Estelle!'

'We got you, man,' said Corey, and while Audra discussed the particular 'challenges' of his Irish skin with the makeup artist, Will allowed himself to be led over to a rail in the corner of the room, where several garment bags hung like vampire bats.

'They always send over a bunch of different options,' said Hector, not pausing to explain who 'they' were. 'Take your pick!'

The tuxedos before him were, without a doubt, stunning. They were also, even more certainly, never going to fit Will, whose proportions were considerably slighter than those of Patrick, Corey, or Hector.

'This isn't going to work,' he said. 'I'll look like a kid who got dressed up in daddy's clothes. And anyway, I'm not even going to the premiere. I'm supposed to just wait here.'

'Never mind that,' said Audra, joining them. 'Will, go take a shower. First door on the left. Then go into the room next door. I have this completely under control. '

Too exhausted and overwhelmed to argue, Will obeyed, taking his duffel into the bathroom. He brushed his teeth with vigour, then stripped down and stepped under the rain shower. He didn't know how long he stood there letting the water cascade over him, washing away what felt like days' worth of grime. When he finally exited the bathroom in a fluffy white robe, he felt like he had been reborn.

Audra was waiting for him in the next room, along with another rack. She had shed her own robe and put on her outfit for the premiere: a glittering silver cocktail dress that, combined with her makeup and tousled updo, made her look like an editorial Tinkerbell; mischief refined and distilled into its purest form.

'Take your pick,' she said, gesturing to the clothes rail. 'They sent me some gorgeous things, but half of them aren't my colour.'

Instantly, Will's attention was captured by an exquisite piece of tailoring among the dresses: a double-breasted suit in a bold vermillion. The trousers, when he pulled them off the hanger and they slid into his hands, were wide-legged and high-waisted.

'Hello, gorgeous,' he whispered. This, far more than the black tie garb donned by Hector and Corey, was his kind of suit. Womenswear as menswear, worn by a man who made his living dressing like a woman. Drag on drag on drag.

'Good eye,' said Audra, turning to face the wall so he could get dressed. Will pulled on the trousers and then slipped the jacket straight onto his bare torso, enjoying the feel of the unlined fabric on his skin. He went to button up the coat, but Audra stopped him, fussing over him until it hung open in precisely the right way, his nipples barely obscured by the broad lapels.

'You have a great body,' she said. 'Show it off a little, won't you?'

'Are you sure?'

'Trust me, I'm an actress,' Audra told him. 'Learning my lines and crying on cue are only the first part of the job. For the women in this industry, the red carpet is the real final exam. And I happen to be something of a prodigy in that department. There, perfect... Now we just need to figure out what to do with your hair. Oh, and you need shoes.'

'What's wrong with my hair?' Will asked, but Audra was already calling in Estelle and the hair stylist, an olive-skinned man in a tracksuit and a topknot named Javier. Corey followed them into the room, excitement written all over his face, and held up a spotless pair of white sneakers.

'I figured we'd be around the same size,' he said, tossing them to Will, who in possibly the butchest moment of his life, caught them with ease.

'Thanks, man!' he replied, genuinely touched by the gesture, and then he was steered towards a chair where Javier sprayed some of the world's most expensive salt into his hair, teasing the damp frizz into slick, bouncy waves, and Audra offered a director's commentary as Estelle lightly contoured his cheekbones. It was not entirely unlike getting ready with the girls upstairs at the Village. And in her own way, he realised, Audra Kelly's job was doing drag just as much as any queen he had ever met.

'I feel like Cinderella,' he said.

'I played her once,' Audra replied dreamily. 'My first gig.'

'Pantomime?'

'Theme park.'

When Estelle had finished lining his eyes with kohl, Audra loaned him several silver necklaces to layer across his bare chest, and a single dangling earring. Once he had put on the sneakers, which had such a thick tread that they were functionally no different from high heels, Will felt as mighty as if he were in full femme mode. Glimpsing his own reflection, his breath caught in his throat: here he was, but so was Grace. Clark Kent and Superman in the same room at the same time, the moon in a midday sky.

He had proudly spat in the face of an angry mob. He had faced his fear and sung live. He had swallowed his pride and won back his dearest friend. Will Wright felt in that moment like he could do anything. Kick down a door, slay a dragon, or maybe even have a conversation with his ex.

Will re-entered the main room to a wolf-whistle from Hector, but the rest of the room was oddly still. Simone, who had been quietly absorbed in her phone since she first escorted him in, now paced the length of the room, hitting call over and over again and exhaling through her nose with increasing force each time that she got no reply.

'What's going on?' Will whispered to Audra.

'It's Patrick,' she replied. 'He's missing.'

36

Patrick had managed to live in Los Angeles for ten years without ever making it out to Venice Beach. He'd pictured some kind of postcard version of the place; bodybuilders working out on the boardwalk, supermodels on rollerblades, hippies with stands selling crystals and tie-dye. Easy magic. As he followed the GPS directions to the home of Ellie Hoffman, what he found instead was a place that looked like it had been forgotten, left to be taken by the tide and the weeds like a crumbling castle from a fairy tale.

Ellie Hoffman's residence was no different. Patrick passed through the open front gate onto her short driveway and pulled up outside a Spanish-style bungalow half-consumed by climbing vines. Wind chimes and dreamcatchers dangled from any surface that jutted out far enough, and when Patrick exited the car an enormous orange cat immediately emerged from one of the bushes next to the porch and padded over to wedge itself clumsily between his ankles.

'Caliban, leave the poor man alone!' came a voice from the front door; the same voice Patrick had heard on his voicemail yesterday. Ellie Hoffman looked more or less exactly how he might have expected her to, given the witch's cottage where she lived. Henna-red hair floated in a frizzy halo around crab-apple cheeks and twinkling eyes. An off-white, sack-like tunic covered most of her sturdy frame in a way that could have made her look like an ascetic nun, had her fingers not glinted with silver and turquoise rings, and Barbie-pink toenails not been poking out from beneath her blue jeans. She could have been anywhere between fifty and seventy.

'Welcome,' Ellie said, smiling brightly and beckoning Patrick inside. 'I made lemonade.'

Patrick followed Ellie inside, down a short hallway and into the living room.

'Should I take off my shoes?' he asked.

'I wouldn't if I were you,' she said. 'I dropped an earring somewhere in here yesterday and haven't found it yet. Wouldn't want to have to take a movie star to the hospital for a tetanus shot if you stepped on it. Why don't you take a seat over there' – she gestured to a threadbare sofa draped in an Afghan – 'and I'll be right back. Just give Caliban a good shove if he crowds your personal space. I love the beast, but he isn't for everyone.'

Ellie vanished, leaving him to sit awkwardly perched on the end of the couch, wondering if he had made a huge mistake. Encountering the occasional weirdo was par for the course in his line of work, but he didn't make a habit of entering their homes. What if Ellie Hoffman came out of that room wielding an axe, claiming to be his number one fan? Would he feel comfortable physically fighting a woman old enough to be his mother?

Caliban did not approach Patrick, but simply watched him intently from under the coffee table while Patrick glanced around the living room at the various Turkish lamps, blue glass evil eyes dangling from doorframes, the menorah and Buddha bookending a small stack of dog-eared paperbacks, the trio of silver urns on the mantle, the vase full of bright pink flowers that looked freshly trimmed from the bushes outside, and framed photographs covering almost every inch of the wall. Ellie was present in many of them, surrounded by people who looked like her children.

Some of the older pictures, faded or in black and white, featured a handsome couple. The man had a broad, pleasing smile in many of them, while the woman, pursed lips and arched brow, had the air of somebody about to say something witty or devastating. A smaller number of photos included a pretty, laughing young woman with a snub nose.

'Your parents?' Patrick asked as Ellie returned, carrying two cardboard boxes. He gestured to a picture of the first woman in a modest dress holding a bouquet, the man standing solemnly next to her.

'Yes,' she said, placing the boxes down on the coffee table with great care. 'They're the reason I contacted you, Mr Lake.' She removed the lid from the first box, revealing a meticulously stacked assortment of papers, some of which were emblazoned, Patrick could see, with the Kismet insignia.

'They were collectors?' he asked.

'Not especially,' said Ellie.

'They certainly seemed to be admirers of Captain Kismet,' said Patrick, reverently picking up what he instantly knew to be an original issue of *Wonder* Magazine.

'In a way, I suppose,' Ellie said. 'They created him.'

Patrick frowned.

'Walter Haywood created Captain Kismet,' he said. 'Everybody knows that.'

'All anybody knows is the story that Walter Haywood told them,' said Ellie, her lip curling up as she said the man's name. Patrick got the impression that in this house, the Haywood name was mud.

'I don't understand,' he said. 'Haywood founded *Wonder* Magazine and all of its proprietary characters.'

'The magazine was his,' Ellie nodded, 'but everything else? All my parents. Haywood liked to say that he came up with the characters himself, and hired writers and artists to help with the work of telling those stories, that they were all his intellectual property.' She pointed to the box. 'Go ahead. Take a look. It's all right here.'

As slowly and fastidiously as possible, Patrick went through the contents of the first box. Early character sketches for Captain Kismet, Axel, Sura, Penny, Omega. Typed pages of Kismet's adventures, covered in annotations, half the words crossed out and rewritten in the margins. And finally, at the bottom of the box, a series of loose pages punched and tied together in the corner with string:

The Adventures of Captain Kismet, #12

'The Omega Issue,' Patrick breathed.

'You sit there and read,' said Ellie. 'I'll fetch that lemonade.'

Patrick tried to read with intention and care, but found himself flipping through the pages like a child devouring their first comic book, unable to believe the story unfolding before him: Penny's hubris, so rarely explored in the fifty years since; Sura's angelic return; and the operatic romance of Kismet cradling Axel in his arms, kissing him back to life.

'It's so... *gay*,' he said moments later, sipping lemonade, the issue safely back in its cardboard tomb.

'Isn't it just.' Ellie beamed, and Patrick felt a tug in his chest. He'd seen a similar look in Will's eyes when he opened his drag closet, had heard that verve in April's voice while they discussed Kismet lore over Margo's kitchen table.

The fragile joy of showing somebody else the thing you love the most.

'There's more,' said Ellie, reaching for the second box of her parents' personal effects and pulling it into her lap. She placed a hand protectively on its lid.

'This is their story,' she said. 'Their whole lives, they didn't want to share it with anybody outside of the family. But I think it's time. And I have a feeling that you might be just the person to hear it, Mr Lake. I've always considered myself a little bit psychic, actually. I used to read palms down on the boardwalk. I was rarely wrong about people, and now, with you sitting here in front of me... It feels right.'

With an even more loving touch than before, she lifted the cover off the second box, and one by one, handed Patrick fragments of the past.

It began with a letter, written in a fine, elegant hand, on paper so old and thin it was almost translucent between his fingers.

New York City
1949

Dear Axel,
I am sorry that it has been so long between letters (not that I really expect you to have noticed my silence). A great deal has changed since I last wrote you: Charles and I are married now, can you believe it? It was only a small, private affair, just the two of us at City Hall. The couple from next-door were witnesses. There were none of the usual blessings, no breaking of the glass, no hora, although we did have a rather excellent lunch at the Bossert afterwards. Mother and Father would have positively detested it, which I am more than willing to admit lent a brighter shine to the occasion.

   My only regret is that you were not there to meet Charles, to have a drink with him and discuss whatever dull matters men always seem to bring up over hard liquor. Baseball and automobiles, perhaps? I asked for a glass of Scotch at the restaurant and toasted my husband, but really, I was toasting you, the only man I've ever known who truly understood me. I sipped the Scotch and my throat burned and I told myself it was the alcohol making my eyes water.

I tell myself all kinds of marvellous stories these days, Axel. I even write some of them down; fantastical tales of castles in the stars and men who fly. Wondrous strange!, as your old pal the Bard would put it.

I showed some of my stories to Charles. Even that felt, for just a moment, like a betrayal – I know you kept asking to someday read my scribbles.

He liked them a lot. So much, in fact, that he took one into his studio – a tiny room in our apartment, little more than a closet really – and came out an hour later having sketched the most tremendous illustrations.

'We make quite a team,' he said, and he kissed my cheek, and I giggled. Me, Axel! Like I was a schoolgirl. Charles sent the story and his pictures to an editor he knew at a magazine. Incredible Tales, I think it's called, or Tales of Wonder. Maybe something will come of it, perhaps nothing will, but if there is one thing I have learned, I daresay we have all learned, from that terrible, terrible war is that if nothing matters, then surely everything matters. It is our duty, I think, to do for ourselves what those who are no longer here cannot do. To grasp opportunity, to

say today that which might be too late to say tomorrow.

There are so many things I never told you, Axel. About me, about who and what I really am. I tell myself I didn't have the words, but that's another lie.

The truth of the matter is I was afraid. And now it is far too late to tell you anything, which I suppose is why I am sitting here in my nightgown by candlelight like some Gothic heroine, writing a letter to a dead man. In the hope that by putting ink to paper, this simple act of creation will somehow carry a part of me to a place where even the tiniest fragment of you might still reside. That is just one more story, I suspect.

But isn't it a pretty one?

Your sister,
Iris

'Axel,' Patrick breathed.

'My uncle,' Ellie said. 'He died long before I was born. I'm not sure my mom ever got over it. I suppose that's why he's everywhere in her work. She gave him a second life, a destiny far greater than the one he was saddled with. Her shining prince from the heavens.'

Patrick handed the letter reverently to Ellie and picked up the next artefact from the box: a photograph of the second young woman from the wall, hands perched on top of a baby bump. 'Her name was Eleanor,' said Ellie. 'They named me for her.'

A story began to form in Patrick's mind, each new piece of its puzzle falling into place.

Postcards that Ellie's father Charles had received sporadically throughout the years, bearing stamps from all over the world, unsigned, only ever containing one or two lines, from an anonymous correspondent who appeared to have travelled extensively.

You would love Paris.

I find myself once again walking in the city of the seven hills. I sometimes think I never left.

The moon is so bright here in the desert. I never imagined there could be so many stars.

'I think I'm starting to understand,' said Patrick, passing the final postcard back to Ellie. They both held it between them, and Patrick realised he didn't want to let it go. Eventually, Ellie released it into his hands.

'Charles and Iris,' he said. 'They were both...?'

'Yes.' Ellie nodded. 'Haywood chased them out of New York when he found out. They both took my mother's maiden name, Hoffman, when they moved out here. It was a horrible time. Mom told me about it often. How people were being hunted on home soil like they had been in Europe, but all in the name of decency. The hypocrisy!' She laughed and shook her head. 'God, I sound just like her. I miss her.'

'And Eleanor was her...'

'Lover?' Ellie blinked nonchalantly. 'Of course. She came from New York with them too. She was my birth mother. She died having me. They both loved her dearly and promised to always take care of me. I think there was some fudging of official records, because it's their names on my birth certificate, not hers. I imagine that was easier to do in those days. They wanted to make sure nobody could take me away. So they became my real parents.'

She said it with the casual familiarity of somebody who had grown up with the story, but for Patrick it took some processing.

'Wow,' he said.

'Yeah. Wow.' Ellie tucked a stray curl behind her ear.

'And the man from the postcards?'

'What about him?'

'Why didn't he come to LA with them?' he asked.

Eleanor sighed. 'That was one of the great unanswered questions of my father's life,' she said. 'Do you want to know what I think?'

Patrick nodded.

She looked him dead in the eye. 'He wasn't brave enough.'

Patrick's breath grew short, and he thought back to the tall tale he had just read, of Penny's essence being scattered across time and space, the same life playing out again and again. Wasn't that the whole business of comics, at the end of the day? A story being told over and over again until someone got it right?

'Does it feel strange?' Patrick asked. 'Knowing that your family was built on a lie?'

Eleanor laughed. 'A lie? Oh, you're a funny one. My family may not have looked like everybody else's, and certain pretences may have been upheld in public for the benefit of a quiet life, but I assure you, Mr Lake, we never lied to each other. Or ourselves.'

Patrick continued to look down at the postcard in his hands, turning it over and over as if doing so might reveal an as-yet hidden message.

'You're a large man, Mr Lake,' Eleanor continued. 'Does it ever get uncomfortable? A little tight across the shoulders?'

Patrick looked up at her, his brows a question mark.

'The constraints you place on yourself, my dear.'

Patrick's breathing grew even more rapid, his chest tight, and he only knew he had burst into tears when Ellie enveloped him in an embrace, clutching his head to her shoulder, and he saw his tears damping the fabric of her tunic. She held him like that for several minutes while he wept, like a mother might a child, or a hero saving a helpless damsel, until finally the tears ran dry and he withdrew, wiping his puffy eyes, a cloud of embarrassment already forming.

'I'm sorry,' he said. 'I don't know what came over me. I never cry like this.'

'Silly boy,' said Ellie, cupping his cheek with genuine affection. 'Maybe you should.'

37

'What do you mean, missing?' Will asked.

'He isn't answering his phone,' said Simone. 'He always takes my calls. Always.'

'Even when he's mad at you?' asked Hector pointedly. Simone cast a searing glare at him, and nodded.

'Yes,' she said. 'Even when he is mad at me. Because this kind of sulking endangers the work, and the work is what matters. He and I have always been on the same page about that.'

'I think that might have changed, Geppetto,' said Corey. 'Your Pinocchio is a real boy now.'

'Patrick is a dreamer,' said Simone. 'Somebody has to be the grown-up.'

'Hard disagree,' said Audra. 'This is LA!'

'Never mind that,' said Will. 'Where *is* he?'

A carousel of increasingly grave scenarios began to spin through his mind: Patrick being pursued by paparazzi in such a frenzy that his car went off the road; Patrick being accosted by a deranged fan; Patrick falling from the top of the Hollywood sign. What on earth Patrick would have been doing atop the Hollywood sign in the first place was beside the point. If he had fallen, then he could have broken both his legs, might at this very moment be clinging on to life, and here they were at the Chateau bloody Marmont playing dress-up when they should be out forming search parties!

'I'm going to go look for him,' Will declared, marching towards the door as if he had any idea where Patrick might be, or where to even begin his search, or even any knowledge of this city at all.

He hurled the door open, and as if by magic there Patrick was, standing in the hallway, hand outstretched, caught in the motion of entering. It had been just a few months, a handful of long weeks since they last saw each other, but he looked different somehow. Taller, maybe?

'Will,' Patrick's eyes widened in shock, and Will said the first thing that came to mind, the only words he felt capable of getting out in the right order:

'What time do you call this?'

'LA traffic,' said Patrick. 'I was at the beach, and getting back took forever, and...' He smiled lopsidedly, a single dimple creasing the left side of his face. 'And gay men,' he announced, 'are simply incapable of being on time.'

'That's a stereotype,' Will replied with a smirk. 'I thought you were above those.'

'There you are,' Simone's voice behind them sounded infinitesimally gentler now that her client was present. 'Where have you been?'

Patrick's eyes drifted from Will's.

'Venice,' he said. 'Traffic. I'm sorry.'

'What were you doing out there?' asked Simone. 'You know what, never mind, we don't have time. Patrick, there's a tux over there with your name on it. You have' – she checked her Cartier watch, 'five minutes to get premiere-ready – and then we are all leaving.'

'Five minutes,' Patrick repeated. 'Sure. Can do.'

He brushed past Simone towards the room where Audra had helped Will get ready, and once more Will questioned what on earth he was doing here. This was not his world, and certainly not the time to be distracting Patrick.

'Will?' Patrick called. 'You coming?' His expression softened. 'I think we need to talk.'

'Yes,' said Will, crossing the room to meet him. 'Yes, we do.'

Patrick closed the door behind them, and Will braced himself. He remembered, with sudden horror, how things had ended the last time Patrick walked into a hotel to find him dressed in red.

What he did not expect was for Patrick to grip him in a crushing embrace, arms vice-like around his back, face buried in his neck. Will curled his arms around Patrick's shoulders, closing his eyes and gladly using one of the five minutes allotted to them by Simone to remind himself of Patrick's smell, the way he felt, the sheer solidness of him.

This, he thought, *was worth crossing an ocean for.*

'You crushed it,' Patrick said into his neck.

'Excuse me?' asked Will, pulling away, and realising with some amusement that Patrick appeared to be as scrambled as he was.

'Your song,' said Patrick. 'I saw you, Will. I heard you sing. It was amazing.'

'What?' Will asked incredulously. 'How?'

'Jordan sent it to me. He seemed to think I might find it relevant to my interests.'

Will's heart swelled. He resolved to bring Jordan back a truly ostentatious souvenir from Los Angeles.

'He also said something about a guy called Maurice?' Patrick continued. 'Do I need to get all jealous? Because I totally will.'

Will laughed, and said: 'That reminds me; you still owe me twenty quid.'

'I owe you so much more than that.' Patrick said sombrely. 'I'm sorry, Will. So sorry, you'll probably never know.'

Oh, shit. They were really doing this.

'You hurt me,' said Will.

'I know.' Patrick nodded.

A harsh knock rapped three times against the door.

'*Two-minute warning*,' Simone called.

'Roger!' Patrick yelled. He pulled off his T-shirt and began to unbutton his jeans, and at the sight of that body, Will once again felt his brain hit Shuffle.

'Tell me,' he said, taking a seat on the end of the sofa. 'Please. Tell me what happened. What was going on with you?' Under slightly different circumstances he might have felt guilty about asking such a loaded question while he was fully dressed and Patrick stood before him in his underwear, but hey, time was of the essence.

'That night,' Patrick began. 'In my hotel room...'

'Did I push you?' Will asked. 'Make you do something you didn't want to?'

'The opposite.' Patrick shook out the neatly pressed pair of suit pants and stepped into them. 'I have never, in my life, trusted somebody the way I trust you. Never felt so seen or understood.'

'Then I really don't get it.'

Patrick threw on a white shirt.

'I was afraid,' he said, focusing first on the buttons and then the cuffs. Finally, when he felt ready, he looked at Will. 'I was afraid that being so deeply known would make it harder to hide who I am from the rest of the world. That I wouldn't even want to, anymore. Because being with you is the first time in years that I've felt really myself. And actually *liked* myself. How could I go back to the way things were after that? Shut myself away after finally breathing clean air?'

Patrick donned his black jacket, and then began to fiddle with the black bow tie in his hands.

'Let me,' said Will, standing and taking it from him. He looped the fabric around Patrick's neck. 'I'm sorry too,' he added.

'For what?' Patrick asked, his eyes fixed somewhere over Will's shoulder.

'That day on set. I knew you weren't ready to come out, that it would mean all kinds of trouble for your career, but I got so insecure that I put pressure on you anyway. It was very unchic of me. I should have known better.'

Will stepped back, inspecting the job he had done on Patrick's bow tie.

'Not bad,' he decided.

The door clicked open.

'We are leaving,' said Simone. 'Now.' She vanished from the doorway, clearly confident that Patrick would follow.

'Looks like we're out of minutes,' said Will.

Patrick smiled sadly. 'Wasn't that always our problem?'

'Hey guys...' Audra edged into view in the hallway outside, one hand covering her eyes, the other splayed out in front of her as she inched forward blindly. 'Simone says we need to get going...' She parted the fingers obscuring her view and sighed. 'I thought you might be fucking,' she said, not bothering to hide her disappointment. 'Come on!'

They all exited the suite in a flurry of activity, and Will allowed himself to be swept along in the tide of people, Simone's edict that he stay behind all but forgotten.

A limousine awaited them in the courtyard, and Will and Patrick piled into the back after Audra, Hector, Corey, and Simone.

'I feel like I'm on my way to prom!' Audra said. 'Champagne, anyone?'

'Will, I have to tell you something,' said Patrick. 'Actually... all of you.'

'You're gay,' said Audra. 'We know, sweetie. We already did this, remember?'

'It's not about *me*,' said Patrick. 'It's about Captain Kismet.'

'What is it?' asked Will, thinking that if he ever heard the name Captain buggerfucking Kismet ever again, it would be too soon.

'It's the reason I was out in Venice,' Patrick said. 'The Omega Issue. I found it, Will. And get this...' He took one of the glasses of champagne that Audra was passing around the back for the car, and held it out in front of him. '*They* were gay too.'

'Who?' said Hector.

'Say more!' cooed Audra.

Patrick explained what he had learned from the woman out at Venice Beach, showing them all pictures on his phone that she had permitted him to take of the hidden proof of Captain Kismet's real origins, and in watching him speak, Will felt his eyes threaten to fill. He looked like a man who had just come home.

'We've always been here,' said Patrick. 'I know that shouldn't surprise me. But it does. To know that in some small way, the reason I'm here, in this car, with all of you, is because of them. It feels like...'

'Lineage,' said Will.

Patrick smiled, and it was a shining, glorious thing. 'Yes. Lineage.'

'This is incredible, Patrick. I'm so happy for you.'

'That's not all,' Patrick said. He put his hand on Will's knee and looked over at Simone. 'I want to come out.'

For the first time since the elevator doors opened, Will saw Simone's perfect façade crack, a flicker of panic crossing her eyes. Or was that genuine concern?

'We've talked about this,' she said.

'I know,' said Patrick. 'And I know I told you this was what I wanted, that I was OK with it. But the truth is, I'm not.'

Simone took a deep breath, as if she had been preparing for this conversation for a long time but was still not eager to have it.

'Things will change,' she said. 'The roles that get offered to you. The opportunities. You might even lose the *Kismet* movies.'

'Money, money, money,' said Patrick. 'You're always talking about the money we'll lose by being honest, the opportunities that will dry up, the people who'll boycott, the markets who'll drop me. But what about the people who don't? The ones whose lives might even be improved, who might feel less alone?'

'You're certainly putting a lot of stock in your own significance,' said Simone.

'That's just the thing!' Patrick said, his voice rising. 'It's not about me! It never was! It's about all of us. How can we ever expect to change anything when we keep playing by other people's rules? Fuck them!'

'I don't know what to say.' Simone's impassive demeanour finally gave way to a crease at the eyes, a pursing of the lips. 'I've never seen you like this.'

'Me neither,' Will echoed.

'I'm just full of indignant rage,' said Patrick. 'And I also haven't had sex in several months. Well.' He turned to Will. 'There was an aborted encounter in a bathroom stall that I'll tell you all about later, and it didn't mean a thing, and we were broken up, and—'

'I'd be disappointed if you didn't try to get over me by getting under someone else,' said Will. 'Don't worry about that.'

'I appreciate where you're coming from,' said Simone, 'but representation is just the start. It's the bare minimum, Patrick. If you want to do this, I will be right there with you, but being an openly gay celebrity is a whole gig by itself. People are going to have questions. And the community will have expectations. The handsome white man is going to need to have a clear stance on all the issues. Book bans. Trans rights. "Don't Say Gay" legislation. Are you ready for that, renaissance man? Actor, activist, role model?'

'I'm ready to do the work,' Patrick told her. 'I have a lot to make up for.'

'You don't owe me anything,' said Will, putting his hand over Patrick's.

'It's not just you,' said Patrick. 'I feel like I owe *them*. Iris and Charles. They had to lie and hide to be happy. Their story had to be a secret. If after all this time, I'm doing exactly the same, I can't ever expect anything to change, can I?' His strident tone dropped. 'I couldn't hide and be with you.'

Will looked around the car, at Audra and Hector and Corey and Simone's expectant stares, and realised that he and Patrick were going to have to have the most intimate, awkward conversation of their relationship with an audience. Which felt perversely apt.

'We don't have to talk about this now,' he said.

'Don't we?' Patrick raised an eyebrow. 'Then what did you fly all the way to Los Angeles for? The food?'

'I just don't know how this would ever work,' said Will, flapping his hands around the back of the limousine. 'Not to be dramatic, but we're from different worlds. You make movies in Hollywood, I sing and dance in a dive bar wearing a dress.'

'And yet here you are,' said Patrick, 'on your way to a premiere with me.'

'Yes, and I wouldn't want to be anywhere else in this moment. But what about all the other moments after this one? How do we make it work, day to day?'

Patrick said nothing.

'All I know,' Will continued, 'is that before any of this, before the secrets, before you kissed me in the back of that cinema, you were my friend.'

'The back of a movie theatre?' Audra remarked. 'That is a throwback.'

'I think it's romantic,' Hector said.

'You think *everything* is romantic,' Audra said, leaning into him. She tapped the end of his nose. 'Don't you *dare* kiss me right now, Mr Ramirez. You'll smudge my makeup.'

Will cleared his throat, and the two of them hushed apologetically.

'I just want you to know,' he said, turning back to Patrick, 'that I am still your friend. I always will be. Whatever happens between us, whatever form it takes and on whatever terms, please just know that I'm here for you.'

He paused, realising he'd never actually said it out loud. Had been so obsessed with not seeming too needy, of misreading what was there, of being the silly little gay boy who deluded himself into believing a real man might want him.

But what the hell? He'd flown around the globe to have a single conversation. If Patrick hadn't deduced by now how Will felt about him then he never would.

'I love you, Patrick.' he said. 'I adore you, in fact.'

Will didn't look away from Patrick, knowing that the next words out of his mouth could change everything.

Except he said nothing. The car stopped, and the door opened before Patrick could answer. The limousine's interior was illuminated from the outside in a series of rapid flashes: fractured light from strange stars. The world premiere of *Kismet 2* was about to begin.

'Showtime,' said Simone.

38

It was time to get out of the limousine. Patrick watched numbly as Corey climbed out first, then Hector, who held out his hand and assisted Audra's exit from the car in one single, fluid, ladylike motion. Through the open door, Patrick could see the Chinese Theatre on Hollywood Boulevard. This was it. Everything he had been working towards. What he usually thought of as the absolute best part of his job, when he and everyone he worked with were finally able to share their labour of love with the rest of the world.

And yet all he wanted to do was stay in the car.

Patrick turned to Will, hating how helpless he felt.

'I wish we had more time,' he said.

'It's OK,' Will told him. 'Go. Do the red carpet thing. We can talk after.'

He smiled encouragingly, and Patrick never wanted to look away. Will was really *here*. In LA.

'I'll arrange a seat for him in the screening,' said Simone. She looked, by every measurable Simone standard, sincere. Patrick looked across at her for a moment, wondering if she had meant everything she'd said about supporting him if he took the plunge. Or if she would cynically cut him loose the way so many other managers had when their clients stopped playing by the rules of an unwinnable game.

'Snacks are on me when we get inside,' Patrick told Will. 'Best popcorn in the world, remember?'

'It's a date.'

He squeezed Will's knee and kept his hand there, taking in how solid he felt. *Drive*, he wanted to shout. *Take us far away from here, I don't care where. There is no place on earth I could not be happy with this man.*

Patrick forced himself up and out of the limo, following Simone to the small patch of cordoned-off space that preceded the red carpet proper, where reporters and photographers clamored. He hung back at the edge of the carpet while Audra took centre spot, escorted by Hector, and watched her posing for the cameras, pretending to laugh at something Hector whispered in her ear, America's sweetheart from head to glittering toe.

Then it was his turn.

Patrick straightened his tux, glancing down just long enough to notice for the first time where he was standing. The red carpet had been laid over almost the entire historic front courtyard of the Chinese Theatre, obscuring the handprints and signatures of some of the biggest names in Hollywood royalty. But here, at the edge, some of those stones were still visible. Patrick's legs very nearly gave out as he read the autograph beneath his feet.

Rock Hudson.

Patrick didn't believe much in signs or omens. He did not visit a psychic or get energy healing, nor did he make decisions based on Tarot or entrust his fate to crystals. But when the entire cosmos cried out for a man to take a damn hint, only a fool would refuse to listen.

'Will!' he called, turning back to the car. 'Will!'

'What's going on?' asked Will as Patrick clambered back into the limousine, breath short and heart racing.

'Did I ever tell you why I auditioned for Captain Kismet?' he asked, sidling up so that he was practically on top of Will.

'What? Patrick, you need to get out there.'

'I always thought I had something in common with him,' said Patrick, ignoring Will's protests. 'That alter ego, you know? The persona that Richard Ranger took on when he needed to be strong. I've been pretending to be some version of that my whole life. I figured I had a pretty good idea of where Kismet was coming from. But I was wrong. These last few months, I've found myself channelling someone else.'

Will narrowed his eyes. 'Who?'

Patrick laughed. Will knew damn well, but he wanted to hear Patrick say it. And he *should* say it. He should be racing to the top of the nearest, tallest building and proclaiming it to the entire city.

'You,' he said. '*You're* my better self. You're the person I think of when I need to be funny or brave or strong. I'm trying to summon some of that strength right now, because I have something to tell you that I have never told anyone before.'

He took a breath.

'I love you too, Will Wright,' he said.

Will's eyes filled with tears, and Patrick leaned in for a kiss… and flinched as his thigh was slapped. Quite hard.

'You couldn't have said that *before* you got out of the car?' Will exclaimed. 'I've been sitting here having the world's best-dressed nervous breakdown.'

'I'm sorry!' Patrick said. 'But it's true. I'm in love with you, Will, more than you will probably ever know. And you're right. I should have said it sooner. You shouldn't have had to fly halfway around the world to hear me say it. But now that you're here…'

He held out his hand and nodded to the open doorway. 'Come with me,' he grinned.

Will, eyebrow raised, took his hand, and allowed himself to be helped up out of the car.

'Where exactly do you think you're going with me?' he asked, his eyes wide at the sight of all the cameras, of all the reporters who were so enamoured of Audra doing her thing that they had yet to spot the two of them.

'Come on,' Patrick repeated.

'Patrick...' Will eyed the crowd nervously. 'Where are we going?'

'Where do you think?' Patrick jerked his head towards the red carpet.

Will gripped his hand harder.

'Are you sure about this?' he asked.

Patrick took both of Will's hands in his own, conscious that more and more stares were turning in their direction. He felt his lover's skin on his and imagined it was physically possible to draw strength from the contact; Kismet willing Axel back to life with the force of his love.

'You're my hero, Will,' he said. 'Now it's my job to make sure I'm worthy of you.'

He began to walk backwards, leading Will step by step towards the carpet.

'I promise we'll figure the rest out later,' he said. 'But right now, you are the most beautiful person here, and I want to show you off. If you would do me the honour?'

He released Will's hands, and held out his arm.

Will laughed. 'Well, I did get all dressed up,' he said, taking Patrick's arm.

'Out of the closet,' Patrick whispered, 'and into the fire.'

They stepped onto the carpet together, all eyes turning to them. Patrick paused midway and turned to Will. He cupped his cheeks tenderly and drew him in for a kiss. The air around them exploded in clicks and flashes, a hundred cameras capturing forever the moment that he went from just another actor in yet another superhero movie to Patrick Lake, Homosexual.

'I love you,' he whispered again in Will's ears.

'I love you,' Will whispered back, followed by: 'Good God, I need a drink.'

'Patrick!' the press called out. 'Patrick! Patrick! Who's your friend!'

'This is Will,' Patrick told them, his voice clearer and steadier than any line reading of his career. 'He's my date. Actually… he's my boyfriend.' This invited more clattering and a constellation of camera flashes. More questions, too. *How long have you two been involved? Are you coming out right now? Are you a member of the LGBT community? Are things getting serious between you?*

Is this love?

Patrick turned to look at Will again – his prince, his queen, his favourite person in this or any universe – and simply said: 'I'm his biggest fan.'

ACKNOWLEDGMENTS

I spent well over a year working on my Difficult Second Novel, convinced that I had some very serious and important thoughts to share about queerness, identity, and the state of the world. Thank god, then, for the people who reminded me that a romcom is supposed to be fun.

Love and thanks, first and foremost, to my dear friend Sam Sedgman, who helped me figure out countless thorny plot and character details over margaritas while on a "research" trip to L.A., and who pretty much has shared custody of Will and Patrick at this point. Look at our boys, Sammy!

All of the drag queens in *We Could Be Heroes* are products of my own imagination, but some names are borrowed, like Julie Madly Deeply and Alesha Tryed. A great big kiss to them and all the bastard queens of Birmingham.

While April and her dream job at *FanFam* were fabricated, her story was inspired by so many amazing Black, Latinx and queer creators I've had the pleasure of following in the fandom space, not least of all DJ BenHameen, Tatiana King Jones, and Ian Carlos Crawford, who I am now lucky to count as a close friend.

We Could Be Heroes has benefited from an *Avengers*-style team-up of real-life champions in publishing on either side of the Atlantic, including Daisy Watt at HarperNorth, Kate Dresser at Putnam, Florence Rees at A.M. Heath, Maria Whelan at InkWell, and Emma Obank at Casarotto.

This story wouldn't exist were it not for the inspiration of one of my favourite novels of all time, *The Amazing Adventures of Cavalier & Klay* by Michael Chabon. If imitation is the sincerest form of flattery, then consider *We Could Be Heroes* my own humble attempt at cosplay.

It goes without saying at this point, but I'll say it anyway: thank you to my family, biological and otherwise, for all that you do. I also happened to fall in love while working on this book, and can't pretend some small part of the final product isn't art imitating life. Kieron, thank you for being you.

And because no superhero movie is complete without a post-credits scene...

EPILOGUE

One Year Later

'Could somebody zip me up, please?' Will called from his seat at the High Table.

'I've got you,' said Faye from his left. To his right sat one of the new girls; a quiet, skittish thing called, ironically, Wanda Talk. She'd painted so dreadfully her first night here that Will had exhorted 'Absolutely *not*' in a tone that was not unlike Margo's, and steered her away from overhead lighting and into the stool next to him so he could help her fix her face. Now Wanda followed him around like a baby bird that had imprinted on its mother, and Will pretended to be annoyed whenever she asked his advice.

Behind them, facing the back wall that had finally been fitted with vanities, Julie Madly Deeply, Raina Shine and Sadie Chatterley lovingly took in their own images like budgies. The Village had been given a temporary stay of execution, but as long as at least three witches sat before the mirrors in the shoddy dressing room, Will felt it would not fall.

Maiden, mother, crone. It was the way of things. Not that he particularly liked the idea of being anyone's mother. It made him feel old, and he could not remember any valuable lessons his own may have taught him. A big sister, perhaps. Everybody should have one of those.

There came a tap from the doorway, but Will was too engaged in attaching a particularly calcitrant eyelash to pay much attention until Faye cleared her throat.

'You've an admirer at the stage door, my duck.'

Will looked past his own reflection and there, over his shoulder, standing on the threshold holding a single red rose, was Patrick.

Wanda gasped silently, but the other queens paid no mind. Patrick had become a frequent visitor over the last twelve months, and while his first appearance still lived on in internet infamy, the queens were no longer impressed. They were the headliners here, after all. What was one more star in such a bright sky?

'You're here!' Will rose from his seat and embraced him. 'You're *early*. I thought you weren't getting here until tomorrow?'

Patrick laid a gentle kiss against his ear, where it would least disturb his makeup.

'I wanted to surprise you,' he said. 'It's been a while since I've seen you perform. It's not the same watching the videos.'

'You are the sweetest man in the world.' Will took the rose and tickled Patrick's chin with it. 'I've missed you.'

'I've missed you too. A lot. I can't wait to be full of Grace later.' Patrick's grin was impish.

'I am taped in too many places to be having this conversation,' Will scolded. 'And as a matter of fact, I will have you know I am a *very* pious woman.'

'That's not what I've read on the bathroom wall,' quipped Wanda, seemingly surprising even herself with this jibe. Faye cackled.

'Are the others here?' Will asked, looking past Patrick to the stairwell.

'They're all downstairs,' Patrick told him. 'Margo and April are already talking about doing shots, they've got Owen staking out the best spot right in front of the stage, and Dylan is pretending not to be thrilled that Jordan is letting them have a beer even though they're not eighteen yet.'

'Oh, that reminds me, Dylan's band has a gig in a few days,' said Will, patting down his dress for non-existent pockets. Where was his phone? He'd made a note of this.

'I saw in the shared calendar,' said Patrick. 'What are they calling themselves now, anyway?'

'The Gory Details.'

'Ooh, I like it. That one has got to be a keeper.'

'Who knows with that kid. Everything is so...' Will froze.

'Babe?' Patrick rested a hand on Will's hip, thumb rubbing against his padding.

'Sorry, I just realised something.' Will batted his eyelashes to keep from crying.

'What's that?'

'I am so fucking happy.'

Patrick's sly smile waxed into a grin as bright as the sun.

'Me too,' he said.

Future plans for the Wonderverse had stalled in the aftermath of some middling reviews for *Kismet 2*. Which was fine for Audra, as she was now the face of a famous, cruelty-free skincare brand and was garnering universal acclaim for her 'down-to-earth', 'deeply relatable' performance in this summer's big romantic comedy. She really *was* a consummate actress. And the entire world seemed to have noticed a change in Patrick Lake in the last year; he was funnier, everybody agreed. Impossibly, even more charming. He had just signed on to a limited revival of *Torch Song* on Broadway, and Will knew he was brimming with excitement at getting started.

Captain Kismet would be back someday, played by some other devastatingly handsome actor, and the cycle would begin again.

There were only a limited number of stories in the world, and Will and Patrick had played their role in this one.

Now came the less glamorous but no less thrilling part, where they divided their time between the Second City and the City of Angels, flying back and forth, delirious on jetlag and each other. Tonight they would go to bed and do all kinds of wicked things, and then in the morning they would look at their calendars, and in the moments between Patrick's rehearsals and Will's growing list of gigs, they would figure out who would travel to who, ensuring that they never went longer than a few weeks without seeing each other. They'd stitch those moments together until there came a day where they would turn around and realise they had built a life.

But first...

'I should finish getting ready,' Will said. 'Everybody will be expecting a show.'

'That's my girl.' Patrick squeezed Will's hand and kissed him tenderly on the lips. Then he turned in the doorway and walked down the stairs to join the rest of the crowd where their family were waiting for him, ready to cheer on the person they all loved.

ALSO BY PJ ELLIS
LOVE & OTHER SCAMS

'Mischievous, magnetic and heaps of *fun*. No matter how you're feeling, the pages instantly cheer you up' **EMMA GANNON**

'Hold onto your diamonds – the romcom of the year is here, and it's an absolute riot. I am PJ Ellis' number one fan' **LIZZY DENT**

'Some of the funniest dialogue I've read in a long, long time… A heisty romp of a romcom that brilliantly skewers marriage, class and love. PJ Ellis is the real deal' **GRANT GINDER**

'I completely adored *Love & Other Scams*. I can't wait to tell everyone I know to read it immediately – because this book is all I want to talk about. PJ Ellis is officially a genius' **LUCY VINE**

'The most brilliant read. Blisteringly funny, genuinely sexy, cancel-all-plans gripping and with tender moments so beautifully written I'm still a little weepy. The solid gold article, no grifting here!' **LAUREN BRAVO**

'I devoured this delicious debut in one sitting … *Love & Other Scams* deserves to be a huge bestseller' **SARRA MANNING**

'I don't think I've ever had such a blast reading a romcom. Totally outstanding – it will, for sure, be the book of the summer' **LAURA JANE WILLIAMS**

'A sparkling diamond of a novel' **ERICA JAMES**

'A dose of unbridled joy' **AJ WEST**

'Fresh, fast paced and funny with a wonderfully warm cast of characters – it's everything you want and more from a book about diamonds, deceit and desire. I adored it' **LAURA KAY**

'If you've ever had your weekend ruined and your budget broken by a so-called friend's over-the-top wedding, *Love & Other Scams* is the book for you. You'll feel seen in the best possible way' **KATHERINE HEINY**

'An entertaining romantic caper with heart, heat, and sass – perfect for anyone who's ever dreamed of taking revenge on perfection' **JUSTIN MYERS**

'Sharp and entertaining … puts the con in unconventional romance' ***BOOKLIST***

'Ellis combines a heist with a romantic comedy and creates something exciting and vibrant … laugh-out-loud hilarious. A delightful, fast-paced escapade full of snappy dialogue' ***KIRKUS REVIEWS***

'My favourite read in years. An absolute belter' **HEIDI STEPHENS**

'*Love & Other Scams* is the definition of a rollicking romp! Ellis' sharp wit and masterfully drawn characters completely sucked me in from the first page. Full of hilarious hijinks, yet also tugged every one of my heart-strings. It's a pure delight!' **FALON BALLARD**

'A blast from start to finish. I loved every minute of it!' **ALICIA THOMPSON**

'Two con artists. A scam. A cat-and-mouse game. And yet the real heist here is debut author PJ Ellis' ability to so fully capture a reader's attention with vibrant characters and the seasoned skill of a pro. I was laughing from page one and I already can't wait to read what he writes next' **STEVEN ROWLEY**

★A BOOK OF THE MONTH IN
RED, *GLAMOUR* AND *COSMO*★
★ONE OF *CRIMEREADS*'
MOST ANTICIPATED NOVELS OF 2023★
★ONE OF *PASTE'S*
MOST ANTICIPATED ROMANCES OF 2023★